Someone called out, "Hey! You! With the clothes!"

I was almost out of the parking lot when one of the newsies thought to step in front of me. I revved the Jeep's engine. He blinked once, twice, must have seen that I wasn't blinking once, or twice. He jumped aside.

By then, a silver sedan had pulled up to block the exit onto the street. Bouncing over the curb, I gunned down Oak Street. I ran a red light at the next intersection and turned left. I shot a glance into the rearview mirror. I'd lost the sedan.

Suddenly, my whole body started to shake. Squeezing the steering wheel to keep the Jeep in control, I drove east. Newspeople would be at my place, too. Some would have even remembered the way from the last time. The old can was going to be pried open; the worms were going to dance in the glare of the lights again. That long-ago man who'd been thought to have falsified evidence was going to be back bigger than ever. Pressure would build. Plinnit would have to act. I'd have to be charged….

JACK FREDRICKSON

HUNTING SWEETIE ROSE

W🌐RLDWIDE.®

TORONTO • NEW YORK • LONDON
AMSTERDAM • PARIS • SYDNEY • HAMBURG
STOCKHOLM • ATHENS • TOKYO • MILAN
MADRID • WARSAW • BUDAPEST • AUCKLAND

For Lori and for Jack

Recycling programs
for this product may
not exist in your area.

HUNTING SWEETIE ROSE

A Worldwide Mystery/April 2014

First published by Thomas Dunne Books for Minotaur Books, an imprint of St. Martin's Press.

ISBN-13: 978-0-373-26891-7

Printed in U.S.A.

Acknowledgments

Patrick Riley, Mary Anne Bigane, Joe Bigane, Eric Frisch, Missy Lyda, India Cooper, and Marcia Markland tried their best to remove the muck from the manuscript.

Susan did too, as she does with everything that matters in my life.

What remains is solely my fault.

PROLOGUE

THE *ARGUS-OBSERVER* was the only Chicago newspaper that dared run the pictures of the clown going off the roof, screaming.

It happened at the start of the evening scramble, that time when floors and floors of appropriate business attires are let out to charge Union Station for trains southwest to Willow Springs, west to Brookfield, or north to Glenview, Deerfield, and points richer beyond.

Waves of hurrying heads turned up to laugh at the daredevil clown—red-nosed, orange-haired, dressed in huge green dots—prancing antics atop the old Rettinger Hardware Supply building. Dozens paused longer, to snap a cell phone picture, new proof of their wacky, rush-hour lives.

Until 4:41, when it went wrong.

The first of the *Argus-Observer* photos showed the daredevil clown with his left hand outstretched, waving at the commuters five stories below. His right hand was raised high, clutching a bouquet of red, blue, and yellow balloons. It would have been a happy summertime photo, a clown cavorting high against the blue of a summertime sky.

Except for the rope.

It was supposed to be taut behind him, tethering him as he leaned out to thrill the crowd.

It wasn't. It had started to fall, a limp, worthless tail. Anchoring nothing.

The middle picture, shot just a second later, captured

the instant the clown pitched out past the point of return. He'd started to twist, to look back at the roof. His big red and white clown-mouth still smiled, because it was painted on that way, but now there was a dark hole in the middle of it, the start of a scream.

The last photograph showed him plummeting, upside down, arms out, grabbing at the air. The balloons had escaped his pink glove. Only the rope, loose and useless, was following him down.

The *Argus-Observer* ran no more of the photos. Not even that raunchiest of scandal sheets had the stomach to print the ones of him lying crushed and leaking on the sidewalk.

Nor did they even think to call it murder.

ONE

TWO WEEKS LATER, late one afternoon, I was standing outside Rivertown's city hall, about to watch another clown—this one relentlessly alive—being hauled away by earnest young men in dark suits.

I'd been drawn across the lawn by the arrival of a Channel 8 News van. Nothing at Rivertown's municipal offices had ever interested the press before. The corruption there is pathetic in its cheesiness, not nearly as dramatic as the big-scale shenanigans in Chicago, just to the east. So whatever it was that had finally drawn the newsies was enough to interest me. I scrambled down the long ladder, capped my paint, and hoofed it across the broad lawn that separates my turret from city hall.

I got there just as a young woman got out of the van. She was dark-haired, slim, and taut of skin and sweater. I watched her from twenty feet away, a crowd of one, as she smoothed the wrinkles from her black skirt and touched at the matching luster of her hair.

I no longer recognized most of Chicago's field reporters. The local television stations were purging their stock, replacing crinkled, mostly male veterans with unmarked females. Some of the new ones looked and sounded young enough to be on work-study rotations from the local journalism schools.

Not so the one who'd gotten out of the van. She was young, but not college-young, and on television, she came across smart, way past school-smart. It didn't hurt, either, that she was one of the best-looking women in Chicago news. Up from weekend weather, she was now doing small features, but I imagined her bosses had her pegged for a local anchor slot. She was a comer, someone to watch. She was Jennifer Gale.

Her cameraman, a burly fellow with a scruffy beard and a Taste of Chicago T-shirt, shouldered a video camera and motioned to her to step into the frame he was making of the front entrance of city hall. He squinted through the viewfinder, nodded, and she began speaking into a hand-held microphone.

"I'm here in Rivertown, just west of Chicago, where today Elvis Derbil, building and zoning commissioner, is being arrested for unlawfully relabeling and selling thousands of bottles of out-of-code Italian salad dressing. Allegedly, the labels were falsified not only to redate the stale product but also to disguise its true fat and caloric content. Commissioner Derbil, a longtime Rivertown employee, is a nephew of the mayor."

The cameraman nodded, and she stopped speaking. For two or three moments, nobody moved. Not Jennifer Gale, who stood fixed in the shot that had been set up. Not the cameraman, hefting what looked to be a heavy camera. Not me, the crowd.

Then the front door of city hall opened and two dark-suited young men marched Elvis Derbil outside.

They had him handcuffed, the current fashion for parading a white-collar perp past a television camera. Except Elvis's collar wasn't white. It was a purple plaid, which contrasted arrestingly with his green denim jeans and turquoise-studded brown cowboy boots. I could only hope that Elvis had not been tipped about his arrest. To think otherwise, that he'd deliberately chosen those colors for his day on television news, would have been unkind.

Microphone raised, Jennifer Gale charged the trio. "Mr. Derbil, did you alter labels to resell stale-dated salad oil?"

Elvis gave her a yellow-toothed grin, but he'd pointed it a foot below her chin. Elvis never shrank from looking like a fool.

When he didn't answer, she aimed her microphone at the suit closest to her. "Are more arrests pending?"

The young man shook off the question and hurried ahead to open the door of the black Impala parked at the curb. I turned to watch the suit that stayed with Elvis. As I'd hoped, he was raising his hand to protect the top of Elvis's head as he nudged him down onto the backseat.

This part would be especially wonderful.

It was. The young man's hand made contact, and suddenly his face contorted as if he'd just palmed steaming roadkill.

Mercifully, I'd never had to touch Elvis's head, but I'd long been familiar with its sheen and could imagine its stickiness. Back in high school, Elvis had greased the sprouts atop his narrow head with Vaseline, slick jelly that made his hair and the tops of his ears glisten like newly lubricated machinery. Speculation had it then that any insect landing on Elvis's head would dissolve in the petrochemical ooze before Elvis could think to scratch.

Years later, when my own life had dissolved and I retreated back to Rivertown, I had to go to Elvis, now Rivertown's building and zoning commissioner, for an occupancy permit to live in the turret, and I saw that the years had not been kind to the top of his head. His forehead had retreated substantially, forcing him to abandon petroleum jelly for a scented hair spray, which he used to starch his cowering hairline up into a kind of wall, halfway back on his scalp. Like his beloved Vaseline, the spray had gloss, so he was able to maintain a sheen. Gone, though, was the mixed mechanical smell of grease and whatever had perished in it. Elvis now smelled of coconut, freshly shredded. It was that sticky, coconut-smelling residue that the young suit had just palmed.

Furious at what was now on his skin, the young man slammed the door on Elvis and spun, holding up his hand as though wounded. His eyes were wild and darting, desperate for a place to wipe his palm and fingers. His eyes found the grass. He began to kneel. Then he stopped, for he'd suddenly realized that Jennifer Gale and her cameraman might still be running tape, not ten feet away. Straightening up, he mimed a ludicrous nonchalance as he walked around to get in the passenger's side of the car.

The Impala sped away, but I expected it wouldn't speed long. My money was on a screeching stop at the nearest gas station, for the sticky-palmed young man to make a fast, one-handed dip into the windshield wash.

Jennifer Gale finished her concluding remarks and handed her microphone back to the cameraman. As he headed for the van, she smiled at me and walked over.

I noticed fine lines around her eyes, and a couple more, the good kind, from laughing, around her mouth.

"I saw you get off the ladder. You work for the city?" She pointed at the turret behind me.

"I live there."

She frowned. "That's a city landmark. It's on their letterhead. They let you live there?"

"My grandfather built it. I inherited it."

Her eyes told me she didn't believe me. "Interesting. Are you surprised about Elvis Derbil?"

"Nothing about Elvis surprises me."

I was surprised, though. Altering salad oil labels required ingenuity, and that wasn't Elvis. He was a subterranean operator, a minion directed to trade zoning and building permits for cash. Beyond that, he wouldn't move without instruction.

She turned to look behind her, at city hall. "I suppose your grandfather built that, too?"

I was used to the question. City hall was built of the same stones as the turret.

"They appropriated my grandfather's pile of limestone and most of his land at the end of World War II. They didn't want the turret."

After another glance at the turret, she made a show of studying my paint-splattered jeans and torn T-shirt. "Are you eccentric?"

"Only until I get enough money to act normal. Why?"

She pointed to the turret behind me. "Because I'm wondering if you use a chauffeur." A smile played at the nice faint lines on her face.

I turned. A long black Lincoln limousine was parked behind my Jeep, and a liveried chauffeur, in full gray uniform with a black-visored hat to match, was knocking on my timbered door.

Never at a loss for snappy repartee, I said, "I use him for odd jobs, fetching pizzas, picking up my other pair of jeans from the laundry." I wished her luck in unraveling the greasy strands of Rivertown and headed for the turret.

"Until tonight, at nine," she called after me.

"I never miss the news," I called back.

TWO

"Mr. Vlodek Elstrom?" the chauffeur asked as I walked up.

When I nodded, he nodded, but at someone in the car's backseat. The door opened, and a tall man, thickset enough to have played professional football thirty years earlier, got out. He stuck out his hand. "Tim Duggan," he said. "Let's go down and look at the river."

His suit coat was cut wider than he was. He was carrying, probably in a belt holster.

"This is all very dramatic," I said.

He made a smile that didn't move his cheeks. "I just like rivers."

We walked down to the Willahock. For a minute, we said nothing, just rocked on our heels and watched empty motor oil quarts and opaque milk jugs frolic inside the half-submerged tires and tree limbs at the opposite bank.

"You keep your side of the river clean," he said.

"I try to do one moral thing a day."

"I understand you do investigations."

"From whom do you understand this?"

"Here and there. The newspapers, too, some time back."

"I try to avoid the newspapers," I said.

He nodded. He understood that, too.

"I'm not licensed," I said. "Mostly I do insurance work, examine accident scenes, research court records."

I left out that, for a time, I'd also written an advice column, masquerading as a woman, for a freebie supermarket rag masquerading as a newspaper. I'd quit that some months before, because the column was making me too aware of the kinds of minds that were loose across America.

"You hear about that clown that went off the roof a couple of weeks ago?" he asked.

I looked at his broad, tough face. "There was only a single paragraph in the *Tribune*. They called it a tragic accident."

"The *Argus-Observer* was the only one that gave it any real play. The story pretty much disappeared."

"I don't read the *Argus-Observer*."

He made another smile. "So I would imagine."

For sure, he'd checked me out.

"What is it you want, Mr. Duggan?"

"What do you charge?"

"It depends on how forthcoming my clients are." I was developing an aversion to Duggan's cementlike demeanor. "For standard stuff, photographing accident scenes, running down records, I'm reasonable. For others, I bill premium—two hundred dollars an hour."

It was a laugh. It had been a long while since I'd billed anybody for much of anything. Thanks, in huge part, to the *Argus-Observer*.

"I'd like you to look into that clown's death." He took a white envelope from his suit jacket. Holding it out, he said, "There's two thousand dollars in there."

"Do you represent the building's owners?"

He gave that a noncommittal shrug.

"You'd do better going to the police, get their information," I said.

"I'm looking for discretion."

Something itched on my face. I touched my cheek, and a small piece of caulk fell off.

He noticed. He raised the envelope higher.

It was enough. I took his envelope, and we started up the hill to the street.

"How will I get in touch with you?" I asked, at the limousine.

He handed me a business card. It read, TIMOTHY DUGGAN. SECURITY.

"You do security for the building?" I asked.

"If your billing exceeds the two thousand, let me know." He got in the car.

Unlimited budget. Limousine. A cash offering. He wasn't my typical client, not even before my life collapsed.

As he was driven away, I pulled out my cell phone and called a man I'd once done a favor for. He worked for the State of Illinois and had nothing to do with vehicle licenses, but he had access to the database. It's like that in Illinois government; everybody has access to everything. It's why so many of the state's workers, right up to the recent governors, retire in prison.

My contact put me on hold, came back in a minute. "The limousine is registered to Prestige Vehicles, in Chicago," he said.

"Leased?"

"Most likely. You're wasting your time. Those outfits don't disclose information. Some of their clients are pretending rich, and don't want it known they get carted around in leased cars."

"Me, I own what I drive," I said.

"You still driving that heap of a Jeep?" He chuckled, proud of his rhyme.

"I just put fresh duct tape across the rips in the side windows. It looks almost new."

"Newly slashed, you mean." He hung up before I could

brag that I'd primed the rust spots in the same shade of gray as the tape.

I went into the turret and onto the Internet. Google, that collector of all lint, had a dozen Timothy Duggans in Illinois. One was an actor, another owned a restaurant, a third coached high school soccer. None ran a security firm. Duggan's operation must have been small, and very private. He worked at not getting noticed.

I then keyed in "Clown, fall, Chicago." The first listings belonged to the major newspaper Web sites. The *Tribune*, *Sun-Times*, *Reader*, and *Southtown Star* all had carried the story, two weeks before. Each had given it a bare few sentences, seeing the death as an obvious accident or, unmentioned, a possible suicide. None had updated the story since.

I scrolled down the screen to the *Argus-Observer*'s site and saw the three photos they'd run. A clown dancing, a clown tipping, a clown dropping.

Just that morning, they'd updated. John Keller, the bastard who wrote a two-inch-wide column called "Keller's Korner," had posted one of his trademark teasers: DIVING CLOWN? WHY DON'T COPPERS COP?

As always, he'd written in his usual breathless style, using fat letters to take up the space where the facts should have gone. Keller's teasers never had middles or ends, just boldface beginnings followed by his signature tagline, "Details to follow." Except details never followed; Keller never wasted time on research or probing credible sources. The nuggets that appeared in his daily "Keller's Korner" were a vile mix of half-baked truths, served up in thick print.

I knew John Keller. I'd felt the burn of his acid-etched innuendos years before, when I'd gotten caught up in a false evidence scheme during the trial of a suburban mayor.

He'd raked me over live coals because, at the time, I was the son-in-law of one of the major industrialists in Chicago. I was innocent of any wrongdoing, and exonerated within a week, but those were the sorts of details that never followed in "Keller's Korner."

Still, there had been truths, between the lines, in Keller's teasers about me. Evidence had been falsified in the Evangeline Wilts trial. Just not by me.

I wondered how much truth Keller was hinting at now, about the clown.

I went back outside, finished the window I was painting, did another, and then it was dusk and time to knock off. I climbed the stairs to the semifinished kitchen on the second floor. It awaits new countertops and nonrusted appliances, which await more than the two thousand dollars I'd just gotten from Duggan.

I heated two generic local frozen entrées—one fish, one lasagna—in the dented microwave, not because I love variety, but because they were what I had. I took them, smoldering, across the hall.

The other half of the circle that is the turret's second floor will one day be a library, or a dining room, or whatever anyone sporting enough money wants it to be. For now, it is my office, lounge, and occasionally the place where I sleep, in the electric blue La-Z-Boy that I'd acquired, like the room's other furnishings, the card table and the tilting red desk chair, truly used. I shifted the La-Z-Boy into full recline, picked up my microtelevision from the floor and balanced it on my lap next to the first of the evening's delights—the radiated fish—and turned on Channel 8.

Jennifer Gale's segment came on at 9:08. As I'd noticed outside city hall, the cameraman had done a nice job of framing her in the video. Even as Elvis was being led out, the cameraman had filmed over Jennifer's shoulder, keeping the side of her face in the shot, as befitted the station's objective of delivering beauty with news.

Sadly, the piece ended without showing the horror on the young suit's face as he palmed Elvis's head. I supposed the news director felt that showing an agent recoiling from a sticky scalp would be a discourtesy to the courage of steel-jawed lawmen everywhere.

Leo Brumsky called ten seconds after the segment ended. "Dek, you're not gonna—"

I stopped him because I'd known he would call. We'd been one-upping each other since seventh grade.

"Elvis," I said, casually readying my bait. "You saw him on the news, too."

Gently, I dropped my hook into the pool of his imagination. "Better. I was there, outside city hall."

He paused, his waters beginning to roil. I knew what he was thinking. Though Leo's girlfriend, Endora, is beautiful and has a genius IQ to match his, the adolescent lust of the young male, no matter how old he has become, never fully withers.

"How close?" He wasn't asking about my proximity to Elvis.

Slowly, I began taking up my slack. "Close enough to smell her perfume," I murmured.

"Jeez." Envy burbled up, coating the word like syrup.

I pulled harder, still patient. "I talked to her."

"Jeez," he said again.

"You want to know what we talked about, Leo?" I asked softly, ready now.

"Yes." It was a whisper. A seventh-grade, testosterone-revved, prepubescent kid's begging whisper.

"Salad oil," I murmured, jerking, hooking him tight. "About how salad oil, slick oil, delicately warmed, might feel…"

He hung up, destroyed. Seventh grade went away. For the time being.

I picked up the second generic cuisine and scraped back some of the topping that could have been marinara or ketchup or thin red latex paint. The lasagna noodles that lay beneath were the same pale beige as the fish I'd just eaten. In fact, it could have been the same substance, merely pressed into a corrugated pasta shape. I took a bite. It tasted like the fish, too. I scraped back more red, looking for signs of gills. I found none. Still, I finished it quickly, pushing away the thought that my lasagna had once swum in the sea.

I climbed the curved metal stairs to the third floor. It's where I have a fiberglass shower enclosure and the bed Amanda and I shared during our marriage.

I looked out the window. A half-moon was high over the Willahock River. Its light was soft, enough to mask the debris on the opposite bank and make the gently rippling water appear clean. I dropped my clothes onto the chair I use as a closet and slipped under the blanket.

I thought again about the Willahock, and the death of a clown, and how, like the camouflage of a soft moon, a dark limousine might be so very excellent at hiding truths.

THREE

The Rettinger Hardware Supply building was an old sand-blasted, redbrick, nuts-and-bolts warehouse that looked to have been gentrified into four floors of residences and street-level stores twenty years before. I parallel parked between two BMWs, waited next to the door that led to the upstairs condos, and slipped in when someone came out. A narrow stairway on the fifth floor led up to a little hutch on the roof. A door that was flaking old green paint opened to the outside.

The roof was flat to the edge, covered with tar and enough loose gravel to make it a fool place to go tap dancing. I walked around, staying well back from the edge. There were no marks on the gravel, no scuffs or scrapes at the edge that indicated the clown had tried to grab or kick his way back onto the roof. Either he'd gone off the roof on purpose, a suicide, or he'd gone off surprised, the victim of a bad knot or a frayed rope.

Or as Keller had vaguely implied, the victim of murder.

I thought back to the slim paragraphs in the news accounts. The commuters heading to the trains had assumed, naturally enough, that the clown's act was an advertising stunt. Yet none of the newspaper or Internet reports had mentioned what the clown was touting. It was a question for the cops.

I took another turn around the roof. There were no rings or cleats. I walked back to the hutch, looking for the place where the clown had tied his rope.

Most of the green paint on the door had weathered away, exposing wood that had gone gray from the sun and the wind and the rain and the snow. I looked closely at the edges. Several faint indentations, exposing fresh yellow wood that had not yet weathered, were visible above the top hinge. It was the place where the clown had looped and tied his safety rope.

I pressed my thumbnail against the door. It easily cut a semicircle into the spongy wood—and that was a problem. There were no deeper marks in the wood, no rough abrasions that should have been made by the rope rubbing back and forth as it worked itself loose.

I went down the stairs.

THE DISTRICT'S POLICE station was one of Chicago's older cop houses, set in the middle of a block. I parked between a Pontiac that had one headlight and an Oldsmobile that had no bumpers at all. I imagined I heard the Jeep sigh, settling in comfortably among its own, when I shut off the clatter of my engine.

The desk sergeant frowned as he read my business card. "Records researching what?"

Records researcher is a vague title. Illinois government, rarely picky about much at all, ethics-wise, is uncharacteristically careful about licensing private detectives. A law school degree or law enforcement experience is required. I have neither. So I avoid even the inference of working as a private investigator. Records researcher does well enough as a job title, and it sounds harmless.

"The insurance file on the clown that went off the roof at the Rettinger building," I said.

"You trying to make him a jumper so your company won't have to pay?"

"Nothing like that." I gave him one of my winning grins. "Is the officer in charge in?"

"Later this afternoon," he snapped.

"You'll give him my card?"

"Even if it's with my dying breath."

Walking out, I looked back. He was leaning over, to drop my card in a wastebasket.

There was a Plan B. The Bohemian's office was less than a mile away.

THE BOHEMIAN'S NAME is never in the papers. Anton Chernek values secrecy the way Midas valued gold, except with more fervor.

He is an attorney, a CPA, and a certified financial manager, but his degrees suggest only that he manages high-dollar investment portfolios for high-dollar clients. His real responsibilities reach much further. For those whose net worth transcends tens of millions, he can be a facilitator, a fixer, an overseer of entire lives—the go-to guy when trouble erupts. An errant child, a sticky business partnership, an even stickier personal partnership; those are Chernek's real domains. He resolves difficulties quietly, compassionately, and almost always fairly. He is first-generation American, old-world courtly, and very quietly essential to the well-being of many of Chicago's most prominent people.

I first met him at the conference my ex-wife's lawyers called to work out the details of our divorce. He'd come with Amanda's lawyers, sat in the background, said nothing. I came alone. He liked that I didn't want anything from her. I think he also liked that my first name, always unused, is Vlodek. It is a solid Bohemian name, like his own.

His are the only offices on the top floor of a yellow brick former bicycle factory. The elevator let me off into his reception area, a dark expanse of money-green leather furniture, burgundy carpeting, and blue-suited financial fund brokers, hoping to see the Bohemian but willing to settle for one of his staff.

His personal secretary didn't keep me waiting. She's a formidable, helmet-haired woman with a British accent and a Transylvanian demeanor. Her name is Buffy, and that is the only laugh she offers the world. She smiled an eighth of an inch to express her ecstasy at seeing me again and led me back to his office.

"Vlodek," the Bohemian called out, exaggerating the syllables—Vuh-lo-dek—on his tongue. "What a pleasant surprise."

He is sixtyish, six-four like me but thirty pounds thicker, tanned almost to mahogany, and always better dressed. That day, he wore a peach-colored dress shirt with a white collar, a deeper-colored peach tie, and midnight blue suit trousers. The matching suit coat was hung on an antique mahogany rack next to his mahogany credenza. The Bohemian wears mahogany like he wears money, very well.

I sat down on leather taken from a burgundy cow.

"How is the lovely Amanda?" It is always his leadoff question, and it is never idle or social. My ex-wife is the daughter of one of his most prominent clients, the tycoon Wendell Phelps.

"Very busy."

"I understand she is doing a marvelous job."

Amanda had recently joined her father's electric utility, directing its charitable endeavors. It left her little time for teaching at the Art Institute, or working on one of the art history books she occasionally authored. Or me.

"That's good to know," I said.

"It will settle down, Vlodek."

"Of course," I said.

He smiled. "Anything I can help you with?" He knew I would not drop in merely to chat.

"I'd like a phone call from the officer who's in charge of investigating the death of that clown two weeks ago."

"The poor man who fell off the roof?"

"Yes."

"Not much press on that. Just a few words in the paper, as I recall."

I nodded.

He didn't ask why I wanted to know, and I offered no explanation. It was like that between the Bohemian and me. He just smiled, and I smiled, and not a confidence was broken.

FOUR

LEO CALLED, SAVING me from an edgy afternoon of waiting for the phone to ring.

"Busy today?" he asked.

"Waiting for a phone call."

"A potential client?"

"A real client, flashing cash."

He whistled. "Happy times are here again. You can tell me about it when I pick you up. I need your brawn."

"It comes with brains."

"Rarely necessary. Your tools would be nice, though."

"Which tools?"

"Anything to cut metal tubing. Plus a power screwdriver to attach things to ceilings and floors. You can ride with me to the hardware store?"

I told him that would be fine.

An hour later, a motor sounded outside. It wasn't the strong, full-throated Porsche I was expecting. This engine was tinny and weak. I looked out one of the slit windows. A light blue pickup truck, accented with irregular splats of rust and fitted with a rack to haul lumber, was idling at my curb. I'd never seen the truck. Inside it, though, were familiar flashes of outrageous color—this day, a yellow Hawaiian shirt and lime green trousers, obnoxiously bright even through the double filters of the truck and turret windows. It was Leo, in bloom. I went out, set my toolbox in the truck bed, and got in.

"Where the hell are we going?" I asked, by way of a greeting.

His thick, bushy eyebrows cavorted on his narrow bald head like overcaffeinated caterpillars. "I've had a flash of genius. We're off to get fitness equipment, for Ma."

He is five foot six and weighs the same one-forty he did in high school. Also like in high school, he lives with his mother in her brown brick bungalow in Rivertown because she won't consider living anywhere else.

His expertise is in establishing provenance. The big auction houses in Chicago and on both coasts pay him in excess of a half-million dollars a year to establish the lineage of the pieces they offer to their bidders. For Christie's, Sotheby's, and the others, he wears Armani suits selected by his girlfriend, Endora, an exotic onetime model and current researcher at the Newberry Library. For me and his other friends, he selects duds from the back rack at the Discount Den, Rivertown's retailer of odd lots of hardware, appliances, canned goods, and occasionally clothing that no one but Leo wants.

As he headed toward Thompson Avenue, Rivertown's seedy adult playground, I studied the day's ensemble. Regrettably, I'd seen the lime green pants before, as I had the black-and-white saddle shoes. The shirt, however, was new. It was no ordinary tropic yellow. It was covered—or perhaps more accurately, infested—with multilegged insects, the color of blood. Like all of his casual shirts, he'd purchased it in double extra large. He won't admit it, but I believe he buys them wretchedly oversized so he can crawl into them without unbuttoning them first.

"Fitness equipment, for Ma?" I asked.

"You've got a client?"

It wasn't like Leo to dodge any question, but I went along. "A security guy came by in a limousine yesterday.

He hired me to look into the death of the clown that went off the Rettinger building."

He looked over. "It wasn't an accident, like the paper said?"

"He didn't say what he thought. Nor whether he's inquiring on his own or for somebody else."

"A negligence liability issue for the building's owners?"

"That's what I would have thought, but there's something else." I told him about the door on the roof. "It should have been marked by the rope pulling away. I'm waiting for a cop to call, to tell me what they're thinking." I turned on the seat. "So, fitness equipment, for Ma?"

"A healthier body can lead to a healthier mind." His eyes stayed fixed on the road.

For years, Ma Brumsky—a low-slung, gray-haired babushka who favors catalog housedresses and furry slippers—had run a proper Polish, fish-on-Fridays Catholic home. She played bingo at the church, knitted for charity, and had other Polish ladies—all but one widows like her—over for cards every eighth Saturday evening. Other than tippling at Leo's whiskey, and stealing the occasional coffee cup or silverware setting for two when Leo took her out to dinner, the woman had led an exemplary life.

Until Leo bought her a big-screen television.

It loomed in their front room, taller even than the high-backed sofa Ma had kept pristine for decades under a succession of clear plastic slipcovers. With its side speakers, the set was almost as wide, too.

It wasn't the size and the sound of the new TV that took over Ma's life, though; it was the adventure it summoned. For, after a week, possibly two, of marveling at how her regular shows—the soaps, the realities, the cop dramas, even the shopping channel—had been transformed by being quadrupled in size, Ma Brumsky ventured toward newer horizons. She found channels she'd never seen before. She discovered soft porn.

Out went having her friends over for cards every eighth Saturday evening. In came big-screen events for Ma and the other ladies, every night there wasn't bingo at the church.

At first, Leo saw it as harmless. On those movie nights when he wasn't staying at Endora's condo, he worked in his basement office, willing to dial up the volume on his bossa nova CDs to drown out the excited Polish chattering and occasional stomping of an orthopedic shoe or metal walker leg just a few feet above his head.

Then Ma's tastes in videos expanded even more. She discovered hard-core, pay-per-view. Suddenly, she was witnessing twosomes and threesomes and foursomes interact in ways she and Pa Brumsky, rest his soul, never would have imagined in the dark beneath their goose down comforter.

Out went the tame romance novels from the library; out went the Polish-language newspapers. Out went words in general. Daytime hours were now for rest, so that she could be fully alert and observant far into the night.

Leo became concerned.

"A healthier body can lead to a healthier mind," Leo said again, working his lips as though mumbling an incantation, as he pulled into the Home Depot.

He had me wait in the truck. Fifteen minutes later, he came out pushing a contractor's cart. On the cart were long lengths of metal tubing and a box filled with metal parts. After strapping the pipes onto the truck rack, we started back toward Rivertown.

"What's with the pipes?" I asked, ever the ace investigator.

"Surely it's obvious."

"A fence?"

"Some detective."

When I pressed him, he offered up a sly smile and changed the subject to an exhibit Endora was curating at the Newberry Library. "Female literary provocateurs of the 1920s," he said.

"Endora is no mean provocateur herself."

"Amen to that."

He parked in the alley behind his house. We carried the poles, hardware, and my tools through his back porch, past Ma's cases of diet soda, cheese curls, and All-Bran, and down the basement stairs.

Where I stopped, stunned, at the bottom.

Through its unfinished door opening, Leo's office was as it had always been, a mismatched medley of cast-off furniture and state-of-the-art magnifiers, enclosed by untaped, unpainted drywall. The rest of the basement, though, had been ruined.

Leo's basement had always been a jumble of the artifacts of the Brumskys—the fake, small Christmas tree they used to shake off and put on the television, before the big screen; boxes of old dinner ware, some bought, most liberated by Ma from one restaurant or another; the model train layout on green-painted plywood I'd helped Leo put together in grammar school, on one of those many afternoons when I'd sought sanctuary at his house instead of trudging to whatever aunt's apartment I'd been assigned for the month. As a child, I'd envied Leo his basement clutter of family things. As an adult, I envied him his clutter more, because it showed good in his past.

No longer. The basement had been cleared out. Ruined.

"What did you do with all of your nice things?" I waved my arm at the newly denuded space.

"I rented one of those big storage spaces. That's where I got the truck."

"For what?"

"I decided Ma and her friends need an exercise room," he said simply.

"And less movies?"

"Absolutely."

I touched the toe of my shoe to one of the pipes we'd just set on the floor. "So these are…?"

He pointed up to the ceiling. He'd chalked eight circles on the wood joists. One for each of the pipes he'd gotten at the Home Depot.

"For stretching, kicking," he said.

I looked down, then back up. An outrageous image had blown hot into my head.

"No," I managed, but it was tentative.

Leo's lips widened into a sly smile. "Brilliant, huh? Low-impact workouts, easily done, standing up."

"Not pipes." I pointed to the hardware on the floor. "Poles."

His smile broadened until his head was half teeth. "Ma's lady friend Mrs. Roshiska has a nephew, Bernard. He's an accountant. He told me it's all the rage. Excellent exercise, particularly for older ladies."

"Septuagenarians?" I started laughing. No, not laughing; shrieking. The picture forming in my head, of Ma Brumsky and her lady friends, struggling to work poles like the torsos who pranced in the joints along Thompson Avenue, was going to blind me.

"Just muscle toning, you letch," Leo sputtered, trying not to lose control himself. "Bernard—"

"I know." My eyes had filled with tears. "Bernard, the nephew accountant, says it's all the rage."

With great will, I calmed myself, and we went to work.

Periodically, though, I had to pause, to wipe my eyes, and to convulse.

It took less than an hour to mount the eight pipes to the floor and ceiling. When we were done, I stood back to study the loose maze we'd created. Almost all of the poles were within five feet of each other.

"They're too close together," I said. "They can't really kick high."

I chewed my lower lip. "What about that one?" I asked, when my breathing had steadied. One of the poles was set farther apart from the others.

"Mrs. Roshiska's. She needs a walker."

That did it. I howled all the way up the stairs, across the yard, and into the truck. I was still laughing when he threw me out in front of the turret.

A Lieutenant Jaworski called at six fifteen that evening.

"I was told you had questions regarding the death of James Stitts." His words were clipped, impatient. The Bohemian's clout must have come down hot from someone important.

"James Stitts was the clown?"

"You don't even know his name?"

"Actually, I have very few questions."

"Insurance questions?"

"Any doubt as to cause of death?" I asked, sidestepping.

Jaworski took a minute, evaluating my obvious evasion.

"Lousy Boy Scouting," he said, finally. He must have decided I wasn't worth more anger.

"Pardon me?"

"Mr. Stitts never learned his knots. He tied his safety rope around the door on the roof. The knot came loose, the rope came away, down he went. Simple carelessness. Death by poor knotting."

"You checked the rope?"

"Brand-new, no frays. He tied a lousy knot, was all."

"And you checked the door?"

"Solid enough to hold a rope. Nothing gave way."

"What was he doing up there?" I asked.

"For Christ's sake, Elstrom."

"An advertising stunt?"

"Must have been. Stitts did birthday parties, car dealerships, store openings. Lots of balloons. His wife said he got two or three gigs a month."

"What was he trying to advertise, up on that roof?"

"How the hell would I know that?"

"By what he left behind."

"He left nothing behind."

Not even a mark of a rope pulling off a door, but that observation I owed to Timothy Duggan, not to a cop.

"So you don't know who hired him?" I asked instead.

Jaworski paused. "What does that have to do with insurance?"

"Routine, for the file."

"I told you, I don't know what he was pushing," Jaworski said.

"You asked his wife?"

"Sure," he said, after enough hesitation to mean he hadn't.

"Now you're at a dead end?"

"Not a dead end, damn it. The man's rope came loose, and he fell." He took a breath. "Now, if that's all…"

"What does John Keller know that you don't, Lieutenant?"

He hung up before I could anger him further.

FIVE

THE ONLINE DEATH notice, at the *Tribune*, said James Stitts loved being a clown. It also said he loved his wife, Bea, and their two children. It did not mention that he loved working in human resources, which he did full-time, for a large suburban firm.

He'd lived in Arlington Heights, northwest of Chicago, in a beige split-level home on a cul-de-sac. A kid's red bike lay on the blacktop driveway, in front of a silver minivan. I got there at nine o'clock the next morning.

A dark-haired woman in her midthirties answered my knock at the front door. She wore no makeup, had only smudges under her eyes.

"This has to do with James's insurance?" she asked, after she'd studied my card.

"I'm not with his insurance company, and there are no irregularities with his policy, as far as I know. I'm just pulling together some general information."

"For who?"

I thought of the lies I could offer. I skipped them all. "For someone who wants to know exactly how he died."

"For who?"

"I don't know. I got hired by a security firm to look into your husband's death."

"The condo owners in that hardware building, then, worried about a lawsuit?"

"I don't know."

She considered that for a minute and then opened the screen door. "Let's talk in the kitchen."

She led me through a living room strewn with electronic game controls, a basketball, and one small Nike high-top half hidden under a chair. It was a room for kids and play. Except now, a boy's small dark sport coat also lay tossed across the back of a chair, a clip-on necktie dangling from its pocket. Funeral clothes.

She waved at the mess as we walked through. "I've had my hands full since James died, and I don't have the heart to yell at the kids to pick up."

She poured coffee into yellow mugs, and we sat at an oak pedestal table.

"The police said his death was an accident," she said. "They said the rope he used to anchor himself became undone, and he fell from the roof."

Her eyes locked onto mine, perhaps challenging me to accept it as truth.

"No chance it was…?" I stopped to hide behind a sip of coffee, because I didn't have the guts to finish the question.

"Suicide? No way in hell."

"Accident, then, for sure?"

She said nothing but kept her eyes hot on me.

"No way in hell, either?" I asked, after a moment. It was why she'd let me in the door. I wondered then if she'd been the one who'd fed the nugget to Keller about the cops giving up too soon on the case.

"What could the person who sent you here think, Mr. Elstrom?"

"I would imagine that person, like me, like you, wants more facts."

"James's insurance company, must be."

"Most insurers are straight up. I don't think one would hire me blind."

"James's life insurance company is holding off, saying he was engaged in a high-risk activity. They might not pay on the policy."

"They can do that, if their insured person routinely engages in something high risk, something they wouldn't ordinarily cover."

"James was a careful man. He wouldn't have tied a poor knot. He wouldn't even start his car until his seat belt was fastened."

"Did he perform that way often?"

"At the edge of a roof? Never. I told you, he was not a risk taker. He did it this time because the money was good." Her eyes were still defiant. "He knew how to tie a damned knot. He practiced a dozen times on the rope he bought."

"How good was the money?"

"One thousand dollars, for two performances. Each was to be done on a different rooftop. He got paid half up front."

"Who hired him?"

"I don't know who she was."

"She?"

"Some woman who had big plans. She told him she wanted to build a buzz, generate some interest. The first performance was to be spontaneous, no product brochures, no bullhorn, just a clown dancing, downtown, on a roof during rush hour. She thought the newspapers would love the mystery of why he was up there, maybe enough to publicize the second performance. Then she could adver-tise the hell out of it, and all kinds of people would show up, curious, and she could capitalize on whatever she was selling."

"You have no idea what that was?"

"No. She just told James to find two rooftops downtown that were low enough to be seen from the street, and get things rolling."

"Do you think James knew her name?"

"If he did, he never said. She was a secretive lady. She paid cash."

"Do you know where she worked?"

She gestured out past the living room. "She came here?"

"In a limousine. Had a chauffeur all dolled up in a gray suit, gray cap."

"What did she look like?"

"I couldn't see her, for the dark-tinted windows." She shrugged. "Just rich, I suppose. Everybody looks rich in a limo."

I finished the last of my coffee. I still thought it possible she'd been the one who'd tipped Keller, to fight off any talk of her husband committing suicide, but it was just as likely she hadn't heard yet about the column at all. She would, though, from a neighbor, a friend, or some mere acquaintance with a nose. I didn't envy her that.

I drove away thinking about limousines. My world is not filled with long dark cars. My only encounters with them had been to dodge them, with Amanda, when we'd been crossing the street, in front of the Goodman Theater or Symphony Center, downtown in Chicago.

Yet now two of them had driven into my life. The first was Duggan's, two days before. Now, a second, one that had brought a woman to hire James Stitts to dance on a roof.

Maybe to hire him to die.

SIX

THE RESPONSIBLE THING to do, when I got back to the turret, was to report to Duggan.

To tell him the cops liked Stitts's death as an accident from a poorly knotted rope and that they saw no reason to investigate further, especially not if that might lead to a suicide finding that would null an insurance payout to a widow.

To tell him, too, that Stitts's widow was having none of that. Her husband had been a careful man, meticulous enough to practice knotting his new rope until he'd gotten it right. Nor was there any chance the man was suicidal.

I'd tell him I was with the widow on both counts. The door had not been marked, abraded by a poorly tied rope pulling away. It had been no accident.

Just like it had been no suicide. The *Argus-Observer* photographs showed Stitts had been at the edge of the roof when the rope began to fall behind him; he was too far away from its other end to have untied it himself.

Not an accident; not a suicide. Someone at the other end had loosened the rope.

Likely as not, Timothy Duggan already suspected that—and that, I wanted to think through.

So I made no call. I retreated instead to what I often do, when too much is banging around too loudly in my head. I cut wood.

Cutting, sanding, and staining allow me a degree of

mental drift. Busying my hands sometimes calms whatever is loose in my brain.

Not that afternoon. After three hours, all I'd finished
was six pieces of ceiling trim. None had been accompanied by any mental breakthrough.

Then I cut one piece too short. It looked all right, at first.
When I held it up to the kitchen ceiling, though, I saw it
was an inch too short.

That snapped my lazing brain back to the door on the
roof of the Rettinger building, and to how a rope could
come loose without leaving a mark.

Lieutenant Jaworski said the rope appeared to be in excellent shape. That there'd been no rips or frays supported
his conclusion that the knot had simply worked itself loose.

I called Bea Stitts. "Just a small detail, ma'am: That
rope your husband practiced knotting, then brought to the
Rettinger building? You said it was new?"

"Brand-new. He bought it at the True Value here in Arlington Heights. Is that important?"

"I like to be thorough." I hung up before she could ask
anything else.

The man who answered the phone at the True Value
sounded proud of their selection. They stocked rope in
three different thicknesses, he said. Each came in ten-,
twenty-five-, and fifty-foot lengths.

Calling Lieutenant Jaworski, to ask about the length of
Stitts's rope, would excite him into asking why I wanted
to know. I was not ready to discuss what was still a small,
but growing, burr in the blanket under my brain.

I called Jennifer Gale at Channel 8. The receptionist
took a message. Jennifer called back in ten minutes. She
remembered me. I told her what I needed.

"Why do you need them?"

"A liability issue."

"Insurance? You're working for the building owners?"

"I don't know for sure. I got hired by an intermediary."
It could have been true.

"Odd, though, that you of all people would get hired to
check that clown's death."

"I don't just paint windows," I said, trying to sound
mildly offended. "My primary business is insurance investigation."

"Of course it is," she said soothingly, as though wishing
I were nearby so she could pat me on the head.

She thought for a moment and then said, "You'll have
to trade for them. You have something I need, as well."

The dim little red warning bulb in my mind flickered.
"What might that be?" I asked, as if I didn't know.

"Background on your zoning story. I've done a little
research. You really do own that turret. Yet it's zoned as
a municipal structure."

"A television story on me will rile the lizards that run
the town. They might never change my zoning to residential, which means I might never unload this place."

"The exposure might make them change your zoning
back to residential."

Her logic was at least as good as mine, maybe even
better.

"Background for now, nothing for broadcast until I approve?" I asked.

She said that sounded fine, for the time being, and told
me she'd see what she could do.

THAT EVENING, JENNIFER GALE did a piece on the horrors of
living rich. A new resident of an upscale golf course sub-
division, having plunked down a number of millions for a
mansion along the fourth fairway, became enraged by the
frequency with which wildly hit golf balls were striking his

dream home. Finally, after yet another ball had ricocheted off his plate glass, the mansion owner's fuse had fried. He charged out, waving a pellet gun to scare the golfer, who was now on the property, searching for his ball. As luck had it, though, the mansion owner slipped on a spot made slick by a number of visiting geese. Falling, he accidentally discharged his gun. The pellet hit a goose. The golfer ran away, unharmed. Not so the goose. It died. A bird-loving neighbor saw it all and called the police, who arrested the mansion owner, now smeared and reeking and glistening, for killing the goose.

Jennifer Gale reported it all with a straight face.

It was a laugh, and it was not. When it was over, I played with my television for another few minutes, switching channels with no real interest. Finally I shut it off, worn down once again by what wasn't on TV.

I started up the stairs to bed. Then someone began pounding on my door. It happens in the late evening, occasionally. Fun lovers, boozed and woozed along Thompson Avenue, sometimes lose sight of their neon guideposts and stagger across the spit of land to the turret, thinking it might be a place for more amusement, or at least a secluded spot to urinate.

This time, though, it was no drunk. It was Jennifer Gale, dressed in a tight-enough pink sweater and considerably well-tailored blue jeans. She carried a laptop computer.

"This is a sort of ambush journalism," she said. "I have what you want, and I have questions. I am hoping I caught you late enough that you are not at your sharpest."

"I don't sleep well," I said, holding the door open for her to come in. "I am never at my sharpest."

She paused as soon as she got inside. First-time visitors do that. The turret's curved, rough limestone walls cast dramatic shadows, no matter what the time of day or type of light. Respecting that, I'd furnished the first floor simply, so as not to detract from the architecture, with two white plastic lawn chairs and a table saw.

"Neat," she said, staring up at the dark beamed ceiling.

"The chairs I found in an alley," I said, drawing her attention to my own contributions. "The table saw came from Sears, originally. I bought it used."

She walked over to the enormous stone fireplace. There is one on each of the five floors.

"This has never had a fire," she said. She leaned in to look up at the flue.

I looked away, so as to not stare at her leaning in, in those considerably well-tailored blue jeans.

"Until me, this place never had a human occupant," I said, my thoughts almost under control.

She pulled a small digital recorder out of her pocket. "For notes, not for broadcast?"

"You've brought me pictures?"

"As you requested."

She set her laptop on my table saw, and we sat on the plastic chairs.

"Let's begin with your background, and the history of this place," she said.

"My grandfather, trained as a brewmaster in the old country, was transformed by Prohibition into becoming a minor bootlegger. He had no Outfit aspirations; he merely sought to brew premium beer for the Slavs and the Czechs who worked at the Western Electric plant in Cicero. The big gangs that controlled whiskey and beer in Chicago didn't mind him much, because his operation was so small. However, they did begin to mind each other, and for a time, they quit brewing and distilling and distributing to concentrate on killing each other. Which left my grandfather's business to blossom. Money rolled in. With his newfound wealth, he did what anyone with a lunatic sense of grandeur would do: He started building a castle along the Willahock River. Sadly, the big guys soon came to an accommodation and resumed deliveries. My grandfather's business tanked. He died, after having finished only this one turret."

"How did this place get zoned municipal?"

"How many pictures did you bring?"

She pointed at the laptop on the table saw. "Every one the *Tribune* received, though they published none. I would imagine they're the same ones the *Argus-Observer* got."

I went on. "After my grandfather died, the title for the land, the pile of limestone, and this turret went to my grandmother. She tried to sell it, but no one wanted part of a castle. After she died, title passed to her daughters, who did not think it necessary to pay the property taxes. Years went by, no taxes were paid. Then, right after World War II, it occurred to the lizards—"

She held up her hand to interrupt. "You keep calling your city administrators lizards."

"They operate low to the ground, and out of sight."

"Ah." She motioned for me to continue.

"After the war, it occurred to the lizards that they'd need a thick, dark, soundproof place to collect graft from what they were hoping would be a postwar business boom. They appropriated most of my grandfather's land and his mountain of limestone for nonpayment of taxes and built the magnificent temple of enormous offices and tiny public rooms you see across the lawn."

"They didn't want the turret?"

"No. It sat for another sixty years, accumulating rodent excrement and more unpaid tax bills, until the last of my grandmother's daughters was near death. My last surviving aunt didn't want to burden her own children with old tax bills, so she cut a deal with city hall. They wouldn't come after her estate for the unpaid taxes if she would approve changing its zoning to municipal. The lizards didn't want to own the turret; they merely wanted control of its exterior to use as a city icon."

"So, zoned as a municipal building, which made it worse than valueless, she left it to you?"

"She never liked me. It was her last flush, on her way out of the world."

"You moved right in?"

"I ignored it for a few years. Until I needed a place to live."

"After your life with Amanda Phelps fell apart."

That was new territory, beyond our agreement. I stood up and moved toward the laptop on the table saw.

"Fair enough, for starters," she said, coming over to join me.

She switched on the computer. The first dozen photographs appeared on the screen. "As you asked, every one, on the roof and going down." She grimaced. "Plus some of him on the sidewalk, after he hit."

"I need copies of my own."

"This is merely an insurance liability issue?"

"As I said, I got hired by an intermediary."

"You'll tell me eventually?"

"No."

She sighed and bent over the laptop. "Your e-mail address?"

I gave it to her. She typed it in and forwarded the pictures.

She smiled then, closing the laptop. It was a lovely smile—and probably made of the hardest steel.

"I'm going to be mad as hell if John Keller scoops me on this clown story," she said at the door.

Of course she would have known about Keller's taunt to the cops. She would have researched the Internet, after I'd asked for the pictures.

"What's the matter with geese?" I asked.

She looked up at my face in the light of the outside lantern, taking a last measure of her odds of extracting more information from me. Then, gently, she shook her head in mock resignation.

"Entirely too slippery," she said.

SEVEN

I ALMOST PHONED when I got your pictures," Leo said when he called the next morning. It was late enough that his voice shouldn't have been muffled and scratchy.

"You were up at three in the morning?" I'd stayed up long after Jennifer Gale had left, studying every picture that showed the rope trailing behind the clown. Then I realized I could study them for decades and still not be able to learn what I needed to know. So I did what I do sometimes when a problem gets too thorny. I dumped it on Leo. I e-mailed him the pictures.

"Ma's friends didn't leave until after two," he said now.

"Double-feature dirty movie night?"

"No. They were exercising."

"No doubt healthier than dirty movies, but until two in the morning?"

He yawned. "The ladies didn't arrive until nine. Then they had to have vodka. Then it took them an hour to make it down to the basement. Then they had to have more vodka—"

"Vodka? To do stretches, partial knee bends, the occasional pirouette?" I made a noise that sounded like a giggle, but then, I was short on sleep, too.

He yawned again. "Come over, and bring your tools."

"For what this time?"

"Two of the poles fell down."

"How energetic did they get?"

"It was the vodka, and Mrs. Roshiska's CD of Polish folk tunes. Very spirited."

"What about the questions I sent with the pictures?"

"Come over with your tools. We'll tighten the poles so none of Ma's friends will die, and I'll show you what I learned."

As he hung up, I thought I heard another yawn.

I put my toolbox in the Jeep and drove to Leo's.

LEO'S BASEMENT HAD undergone more change. Curtain rods had been hung on the walls, and the floor, good enough as bare concrete for almost a century, had now been covered with red tiles flecked with specks of gold.

"All this for exercise?" I asked.

"Ma got the handyman in yesterday. She said she wants to soften up the place."

"Nice television," I said, pointing to the other big change in the basement. A new big-screen television, slightly smaller than the monster in the living room, sat on a long table at the end of the room.

"Ma decided they need instruction videos to exercise right."

I stepped over the two poles that lay on the floor like trees felled by a tornado and looked up at the ceiling. "The bracket screws came right out of the wood joists?"

"A couple of Ma's friends tip in well over two hundred and fifty."

"I thought they were going to just lean against the poles, to steady themselves."

"Apparently, vodka and Polish folk tunes really rev the metabolism."

I wished I could laugh, but it wasn't going to be that kind of morning. Not with what I feared he was going to tell me about the rope.

I reattached all the brackets, top and bottom, with stronger screws. It was only after I took a turn on each pole that he pronounced my work satisfactory.

"Ma's having the handyman back today to give me a door," he said, as we walked through the rough-framed entrance to his office.

"Considerate of her," I said.

He yawned.

I dropped into the huge green overstuffed chair he kept in his office for visiting elephants. He pulled down a projection screen and keyed something into his computer. A picture of the clown falling appeared on the screen.

"You asked about the length of the rope." He pointed a yellow pencil at the screen. "There were actually a dozen shots, taken from far enough away to be good for our purpose. I began by establishing the dimensions of everything in the background, the bricks, the windows, the mortar joints. From those known factors, I calculated how far your unfortunate Mr. Stitts was from the building as he was falling, so I could adjust for the depth of the field in the photograph."

"You mean, how far the rope was from the background of bricks?"

"Yes. Every dimension in the picture has to be known. Once I had those, it was easy to calculate the approximate length of the rope."

"And?" I asked.

"Forty-three feet, maximum."

"You're sure?"

"Give or take a foot, to allow for miscalculations of the slight curves of the rope as it trailed, but yes."

"How about my other question?" I asked after a pause.

"The condition of the trailing end of the rope? I couldn't see any frays, but I can't tell if it had been dipped in something at a factory to prevent it from unraveling. You'll have to inspect the rope itself for that."

He hadn't confirmed it all, but he'd confirmed enough.

"What are you thinking?" he asked, after I'd said nothing.

"A fifty-foot rope, wound and knotted around a thirty-inch door."

"Subtract a little more than five feet for the loop, another two for a double knot? Leaves forty-three feet, exactly what I calculated."

My mind jittered over the scenario. One second the rope was taut, securing the clown as he danced high at the edge of the roof. The next, it was falling behind him, cut away by someone hiding in the small rooftop hutch. Best of all, the unseen killer would have taken the evidence—the seven feet of rope that had been cut off—away with him.

Leo's voice intruded from somewhere distant.

"It means a cut rope?" he was asking.

"It means murder," I said.

EIGHT

I THREATENED DUGGAN from the Jeep. "I'll come to your office, give you my report."

"Tell me on the phone."

"I need to report in person, to you…" I paused, then added, "And your client."

"Impossible," he snapped.

"Necessary," I said.

"Tell me, damn it."

"You mean like John Keller told you?"

It had been no coincidence that Duggan had hired me just a few hours after Keller's taunt to the cops came out in the *Argus-Observer*. Keller had turned up the burner under the clown's death, and Duggan's client had felt the heat. Enough to send Duggan to hire me, that same day.

The question I wanted answered was why.

"You, and your client," I repeated.

"This is unprofessional, Elstrom."

"Damn right," I agreed, affably enough.

He swore. "Hold for a minute."

It wasn't for a minute; it was for five. When he came back, it was only to say, "I'll call you," before he hung up.

Maybe he hadn't gotten through to his client. That was fine; he'd already not said enough. He hadn't asked the one question he should have, right off the bat. He hadn't asked if the clown had been murdered.

He hadn't asked, because he already knew.

A GREEN TOYOTA PRIUS was parked at my curb when I got back to the turret. Jennifer Gale was parked on the bench down by the Willahock.

I didn't recognize her at first. Gone was any trace of makeup. Gone were the on-camera clothes, and the well-tailored jeans she'd worn the evening before. This day, she wore a long-sleeved Chicago Bears jersey, baggy denims, and scuffed running shoes. Without makeup, the lines on her face were pronounced, and I adjusted her age upward by another five years. I thought that made her more beautiful.

"A newspaper reader," she said, looking at the *Argus-Observer* I'd stopped for on the way home. "I thought you were all extinct."

"I don't subscribe, for fear of commitment. I buy from the box, once or twice a week, and then usually the *Tribune*."

"Except today you bought the *Argus-Observer*."

I sat down. The bench was not long, but it could provide sufficient distance between two people, if one of them remembers he loves the woman he's used to sharing it with, even if she's his ex-wife and has trouble returning his phone calls.

"You needn't bother," she said, tapping the *Argus-Observer* I'd set on the bench between us. "I already looked through it. There's nothing new from Keller."

She'd seen through the smoke I'd sent up about wanting the clown photos for an insurance matter.

"You just happened to be driving by?" I asked, thinking a diversion might be productive.

"Nice view, if they'd clean it up," she said, of the containers and jugs bumping against their tire prisons.

"They did once. They hired high school kids to haul out

all the debris. Then the lizards held a series of soirees, pitching the idea of a Rivertown Renaissance to developers."

"I've seen those Renaissance banners on the light poles along Thompson Avenue. They're tattered." She grinned suddenly. "How perfectly medieval: They need your turret for their Renaissance."

"The developers never bought into the idea. Only the garbage came back." I turned to look at her. "You didn't come to enjoy the Willahock."

"Driving by, I thought I'd stop in, see what I can learn about a death that everyone, except John Keller and you, thinks was a tragic accident."

"I'm really supposed to accept that you were just driving by?"

"It would be convenient."

Just like I hadn't figured her for just driving by, I couldn't figure her appearance. The two previous times I'd seen her, Jennifer Gale had been impeccably dressed and made up. Though both times had been for a camera— when Elvis had been arrested, and then, last night, immediately following her broadcast—I didn't imagine she went anywhere without makeup, dressed in baggy, worn clothes. Unless, that morning, she was deliberately trying to avoid recognition.

"Trying for incognito this morning?" I asked.

"So, what did the photos show?" she asked, dodging.

"I just got them last night," I said, dodging as well.

"Yes, and you told me you never sleep."

I shrugged.

"OK," she said. "Let's talk more about you and Rivertown."

"Nothing more to tell."

"Rivertown has always been known as a harmlessly

crooked little town. Run tightly by the same expanded family for decades. Word has always been that no one much minds, because the place is so small, and its greasy goings-on—the hookers, the gambling, the payoffs—never seemed to affect anyone outside the town limits. So I'm wondering why the mayor's nephew, a dullard by all accounts, would now venture beyond the safety of those town limits."

"You're suggesting Elvis didn't come up with this scheme on his own? I agree. Yet I don't see the lizards risking scrutiny over something like salad oil."

"You don't like scrutiny, either, Mr. Elstrom," she said after a moment.

I turned to watch the milk jugs dance with the oil containers.

"You used to have a tidy little business," she went on, "researching, photographing, working for law firms and insurance companies. You married Amanda Phelps, daughter of Wendell, one of the biggest movers and shakers in Chicago. You moved into her mansion at Crystal Waters. You were living the golden life."

"Every day was sunny, for sure."

"Then you were accused of validating false evidence in the Evangeline Wilts trial."

"I was duped. I was exonerated."

"Yes, and fairly quickly, but only after being trashed by John Keller in the *Argus-Observer*, and that ruined you, of money and business. And perhaps of Amanda Phelps, because you brought dishonor to the doorstop of the powerful Wendell Phelps. She dumped you—"

"Actually, I dumped myself," I cut in. "She just had me rolled out the door."

"You returned to the town of your youth, to huddle in your grandfather's turret."

"Awaiting the Rivertown Renaissance."

"At which time you can sell your turret for a princely sum?"

The banter was giving me a headache. "That's the plan."

"Except your turret is zoned as a municipal structure, even though you own it. Who would buy it, if it's zoned only for city use?"

"Where's this going?"

"Right back to Elvis Derbil, salad oil king and zoning commissioner. He's got you under his greasy thumb. Your story will make a heck of a follow-up to the piece we ran on Derbil."

"You're not pushing for my little story, though."

She smiled. She hadn't come to follow up on Elvis; she was scratching for leverage, to find out what I knew about the clown.

"I'll be more direct: You want to come with me to see the rope?" she asked.

"What?" I managed, but it was too late to play dumb.

"You wanted the pictures because you think the clown was murdered, right? You're thinking the rope was cut?"

I kept my eyes on the oil containers and milk jugs, but they offered no counsel on how to deal with someone who thought as fast as Jennifer Gale.

"I'm going to check out the rope," she went on. "I can get you in, too—but you've got to give me what you know."

"I don't know anything, not yet," I said.

"You know enough to suspect that rope was cut." She checked her watch and stood up. "I'll call you when everything is arranged," she said and walked up the hill to her car.

NINE

A MESSENGER CAME an hour later. He handed me an envelope. I was expecting a termination letter from Duggan, firing me for demanding to get close to his client. It wasn't. Handwritten on the upper left corner of the envelope, where the return address goes for people who don't use messenger services to deliver their mail, was lettered, simply, "Sweetie."

The note inside was written on thick cream-colored stock that matched the envelope. "Dear Mr. Elstrom, I apologize for the lateness of this, but Amanda Phelps suggests that you are a person I should know. Can you join us at a small get-together this evening, at seven o'clock?" It named an address off Michigan Avenue, on Chicago's Gold Coast, and was signed "Sweetie Fairbairn."

I looked up. "Thank you," I said.

The messenger made a polite cough. "I'm to wait for the favor of a reply, sir."

It was easy enough to do. I didn't know Sweetie Fairbairn, but I did know Amanda Phelps, my dark-haired, sparkling eyed, vixen ex-wife.

The messenger was resolutely keeping his eyes away from my paint-splattered, caulk-encrusted clothes. He probably learned that kind of self-control in messenger school.

"Tell Miss Fairbairn I'll be happy to attend."

He nodded and went to his car. I went inside, to my computer.

Google reported that Sweetie Fairbairn was the widow

of an important industrialist, Silas Fairbairn. She was a socialite, a board member, and seemingly a friend to all of Chicago's rich and famous. Mostly, she seemed to be a philanthropist, judging by the number of charity Web sites that showed her, an attractive, middle-aged blond woman, quite short, posing with other attractive, middle-aged blond women, almost all of whom were at least half a head taller than she was. They all appeared to be wearing clothes that cost more than the kitchen appliances I couldn't afford.

I went outside and climbed up my ladder. It was where I belonged. I didn't know people who traveled in Sweetie Fairbairn's circles, except for that most exquisite lady she'd mentioned in her invitation—and that one wasn't even blond.

AMANDA HAD BEEN raised rich, by a man who controlled Chicago's largest electric utility but was indifferent to raising his daughter. I'd been raised indifferently, too, but poor, by a trio of aunts who shuffled me around like a suitcase left behind by a long-gone relation. The relation was their sister, my mother, who took off the day after I was born.

I met Amanda when I was making a stab at what I imagined was the good life. I was living downtown in Chicago, driving a used Mercedes, building up a small research firm that serviced lawyers and insurance companies. I thought I was done with Rivertown forever. She was living in a gated suburban community, in a micromansion mostly unfurnished because she'd blown her grandfather's inheritance on the eleven million dollars' worth of art she hung on the walls. We married because we didn't think seriously about the differences in our backgrounds. We divorced a year later because, by then, we could think of nothing else. And because I'd been portrayed as a fool in the newspapers, after being falsely accused of rigging evidence in a suburban mayor's trial. I'd blamed the bad publicity on Amanda, reasoning—in an increasingly sodden state—that my notoriety was her fault because her father was such a prominent man.

The love, though, never left. It survived the Wilts trial, and my reckless days that followed. It survived our divorce, and later, a crazed man's attempt to blow up her gated community, one house at a time. It survived a reappearance, of a sort, of a girl I'd once been suspected of killing, years before.

It had survived all of that, and we'd actually begun nibbling at the notion of living together again, when her father, always a distant shadow when she'd been growing up, experienced some sort of come-to-the-mountain moment. He shed his indifference and set out to take over his daughter's life as craftily as he took over the smaller, less defensible utility companies he routinely added to his conglomerate. He offered her the directorship of his organization's multimillion-dollar charitable works programs. They both knew it was a guilt play—his, at not having been around when she was growing up—hers, if she passed on an opportunity to help thousands of people.

She took the job. Gone went the classes she taught at the Art Institute, gone went the book on Renaissance art she'd been working on. And gone, maybe, was the time we needed to rebuild what had been between us. We now communicated through the buffers of answering machines—mostly hers—and e-mails…and now, through an invitation from one of her friends.

It was good enough.

I CALLED AMANDA'S office at four o'clock, intending to leave the message that I'd see her at Sweetie Fairbairn's that evening. Amazingly, her secretary put me right through.

"Thanks," I began, when Amanda picked up.

There were voices in her background. "For what?" she said, after she did something to quiet them.

"For Sweetie's party."

A voice near her got louder. "Sure, that will be fine," Amanda said. Then, to me, "Sweetie called an hour ago to tell me it was a bit of a last-minute thing, but that you'd accepted her invitation for tonight."

"I'll bet she gets through to you easier than I do." It came out cranky, and I regretted it.

"Listen, Dek—"

"I know you're busy, Amanda."

"Don't patronize me."

"OK; you're not busy."

"And don't be your usual smart-assed self."

I shut up, and waited.

After a few seconds, her breathing slowed. "Look, I'm sorry I haven't returned a couple of your phone calls. It's just that this is becoming so much more than I imagined…" Her voice trailed off.

"You don't have to be doing it."

"I should go back to indulging myself at the Art Institute, a princess with millions in art and no conscience?"

It was an argument we'd had, a dozen times. I skipped my usual self-righteous pronouncement that her father was bribing her, saying instead, "Forget it. No big deal, if you've been busy."

"Thank you," she said, too simply.

"And thank you, for engineering that invitation."

"You started to say that before. What do you mean?"

"Snagging me the invitation to Sweetie Fairbairn's party. A date's a date, no matter where we have it."

Something buzzed; probably her phone. "Hold, please."

She parked me in the ether so quickly it took me a second to realize I was listening to dead air.

After a long three minutes, she came back. "I did not 'engineer' your invitation, as you say. I met Sweetie a month ago, at a dinner. I'm afraid I put the arm on her for the new children's wing at Memorial Hospital. We traded histories a little; she wants to know about the people who hit her up for money. In the course of things, I must have mentioned you. That's it, Dek. I had no idea you'd be attending this evening until an hour ago, when she called to tell me."

"Perhaps she learned I am someone who could add a little gravity to her circle of friends."

She laughed, for the first time I'd heard in a month. "I'm sure it's just a little background checking."

"To put a face to the man you're seeing?"

She paused one heartbeat too long to be encouraging. "More likely to be sure I'm on the up-and-up. Sweetie is very particular about her donations."

"I could be a liability?"

"There'll be food, Dek. She'll give you an air kiss, spend two minutes talking to you, and leave you thinking you are the most important person she's ever met. She's nice."

"Then we can slip away, have a drink someplace?"

Again, a pause. "Not tonight, I'm afraid. There'll be people from foundations there, people who can get things done."

"Tomorrow night, then?"

"A dinner with the board of the Metropolitan YMCA."

I didn't bother to ask if she was free for dinner any other nights. That's what bothered me the most, after we hung up.

That I hadn't bothered.

TEN

THE GOLD COAST of Chicago, those blocks along and surrounding Michigan Avenue north of the river, is studded with solid midwestern values, so long as the midwesterner is a millionaire and values huge-buck condominiums and glitzy stores that offer hundred-thousand-dollar necklaces and thousand-dollar shoes.

Once, early in our relationship, Amanda and I were walking along Michigan Avenue. It was a splendid spring evening, and we paused to look at the men's clothing displayed in the window of one particularly expensive-looking place. Go in and look around, she taunted, knowing full well that although I liked good, grand made me itch. A dare was a dare, though, so I took it. We went in, and I moved around trying to appear like I belonged, all the while avoiding looking at what I was sure would be a smirk on her face. At one point I stopped to finger the cuff of a two-thousand-dollar sport coat. A salesman came up and inquired whether I liked it. Indeed I did, I said, but then inspiration struck. I told the man I was wondering about the pants. Sir? he asked, confused. The pants, I responded; surely, for two thousand dollars, the coat came with about fifty pairs of pants? Amanda lost it then. Choking with laughter, she hustled me out of there quick as lightning, and proposed that we never walk along Michigan Avenue again.

Sweetie Fairbairn's address was in the middle of all that, on Oak, a side street. I drove past it three times before I realized she lived in the Wilbur Wright. It was an old, ten-story hotel built right after the Wright Brothers' first flight and named after one of them, though whether Wilbur was the one who flew the contraption or jumped up and down on the ground, I couldn't remember.

The doorman didn't come over when I pulled to the curb. He might have been reluctant to offer encouragement to anyone lingering in such a battered vehicle, or perhaps he was confused about how to communicate through a plastic side window criss-crossed with so much silver tape.

I unzipped the window corner and fluttered my hand out in a beckoning fashion. It was enough. He nodded, came over, and bent down to put his mouth to the small triangular opening.

"Sir?"

"Does Sweetie Fairbairn live here?"

"We're not allowed to give out..."

I'd spiked her invitation on a wire that used to connect to the radio. I pulled it off and held the paper to the opening.

What I could see of his mouth softened as he reclassified me from poor to strange. "Very well, sir. We have valet parking."

I got out and handed the key to the kid who came up. "Anything falls off, put it in back, on top of the Burger King wrappers."

The kid nodded like that was a usual request, and I walked inside.

The lobby was small, polished stainless steel and shiny black marble. The concierge was a young man with glossy black hair, hired perhaps because he matched the marble. I flashed Sweetie's invitation, punctured though it was.

"Sweetie Fairbairn's suite," I said, not only using the S words symmetrically, but announcing as well that I had enough class to know hers would not be some closet-sized room facing an air shaft.

"Penthouse," the glossy young man corrected, raising his nose a half inch. "Not suite." He pointed to the last elevator down a short corridor, where a broad-shouldered man was talking to two slender blond women.

They turned as I approached, anticipating a fellow social traveler. It wasn't just the man's shoulders that were broad, I saw; his whole suit coat was cut wide. He had a gun on his hip.

All smiled—the man carefully; the women uncertainly, and then only after all four of their eyes had lingered on my necktie. I'd taken special care with my outfit, going over my blue blazer twice with my Shop-Vac to make sure I'd gotten up all the oak dust. The khakis were selected as being the cleanest from the pile on the chair by my bed, though I supposed their wrinkles might have caused the pickiest of observers to wonder if I'd slept in them more than once. Finally, I'd selected the new-looking floral necktie because it matched my blue button-down shirt. Also because it was the only tie I owned.

The elevator had barely begun to rise when first one woman, then the other, began sneezing. Apparently, I'd not vacuumed enough. I took a discreet step back into the corner, to give them better air. It didn't work. They sneezed, almost in unison, a second and then a third time.

Mercifully, the door opened after that. The women fled. The guard remained, motioning me out.

I stepped into a small foyer papered in red silk. A young man in a tuxedo offered me a flute of champagne from a tray. I took it into an enormous, softly yellow living room.

At least a hundred people were there, chatting and laughing and bobbing their heads with such animation that they could well have been filled with helium. There was lots of tan cleavage—some wrinkled, some not—white teeth, and glittering jewelry, but no formal evening gowns or tuxedos other than on the waitstaff, I was relieved to see. The room smelled of the fresh cut flowers that seemed to be everywhere, and, I supposed, of the smug self-assurance that comes from mingling with one's affluent own.

I'd paused, unsure where to go, when a hand gently touched my arm. It was a lovely hand, attached to an equally lovely arm, all part of my most favorite terrain on the planet.

"I've been watching the door, hoping I could stop you before you belly flopped onto the buffet table," Amanda whispered.

She was, as always, magnificent. She wore a simple black dress that matched her hair, and a garnet and diamond pendant that caught the flecks of fire in her eyes. The skin around them was taut, though—and wary. She looked tired.

"You look tired," I said.

She squeezed my arm. "I told Sweetie you'd want to bolt as soon as you saw the crowd."

She led me to a quiet place by a tall window that looked out over the city. Even though the Wilbur Wright was small—ten stories is nothing in any city anymore—the Wright Brothers for sure would have been impressed. I was standing higher than they first flew, and I'd made the ascent without getting a single bug stuck to my teeth.

Amanda made a show of standing back and looking at my outfit. "Same blazer, same pants, same shirt, same tie," she said.

"I remain unchanged."

She winced slightly at what she took to be a small pettiness.

"I didn't mean that the way it came out," I said quickly.

"It won't last forever, Dek. Just until I get settled into whatever it is I'm settling into."

"Good deeds."

"Good deeds."

For a minute we both stared out the window like strangers new to town.

"Ever hear of the heiress who built that penthouse?" She pointed at another hotel, across Michigan Avenue.

"Never."

"Airlifting the construction material by helicopter required F.A.A. approval."

"Sounds like a reasonable use of an inheritance."

"Sweetie heard about that. Ten years ago, she and Silas bought the roof on this place and did the same, helicopters and all."

"Airlifting two-by-fours doesn't impress."

"It does them, the social creatures. They take their cues from one another. That means outrageous things, sometimes. That can also mean big donations. One person gives; others follow. A lot of money is raised for charity that way." She turned away from the window. "This can be my chance to make something positive out of my father's wealth and connections." She smiled at me with those weary, beautiful eyes. "How about a movie, a week from tomorrow night?"

"And dinner."

"At our trattoria," she added, smiling. It was where I'd proposed, after so very few dates.

Before she got snagged by charitable works, we'd started going back there, first tentatively, then frequently, after our divorce. The reminding was part of the rebuilding.

"All right," I said, rolling my eyes with exaggerated reluctance, "but don't expect anything afterward."

Her laugh was loud then, and genuine. It warmed the room, and my core, where I keep my sense of well-being.

"I must go, schmooze with rich people," she said. "The buffet is against the far wall."

"What about Sweetie Fairbairn?"

"I told her you'd be by the food."

Then she was gone.

Having subsisted on modestly portioned, microwavable meals for too long, I found the buffet with the urgency of a falcon diving for a mouse. The table was twenty-five feet long and filled with the usual caviar, squiggly little pastries stuffed with squiggly little cheeses, veggies, and meats that were not at all usual to me. At the far end, there was a goodly portion of a steer up on its side, attended to by a fellow with a white hat and a long knife. Most exciting of all, nothing on the table appeared to have been painted red to disguise marine origins.

The item in the center of the table, though, gave me pause. It was long, orange, and shaped like a paving brick.

The color was right, the shape perfect. A bizarre thought formed. I gave the table a nudge with my hip, but the thing did not quiver, at least not convincingly.

"Wondering?"

A short blond woman in a black dress and a single strand of small pearls had come up.

I turned. "Yes."

She picked up a bone china plate—no paper for those digs, high atop the Wilbur Wright—and a linen napkin. "Let me help you," she said. Her voice had a slight lilt, a trace of something Scandinavian.

She could have been forty, she could have been fifty. She could have been beautiful, or perhaps not. Certainly her makeup had been artfully, and maybe professionally, applied. As she started filling the plate, I noticed faint age spots on her hands, spots that no creams could completely hide.

She filled the plate quickly. At the caviar, she paused, raising an eyebrow.

I thought back to the lasagna I'd eaten, not that many nights earlier, and shook my head. "I've had too much seafood lately." She nodded and continued adding to the plate. She finished at the end of the table, when the white-hatted man laid a large slice of rare roast beef over the mound on the plate, as though trying to hide an embarrassment of too much food with a blanket.

"You deliberately avoided that?" I asked, pointing at the brick on the table's center.

She smiled and nudged the table with her hip as she'd seen me do. Again, I could not tell if the yellow-orange thing had quivered.

"It's getting old," she said, sighing. "A connoisseur?"

"I know certain delights." I shrugged modestly. "No one else seems to be interested in it, though."

"They don't know what it is. I set it out every time, but no one takes."

"Same brick?"

"I'm afraid it's lost some of its suppleness; it no longer jiggles."

"Velveeta," I said.

"Velveeta," she confirmed.

With that, I felt as though I'd liked her forever.

She carried my mounded plate past a man standing at the head of a short hallway. He, too, wore a square suit, like the guard who'd ridden up in the elevator.

She opened a door, and I followed her in. The room was small, no bigger than the one I had in college, and decorated about as well. A laptop computer sat on a beat-up wood desk backed against a wall. Above the desk, a huge corkboard held a large calendar that was penciled in with dozens of appointments, and a worn picture postcard of a covered bridge that had octagonal windows.

Next to the desk, a metal typing table held an old red IBM Selectric typewriter. A row of high beige filing cabinets ran along an adjacent wall.

I'd seen crummier-looking home offices, but not many.

She motioned me to a worn wood armchair that creaked when I sat down. After handing me my plate, she went to sit at the desk, in an ultramodern black mesh chair that appeared to be the only expensive furnishing in the room.

"Welcome to Shangri-La, Mr. Elstrom."

"It does feel quite comfortable," I agreed.

"I can think in here."

"I do my thinking on my roof," I said, as though that made sense.

"Eat, Mr. Elstrom," she said. "Amanda told me you like to eat."

The beef blanket was tender enough to cut with my fork. For sure it had never developed muscle swimming in the sea.

I chewed, and waited to chit and chat.

"You're still very close to Amanda," she said.

"You heard this from Amanda?"

"Not in so many words."

I looked up from a particularly interesting little piece of cheese. "I like to think we're still close, yes."

"Sometimes you appear in the newspapers."

Amanda wouldn't have told her that. Sweetie Fairbairn had done research.

"I try to avoid publicity." I chewed faster, to clear my mouth. Our small talk, even mitigated by fine nibbles, was presenting the potential to turn nasty.

"I'm considering making a rather sizable contribution to an effort she's leading," she said.

It was as Amanda had said. Sweetie Fairbairn wanted to make sure I had no way of getting at any of the money Amanda raised.

"We never did share checkbooks, Ms. Fairbairn. Anyway, we're divorced."

"I don't wish to offend, but I must be careful."

"I understand."

"Are you really an understanding man, Mr. Elstrom?"

"Unfortunately, I've demanded to be understood more than I've learned to understand," I said. It was one of the things I thought about, up on my roof.

She smiled faintly and stood up. "Thank you for coming," she said. She'd satisfied herself about me in record time.

We went out into the hall. She aimed for a cluster of glittering people. I moved toward the window where Amanda and I had stood a few moments earlier.

I watched Amanda's reflection in the glass. She was engrossed in conversation with one very thin woman and two distinguished-looking, silver-haired men. She looked happier than I'd seen her in months, and seemed to especially enjoy the witty asides of one of the distinguished men.

I tried to concentrate on the drama of the view she and I had enjoyed just a few minutes before, but the picture out the window had been changed by the superimposition of Amanda's reflection on the glass. Chicago no longer sparkled. It looked like a cold, hard town, a place of dark shadows and too bright lights—the kind of place where a guy could lose his girl, or a clown could go off a roof, and nobody would much mind.

My appetite was gone. I set my plate on an end table, and left Sweetie Fairbairn's penthouse as quietly as if I were sneaking away with a pocket full of silverware.

The same guard who'd ridden up with me was waiting

when I got out of the elevator. Across the lobby, outside the glass door, someone's black limousine had pulled up under the canopy.

It prompted an inspiration.

"Tim Duggan around?" I asked the guard.

"Somewhere," he said.

I pulled out the little spiral notebook I am never without. I wrote two words on a sheet, signed it, and tore it out. I folded the little note in half and handed it to him.

"For Ms. Fairbairn," I said, and walked out, quite alone, into the night.

ELEVEN

IT SHOULD HAVE been a clown tumbling off a high roof, or Sweetie Fairbairn murmuring lies, or Amanda ecstatic at the wit of a finely dressed man, but it was a dream of Elvis Derbil that tore me, sweating, from sleep at four thirty the next morning. He'd been kneeling on the far side of the Willahock, filling empty salad dressing bottles with the muck that moved cloudy at the bank.

It didn't matter. Most nights, one dream or another usually wakes me earlier than four forty. At least Elvis had the decency to let me sleep until almost sunrise.

I pushed myself out of bed, rang the curved wrought-iron stairs going down to the would-be kitchen, and awoke Mr. Coffee. Leaving him to burble, I went outside, crossed the street, the spit of land, and Thompson Avenue, and bought an *Argus-Observer* from the box under the red and white Jiffy Lube sign. The coffee was ready when I got back. I took a travel mug's worth and the paper up to the roof. I keep a lawn chair there for when faces awaken me in the night and I go up to wait for the sun to make them go away.

Rivertown is best in the dark just before dawn, when the neon and the noise from the honky-tonks along Thompson Avenue have shut down; when the girls who work the curbs have shut down, too, gone to the rooming houses back of where the factories used to light the night, to lie for a few hours blessedly alone. It is a good time to think.

I started with the strong probabilities. Sweetie Fairbairn

learned I did investigations from some earlier, innocuous comment of Amanda's. Supposing I'd be as good as anyone to take a fast, anonymous look at the death of James Stitts, she sent Duggan to hire me. I'd become troublesome, insisting on meeting with Duggan's client. That demanded an inspection by Sweetie Fairbairn, before she proceeded with me. Or not.

After that, my certainty floundered. If Sweetie Fairbairn was innocent of any knowledge of the clown's death, she would have gotten better and faster results using the connections a woman like her must have had to the highest levels of the Chicago police.

If she weren't innocent, she'd never respond to the note I left at the Wilbur Wright.

My mind flitted then, back to the party and the delight on Amanda's face, as she laughed at a slick man's joke. I pushed the image away.

The sky had begun to lighten to the east. The tonks, liquor stores, hockshops, and the bowling alley were beginning to materialize, gauzy and indistinct, in the dim, growing light of the new morning. There was enough light to read now. I picked up the *Argus-Observer*.

As usual, the rag carried little serious news. Keller teased about a supposed kickback scheme in Chicago; another columnist wrote of a diet regimen gone wrong in Hollywood. The longest story was on the third page, about a cat that could play the piano. Or not.

There was nothing about the clown. I tossed the remains of my cold coffee over the wall and went inside.

"YOU LOOK LIKE hell." Leo said a couple of hours later, stepping out onto his front steps. He wore a neon green sweatshirt with Woody Woodpecker embroidered on it. "Would you like coffee?"

"I've been up on the roof for hours, drinking coffee."

"You have a dilemma?"

I nodded.

He told me to sit on the steps and went inside. We'd sweated a thousand dilemmas on those front steps, spring through fall, since seventh grade.

He came out with two of Ma's scratched porcelain mugs, steaming with coffee. He'd also brought several newspaper sheets, tucked under his arm.

"Coffee with fortifier," he said. "You'll bloom like a rose."

It was a surprise. Coffee and fortifier was coffee and Jack Daniel's.

I took a sip. He'd made it weak, just enough to flavor the brew, because he knew I avoided booze since my divorce.

"My dilemma," I began, after he sat down.

He looked at the folded newspapers he'd set on the concrete between us. "I know."

I set down my cup. "What do you mean?"

"Amanda and that guy. Three times, their photos have been in the papers."

My face must have looked paralyzed. Because his then registered the shock of realizing he'd just told me something hurtful that I didn't know.

"Lovely day today," he said, looking for even the smallest laugh.

"What guy, Leo?"

"I thought that was why you came over." He unfolded one of the newspaper sheets and handed it to me. "Today's *Tribune.* A party, night before last."

It was one of those society lineup photos, fine folks dressed in fine duds to do fine deeds. Amanda stood next to the silver-haired fellow I'd seen at Sweetie Fairbairn's, the guy who'd made her laugh. They'd been at a fundraiser for the Lyric Opera. His hand rested around her waist.

Leo mumbled something about getting us more forti- fier, meaning he was going to give me a minute with the other news sheets. He took my cup, which I'd barely tasted, and went inside.

The man's name was Richard Rudolph. In addition to heading a commodities trading firm, he sat on charitable boards. He looked every bit a rich, do-gooding son of a bitch. In each photo, Amanda looked delighted to be with him.

Leo must have been waiting just inside the screen door, because he came out the instant I looked up.

"It doesn't have to mean anything," he said, setting down the coffees. "Those people travel together, in packs."

"Not with their arms around each other."

I picked up my cup, took a taste. He'd added only more coffee. He was my friend.

"That was only in today's photo, Dek."

"Maris Mays?" I asked, keeping my eyes on the shutters of the bungalow across the street. Maris was a girl Leo and I had known. She'd disappeared right after high school. Years later, someone hired me to execute a will, and that led me back to those very old times. Maris haunted me during that investigation, and that had haunted Amanda.

"Maris didn't reorient Amanda's world," Leo said. "Wendell Phelps did. Old Dad brought her into his com- pany, and into his life. Those pictures don't have to mean anything."

"They meant something to you; you saved them."

"I was thinking you'd seen them, and would want to talk."

"Shit, Leo."

"Tell me about your dilemma," he said.

"You mean my other dilemma?" Whining, self-indulgence, and churlish words were still called for.

"OK. Your other dilemma."

"Ever hear of Sweetie Fairbairn?" I folded the news sheets so I wouldn't have to look at the photos of Amanda and the silver-topped gigolo.

"I did work for her once, part of a team she'd hired to authenticate two Jackson Pollocks she wanted to buy for the Art Institute."

"Jackson Pollock? Was that the guy who threw paint?"

"Boor." He laughed too hard and too long at my feeble joke. Then, "Why do you ask about Sweetie Fairbairn?"

"I went to a party at her penthouse last night. Amanda was there, and at first I thought she'd arranged the invitation, so we could steal a few moments."

"Go on," he said, after I'd paused for too long, thinking about naïveté.

"Sweetie herself took me aside for a short, intimate chat, ostensibly about my relationship these days with Amanda."

"Ostensibly?"

"She told me she was considering donating to one of Amanda's projects, and asked certain perfunctory questions about how close we were."

"Meaning whether you could get your lunch hooks on money Amanda took in?"

"That's what I was thinking, yes."

"Can you blame her? Look at the way you dress, as opposed to someone with refinement." He touched Woody Woodpecker's beak. He was going to get a laugh out of me, no matter how long it took.

"She satisfied herself about my trustworthiness too quickly."

"Your winning smile, working at its usual warp speed?"

"She'd been sizing me up, all right, but it had nothing to do with Amanda. Sweetie Fairbairn is my client."

"The clown case? She was the one who hired you?"

"To be certain, I asked one of last night's guards if Duggan, the guy who'd hired me, was around. He said yes."

"What's the dilemma? That Sweetie Fairbairn somehow knew the clown?"

"The widow Stitts told me her husband had been hired by a woman who rolled up in a chauffeured limousine."

"Come on, Dek. A lot of women in this town get around in limos."

"Only one invited me to a party to give me the once-over."

"Now you're thinking she hired you to see if there's evidence that ties her to the clown's death?"

"The scenario works."

He gave that some thought and said, "That's a humdinger of a dilemma."

"For sure."

"What are you going to do?"

"If my client's a killer…" I let the thought fade.

I shook my head, he shook his, and we walked—two bobble-heads—down to the sidewalk.

"Seriously, what are you going to do?" he asked through the open door, after I got in the Jeep.

"I already did it. I left her a two-word note, last night: 'The Clown?'"

"What if she doesn't respond?"

"Then what I'd like to do is wait after school for the silver-haired bastard who's sniffing around my girlfriend, and beat the shit out of him on the playground."

TWELVE

JENNIFER GALE CALLED right after I got back to the turret. "Let's meet for lunch," she said.

"The rope?"

"I've got news."

She would also have questions about the clown's death, Rivertown, and my zoning. She would dig at all kinds of things I didn't want to talk about.

At that moment, sour and cranky from thinking about Amanda and her silver-haired friend, the idea of being interrogated by Jennifer Gale about anything at all sounded splendid. I agreed in less time than I should have.

"We'll meet at noon," she said. She gave me directions to a place I'd never heard of, adding, "Typical gourmet: miniscule portions and enormous prices, but there's never a crowd. It's a great place to talk. I hope you'll be dressed appropriately."

"I never am, not for a gourmet place." I was wearing one of my three pairs of khakis and one of my three blue button-down shirts.

"See you in a half hour."

I put on my floral tie and my blazer. Then, mindful of the sneezing I'd set off in the elevator rising to Sweetie's penthouse, I lingered for a moment outside, in the cleansing breeze off the Willahock, before getting into the Jeep.

The name of the place, Galecki's, matched what she'd given me, but everything else about it was wrong. The walls were paneled in fake knotty pine, worn yellow-and-white-checkered oil-cloths covered the tables, and the place was mobbed with enough blue collars to make me think the food was good and reasonably priced. The day's special, stuffed cabbage rolls, was chalked on a board above the cash register, in English and in Polish.

I'd been had, by a woman who might be as playful as she was beautiful and threatening. I took off my tie, jammed it into my blazer pocket, and worked my way through the crowd to add my name to the waiting list.

"Elstrom?" The hostess looked me up and down as if she were inspecting beef. She was a babushka with a heavy Polish accent, another Ma Brumsky, though ideally she possessed a more refined taste in movies.

"Elstrom?" she repeated, holding out the menu like she was going to jerk it back if I answered wrong.

"Yes."

"Miss Fancy Pants Gale phoned, tell me to seat you at her special table." She led me through the packed dining area to a tiny, two-person booth behind a floor-to-ceiling shelf filled with napkins, dishwashing detergent, and enough bottles of ketchup to disguise all the fish and lasagna I'd ever microwave.

Jennifer Gale had been straight about one thing. The booth was secluded enough from the din to be the perfect place to talk.

The hostess left me with the menu. A moment later, a waitress brought me coffee with a knowing smile. Obviously, not everybody got to sit behind the ketchup at Ms. Fancy Pants Gale's special booth.

Jennifer breezed in five minutes later, followed closely by the hostess. She wore a green sweater and khakis, though her khakis had been pressed more recently than mine, perhaps that very day. Perhaps even, judging by their perfect fit, while she was inside of them.

Fancy pants, indeed.

She slid into the booth, saw the hostess looking closely at me.

"Forget it," Jennifer said to the babushka. "He's got a rich girlfriend."

The older woman pursued her lips. "How rich?"

"Mama!"

The hostess shot her a dark look, winked at me, and left.

"That's your mother?"

"Who else but a mother would act so blatantly? I tell her I'm happy with my career. She can't imagine how that can be, if I don't already have three kids and am not pregnant with a fourth."

"It's Galecki, then, not Gale?"

"My maiden name. I thought Gale sounded better for the news."

"You're married?"

For the briefest of instants, her features froze. "He died."

The waitress came back with coffee for Jennifer and a refill for me. Jennifer said something to her in Polish. The waitress smiled, took my menu, and went away.

"What am I having?" I asked.

"The cabbage, but everything's good here."

"Especially Mama?"

She smiled. "Especially Mama." She took a sip of her coffee. "If Elvis Derbil is a minion, not a born risk taker, who is telling him what to do?"

"I don't see anyone at city hall telling him to venture past the town limits."

"Who, then?"

"I can't imagine."

"Then tell me about the clown's rope."

"You're the one who wants to go see it," I countered.

"Work with me, Dek Elstrom. I have resources you can't match."

"To use for broadcast, unfortunately."

"OK. Same deal as we have with your zoning story: nothing about the clown for broadcast, until you say— but not for forever, and you must bring me along, every step of the way."

Her conditions were reasonable, and I did need to see the rope to be sure.

"As you suggested the last time we met, I think the rope was cut," I said.

"Murder?"

"I have no idea who would have motive."

Our lunch came. Mine was four cabbage rolls, set on a pile of potato dumplings. Hers was a small cup of broth, clear enough to pack no threat to her exquisitely tailored khakis.

We ate. I was hungry and diligent, and gave up after finishing only a quarter of what I'd been served.

The waitress frowned as she took my plate away.

"The rope?" Jennifer Gale asked.

"Yes?"

"I'll be apprised, every step of the way?"

"Yes."

She smiled, victorious. "We'll go right now."

The waitress came back with two square foam containers. I hadn't told her to pack what she'd taken away.

Jennifer leaned forward. "Open them."

Inside the first was what was left of my cabbage rolls and dumplings. The second contained a stuffed green pepper, some kind of sausage, two potato pancakes, and a thick slice of ham.

"A sampling of what could be in my dowry." She laughed, and we got up.

At the cash register, I wanted to pay, but Jennifer would have none of it. She wanted to pay, but Mama would have none of that.

"It's not going to work, Mama. His girlfriend is rich, real rich," Jennifer said.

Mama ignored her, turned to me. "You come back?"

"Thank you. I will."

Mama wagged a finger. "But not with any rich girl-friend."

Jennifer grabbed my arm and pulled me out of there.

I FOLLOWED HER south, to the police station I'd visited before. We walked in together. Fortunately, a different desk sergeant was on duty. He took our names, made a call. A minute later, another sergeant came for us.

She was tall, over six feet, and as rail thin as some of the rich women I'd seen at Sweetie Fairbairn's party. Clearly, she'd never dawdled over dumplings at Galecki's.

"Jennifer Gale, it's a pleasure," she said, sticking out her hand.

Jennifer introduced me simply as an associate, and we followed the sergeant down a tiled corridor to a dark-stained door that had a thick wire-mesh screen screwed behind its frosted glass. The sergeant opened the door, told us to wait by the counter just inside, and walked back between the rows of shelves. She came back holding a plastic tub.

"This lockup isn't staffed full-time?" Jennifer asked.

"We don't keep key evidence in here. Just the ancillary stuff." The sergeant took the lid off the tub, withdrew a plastic bag big enough to hold a roast, and hefted it onto the counter. Inside the bag was a coiled rope.

"The rope stays in the bag," the sergeant said.

Jennifer looked over at me. I nodded that it was all right. I was confident that Leo's calculations had been accurate enough to show that the rope had been shortened.

I lifted the bag and held it up to the fluorescent lights. Though the bag was new and clear, I couldn't make out the condition of the ends.

"Could you open the bag enough to let me see inside?" I asked.

The sergeant looked at Jennifer. "You do understand, we're just talking a bad knot here?"

"Accident, no doubt," Jennifer said. "As I told you on the phone, there are rumors of people suing the owners of the building. For what I don't know, but I want to be ready in case. I have a look at the rope, see for myself to make sure it isn't frayed or anything, so I know, in case I need to know." She shrugged.

It was an effective performance. Jennifer had said nothing, but she'd said it in a Chicago neighborhood-speak so effortlessly that the sergeant had begun nodding along, in time with her cadence.

The sergeant put on blue plastic gloves and opened the bag so I could see in.

One end was immediately visible. It had been dipped in some kind of gluelike substance. It was a factory-sealed end.

"Can I see the other end, please?" I asked.

"For frays?" the officer asked, unconvinced.

"For frays," Jennifer said quickly.

The sergeant maneuvered the opening in the bag until the other end was visible.

That end was raw, unsealed. Freshly cut.

Jennifer thanked the sergeant, and we left.

"Someone cut that rope," Jennifer said outside, on the sidewalk.

"No doubt."

"Your client, that security guy? Or someone he's fronting?"

"I can't imagine," I said.

THIRTEEN

I CALLED DUGGAN after Jennifer pulled away.

"Nice note," he said, right off.

"It didn't get me a meeting with your client, Sweetie Fairbairn."

He covered the mouthpiece of his phone. A minute later, Sweetie Fairbairn came on the line.

"Thank you for your note, Mr. Elstrom." Her voice was soft, tentative.

"Thank you for a lovely party."

"What put you onto me?"

"You didn't question me enough about my relationship with Amanda."

"Can you drop by?"

I told her I could, and would, and pointed the Jeep toward the Gold Coast.

IT MUST HAVE been a fine day for bargains—perhaps thousand-dollar shoes were being dumped for nine hundred—because Michigan Avenue was packed solid with shoppers. Great throngs of them choked the sidewalks and the crosswalks, swinging bright bags filled with things sure to improve their lives.

A different valet was on duty at the Wilbur Wright. This one came right over to take the Jeep, but his narrowed eyes betrayed his concern that I'd be hunting under the floor mats for a quarter to tip him when I came out.

Again, a guard stood by Sweetie's private elevator. The

previous evening, I'd wondered if the elevator guard had been hired special for the party—to keep out riffraff, or perhaps to quell a riot, should the swells spill down from the penthouse, ginned up, and start spoon-flicking bits of caviar at guests in the lobby. Those thoughts had disappeared when I'd gotten upstairs. There'd been more guards, too many more for ordinary security, in the penthouse. Sweetie Fairbairn had mysteries. What I couldn't figure was why those mysteries needed full-time protection.

I gave the guard my driver's license before he could ask. He took a careful look at the beaming face I'd presented to the Illinois secretary of state's photographer, before the secretary of state had become governor and then gone on to prison, and announced my arrival into a small walkie-talkie.

Timothy Duggan's frown was waiting up in the foyer.

"You're something, Elstrom," he said.

"I, too, marvel at myself."

He told me to sit on an orange velvet settee just inside the living room. I supposed that was so he could keep an eye on both the elevator and myself.

I looked around the room. Just the night before, it had been filled with a hundred rich people, drinking and chewing. Yet now every piece of furniture—the two dozen sofas, settees, and chairs, all upholstered in sunny summertime yellows, greens, and oranges—along with the endless expanse of beige carpet, appeared spotless. I could not spy the slightest pink remain of cocktail weenie or black speck of caviar anywhere. Either rich people were very careful chewers, or someone had come along with a Shop-Vac, much as I did to clean my clothes.

"Are you terribly angry with me, Mr. Elstrom?" Sweetie Fairbairn asked softly.

I hadn't heard her enter. She looked wan. As she took

my arm, I had the suspicion that Sweetie Fairbairn wasn't guiding me toward the hall so much as she was hanging on to me, for support.

"Not yet, but there's still time."

"Yes," she said.

We went into the kitchen. It, too, was large, obviously outfitted to feed as many people as the living room could hold. There were two stainless steel refrigerators, a gas stove with many burners and ovens that looked like an antique but probably wasn't, and several long counters. The four dainty white chairs set at a small table in the corner looked like an afterthought, incongruous in such a large room.

She walked to a cabinet. "Wine, Mr. Elstrom?"

"I try to avoid it." I saw no need to add that I'd had whiskey in my coffee that morning.

"Good idea." She took out a bottle and poured three inches into a glass on the counter.

"You have guards on staff?" I asked.

"None on staff. Tim hires them, as needed." She walked us to the table. "In fact, I no longer have any live-in help."

"Neither do I," I said, to be sociable.

Her eyes widened for only a second, until she realized I was having her on. She offered a faint smile. "Most of my life was spent being the help, not having it," she said.

Part of me wanted to like her for that, as I had for the Velveeta and her tacky office with its crummy furniture and worn postcard of a covered bridge. First, though, I needed to know she wasn't a killer.

We sat across from each other, in the strong light of a low overhead fixture. Just like on the previous night, her age was impossible to determine, even in the bright light. She could have been forty, she could have been fifty.

She noticed my scrutiny. "Fifty-eight," she said.

"Wow," I said.

"Wow for not looking that old? Or wow for not looking that young?"

"Wow for your ability to read minds."

"Excellent, and very diplomatic." She took a slow sip of wine and asked, "Was the clown murdered, Mr. Elstrom?"

"His name was James Stitts—"

"I know that. Was he murdered?"

"It would be tough to prove, but yes."

Her hand shook, just a little, as she set down the glass. "You're certain?"

I told her the safety rope had been cut, its severed end taken away. It was information she'd paid for.

Her face had paled. "Murder, no doubt."

"Stitts's widow said it was a woman who'd hired her husband to go up on that roof. She came to their home in a chauffeured limousine." I watched her face.

"The woman was blond, of course?"

"Bea Stitts couldn't see inside the car."

"She was blond, Mr. Elstrom. That detail would not have been overlooked."

"You're being set up?"

She put her hands on the arms of her chair and pushed herself up like she weighed a thousand pounds. "Thank you, Mr. Elstrom."

I didn't get up. "You're being blackmailed?"

She started out of the kitchen as though she hadn't heard me. I'd been dismissed. I got up and followed her across the living room because there was nothing else to do.

Duggan already had the elevator door open. Sweetie Fairbairn turned around and walked away.

I went into the elevator. The door closed, and I was sent descending.

I thought, then, of an old comedian's slurred, confused

retort in a drunk-at-a-tavern routine. "I've been thrown out of better places than this," the drunk had bragged, looking around confused but proud, as he'd been tossed onto the sidewalk.

I doubted I'd ever been tossed from classier digs.

Still, I was as confused as the drunk, not at all sure what had just happened.

FOURTEEN

AMANDA SURPRISED ME later with a call. "You doing anything this evening?" Her voice sounded small.

"Nothing I like."

"Dinner?"

"You told me last night you were booked up until the next millennium, or at least until our date next week."

"I canceled for tonight. I'm craving simplicity."

"So you thought of me."

She laughed. It wasn't much of a laugh, but it offered promise.

"Actually, we have something to celebrate. You must have impressed Sweetie Fairbairn. She called, asked very few questions about the children's wing at Memorial Hospital, and then said she'd be sending a donation. She hinted it might be larger than what we'd discussed."

"What time?"

"I'm thinking around eight."

"No, I meant what time did Sweetie call?"

"An hour ago. Why?"

"Did she mention me?"

"Mention you? What's going on, Dek?"

"Our trattoria, at eight?" I asked, sidestepping.

"Somewhere else." She named Rokie's, a barbecue sandwich place nestled next to a forest preserve, northwest of the city. We'd been there once, after a movie or something. It had no history for us.

History or not, it was a start. Or maybe a restart. Whatever it was, I decided to think of it as progress.

AMANDA WAS ALREADY there, waiting in her white Toyota at the far corner of the lot. I pulled up alongside and got out.

"Shall I slip the maître d' a twenty for a table away from the window?" When we'd last been there, we'd laughed about the grease on the windows.

She gave me a hug. "I'm thinking al fresco." She pointed at the row of picnic tables across the parking lot.

It was a nice night. It would be fine.

I went in and got two beefs, two Cokes, an order of fries, and one squirt bottle of barbecue sauce to color our lips and chins the shade of congealed blood.

"This is a wonderful surprise," I said when I got back to the table.

"I needed a night."

"You can have more than one."

"I know." She reached across the table to put her hand on mine for a moment. "I know that a lot."

I ripped open the bag, handed her a beef, and spread the fries between us. The beefs were good; the fries were good; squirting everything with barbecue sauce was superb.

"Ever get back to the Art Institute?" I asked after I'd gotten my hands sufficiently sticky. The Art Institute was where Amanda used to spend her time, teaching and writing. When she wasn't sleeping. Or with me. Or both.

Her face became guarded. "I gave up my last class a month ago."

"Do you miss it?" I asked it casually. I'd told myself, driving over, that I wouldn't push against her new life.

"That's the thing, Dek. I don't know. Every time I start thinking about the way I'd been living, one thing keeps coming up: selfishness."

"You taught. You wrote. You lived a frugal, almost ascetic life."

"With eleven million dollars' worth of art hanging on my walls."

"And hardly anything on your floor." That had been true both in the gated community and in the high-rise on Lake Shore Drive where she'd moved after the houses in her neighborhood began exploding. Her income from her art books and her teaching had always gone to pay for insurance and a secure habitat for the art, not stuff to walk or sit or lie down on.

"You do understand?" she asked.

"Sure," I said, smiling like I meant it.

Her chin rose, just a touch. She knew well that I didn't understand, not really.

"Here's what else I think I understand," I said. "We're more alike than I used to believe, in that we're both orphans, of a sort. Except your father didn't take off, like my mother. Now you've been given a second chance to connect with him."

"At his instigation."

"Yes, and for that, he is to be applauded. I also think, if given the opportunity, I'd jump at the chance to connect with my mother, or the Norwegian who supposedly was my father."

Her face was still guarded. She wasn't accepting what I was trying to blithely pass across the table as a change in my attitude.

"Sweetie Fairbairn," she said, steering to a safer harbor. "You had a good time?"

"I always enjoy mingling with swells on the tops of buildings. The elevation does something for my appetite."

"Appetite or not, you did well. As I said earlier, she was

all business this afternoon. She's seriously interested in helping the children's wing."

"After I told her you and I never had shared a checkbook."

She laughed, just like old times. "Strange, though," she said. "I've been told Sweetie likes to start out slow with new charities. Ten, twenty thousand dollars, usually. This afternoon, though, she hinted at a donation approaching a hundred thousand."

"How did she sound?"

She shot me a quizzical look. "All business, as I said. Why did you ask if she'd mentioned you?"

The newspaper photos of Amanda and the silver-topped jokester came back at me. She'd appeared happy, in her element. Or maybe it had been something more. She might have become close enough to the commodities man to trade confidences.

The thought cut, that I might have to guard information around Amanda.

"Vanity," I said. "I like to be remembered."

Her face changed. She recognized the brush-off.

"Well, whatever it was, I hadn't anticipated hearing from her for some time. You helped, Dek."

I wondered, then, if we were at Rokie's because she felt she owed me, for not screwing up at Sweetie Fairbairn's the previous evening.

We made small talk. She asked about Leo, and about Endora. I asked more about the children's wing. We talked about my working on the turret, and whether Rivertown would ever become upscale enough for me to make a buck on my rehabbing.

We talked about Elvis Derbil and salad oil, too, because she'd seen Jennifer Gale's coverage of his arrest. In the not-so-long-ago days, she would have called me right away, laughing, incredulous, demanding to know what I knew about what was going on. No longer. Spontaneity had left us; we'd become careful about even the most inconsequential things.

"I met her, you know," I said.

"Met who?"

"Jennifer Gale. The television reporter who broke the story."

"The day they arrested Elvis?"

"She wanted to know about the lizards." Suddenly, I felt like I ought to confess things I hadn't done.

"She's beautiful. Did you like her?"

"She is, and yes. I like her."

She looked away then, at the cars parked in the lot.

"Your picture's been in the paper," I said. It was on my mind. It just came out.

Her eyes flashed back to mine. "Fundraising."

We said more careful things, but I don't remember what they were. We were like two old friends who'd bumped into each other on a street and decided to grab a quick bite before going different ways. For forever.

"We'll have our proper date at our trattoria next week?" I asked.

"That would be nice," she said softly.

Then there was nothing more to talk small about, and we walked to our cars. The night, still young, had become old. She got in her car, I got in mine. She drove east and I headed south, as if we were off to separate planets.

FIFTEEN

I DID SERIOUS time up on the roof, through the night, into the dawn, trying to rationalize Sweetie Fairbairn's behavior. Trying not to dwell on Amanda's.

Sweetie Fairbairn had been too accepting.

Too accepting that I'd developed information that might place her in a limousine, hiring Stitts to dance into oblivion.

Too accepting that she was being blackmailed by someone willing to kill.

She shouldn't have accepted any of it. She should have demanded that things be done. Instead, she'd sent me away.

Dawn changed into daylight. I'd rationalized only one good thing.

I had to take another run at Sweetie Fairbairn.

TRAFFIC ALONG MICHIGAN Avenue was stopped from turning onto Oak. Two police cars had blocked the street. Beyond them, I saw fire engines parked in front of the Wilbur Wright. I gunned the Jeep into a tended public garage, tossed the key to the valet, and ran down Oak.

Three fire trucks and one ambulance, their diesel engines idling loudly, were stopped in front of the hotel. I didn't see hoses and I didn't see smoke. A policeman blocked the door to the hotel.

A throng of people who looked rich enough to stay at the Wright were milling about across the street. They looked angry. I walked over and listened to two of them grouse about false alarms and damned kids.

I'd started to cross back when I saw Duggan. He was down the block, leaning against a double-parked limo. I walked up slowly. He nodded when he saw me, then leaned in the car to say something. After a moment, he got in the front passenger's seat.

The rear window powered down. Sweetie's face appeared, pale against the dark interior of the car. "Mr. Elstrom," she said in a small voice. She unlocked the rear door, then slid over as I got in. She wore a soft pink pantsuit, an even softer pink blouse, and the blankness of shock on her face.

No one—not Sweetie, not Duggan—asked why I was there.

"Some kid pulled a fire alarm?" I said.

She turned her head slowly, to look back at the Wilbur Wright. "Small fire in a powder room, they said. Nothing major, they said. Just something like a forgotten cigarette that set off some tissues, enough to make smoke and set off the alarms."

I settled back in the leather. "No big deal?"

Timothy Duggan shifted on the front seat but didn't turn around.

"It's my powder room," Sweetie Fairbairn said. She took a breath. "We'd just gotten back from a breakfast." She spoke in a monotone, as if the precision of her words, and not their content, were what mattered. "I didn't smell the smoke when we entered the apartment, but Tim noticed it right away."

She leaned forward to touch Duggan's shoulder, in the front seat, as if for reassurance. "Then our smoke alarm went off?"

"Yes, Ms. Fairbairn," Duggan said, not turning away from watching the street and the sidewalks.

By the gentleness in his voice, I realized that he, too, suspected she was on the verge of shock.

"No guard was upstairs?" I asked.

"Not necessary," Duggan said, "when we weren't going to be there."

It was boneheaded reasoning, but I let it go.

One of the fire trucks, then another, rumbled behind us, driving away. Sweetie's driver looked over at Duggan, who shook his head. We'd stay in place. The driver leaned back.

"Tim turned me around right away, and we came back down in the elevator," Sweetie continued. "A half hour later—a half hour, Tim?"

Duggan nodded, still looking restlessly around.

"A half hour later," Sweetie said, "the manager called Tim to say the fire had broken out in the powder room just off the foyer." The last fire truck drove away, followed by the ambulance. Then Duggan's cell rang. He clicked it on, listened, and mumbled something into it. A second later, he nodded, and the driver slipped the limo into drive and we started down the street.

"Robert said there's no smoke damage, Ms. Fairbairn," Duggan said. "He put the exhaust system on high. It will be fine."

"Parties can make a room so stuffy, even now that no one smokes," Sweetie said, staring absently past me out the window as the car circled the block.

I leaned forward. "Who is Robert?" I asked Duggan.

"Robert Norton. One of the contract men I use. Once Ms. Fairbairn was safely back in the car, I called him to come over and secure the residence."

The limo eased to a stop in front of the Wilbur Wright. Duggan walked closely beside Sweetie as they went to the elevator. The contract guard, Robert Norton, was waiting in the foyer of Sweetie's penthouse. I recognized him as the guard I'd seen in the hallway, the night of her party.

Norton had been right. There was no smell of smoke in the air. The room was ready for another party.

"One more look," Duggan said and left us with Norton. Sweetie and I sat on two small chairs by the elevator, silent as kids just home from school, waiting for milk and cookies.

When Duggan came back, he opened a small door. "Can't even smell it in the powder room, Ms. Fairbairn," he said, stepping aside.

A few damp pieces of scorched paper lay in the small antique porcelain sink. It wasn't enough to destroy anything. Except maybe a woman's reluctance to pay a blackmail demand.

"How could someone get in here?" I asked Duggan.

"Broken window in the guest bedroom," he said, pointing past the living room. "This place is set back from the hotel's lower walls. Getting onto the roof gets you to any of the windows."

"There are outside ladders?"

"One. There's another up through a supply closet. Both come from the floor below. The maintenance people use them to get to the roof."

"Does the building have video surveillance?"

"Only in the lobby. The day manager said no one got near her private elevator. Our boy did his homework, went up to the hotel's top floor in one of the guest elevators, then used the outside ladder to get up here."

"You'll call the police?"

Duggan looked at Sweetie Fairbairn. Her face was immobile. "I would expect not," he said, after a few seconds.

There was no point in questioning Sweetie. Her mind was somewhere beyond the penthouse.

Duggan saw it, too. "Best you lie down for a time, Ms. Fairbairn," he said.

She nodded meekly and left.

"Who doesn't like her?" I asked Duggan.

He started to shake his head.

"No, damn it. There's no time left for musing and denying. Someone is coming at her."

"She hired me to do security. That's it."

"You must have heard things."

He thought for a minute. "One name, maybe: Andrew Fill."

"Who's Andrew Fill?"

"I think he used to work at one of her charities. All I know is that I heard Ms. Fairbairn asking one of her advisers about Fill. They were arguing, I think."

"Who was the adviser?"

"A guy named Koros. I gather he stops by once in a blue moon. I don't think he does much for Ms. Fairbairn."

"The exact name?"

"George Koros. I think he's got an office downtown."

"Will he talk to me?"

"I'll call him, tell him Ms. Fairbairn requested it."

I left, without either of us seeing fit to wonder whether I'd been rehired.

SIXTEEN

G. K. INVESTMENT MANAGEMENT was on Upper Wacker Drive, on the fifth floor of a curved glass building that mimicked the bend in the Chicago River. A blond woman was leaving Koros's office, going the other way, as I got off the elevator.

By the quality of the address, I expected a snappy receptionist and big leather chairs, like the Bohemian's office. What I saw, when I pushed open the oak door, was something that would have shamed an insurance agent starting out in a strip mall. The reception room had a worn black two-seat sofa, a small wood desk that held only a telephone, and a lamp table piled with dog-eared old issues of *Fortune* and *Forbes*. The ceiling was decorated with a camera tucked behind a hanging plastic plant. A buzzer was mounted on the inner door frame. I smiled at the plant and pushed the button.

A dead bolt was electronically released, and the door to the inner office opened an inch. I pushed it all the way open and went in.

A gray-haired, thickset man got up from behind a desk. He wore a dark blue suit and a light blue tie, and a face that looked pained by my intrusion.

"Mr. Elstrom? George Koros. Nice to meet you," he said, extending his hand.

The office was spacious, and had a view, through curved glass, of the river and the Merchandise Mart. Like the reception area, it was sparsely furnished, holding only a bare desk that was too small for the large room, a desk chair, and one guest chair. The furniture was old, and cheap for the room. A few weeks of the *Wall Street Journal* were stacked on the floor in one corner.

"Tim Duggan phoned, said Sweetie asked that I help you in any way I can," he said as we sat. "I'm afraid he was quite vague."

Duggan had seen fit to play cagey with Koros.

"Really a minor matter," I lied, "having to do with an anonymous, upsetting note Ms. Fairbairn received. Mr. Duggan told me there'd been some difficulty with one of Ms. Fairbairn's employees some time back?"

"I really don't know…"

"Andrew Fill?"

"Ah, yes."

"A bad act?"

"Hardly. Merely a young man who lost his way for a time." Koros smiled. "Certainly not someone who'd send a threatening note."

"Revenge, jealousy, anger, lust? What's Fill's problem?"

"None of those, Mr. Elstrom. He headed up the Midwest Arts Symposium, a group that Sweetie and her friends formed some years ago. They bring in writers, painters, photographers—all sorts of artists—every November for a series of free public lectures. It's quite well known."

He studied me then, for the uninformed cretin that I was. I could only shrug, cretinously, and ask, "And?"

"Sweetie and her fellow board members had him fired."

"For what?"

"For some missing funds. Sweetie didn't file charges. She suggested that if he repaid the money, he could leave quietly. He agreed."

"Did Ms. Fairbairn do the actual suggesting?"

"She entrusted that to me."

"A lot of money?"

"Enough."

"When was he canned?"

"A couple of months ago. He has much to lose, if this matter ever becomes known. He could be prosecuted. I'm sure he means Ms. Fairbairn no harm."

"I'd like to talk to him."

Koros opened a side drawer, withdrew an address book, and wrote down Fill's address for me.

"You'll find he's quite harmless," he said.

"How long have you worked for Ms. Fairbairn?"

"I don't do much work for her, I'm afraid. I merely manage checking accounts for a few of her charities. However, I've enjoyed Sweetie's friendship for several years."

"You can think of no one else who might bear a grudge against Ms. Fairbairn?"

"Even Andrew Fill is a stretch, Mr. Elstrom. He must have gotten in a jam; gambling, perhaps, or drugs. I can think of no one else."

"Nobody?"

"Nobody at all," he said.

ANDREW FILL LIVED in an old building with black metal windows. It could have once been a factory or a warehouse and was built of Old Chicago Brick, that particular blend of yellowish, grayish, tannish bricks that line the sides and backs of most of the older factories and apartment buildings in the city. There's lots of bland, vagueish in that long-ago blend of brick, except for the dark, burned ones. Those they call clinkers, and they're in the mix, too, because in the years following the great fire, not even overbaked bricks got wasted rebuilding old Chicago, not when they could be used on the dark sides and backs of buildings where no one except the owners would see.

Still, it's always those clinkers that draw the eye, because there's nothing vague—nothing ish—about them. They look stronger and rougher than the others. They don't fit in.

Fill didn't respond to his buzzer. Judging by the amount of mass-mailed flyers piled on the tile floor beneath his little mail door, he hadn't been around to answer his buzzer for quite some time.

Someone had saved a buck on the mailboxes. They were flimsy, made of cheap plated tin. The lid flexed enough to show a box stuffed with envelopes. I pinched two out. One was an electric bill. The other was an investment account check. Both had been mailed almost a month earlier.

They would have arrived about the time James Stitts was killed.

Andrew Fill could have gone away, perhaps on vacation, without thinking to put a hold on his mail. Nothing but an oversight, an act of forgetting.

Or those month-old pieces of mail could have been clinkers. Things that didn't fit in.

I jammed Fill's two envelopes back in his cheap tin mailbox and went out to the Jeep.

I CALLED DUGGAN. "Andrew Fill took some money from one of Ms. Fairbairn's charities, and then he might have taken off. His mail is piling up."

"Did Koros have any other potentials?"

"He didn't even see Fill as a likely suspect."

"All right, then."

"Any luck on finding out who set that fire?"

"The building manager has changed the locks on the doors that access the ladders to the roof."

"That's it? No further investigation?"

"Ms. Fairbairn wants no publicity." He mumbled something about calling me later and clicked me away.

I was sure he would.

When pigs flew.

AMANDA PUT THE last nail into the day when she called that evening. "I've got to cancel for next week."

"We haven't even set a specific day yet. Now you're saying you're unavailable for the entire week?"

Mine was a thin protest, though. Yesterday's evening at Rokie's had been stilted, probably for reasons neither of us quite understood. We'd ended up with nothing to say to one another.

"A group of us are going to be working rather intensely on the Memorial Hospital project," she offered.

"Spur-of-the-moment kind of thing, a sort of spontaneous combustion of good intentions among the moneyed set?"

"Sweetie Fairbairn," she said. She'd ignored my sarcasm, another bad sign.

"What about her?"

"Two other ladies on the Memorial fundraising board got the same kind of call from her that I did. She's become hugely interested, hugely fast. We're going to try to enlist her as a director. If we do that, we raise tens of millions in a hurry."

"That's the way hospitals are funded, so spontaneously?" I pressed, because I didn't quite believe. "You people land a hitter like Sweetie Fairbairn, then do a week's worth of meetings, and presto, a new hospital wing gets built?"

"Honestly, when we talked about a movie and dinner, I didn't know…"

The wise part of my brain, never larger in size than a

speck, told me to let it go. Amanda's life was going through an upheaval. I'd told her I'd support her new priorities, that I'd be as understanding as she'd tried to be when I'd gone through my own upheaval—at least until I'd pushed her away by pickling myself in alcohol.

I mumbled something about nothing at all, and then we hung up, both of us relieved that the call was over.

SEVENTEEN

THE NEXT MORNING, I drove a half-baked plan and a full mug of coffee over to Leo's.

I'd spent the previous evening trolling the Internet, trying to get a fix on Andrew Fill. His mentions were numerous, all accumulated from his stint as executive director of the Midwest Arts Symposium. During the years he'd headed that group, it appeared he'd gotten photographed alongside every writer, stage actor, and opera singer who'd come to Chicago.

He was a thin fellow, with a thin nose and thin hair, and a stoop to his thin shoulders. He didn't look like a killer; he looked like the president of a stamp club. For sure, he looked smart enough to take a freebie Stay-out-of-Jail card offered by a charitable socialite. All he had to do was pay back the embezzled funds. He had no motive for coming back at her.

Certainly, not by killing a clown.

Besides, Bea Stitts had said it was a woman who'd hired her husband, a woman in a dark limousine, perhaps playing out some twisted fantasy.

I had to push my mind away from that. Andrew Fill was who I had.

Unless it was a twisted client.

LEO'S PORSCHE WASN'T in his garage. I knew Endora started at the Newberry Library at nine o'clock. Chances were, Leo was on his way home from her place. I decided to hum show tunes while I waited. That's what one does when one doesn't have a car radio.

I'd just gotten through an eighth rendition of the first verse of "Singing in the Rain," which was what one does when one knows only the first verse, when my cell phone rang, spoiling what I was sure was an improving performance.

"How about buying me dinner?" Jennifer Gale asked.

"I thought you always worked."

"This is my day off." She told me she'd swing by the turret at seven thirty and hung up.

Leo's Porsche's exhaust sounded behind me before I could think to examine how I felt about seeing Jennifer Gale again, or, more futilely, begin another rendition of "Singing in the Rain." Leo had the top down, a straw hat string-tied under his chin, and was sporting the huge sunglasses that, with his pale skin, made him look like a glaucoma patient escaped from a prison eye clinic. He gave me a nod as he pulled into his garage, trailing German exhaust and riffs of Brazilian bossa nova. I pulled up behind the big door and climbed out.

He made a disdainful show of surveying my attire. I was wearing painting clothes.

"Don't start," I said. "Don't dare to stand there in yellow rayon, adorned with purple birds and what look like green tarantulas, and deign to mock my wardrobe."

"*Deign*?"

"Deign," I repeated.

"I consider this"—he fingered the hem of the shiny untucked shirt, which in double XL hung on him like a silk robe—"to be perfect attire to wear when deigning, whatever you might think that word means. More important, though, I am not speckled everywhere with crusted bits of white and black, from sloppiness with a brush."

"It's a disguise," I said. "For breaking and entering, which we're going to do today."

"Unfortunately, my schedule, unlike yours, is cluttered. I must work today."

A series of low beats began pulsing slowly from his bungalow.

"At nine in the morning?" I asked.

He stared at the back of his home, disbelieving. "I had to work last night. Ma had bingo at the church. They came over afterward. All of them. They stayed upstairs at first, having vodka and watching dirty movies. I thought it would be OK; I kept working. Then, at midnight, they came down the basement stairs, liquored up and ready to strut. It was too much. I fled to Endora's."

The bass beats were coming faster now, loud and deep enough to vibrate the clapboards on the old garage. He pointed to the stuff I'd piled in the back of the Jeep. "A stepladder, a paint tray, a gallon of paint?"

"And a brush. It's part of the disguise."

"You're really going to break in someplace?"

I told him about my visits to Sweetie Fairbairn's penthouse, the powder room fire, and my conversation with George Koros. "Andrew Fill had a beef with Sweetie Fairbairn. It's all I can think to do."

He looked back at the house. "I can't go in there."

He was weakening. "A home invasion always brightens the day," I said.

He nodded, and we got in the Jeep.

As I pulled away, he asked, "How about we go out for pizza tonight? Real late."

"Can't."

"Date with Amanda?"

"She canceled, for every night next week. She has meetings about her hospital renovation."

"Important work."

"It might be true," I said.

"Of course," he said, staring straight ahead.

"It might also be that she'll be with that white-haired old commodities trader."

"This will pass," he said.

"I'm having dinner with Jennifer Gale tonight."

He shifted on his seat. "Is that wise?"

"A potential disaster. She charged ahead after she gave me the clown photos. She got us in to see the rope."

"And?"

"The rope was cut."

"Murder for sure," he said. "Does Jennifer Gale know Sweetie Fairbairn is your client?"

"I don't even know if Sweetie Fairbairn is my client. It's touch and go with her."

"You've got to be careful around Jennifer Gale. Hell will pay if all this makes the news."

"She's smart; she'll tumble to it sooner rather than later. For now, the best I could do was cut a deal with her. She stays quiet on everything until I approve. In return, I keep her informed about the clown's death."

"You are a man facing constant dilemmas."

"I like her, Leo," I said, after a minute. "She's straight up about what she wants."

"Jennifer Gale."

"Jennifer Gale."

"She's beautiful. And Amanda is sending you bad signals."

I moved on to tell him about the crime we were to commit.

"So what if his mail is piling up?" he said, when I was done. "He got fired, he swiped some money. He's not finding another job. He might have gone home to see the folks, plot his next move. Or maybe he's on a beach, spending his ill-gotten loot."

"Then he wasn't around to set the fire in Sweetie Fairbairn's penthouse."

"That's reason enough to see if Andrew's been at home?"

"A dead clown, and now a fire in her home. Someone's applying pressure to Sweetie Fairbairn. Right now, Andrew Fill is the only one who's got motive."

"Unless Sweetie Fairbairn herself set that fire."

"There is that," I said.

PEOPLE ARE HONEST. People want to trust. They want to trust working Joes most of all. Getting past the buzz lock in Fill's building was simply a matter of setting my ladder, a tray, and a half-empty paint can in the foyer until an older man opened the door to come out.

"Hold the door for you?" the well-meaning soul asked.

"Thank you," I said, all paint-splattered appreciation. I stepped inside with the paint can. "Thanks again."

The paint and I rode the elevator to the third floor and walked down to Fill's apartment. My hunch that the building's contractor had been as chintzy with the locks as he was with the mailboxes didn't matter. Andrew Fill's door pushed open at the first touch of my Discover card.

"Mr. Fill?" I called from inside, after I shut the door.

Only a smell came back at me, thick and cloying from being shut up in an apartment.

Dead meat.

I took out my cell phone and called Leo in the Jeep. He was watching for anyone who looked like the picture of Andrew Fill I'd printed off the Internet.

"Something smells bad in the apartment," I said.

"How bad?"

"Dead bad. Take my painting stuff from the foyer, put it back in the Jeep. We might be leaving in a hurry."

With my cell phone still on, I took another few steps into the apartment. "Mr. Fill?" I said again, louder this time.

Still no answer. The bad smell was stronger.

Ahead lay the living room. It looked undisturbed. I took a right at the corridor and walked down to what looked like two bedrooms and a bathroom. The smell got weaker the farther down the hall I got.

Both bedrooms were neat, the beds made. No clothes were lying about. The bathroom was immaculate.

Only the kitchen remained. Where the smell was coming from.

I walked in, expecting to see a thin man dead on the floor. He wasn't there. Only a roast was, on the counter, rotting next to two peeled and molding potatoes.

Nothing else.

"You broke in on a roast?"

Leo cackled like a crazed jaybird when I got in behind the wheel. I wanted to laugh, too, but the stench of the rotted meat was still too strong in my nose.

"You don't understand," I said. "The guy's apartment was absolutely neat as a pin. Nothing was out of place. He even puts his toothpaste in a drawer."

"Maybe to keep it from smelling like the roast." He started laughing again.

"A man as neat as Andrew Fill would never leave a roast out."

"Depends on how much money he absconded with."

"Or whether he was abducted. Remember, the door was unlocked."

"What now?" he asked.

"I go see what people don't want to say about this."

EIGHTEEN

LEO SAID THAT working out of Endora's cubicle for the rest of the morning would be preferable to hanging around the backyard of his bungalow, waiting for Ma and her friends to finally exhaust themselves. I dropped him across the street from the Newberry Library.

I called Koros as Leo walked inside.

"How much money did Andrew Fill steal?"

"I'm not authorized to tell you, Mr. Elstrom. Approval has to come from Ms. Fairbairn."

"Call her."

"I'll get back to you."

"I'm fifteen minutes from your office."

"No need," he said quickly. "I'll call you right back."

I shut off the engine to wait for a more forthcoming attitude.

He called back ten minutes later. "I don't understand. She always answers her cell phone."

He didn't know about the powder room fire. Sweetie Fairbairn might very well have been huddled somewhere, not talking to anybody.

"I'll take the responsibility for what you tell me about Andrew Fill."

"I don't know…"

"Fill's mail is piling up."

Koros's voice rose. "He's left town?"

"There's more: He left a roast out to spoil."

Koros laughed. It was forced. "Are you kidding with me, Mr. Elstrom?"

"Andrew Fill is a fussy housekeeper, neat in every regard. He left a roast and two potatoes out, to spoil. Which they've been doing, for some weeks."

"You know this how?"

"He may be in hiding. He may be dead."

He sucked air. "Andrew's alive. He must be alive."

"Why?"

"Because he's been paying—"

"Paying what?"

"Paying back what he took, as I told you."

"How much so far?"

"Twenty-one thousand—but he's late, and he's stopped answering his phone. I've been calling every day for the past two weeks. The voice mail is full. He's not answering anyone."

"How much money did he take?"

"A lot," he hedged.

"How much?"

"Four hundred and eighty-five thousand dollars."

"That's enough to go far away."

"This is my fault."

"His disappearance?"

"The money. I was overseeing the Symposium's checking account. The disbursements looked so regular; travel and meals and lodging for the guests the Symposium board invited."

"Not legit?"

"The bills were very legitimate, and Andrew purportedly withdrew funds from the cash account to pay them in full. Secretly, though, he'd set up a dozen credit card accounts, and arranged to use those to pay only minimums against the invoices. He kept the rest of the cash he withdrew."

"I don't understand why Ms. Fairbairn wouldn't go after a man who stole almost a half-million dollars."

"There would be the personal embarrassment, of course. Technically, she was his boss. Worse for her, though, was that she worried her friends would stop donating to charities she was involved with. So she repaid the fund on her own—and remember, Andrew has started to pay it back." He cleared his throat. "Until he stopped answering his phone."

"When did he stop answering, exactly?"

"Like I said, a couple of weeks ago, maybe longer. I thought he had to go somewhere, out of the country perhaps, to get the rest of it. I wasn't alarmed; he was paying back. But lately…"

"You're very trusting, Mr. Koros."

"I had no idea he'd stop repaying, and I certainly did not know he was sending threatening letters, or whatever. Look, I'm not a fool, Mr. Elstrom. I should have kept better tabs on that account. But really, all I did was make sure the account was properly funded and reconciled every month. As for Sweetie, if she said no to punishing Andrew, then it was not my place to disagree."

George Koros had answers for everything.

I drove the few blocks north to Oak Street, to see if Sweetie said they were true.

THERE WAS NO guard outside the private elevator in the Wilbur Wright. I expected the elevator to be locked out, if Sweetie wasn't home, but the doors opened as soon as I pressed the button.

The motors whirred, the elevator went up. Five seconds later, the door opened into the penthouse.

There was no guard in the foyer, either.

I walked into the living room. I suppose I first saw the familiar soft yellow silk on the walls, and the greens and yellows and oranges on the sofas and chairs, all of the colors made bright by the sun streaming in the windows.

I know I saw the sun glinting off the small ring of keys dropped on the beige carpet. It had a large fob with the letters S and F.

Mostly, what I saw was red. Lots of it, spilling out of the square suit of the bodyguard lying facedown on the pale carpet, wet and glistening in the sunlight.

I saw it, too, smeared, darker, on the arms and on the front of the dress of Sweetie Fairbairn.

NINETEEN

WE STOOD IN Sweetie's kitchen.

"Tell me again, Elstrom. Beginning in the hall downstairs." The man in charge, a lieutenant named Plinnit, was tall like me, and packing twenty pounds too many, also like me. He'd come with another detective and two uniforms seven minutes after I'd called. Rich people got fast service, even in crime.

"I didn't figure she was home, because there was no guard off the lobby," I said.

"She always had a guard?"

"Pretty much." I nodded toward the living room. "Timothy Duggan worked full-time. He told me he hired others, to fill in for events and things."

"Why does she have guards?" His eyes didn't blink.

"She's got a lot of money." It was no time for candor.

"Bullshit."

"You'd have to ask Ms. Fairbairn."

"All right. Go on."

"I was surprised when her elevator opened."

"It was unlocked?"

"Yes." Without thinking, my hand moved to my pants pocket, to finger the keys I'd found lying on the carpet. I dropped my hand. I didn't need to be found with keys that weren't mine.

"You entered the elevator and went up?"

"I expected someone would be upstairs in the foyer."

"A guard?"

"A guard."

"And when you got up here, there was no one?"

"No one."

"Meaning no guard? No live guard?"

"Duggan was dead, facedown on the carpet. You know that."

"Sweetie Fairbairn was here, though, right?"

"Trying to help Duggan. I think you ought to talk to her."

Anger flashed across his face, but just as quickly, he made it go away. "All right, Elstrom. Can you tell me if you've been here before?"

"Three times. First for a party three nights ago."

"Why?"

"She was thinking about hiring me."

"Why?"

"You have to ask her."

"You don't have confidentiality protection, Elstrom. You're not her lawyer. You're not even a licensed investigator."

"Ask her anyway, Lieutenant."

Plinnit looked across the kitchen at the other detective. He was much bigger, at least three hundred pounds of solid Chicago beef, gray-eyed and gray-haired. The other man shrugged slightly. Plinnit turned back to me.

"You came into the living room," he went on, "and saw the guard lying on the floor."

"Duggan. Yes."

"You also saw your client."

"Trying to help Duggan, as I said." I hoped it wasn't a lie. I couldn't really tell what she'd been doing, but I'd seen no weapon.

"Then you called us."

"First I told Ms. Fairbairn to go to her room and lie

down. She was obviously in shock. It was then that I called 911. I waited in the foyer."

"You know shock? You're a doctor, Elstrom?"

"She looked like she was in shock."

"You know her bedroom?"

He was goading, prompting for any kind of a slip.

"No. I just figured it was down the hall. Look, she left the living room. I called 911, for an ambulance, for the police. Then I went to wait in the foyer."

"By the elevator door?"

"Of course. It's a small foyer."

"The whole time?"

"What do you mean?"

"I mean: Did you wait in the foyer the whole time after calling 911?"

"It took only a few minutes for you to get here."

"You believe Ms. Fairbairn will back this up as well?"

"No, Lieutenant, she won't. It was after she headed for her bedroom that I called, and then went to wait in the foyer."

"Ah yes, her bedroom; that bedroom down the hall."

The other detective left the kitchen. I heard him out in the hall, talking to someone. He came back a minute later. Plinnit raised his eyebrows. The other man shook his head.

"We're having a problem getting Ms. Fairbairn to corroborate any part of your story, Elstrom."

"She's in shock. Get a doctor. Sedate her. In the morning, she'll be able to have her lawyer tell you everything you need to know."

Plinnit came to stand next to me. "We'll escort Mr. Elstrom down to our office," he said to the other detective.

Plinnit's hand was strong on my shoulder. I tried to relax. It would not do to make any moves.

"What the hell is going on?" I asked as Plinnit steered

me through the living room, past the live evidence technicians and the dead Timothy Duggan.

"Sweetie Fairbairn is not in this penthouse, Mr. Elstrom."

TWENTY

I DON'T REMEMBER the ride. I don't remember whether it was a marked or an unmarked car, or who drove, or whether there was much traffic. I'd never seen the police station. I did recognize the table. It seemed like every station house I'd been in had the same kind of beat-up, plastic-topped relic, surrounded by metal-framed hard plastic chairs that were tough on the ass.

I knew the questions Plinnit was going to ask, like he knew the answers he was going to get. We'd done it before, in Sweetie Fairbairn's kitchen. Twice. Even so, we were going to slog through them again, and again, until one of us wore down too much to go on.

The gray-haired, gray-eyed man stood at the door. Plinnit and I sat at the table.

He switched on a tape recorder and blew through a Miranda. When I said I didn't need a lawyer, he started with the questions. "Ms. Fairbairn was alive and well when you saw her?"

"She was in shock," I said again.

"You know shock?" he asked again.

"Nothing on her face wanted to move. She barely had the energy to blink."

"You told me you didn't think she stabbed the guard?"

"I didn't think anything except blood. I didn't see a knife. I told her to go wait in her bedroom. I went to the foyer, called 911, and—"

"Waited for us."

I nodded.

"Where is Ms. Fairbairn now, Elstrom?"

"I don't know."

"You want to continue insisting you waited for us by the elevator door?"

"That's where I was."

"In the foyer, right by the elevator, where you would have seen her leave?"

"If she took the elevator—but there's a back stairs, Duggan told me."

"Told you today?"

"No. You know I found him dead today. This was yesterday."

"You were there yesterday?"

"Someone set a fire in her powder room."

"That wasn't reported?"

"Certainly it was reported; fire trucks came. The building was emptied. Ask the Wilbur Wright's manager. Check with the fire department."

"But the police weren't called? It wasn't reported as a home invasion, arson?"

"I don't know."

"There's a boarded-up window in the guest bedroom."

"Point of entry."

"Convenient," he murmured.

"Convenient for whom, Plinnit? Timothy Duggan? He's dead. Sweetie Fairbairn? She's missing. Maybe she's dead, too."

"Convenient for anyone to enter unseen. Like you, Elstrom."

I stood up, daring them to push me back down, daring them to come right out and accuse me of murder. I am not at my brightest, angry.

They let me stand.

Plinnit continued. "It must have been someone big, your size, to have gotten close enough to that bodyguard—"

"Duggan," I said, cutting him off. "His name was Duggan."

"No. His name was Norton, Robert Norton. Duggan's at the station, here. He's giving a statement right now."

It took a moment to digest. "He'll tell you about the fire."

"Norton had a gun, Elstrom. How do you think someone got close to him?"

Everyone—me, Plinnit, the silent slab of gray beef by the door—knew there was only one answer to that.

"Norton knew his assailant, trusted him," I said.

"You," he said.

"You betcha," I said.

"Or her?" Plinnit's eyes were steady.

Both Sweetie and I were a good cop's obvious suspects. Me, because I was being evasive. Her, because I'd placed her in the penthouse, kneeling down over the dead man, and because she'd taken off. I wasn't going to play with Plinnit on that. Missing, even dead, Sweetie Fairbairn was still a client.

"I don't see Sweetie Fairbairn using a knife, Lieutenant."

"Did Norton know you, Elstrom?"

"As I told you, I was there, several times. He would have known me by sight."

"Why did Sweetie Fairbairn hire you?" Plinnit asked, and asked again. It was what he most wanted to know. Each time, my refusal to answer that question signaled the end of the round, that we were going to start it all again.

"Ask her, Lieutenant," I said each time.

So it went, around and around and around, each of us

unyielding, as the afternoon changed into evening, and the evening changed into night.

Until, at midnight, I asked, "Do I call my lawyer?"

He surprised me.

"You can do it from home," he said.

THERE WAS NO offer of a ride back to my Jeep. I didn't protest. I was desperate enough for free air to walk until I could find a cab. I went out the front door of the station house.

Into the sudden glare of television camera lights.

The reporters behind them started shouting.

"Vlodek Elstrom! Will you be charged with the murder of Sweetie Fairbairn?" the loudest of them yelled.

Plinnit had probably tipped them I'd be coming out, a little extra pressure from a cop who'd spent his evening not believing most of what I was saying.

I remembered those kinds of reporter noises, those kinds of shouted questions that could be edited into something else entirely. My livelihood, my Amanda, my future; I'd lost everything in that same kind of din.

I smiled, I waved. I walked swiftly away, into the darkest street I could see. When I was sure that none of the cameramen had been able to keep up, I ran like I was being chased by the hounds of hell, until I couldn't run anymore. Then I walked, chest heaving, gulping air, for six more blocks, or maybe ten. Finally, a cab slowed. He looked me over, real slow, said he'd need cash up front before he'd drive me the few blocks north of the river, to the parking lot close to the Wilbur Wright, where I'd left the Jeep.

There were television lights at the hotel, too. Waiting for news of Sweetie Fairbairn, dead or alive.

I stayed close to the buildings and moved up enough to hear the personalities and their crews talking about what they didn't know.

"She's got to come back, right?" and "Someone said she killed all of them," and "Some guy named Elstrom has been arrested."

Then someone called out, "Hey! You! With the clothes!"

A videocam light swung onto me, followed by another. I didn't understand. It didn't matter. I ran down to the parking lot, stuffed cash—I didn't know how much—into the hand of the late-night attendant, and fired up the Jeep. I was almost out of the lot when one of the newsies thought to step in front of me. I revved the engine. He blinked once, twice, must have seen that I wasn't blinking once, or twice. He jumped aside.

By then, a silver sedan—another newsman—had pulled up to block the exit onto the street. I drove onto the sidewalk, almost striking an elderly pair of late-night strollers into the next life. Bouncing over the curb, I gunned the Jeep down Oak Street. I ran a red light at the next intersection and turned left. I shot a glance into the rearview mirror. I'd lost the silver sedan.

Suddenly, my whole body started to shake. Squeezing the steering wheel to keep the Jeep in control, I drove east, to Lake Shore Drive, then south, paralleling the lake. Newspeople would be at the turret, too. Some would have even remembered the way, from the last time, during the Evangeline Wilts trial. The old can was going to be pried open; the worms were going to dance in the glare of the lights again. That long-ago man who'd been thought to have falsified evidence—accused in big print, exonerated in small—was going to be back bigger than ever. Pres-

sure would build. Plinnit would have to act. I'd have to
be charged.

No turret, not yet.

I drove past the turn to the expressway to Rivertown.

TWENTY-ONE

I SPENT THE rest of the night in the Jeep, parked at the back of the Bohemian's building. Surprisingly, I slept until a garbage truck came to empty the Dumpster. It was eight forty-five. The Bohemian's black Mercedes sedan was in the lot.

His receptionist, a sweet-looking brunette that I would have remembered if I'd been thinking clearly, must have remembered me, because she didn't scream when I walked right through the cluster of startled people parked in the green leather chairs in the lobby and went into the inner offices and past the cubicles. Outside the Bohemian's office, helmet-haired Buffy didn't scream, either. Then again, expressing emotion was not her way.

The Bohemian's door was closed. I opened it. He was sitting with two pale, powdered elderly women, no doubt talking about matters of money.

"Jesus Christ, Vlodek," he said, calmly enough.

It was then that I looked down and saw I was covered with dried blood, from helping Sweetie Fairbairn get up from the body of the dead guard.

"I need your help, Anton," I said, perhaps unnecessarily.

The elderly ladies had gone even paler under their caked rouge. Unhealthy-looking white powder ridges now raked their wrinkled, unnaturally reddened skin.

"Vlodek, may I have Buffy take you to a conference room, perhaps get you some coffee?"

I must have nodded, because the grim-faced secretary instantly touched my elbow.

She took me to a conference room I'd been in once before, back when houses had started exploding in Amanda's old gated neighborhood. I remembered the room because of the English hunting print hanging on the wall. I'd been hired to investigate the explosions, and the dogs in the picture, their noses confidently on the ground, had taunted me with their sureness. They knew what they were hunting; I did not.

Like now.

The door opened and the Bohemian came in, carrying two dainty cups of coffee on saucers pinched between his thick thumbs and forefingers. Overrouged ladies love dainty china. He set the cups on the table and sat down.

Taking a fresh yellow pad of lined paper from the stack on the side table, he uncapped an enormous antique fountain pen. "Now, Vlodek, tell me how you soiled your shirt."

"You've not read the papers, or listened to the radio?"

"I prefer Bach on my drive in." He turned to the laptop computer on the sideboard and brought up the *Tribune* Web site. I could read the headline from the other side of the table: SOCIALITE PHILANTHROPIST MISSING. BODYGUARD FOUND MURDERED.

He scrolled down the text, reading silently and making notes. When he had the gist of it, he turned back to me. "You're a celebrity."

I laughed, after a fashion, and told him all of it, beginning with the arrival of the party invitation, and ending with my arrival at his parking lot just a few hours earlier. He was now my lawyer, the one who must keep the hounds away.

When I leaned back, exhausted into silence, he studied my clothes. "Thirty-six-inch waist, Vlodek?"

"Perhaps no longer."

"Thirty-eight, then," he said, standing up. "Drink coffee. Read the computer if you must. Do not communicate with anyone." He left the room.

I don't know that I thought about much of anything while I waited. Telling everything to the Bohemian had drained my mind—relieved me, at least temporarily, of custody of the mess of loose ends that dangled from the disaster that was Sweetie Fairbairn.

Buffy knocked on the door an hour later, came in, and set a box on the table. "Clothes," she said and left. I opened the box. Inside were khaki trousers, but in a softer twill than I'd ever owned. The blue button-down shirt beneath them was softer as well, and had better stitching than what I kept crumpled in the turret. I changed, then put the blood-stained trousers and shirt in the box. The Bohemian would keep them protected, but inaccessible to anyone from a police evidence unit, with or without the proper paperwork.

He came in after another twenty minutes. "John Peet will represent you," he said, naming the best-known criminal defense lawyer in Chicago. Peet had just finished successfully defending a young third wife accused of murdering her eighty-eight-year-old husband. It had been a sensational trial. Their sex life wasn't brought up, such as it might have been, but the woman's tennis pro lover was, as was the hundred million dollars she stood to inherit. Slam dunk; drumroll, please. Everyone thought she'd be convicted. Except John Peet. Who got her off.

"John is making calls, Vlodek. We'll stay in this room until he tells us what to do next."

We'd barely begun to force conversation—something about the fountain pens he loved to restore, I think—when the phone rang. The Bohemian picked it up and listened. "Of course I'll be co-counsel," he said, after a few moments. I took that to mean he'd guarantee payment of Peet's fee. Then, "Yes. I have them in a box, here…I see… That explains why they didn't take them. Very encouraging, John." He handed the phone to me.

"Mr. Elstrom," Peet began. "Good news, of a sort. The police don't like you for the shooting."

"Shooting?" I asked, confused. "They said stabbing."

"Actually, Lieutenant Plinnit told me he was very careful not to say either. They also let you go on believing and saying, at least for a while, that the murdered guard you thought was stabbed was Timothy Duggan. Not exhibiting knowledge of either the means of the murder or the identity of the victim saved your bacon, so to speak. For now, they're willing to think you walked in on something, nothing more. Still, you're a material witness. They're after what you know and have not said. We must be cautious. Other than Anton, don't talk to anyone about this. That means, doubly, do not talk to the press. Eat at home, Mr. Elstrom. Do not answer your door to friends or strangers. If the police come for you again, don't utter a syllable until I arrive."

"Are we doing better, Vlodek?" the Bohemian, that ever-effective fixer, asked after I hung up the phone.

I told him I truly desired that to be true.

TWENTY-TWO

I TOLD MYSELF that my second bout with bad fame was going to be easier than the first. The Evangeline Wilts trial had erased my business, my marriage, and my custom of wintering indoors with sufficient heat. This time, I didn't have those to lose.

I told myself all these things quite literally—actually speaking the words aloud as I drove toward Rivertown. Feeling free to talk aloud to oneself, anywhere, anytime, without drawing a startled glance is an often-overlooked benefit of the cell phone era.

Used to be, people crossed the street to avoid someone who was moving lips, making sounds, saying words to nobody at all. No longer. Cell phones and earpiece microphones have unchained mankind, not just the lunatics. Nowadays, anyone can chatter on, seemingly to no one at all. Nobody cares, nobody stares; it's assumed the talker is merely on the phone.

I once stood next to a young man, nineteen or twenty, in the cookie section of a grocery store. He kept saying, "I love you," over and over, to a shelf of gingersnaps. True, he was wearing an earpiece, but I did not see an actual phone. He could well have been addressing a beloved, or he could have been murmuring to the gingersnaps. Or, perhaps, they were one and the same. There is no longer any sure way of telling.

Leaving the Bohemian's that morning, I was appreciative of all that. I owned no cell phone earpiece, but I had lots to say, and I was in a fury to get it out. I'd failed to un-ravel any of the mysteries of Sweetie Fairbairn, I told the windshield, and for that her life might now be in danger. As the only person of interest so far, I would become Target One for the press, and that would endanger, maybe even destroy, Amanda's attempt at a new life, along with any hope I had of being part of it. On and on I raged, upshift-ing and downshifting along the expressway, a man alone in a Jeep, frothing at the mess he'd made. The windshield accepted it all, saying nothing, judging nothing. No one, in any adjacent car, paid me any mind at all.

It was therapeutic. By the time I left the expressway, I was calm enough to stop at a supermarket for the micro-wavable nutrition and petrified sugary products I'd need to hunker down with while the world tried on my fit as a mur-der suspect and waited for more news of Sweetie Fairbairn.

Ten minutes later, turning off Thompson Avenue, I slammed to a stop.

The press had come, as I'd expected—but they'd been blocked by City of Rivertown sawhorses, well before the left turn to the turret and city hall. There was no police cruiser minding the barricade, just an orange Ford Maver-ick, more rust than paint, angled in the middle of the street. Against its hood, intimately close to the box of doughnuts beside him, rested Benny Fittle.

Benny was a second or third cousin of a village clerk. Normally he was seen in denim cutoffs and a rock band T-shirt, cheeks inflated by something crème filled, writ-ing parking tickets along Thompson Avenue. The lizards valued Benny for his speed; he rarely slowed to squint at the meters to see if they'd expired.

This day, though, he'd been stuffed into a cop's uni-form, to enforce the barricade.

Protecting me from the press was laudable. And incomprehensible.

I looked past the newsmen, past the spit of land. Something fluttered slowly from a second-floor window of the turret. It was a bedsheet. It pictured a bottle, but the lettering was too far away to read.

Below the sheet moved two bright, multicolored shapes of tangerine and chartreuse and neon yellow. One was small, thin, and topped with an oval of pale, bald flesh that, from a distance, looked like a huge egg. The other was a foot taller, thinner, and topped with luxuriant short brown hair.

Leo and Endora had taken control of the turret. Whatever they'd hung from the second-floor window had stirred the lizards to set up a barricade to keep back the press.

I turned the Jeep around, hoping its cross-taped, milky plastic side windows would obscure my face long enough to escape being photographed, and sped away. I parked four blocks down, alongside the river, and came back low along the weed-choked crumbles of the river walk.

When I got to the back of the turret, I edged forward, staying in the shadows.

"Leo," I called softly.

"Hark, Princess," he said. "Do you hear something?"

"Might it be the master of the turret?" she asked, laughing.

"It might, and a dim master is he. Anyone else would realize the press is too far away to hear, and would not deign to whisper."

Despite the hailstorm of crap that had come down on me in the last twenty-four hours, I started to smile. I remembered using the word "deign" with Leo—and I knew that, like every time I got to talking too fancy, he was now going to come down on me as hard as the hailstorm.

"Deign?" Endora said, in a stage voice. "Deign, with no brain?"

"'Tis insane, to deign with no brain," Leo answered.

"For the pain of the deign will remain," Endora rhymed back.

It was too much. Both were good enough with words to go on for hours. I carried my paper bags of food into the sunshine and looked up at what fluttered from the turret.

It was brilliant.

Leo's grin widened his pale, bald head. "It was I who hung the banner that made the City of Rivertown banish the press from your door."

"It was I who conceived and drew it," Endora said.

Then they both laughed, two kids showing off mega IQs.

The sheet hanging large above the front door featured a bottle of salad dressing, label side out. Beneath the bottle it read, YOU CAN'T ALWAYS BELIEVE WHAT YOU READ.

"The lizards freaked," Leo said.

I didn't wonder. The press, in Rivertown to film me for the Sweetie Fairbairn story, would use the reminder of Elvis Derbil in a sidebar alongside whatever they presented about me. It could be diverting. For sure, it would be funny, to everyone except the lizards.

"They hauled out the sawhorses ten minutes after we hung the sheet," Leo said.

"They don't realize news cameras have zoom lenses?"

Leo laughed, shaking his head. "You saw Benny?"

"Dressed up to guard road and dunkers alike."

"Truly the icing on the doughnut. Rivertown will be on everyone's lips tonight."

Trust Leo to warm even the coldest day.

I turned to Endora. "You're wasting your time with him, you know."

She curtsied. Her sundress of tangerine squid and chartreuse fish cavorting in a neon yellow sea matched Leo's shirt.

I raised one of my paper bags. "Come in. I have Ho Hos."

I made coffee and we sat on the lawn chairs in my kitchen. I gave them Ho Hos on paper plates and a criminal's-eye view of my last twenty-four hours.

"Sweetie Fairbairn is being blackmailed, Dek?" Endora asked when I finished.

"That's what she inferred," I said, "but the way she said it sounded like she hadn't yet received a demand."

"Which she would have been able to pay," Leo said. "The woman gives away hundreds of thousands of dollars a year."

"Easily," I said.

"Andrew Fill?" Leo asked.

"I'm having trouble seeing why he'd need to kill the clown or the guard. He's paying back the money, or was, until he disappeared."

"There's always the scenario that Sweetie Fairbairn killed the guard herself, perhaps because he overheard something," Leo said. "Her running away makes her look guilty as hell."

"I'm hoping it makes her look innocent," I said. "I'm hoping she ran because she had no choice."

MY LANDLINE PHONE rang a minute after they left. The answering machine clicked on to announce that it was full. The Channel 5 reporter on the other end was having none of that. He started arguing. I was tempted to pick up, to tell him that he was screaming at a machine. Then I had a vision of myself, as I'd been but an hour earlier, yelling at my windshield, and I regarded the reporter with more compassion. He and I were fellow travelers on an increasingly bumpy road.

Most of the messages on my machine were from the local television stations and newspapers. Mixed in with them were a call from city hall, saying I had to remove my banner immediately, and one from the local water and sewer utility, telling me my payment was late. Again.

I couldn't afford a municipal citation. I went upstairs and pulled in the offending banner.

Coming down, I thought to check for messages on my cell phone, switched off since I'd gone to the police station. Leo had called twice, before he and Endora had decided to come over. Amanda had called six times, increasingly exasperated that I wasn't picking up. Jennifer Gale had called once, reminding me I'd stood her up for dinner the previous night, and saying that my being detained for police questioning was no excuse for stiffing her on the biggest story in town. Then she laughed.

The one call I really needed—from Sweetie Fairbairn, telling me she was all right, but in hiding—hadn't come.

Nor had the one call I'd expected.

I called his number. The answering machine at his office picked up. I hung up and tried his cell phone.

"Timothy Duggan," he said.

"Dek Elstrom."

"You've got balls, Elstrom, calling me."

"Heard from Sweetie?"

"If I did, I sure as hell wouldn't tell you."

"I'll take that as a negative. We've got to talk to Andrew Fill. In person."

"I wouldn't go anywhere with you. You're radioactive."

"I didn't kill your guard."

"Says you."

"I didn't finger Sweetie for killing him, either."

"You said she was there, kneeling over the body. Same thing." He hung up.

I thumbed the redial button. "You need to find her, to protect her. And we need to find Fill, to learn what he knows."

"Let the cops find Fill. As for Ms. Fairbairn, somebody is out to kill her. She's on the run, unprotected. She's safest that way." The phone went dead.

I walked to the window. Benny Fittle's Maverick and his barricade had disappeared. The news vans hadn't. Four of them had pulled up in front of the turret and raised their broadcast antennae like alien periscopes, ready to transmit the first moment I showed my face.

It wasn't even noon, but I was exhausted. I dropped into the electric blue La-Z-Boy.

I didn't see Sweetie Fairbairn as a killer. I didn't see her hiring someone to cut a clown's rope to drop him off a roof. I didn't see her with a gun, shooting her guard.

I didn't see Andrew Fill for any of that, either. He had a motive—revenge—to want to harm Sweetie Fairbairn, but she'd thrown the man a lifeline, the chance to pay the money back and escape jail.

I rubbed my eyes. It didn't help. I still couldn't see anything else.

TWENTY-THREE

SOMETIMES, WHEN I call Amanda, I forget and think that nothing has changed, even though I'm dialing a new daytime number. The illusion lasts only until her phone gets picked up, because it's never Amanda who answers. It's always her assistant, Vicki, or an electronic device.

"Amanda Phelps's office."

"Hi, Vicki. It's Dek. Is the tycoon in?"

Vicki always laughs at that, but I always suppose that's because she's paid to. That morning, though, she was all business. She must have heard the news.

"I'll see if I can find her, Mr. Elstrom," she said, with just a bit of frost.

Amanda picked up in less than fifteen seconds. "Are you all right?" Like the last time I'd called, there were other voices in her background.

"In the news, but I guess you know that."

"You're safe and being looked after?"

"I've got a high-profile attorney. About the news, they'll probably trot out the old stuff, Amanda."

"It's already started."

"You? Your father?"

"Both of us, popular again." She forced a laugh. It was brittle.

"How badly will it affect what you're doing?"

"It will pass."

"They're waiting, Amanda," Vicki's voice said in her background.

"Just a second," she told her. Then, to me, "Listen, Dek, something's happened."

"What?" I asked.

"Amanda," Vicki said.

"I'll call you later."

She hung up.

No surprise, the one-two shooting of Sweetie Fairbairn's bodyguard and her own disappearance led the noon television news broadcasts. No surprise, either, that in the absence of other developments, they trotted me out, via video. They played footage, recorded the night before, of me skulking out of the police station, then seeing the reporters, waving and smiling like a crooked alderman.

When the video ended, the anchor wrinkled his sincere, spray-tanned brow. "Regular viewers will remember Vlodek Elstrom for his role in the Evangeline Wilts trial. Elstrom, a sometimes records researcher, was accused of falsely authenticating bank records for Mayor Wilts's defense. Elstrom, husband at the time of Amanda Phelps, daughter of community leader and businessman, Wendell Phelps, maintained his innocence. And, in fact, charges were subsequently dropped.

"Now the shadowy Elstrom has reappeared, this time amid the murky details surrounding the disappearance of missing heiress Sweetie Fairbairn. Police are not yet willing to discuss Elstrom's alleged role in the Fairbairn case, saying only that he was brought in for questioning last evening as a person of interest in her disappearance. Elstrom has not been charged in the murder of Ms. Fairbairn's bodyguard, Robert Norton. However, Elstrom has retained the services of John Peet, one of Chicago's most prominent, and expensive, defense attorneys, leading some to question just how extensive Elstrom's involvement is, and who is going to pay for such a high-ticket legal defense. Attempts to reach Peet, Elstrom, Wendell Phelps, and his daughter Amanda, a wealthy philanthropist in her own right, have been unsuccessful."

The anchor then treated his viewers to a professionally whitened smile, and said, "Related to these events, but on a lighter note, there is this: It unfolded just a short time ago, at Mr. Elstrom's residence in Rivertown."

The screen switched to a shot of Benny Fittle, leaning against his corroding Maverick, working his jaws with the strength of an industrial composter on something he'd snagged from the doughnut box. From there, the camera zoomed over his shoulder, to Leo and Endora, in tangerine, chartreuse, and neon yellow, looking up at the turret. The lens then rose, to close in on the king-sized salad dressing label that hung from the second-floor window.

"'You can't always believe what you read,'" the news anchor read, chuckling so that we at home would know to laugh, too. "That flapping bedsheet refers, of course, to the case pending against Elvis Derbil, zoning commissioner in Rivertown. Sources tell us he is about to be indicted for switching out-of-date salad oil labels before reselling the product."

It was diverting, indeed, and it was all the mirth I could stand. I switched off the tiny television, walked to the window to look out. The news vans had all left.

They'd done their work.

I'd hit the fan...and splattered all over Amanda.

THAT AFTERNOON, I worked wood, ate Ho Hos, and listened to my landline phone transfer one reporter after another to my answering machine. The recording device maxed out at five o'clock, which was also when I ran out of Ho Hos. And self-control. At the next ring, I hefted a particularly nicely figured piece of oak that I'd just cut perfectly, and considered throwing it like a spear through one of the windows. Interior carpentry, sugar fueled, can only be battered by a ringing phone for so long.

I edged to the window to look out, at the ready to duck back before some cameraman could record my peeping face. Framed by one of the turret's narrow slit windows, I'd photograph like a man looking out of a prison.

No vans had returned. Only one vehicle had come to park in front of the turret. A Prius. Jennifer Gale leaned against it. She wore a black skirt and a black sweater and was sipping an enormous Starbucks coffee.

She smiled up, raised the cup, and toasted me with it. She was at the door when I got downstairs.

"Dusty," she said, eyeing my work duds. "I've been drinking coffee all afternoon. Can I use your bathroom?"

"It's on the third floor. It is a man's bathroom, a man who lives alone. It's particularly dusty."

"It's a question of need," she said, going up ahead of me.

I waited in my office.

"Besides the dust, closets are also a problem here," she said, when she came down.

"I'll build some, someday."

"You'd better, if a woman is ever to occupy this place." She sat down on one of the card table chairs. "About you standing me up last evening?"

"I got detained."

"So I saw, on the news—our news, in fact."

"I really am sorry. I was looking forward to dinner."

"You were on the news again today, at noon."

"Nothing substantive. Just for comedy."

"We'll have dinner now?"

My instinct was to say no—not with a news reporter; not with a beautiful woman; not now. Then I had the thought that it would give me the opportunity to show off the expensive new duds Buffy Griselda had gotten me that morning. It was rationalization, and it was enough. I went upstairs, showered quickly, and descended, transformed, ready for applause.

"Don't you ever wear anything but khakis and blue shirts?" she asked.

TWENTY-FOUR

SHE PROBABLY TOOK it as gentlemanly that I said I'd drive us to dinner. She didn't complain when we had to walk along the river to get to where I'd hidden the Jeep from the reporters. She climbed into the car without commenting on the splotches of rust, or the strips of duct tape that covered the slashes on the plastic side windows.

After buckling her seat belt, though, she made a point of touching the wires protruding from the dash where the radio used to live.

"You're an outdoorsman, right? A rustic? This vehicle is for fishing and hunting?"

"This is my principal mode of transportation," I said, sounding every bit the college graduate that I am.

"How interesting," she said, though whether it was about the wires or me, I couldn't tell. Then, "Where shall we have dinner?"

"Someplace well lit," I said, a bit too quickly.

Barely a foot away, she smiled. Or at least her perfume, a heady, floral mix, did.

"I meant someplace where I don't have to worry about someone breaking into this fine car," I said, fumbling the joke.

She was too smart. "Rich girlfriend," she said.

"Rich girlfriend," I agreed.

I knew a diner with big windows, lit brightly enough for microsurgery, and parked on the street. "We'll sit by the

window, to make sure nobody peels off my silver tape,"
I said.

"Of course."

We both laughed, getting out, but that just made me
more edgy.

"You're Jennifer Gale," the woman behind the cash register said when we walked in.

The diner was only half full. It was easy to hear. Most
of the heads turned.

Smiling as though delighted to be recognized, Jennifer
turned to me. "That booth in the back corner, away from
the windows, you said?"

"Perfect."

I sat on the side facing the rest of the diner, so people coming in wouldn't notice her. We ordered mushroom
burgers and Cokes, because I wasn't elegant and she was.

"How's your investigation into Rivertown coming?" I
asked, hoping to steer the conversation.

"Elvis Derbil hasn't even been indicted yet."

"The Feds are taking their time?"

"I suppose."

She was being deliberately vague. I remembered the
morning I'd found her sitting on the bench by the Willahock. She'd made herself almost unrecognizable behind
huge sunglasses, wearing dressed-down clothes. She'd said
she'd been in the neighborhood and had thought to drop
by. She'd been evasive then, just like now. Something very
hushed was going on between Elvis Derbil and the Feds,
and Jennifer knew what it was.

"You do recall my bringing you the photos of the clown
going off the roof, and getting you in to see the rope?" she
asked, changing the subject. "How you agreed you'd give
me the complete Sweetie Fairbairn story?"

"I don't recall Ms. Fairbairn's name coming up in those negotiations."

"Well, surely you remember calling the police to her penthouse yesterday?" A smile played on her fine face. "Why are you now trying to divert me from Sweetie Fairbairn, the biggest story in Chicago, and her connection to that poor clown?"

"What makes you think there is a connection?"

"I don't think you're working two separate cases. Just a little over a week ago, you were spending your time painting windows. Clients, for you, are rare."

"Interesting observation."

"Accurate?"

"I have competing commitments. One is to my client— a rock, so to speak."

"Let's call her Sweetie Fairbairn," she said.

"My other commitment is to a hard place."

"That would be me, the all-too-accommodating television reporter?"

Our mushroom burgers came, and with them, the opportunity to fill my mouth with meat instead of an answer.

"How do we resolve this?" she asked, as I raised the hamburger to hide behind it.

I thought quickly; I never like to dither when food has just been served.

"I trust you," I said. "You've not traded on your inside knowledge that James Stitts, the clown, may have been murdered."

"What is the link between him and Sweetie Fairbairn?"

I inspected my hamburger. It looked like it was topped with sufficient mushrooms. Then again, it was why I'd chosen the joint. That, and the big front windows we decided to ignore.

"Impasse?" I asked.

"Only until we're done eating."

We talked of rich people, and people who merely acted rich, and geese, and then she asked something strange.

"Ever hear of citizen boards in Rivertown?"

"Citizen boards? You mean, like in Mayberry, where the town folk get together to help ol' Andy discover who's been sticking hungry thumbs into Aunt Bee's apple pies, cooling on the windowsill?"

She laughed. "That'll work."

"No such thing as citizen boards, not in Rivertown. It's not a democracy."

"I didn't think so."

"You didn't think they existed?" I asked.

"I didn't think anybody would know if there were any."

"Look, corruption is everywhere in Rivertown. Hookers work Thompson Avenue unmolested by the police. Taverns stay open past mandated closing times. I've heard there are at least three chop shops working out of old factories, converting stolen cars into used parts. The lizards have a piece of all of that. They would never risk involving the citizenry in city government."

"You mean any ordinary citizenry."

"How does any of that tie to Elvis?"

"Elvis is small potatoes." She took a bite of her hamburger.

"Is this why you suggested dinner for last evening? To ask me about citizen boards?"

"No; I'm killing time until we can abandon our impasse. Things changed when a guard got killed at Sweetie Fairbairn's, Dek. Now I need to know everything about you, her, the clown, and the guard.

"I'm willing to work for it," she added, after I'd said nothing.

"How?"

"Right now, you're too interesting to the media. They'll watch your every move, at least until something else in the Sweetie Fairbairn case becomes more interesting. Such scrutiny will limit your ability to detect, or whatever it is that you do. As I keep telling you, I've got resources you can never match. I help you find out what you want to know, and you give me the story."

I put down the defense of my hamburger. "Sweetie Fairbairn might show up today or tomorrow and confess she was having an affair with the guard. They quarreled; she killed him. End of another tawdry celebrity miniscandal."

"You think?"

"Not a chance."

"Then tell me what you know, with our same guarantee: I don't use anything you don't authorize. But I need to know everything, now."

She was right: She had resources. But I had a client.

"I'll get the story anyway, you know," she said. "All of it."

"No angle to Amanda Phelps," I said.

"How does she fit?"

"Sweetie Fairbairn learned about me through Amanda, at some social gathering. That's all."

"Ms. Phelps has already been brought into your troubles, mentioned on the news because you were once married."

"I'm hoping that link will fade."

"A chivalrous man. I like that. I agree, so long as your Ms. Phelps has no other direct involvement."

We finished our burgers and left, because I didn't want to talk further in a diner. Driving north, I told Jennifer Gale everything I knew about the clown, the guard, and Sweetie Fairbairn.

"Someone's blackmailing her?"

"It's all I can think."

I pulled up in front of an apartment building.

"What's this?" she asked, when I stopped.

"Inside that building is an apartment. The door upstairs might still be unlocked. The apartment might still stink, from a roast and a couple of potatoes that have gone very bad in too many days of heat."

"Who lives there?"

"A man named Andrew Fill."

"Andrew Fill? Didn't he just resign as head of the Midwest Arts Symposium?"

"He's had issues with some of Sweetie Fairbairn's money."

"She fired him?"

"For theft. It's the best lead I've got for now. I want you to help me find where he might be."

I drove us back to the turret, parked behind her Prius, and we both got out. She looked for a moment at the timbered door, perhaps thinking.

Then she shook her head almost imperceptibly and stuck out her hand. "I'm an old-fashioned girl, Dek Elstrom."

"Thank you," I said.

She drove away, leaving me with just the slightest remaining scent of a heady, floral perfume.

"Thank you," I said again, this time to no one at all.

TWENTY-FIVE

I STARTED WAITING outside Tim Duggan's office at nine the next morning. It was south of the city, on the second floor of a three-story building next to a discount tire store. The green hall carpet hadn't been cleaned in quite some time.

He stepped out of the elevator at ten fifteen and stopped when he saw me. His hand went into his suit jacket.

"What the hell are you doing here?" he called from down the hall.

"Did you read that *Tribune* you've got under your arm?"

"It doesn't exonerate you. It reports only that Plinnit has dropped you as a person of interest. You could still be involved."

"I am involved. Now I need to be effective. Let's go inside and converse."

Duggan looked at me for a long minute, thinking, as I was, that his bulk was better and harder than mine. He could snap me like a twig. Or, more sociably, he could merely throw me into the elevator and press the down button. Either way would remove me effectively.

Instead, though, he said, "I need to call a client. Wait here." He unlocked his office and went inside.

The call didn't take long. After only a couple of minutes, he opened his office door and told me to come in.

The office coordinated well with the hall. Beneath the dented metal desk, one beige file cabinet, and three vinyl chairs, there was more of the same stained green carpet.

I went for truth: "What happened at Sweetie Fairbairn's apartment?"

He went for incredulity. "You're asking me? You were there."

"Your perspective."

"It was my day off," he said. "Bob Norton was a reliable man. No way he'd let anybody into that penthouse."

"Not even if that person had a gun?"

"There's a camera in the lobby, aimed at the penthouse elevator door. One monitor is in a cabinet upstairs, in the penthouse foyer. Bob would never have let the elevator come up without positive ID of who was inside."

"Is there tape?"

"Off the downstairs monitor, maybe."

"The back door, or another broken window?"

"The police won't let me back in the penthouse. They'll have to tell you whether there was forced entry."

"You haven't asked them?"

"It's their investigation. I'll ask when they're done."

"There's another possibility."

"No way in hell Sweetie Fairbairn shot Bob."

"Who, then?"

"I sent you to George Koros, to find out about Andrew Fill. You said Fill embezzled from Ms. Fairbairn."

"Fill has gone away. I don't know where he is."

"I don't have any other names. Nobody has reason to want Ms. Fairbairn dead. She helps people—children, hospitals, doctors. Her only offenses come from her good works, in choosing to help some while denying others. Those aren't motives to murder."

"You had to know she was afraid. She sent you to hire me."

"She never mentioned anything specific. I did what she asked. I provided security. She didn't hire me to ask questions."

Someone knocked on his door. Duggan went and opened it.

It was Plinnit.

"Lieutenant," I said, looking at Duggan, "what a sudden non-surprise."

"It's a lovely day, Elstrom," the lieutenant said. "I've come to take you for a drive."

THE GRAY-EYED, gray-haired man was behind the wheel. He didn't wiggle his jowls or drool in excited recognition when I slid into the back of the unmarked car. He waited for Plinnit to get in, then drove us from the curb.

"Nice of Duggan to call you," I said to the back of Plinnit's neck.

The vinyl upholstery smelled funny, as if it had just been drenched with a cleaner to kill a smell. I reached down to touch the seat. Mercifully, it seemed dry.

"He doesn't like trouble," Plinnit said.

"I was invited in."

"Like the person who killed Robert Norton, I'm sure."

"You never got around to telling me if there was a lobby camera at the Wilbur Wright."

"The quality's lousy, but we could make out you. And Ms. Fairbairn, twice. She went up, apparently forgot something, changed her clothes, and came back down the rear stairs because we don't have that recorded. Then she went up again. She's an obvious candidate for shooting Norton, Elstrom."

"If you ever find motive," I said. "Where are we going?"

"You'll recognize it," Plinnit said.

Five minutes later, I did. It was Andrew Fill's apartment building.

I also recognized Jennifer Gale's green Prius. It was parked down the block.

The car looked empty. So did the sidewalks, except for a red-headed woman in a turquoise coat strolling down the block.

"What's this?" I asked.

"Oh, please," Plinnit said.

In the foyer, Plinnit buzzed someone on the second floor, who let us in. We took the elevator up.

The pleasant older man who'd held the door for me the last time I'd come was waiting in the hall. At the sight of me, he widened his eyes and nodded exaggeratedly at Plinnit. Plinnit thanked him a fraction of an instant before the old man slammed the door.

"Last time, I came cleverly disguised as a painter," I said.

"Ah, Elstrom," Plinnit said. We went back to the elevator and rode it up to three.

"What are we doing?" I asked, too loudly, when we got to Fill's door. If Jennifer was in the apartment, the best she could do now was hide under the bed.

Plinnit gave me a puzzled look and withdrew a key from his pocket.

"Aren't you going to knock first?" I asked, again too loudly.

"Losing your hearing, Elstrom? Or are you expecting Fill to be home?"

We went in.

Fill's apartment no longer smelled of spoiled meat. It smelled of Jennifer Gale's perfume.

"The place has been gone over, so you can touch," Plinnit said, then added, "some more."

"You found my prints?" It was my last loud attempt.

Plinnit laughed. "Certainly not on the roast."

"The door was open. I stepped in, looked around, saw the apartment was immaculate. I left."

"How did you think to come here in the first place?"

"Same reason as you, Lieutenant. Andrew Fill had a dispute with Sweetie Fairbairn. It was in the newspaper."

"George Koros told us Fill took money from something called the Midwest Arts Symposium."

"Sweetie Fairbairn had Koros fire him."

Plinnit's face tightened and then relaxed. "The question is, Elstrom, did you come here to snoop or to abduct?"

"Abduct Andrew Fill? Why?"

"For Sweetie Fairbairn. She could have hired you to muscle the money out of Fill."

"No need. Koros can confirm that Fill has been paying it back."

"Koros did. But perhaps Fill was paying back too slowly for Ms. Fairbairn."

"I got involved in this long after Fill disappeared. He's been gone at least a month."

"The stinking roast gave you that?"

Plinnit was too smart for too many lies. I gave him something he already knew.

"I went through his mail," I said.

"We know. We took your prints off the box. We'll probably add violating federal postal laws to your growing list of crimes."

"I wanted to see how long the mail had been piling up."

"You were thinking Andrew Fill went away for a month, then decided to come back to kill Ms. Fairbairn?"

"I don't know what to think. Koros says Fill is an embezzler, nothing more. I'm just assembling facts that might help find Sweetie Fairbairn."

"Why didn't you toss the apartment, Elstrom?"

"What?"

"When you broke in here before. Why didn't you toss the place, do a thorough search?"

"For what?"

"For all that money, Elstrom. Or for clues as to where Fill might be, with all that money."

Something itchy started working at my scalp.

"Want to know why you didn't need to toss this place?" Plinnit went on. "Because you already knew what was here: Nothing, with a capital *N*. You came back just to make sure the place looked good enough for us. Now there's nothing here for anyone to find."

It was enough. "If you want to talk more, let's invite John Peet."

"Not yet, Elstrom. Maybe soon."

We went down to his car.

Nobody said anything on the ride back to Duggan's office building. As the gray-haired, gray-eyed man pulled us to a stop, Plinnit turned around to look at me.

"Care to guess whose face keeps popping up where it doesn't belong, Elstrom? First in Sweetie Fairbairn's penthouse, then in Andrew Fill's apartment?"

I reached for the door handle. "Thanks for the ride, Lieutenant."

"Don't pop up again until I come for you," he said.

TWENTY-SIX

I CALLED JENNIFER as soon as Plinnit pulled away.

"Housebreaking?" I asked.

"That was close, wasn't it? I'd just come out when you arrived in a very official-looking car."

"That was Lieutenant Plinnit, who's heading the search for Sweetie Fairbairn. He wanted to rub my nose in my trail, to make sure I understood he knew I'd been in Fill's apartment. What were you doing there?"

"Your bidding, remember? You want me to find Andrew Fill. What better place to start than his apartment?"

"How did you get in?" It wasn't important, but the woman was fascinating.

"The building's back door was open. Upstairs, for the apartment, I used picks."

"Aren't you too recognizable for that?"

"I have a wig and a very long coat."

I remembered the red-haired woman in the turquoise coat on the sidewalk. "Good thing you chose subdued colors."

"They draw the eye from the face."

"Not that face," I wanted to say, but asked instead, "Did you learn anything?"

"I'll pick you up. We'll talk as we drive."

"Drive where?"

"Oh no you don't, Dek Elstrom. This one I'm in on from the beginning."

"Don't you have to work?"

"Only until three o'clock. I'll pick you up after that."

I checked my phone for messages. Amanda had called twice. George Koros, once.

I got right through to Amanda. "I need to show you something," she said.

"It's lunchtime," I said.

"I can't do a restaurant," she said quickly.

"I'll come to your office."

"No." She said it just as fast, and then I understood why she didn't want to meet in a restaurant, or in her office. She couldn't afford to be seen with me.

"Messenger it to me, then," I said.

She thought for a minute and said, "The hell with it. Sandwiches, in Millennium Park?"

We used to meet at noon there, back when they were finishing up the grand new park. It seemed that all of Chicago had been excited about what was coming. Like us, before we got married.

"I'll get those roast beef sandwiches with the horseradish mustard, the ones on jalapeño rolls," I said.

"You remember the bench?"

I did. Our bench was east of the bean, that asymmetrical, mirrorlike wonder that tourists and locals alike sought out to see their reflections distorted. Our bench was out of the way, tucked behind some bushes.

I told her I'd pick up the sandwiches and see her there in an hour.

I returned George Koros's call.

"I seem to remember Andrew Fill has a summer place, in Wisconsin, or maybe Michigan," he said.

"You think he's there?"

"I don't think anything, Mr. Elstrom. I had to FedEx something to Andrew once, a Saturday delivery. He gave me the address of his weekend place. When I find where it is, can you get out there right away?"

"It's the only lead we've got."

I GOT TO the park twenty minutes early. Amanda wasn't there yet, so I took the sandwiches for a walk. It had been months, perhaps a year, since I'd last been there. The park looked different. Plantings had been changed, and some stone benches added. It wasn't just that, though. The people looked different. I might have still had cellular communications on the brain, because it seemed everyone was on the phone. Headsets, handsets, everyone appeared to be talking to someone far away. There were no couples simply strolling, that lunch hour, like Amanda and I used to do. Everyone looked to be alone, and on the phone.

I saw her then.

For an instant, I almost didn't recognize her. The spring was still in her step; she still moved with the same purpose and grace. Her features were as fine and as beautiful as I always saw them, though now that was usually only in my mind.

Something, though, had changed. There was a tension to her; she seemed somehow coiled. Perhaps it was me.

Our embrace was too fast; her kiss, on my cheek, was too cordial. We sat on the bench, and I spread out the sandwiches.

"Same sandwiches, certainly," she said.

"But not the same old Amanda," I almost said, but didn't. I bit the sandwich instead.

"How is Sweetie Fairbairn?"

"Still gone."

Strangers on a bench, stiff and formal and guarded.

"No inside dope, things I haven't been hearing on the news?" she asked.

"Nobody knows anything. Especially me."

"Why did she hire you?"

I hesitated, as I had the first time she'd asked about Sweetie Fairbairn, the night we'd met at Rokie's.

"I have a real need to know, before I show you something," she added.

I told her what little I knew, about a blond woman in a limousine, and James Stitts, and Andrew Fill.

"And the dead guard?"

"Sweetie was there, and then she took off."

"She never told you how all this might relate to her?"

"She's extremely guarded. She intimated that someone was impersonating her."

"That woman in the limo, for blackmail?"

"Andrew Fill could have set that up with an actress."

"Why? He already has her money."

"A half-million dollars of it. Maybe he wants more."

"Then this makes everything doubly interesting. It arrived yesterday." She pulled a folded sheet of paper from her purse and handed it to me. It was a photocopy of a check, payable to Memorial Hospital, Children's Wing. The check was handwritten, for two million dollars. Sweetie Fairbairn had signed the check.

"A huge check, dated the day she disappeared." I looked up.

"I'd suggested a contribution of one or two hundred thousand."

"And she gave you two million?"

"Much more than I asked for."

"You were very compelling?"

"It wasn't just me. I know of two other people who also received much more from Sweetie than they'd asked for."

"Checks also written the day she disappeared?"

She nodded. "It will become public today, tomorrow at the latest."

"Tell me, Amanda." I wanted her to say the words so that I'd have no doubt.

"Sweetie Fairbairn is giving away her whole fortune."

TWENTY-SEVEN

THINGS HAD CHANGED in front of the turret since I'd left.

Someone from city hall had put up two NO PARKING FIRE LANE signs. One was directly in front of the turret. The other was across the street.

Also, there was a face-off going on between the drivers of two automobiles. Benny Fittle's Maverick was parked across the street, belching hydrocarbons back at city hall. Jennifer Gale was parked in front of the turret, right in front of the new sign. It was hard to tell if her Prius was running, because hybrids belch nothing, idling as they do in electric mode.

Benny was staring at Jennifer Gale, daring her to leave her car so he could enforce the new parking ban.

I got out of the Jeep. "What the hell, Benny?" I asked, crossing the street.

"Better move your car, Mr. Elstrom," he said through whatever powdered thing he was eating. "Otherwise I got to write you."

"Where am I supposed to park, if not in front of my own home?"

"There's spots south of Thompson."

"That's a half mile away."

He smiled with his mouth open, exposing Boston crème run amok.

I'd fight this new battle another time. I went back to the Jeep, started it, and eased it over the curb to park on the grass in front of my door.

Benny, his cheeks still inflated like a blowfish, gave me a thumbs-up.

I walked over to the Prius.

"What's with the fire lane signs?" Jennifer asked through the open window.

"A consequence of my notoriety. Now no press can park here."

"Really?" She got out.

She wore black jeans and a yellow knit top that was cut a little lower than anything my eyes needed at that juncture in my life. I told myself she looked like a wasp, in that yellow and black, except for the curves. Myself laughed. "Yeah, except for the curves."

She reached into the Prius, took out a press sign, and held it up so Benny could see. He shook his head; the press would not be accommodated in Rivertown.

She placed the sign on her dash anyway. Then she started across the street. To my eyes, she was putting a little something extra into her walk as she approached Benny's Maverick. By the way his face was reddening through his smeared windshield, he saw it, too. He started working his throat, like a snake trying to swallow a pig, desperate to get rid of the last of his Boston crème.

Jennifer got to the Maverick and leaned in. She looked to be saying a few long, slow words. Benny's head started bobbing in agreement. She then straightened up, slowly tugged an imaginary wrinkle from her yellow knit top, and came back smiling. Behind her, Benny Fittle was smiling, too, substantially happier than he'd been the moment before.

"Screw with me, screw with the devil," Jennifer said.

I did not doubt the truth of that. Nor, I supposed, would Benny Fittle, ever again in his life.

"How about some coffee before we go to Indiana?" she asked.

"Indiana? We're going to Indiana?"

"Andrew Fill's place."

"George Koros said he'd sent something to Fill at a vacation place, but he thought it was in Michigan or Wisconsin. How did you locate it?"

"I found a canceled check in his apartment, made out to a homeowners' association. Fill had put his cottage in trust."

"Secretive?"

"Not necessarily. More likely, he was following the advice of some lawyer when he bought the place. Just a quick cup of coffee, then let's leave."

I opened the door, and we went up to the second floor.

"Think I'll ever get all the way to the roof?" she asked, as I turned into the kitchen.

"We can take our coffee up there."

I fed Mr. Coffee new grounds. Normally, afternoons, I just run new water through the morning's grounds—a habit of the financially challenged—but she was the press, and curved. There would be no reruns for Jennifer Gale.

"Interesting collection of appliances." she said, as Mr. Coffee burbled, sounding every bit as happy as Benny Fittle. "Sort of like a museum of what people used to have in their kitchens."

"I've had them longer than I'd hoped. That avocado-colored refrigerator I got from an alley. The microwave I bought new, but dented. It might leak radiation, but we won't know that for years."

I poured coffee in travel mugs and capped them. "The roof?"

"Yes, please."

I led us up two more flights of stairs, then up the ladder to the fifth floor.

"Why not stairs all the way?" she asked, as I went ahead, up the next ladder, to the roof.

"My grandfather's thinking was not always clear." I pushed open the trapdoor. "One of my aunts said he was going to distill up here and wanted to make sure he could drop a door on any charging police, then pull both ladders up to the roof with him."

"Wouldn't he then be trapped?"

"As I said, his thinking wasn't always clear."

"Wow," she said, when she got up.

"Best view in town." I leaned against the wall.

She worked her way around the roof, taking in the views from each direction.

"You think Andrew Fill could be in Indiana?" she asked, finally.

"I'd be surprised if he's that close. The man's got a half-million dollars, enough to run far away."

"Maybe we'll find a cottage abandoned like his apartment."

"I think I should tell you about a development that might make you want to forget Indiana and head back to Channel 8. Sweetie Fairbairn wrote very big checks to several charities the same day she disappeared."

"You know this how?"

"One of the recipients got a charitable donation that was way more than what she'd asked for. That person said two others also got substantially more than they requested. Sweetie gave away millions that last day, Jennifer."

"How many millions, do you think?"

"Maybe most of what she had."

"This recipient will verify what you're telling me?"

"Off-limits," I said.

"I figured as much," she said, knowing who it was. She took out her cell phone and flipped it open. "Who else knows?"

"I don't know, but it will get out today."

Jennifer called her news director. After repeating what I'd told her, she nodded a couple of times, frowned, and hung up. "They'll check it out."

"That's it? No on-air time for you?"

She shrugged. "Your tip is unsubstantiated; there's no second source. The news business is changing. We got our news director cheap."

"Indiana, then?"

"Indiana, for sure."

We'd just gotten out the door when Leo rumbled up in his Porsche. The convertible top was down, the bossa nova was up. He turned off his CD player.

Across the street, Benny Fittle leaned his head out the side window.

"Jennifer, this specimen is Leo Brumsky. He is my friend."

Below his summer standards of a wide-brimmed straw hat and big wraparound sunglasses, Leo wore a plum-colored Hawaiian shirt, forested with bright green palm trees that, amazingly, bore bright red apples. Jennifer laughed as she held out her hand.

"Run away with me to the south of France," he said.

"Apples on a palm tree, Leo?" she asked.

"That's artistic license, my dear. I wear only designers with expanded imaginations."

"How much did you pay for the shirt?" I asked, to cut the crap.

"Because of the apples, only a dollar ninety-nine." He extended his chest. Outside his spare 140 pounds, the XXL shirt didn't move.

"We're off on a trip," I said.

Leo still hadn't taken his eyes off Jennifer Gale. "You look…" He stopped.

"Older than I appear on television?"

"Even more newsworthy." He fluffed out the front of his shirt and grinned, a letch covered with apple-laden palm trees. "There's room in here for both of us."

She laughed, charmed. Everyone is, with Leo.

He started to reach for the gear shifter, then stopped. "You do know your Jeep is on your lawn?" he asked me.

"Yes."

He nodded, turned on the bossa nova, and gunned the Porsche back toward Thompson Avenue.

Benny Fittle withdrew his head.

Jennifer Gale and I set off to find Andrew Fill.

TWENTY-EIGHT

WE TOOK HER Prius because, as she put it, she'd already experienced my Jeep.

"What do you want to talk about?" she asked, when we crossed into Indiana. We'd drifted into our own lulls once we left Rivertown.

"Not murder," I said.

"That would be best."

I turned, surprised, to look at her. "Why?"

"I want to show you I'm not all business, ever on the lookout for scoops to further my career."

"Is that true?"

"Of course not, but it's what I want to show."

I laughed and turned back to look out the windshield. The expressway through western Indiana looked the same as when I'd last driven it, the roadside dotted as always with billboards advertising buxom females with come-hither pouts, welcoming gentlemen to stop at gentlemen's clubs. Outside the Prius, inside the Prius, there seemed to be no place for a testosterone-revved man, on the outs with his girl, to rest his eyes.

So I spoke about murder. "The police would like me as a suspect."

"For the guard's murder?"

"Or for Sweetie's disappearance."

"They'll take what they can get, to show progress," she said. "The story is huge. A prominent socialite disappears, following a murder. Now comes word that she dumped most of her fortune on her way out the door? Big-time heater case for sure; lots of pressure on the police." She looked over at me. "Do the cops suspect the link between Sweetie Fairbairn and the clown?"

"Because it was a blond woman in a limo who hired James Stitts? I don't think they know about that yet."

She got off the interstate a few miles west of Michigan City, picked up Route 12, and for several miles we followed the narrow blacktop as it curved under Lake Michigan. The old two-laner was tranquil and arched with trees, a road to take to a picnic on the beach, not to hunt down an embezzler.

Just before Beverly Shores, she turned left and drove along ancient streets that ran through marsh.

"I thought you said he was in the dunes."

"These are the dunes," she said, "just the wet section. According to my computer map, there's a trailer park in here."

"Exuberant mosquitoes, too, I would bet."

We found the trailer park on a crumbling cross street, two dozen tired mobile homes hunkered down on flat tires and cinder blocks. There was no office, no directory at the entrance. Two rows of arched rural-style mailboxes had been screwed to a rack of two-by-fours. The red flags were up on a quarter of them. There was only one car around, a tan sedan parked down the road, well past the entrance.

Above the mailboxes, a faded sign read LAKE VISTA ES-TATES. I double-checked the views toward the lake. Lake Michigan hadn't been visible from that spot since the dunes were formed, some number of million years before. Then again, the sign might have referred to the stagnant green water that covered the acres of sodden tree stumps and cattails we'd just driven through.

Jennifer glided the Prius to a silent, electric halt. She

reached for a sheaf of pink-colored leaflets from the back-seat and handed half to me. They were flyers for a missing schnauzer, Wilma, and listed her age as six. The black-and-white photo showed she was adorable.

Jennifer grinned at my confusion. "This only works if the day's mail has been delivered. I got the dog's picture off the Internet. The contact name and phone numbers I made up. Take your time folding one into each mailbox."

"You keep these with you?"

"Always."

It was a slick way to read the names on the mail inside the boxes, because no one would roust someone for hand-delivering such flyers.

I took the right section of boxes, she the left. Five min-utes later, she said, "Step it up, Dek; we're done." She'd found Andrew Fill, on the top row.

We jammed flyers into the rest of the boxes and got back in her Prius. "Space twelve," she said, starting the engine. We followed the road to the left, reading the num-bers. There were no cars parked in the little enclave, no towels hanging on any lines. And there were no people.

"Ghost trailer park," I said.

"Beach access, down the road and on the cheap. The place must come alive just on weekends."

The trailer at number twelve was small, like all the oth-ers. Once bright white, it had faded to the same chalky gray as its corroded aluminum windows and sat slightly tilted, barely a foot above its slab. A disconnected tele-phone wire dangled limp from a pole twenty feet away. It did not look like a place someone with a half-million dol-lars would ever return to.

"I can't imagine he's there," Jennifer said.

"I'll deliver a pink flyer anyway." I started up to knock on the pitted aluminum door.

"He ain't home," a voice, squeaky for a man's, said behind us.

At least I supposed it was a man's voice, because when I turned to see who had spoken, I saw someone who was barely five feet tall. His hair, such as it was, was pulled taut into a pattylike clump on the top of his head. He wore blue jeans and an oversized plaid work shirt. A plastic bag filled with crushed aluminum cans dangled from the handlebars of a boy's black bicycle.

"We'll try to reach him at work," Jennifer said to the little man.

"What do you want Andrew for?" he asked.

"He called, said he might have seen this dog." Jennifer walked the few feet to the street, holding out a pink flyer.

"You said he called, from here?" As the bike rider looked up at the disconnected phone wire, his voice registered disbelief. "When?"

"Some time ago," I said. "We've come by before, but we never seem to find him at home. So we thought we'd leave flyers. Maybe one of his neighbors saw the dog."

"He's just here weekends. He's got another place somewhere in Chicago."

"Do you know where?" I asked, because it was expected.

The bicycle rider leaned down on the handlebars, studying the picture. "Andy seen this dog?"

"Some time ago. We're hoping he might know who has him now."

The bike rider looked up, into my lying eyes. "Andy ain't been around, not for a month, maybe more, judging by the cans."

"Cans?"

He tapped the bag hanging on the handlebars. "Cans.

Andy's always good for a dozen Mountain Dews every weekend. Been no empties for weeks."

I pulled a fifty from my pocket and handed it to the rider. "What's this for?" the man asked.

"Help with the cans."

The rider gave a small snort, took the bill, and pedaled, strangely and silently, away.

"That was a man, right?" I asked.

"I think so."

We stood watching until he turned the corner.

"For a guy who can't afford heat, you were generous," Jennifer said.

"It might erase a memory of us being here."

"Why?"

"Because I want to break in. I caught a smell when I was close to the door."

"What kind of smell?"

"Bad."

I walked back up to the trailer door. The latch gave with a whisper; the door swung out.

I stepped into a trailer that was swarming with flies and stinking of life gone away.

The place was as neat as Andrew Fill's apartment. No food lay out in the galley kitchen; no dirty dishes were piled in the tiny stainless steel sink.

Yet there were flies, thousands of them, and the smell that was sticking onto the back of my throat. I looked past the kitchen.

It only took a few steps to get to him.

He was lying on his back. His face was red and raw, pocked long and deep by the swarms of flies. Waving my left hand to keep them from my face, I jabbed my right hand under him and found a wallet in his hip pocket. A quick flip opened it. His driver's license was beneath a little plastic window in the worn black leather.

Hurrying past the tiny kitchen, I grabbed a neatly folded dish towel, wiped the door handle, and pushed it open. Down on the ground, I made a fast wipe at the outside door handle as well, rubbed my hands with the towel, more for my mind than my skin, and threw it underneath the trailer.

It might have been the horror on my face. It might have been the stench of too-long-dead flesh that followed me out of the trailer. Or it might have been the furious way I toweled my hands before damned near running for her Prius. Whatever it was, it was enough for Jennifer. She hurried to get in behind the steering wheel and started the car.

It wasn't until we'd breezed five miles with all the car's windows open that she chanced a look at me.

"Andrew Fill is gone," I said.

TWENTY-NINE

"WHY WON'T THAT damned smell go away?"

Her voice came unnaturally high, and her hands were shaking jackhammer hard on the steering wheel. I told her to pull over, onto the narrow shoulder of Route 12. Neither of us had said a word for the first miles, speeding away from Fill's trailer.

She shut off the motor and put her forehead against the wheel. "What the hell, Dek?" she said, her voice lower now.

"Andrew's wallet." It lay on the floor behind her. I hoped the stench came from the wallet, and not from me. I didn't want the smell of Andrew Fill's corpse to be on me.

"Why do you need his wallet?"

"See what's inside." My words somehow sounded ridiculous.

She raised her head to look at me. "I'll pull into the next gas station so you can look. Then throw it away."

"No gas stations. They've got security cameras."

"We've got gas, right? Christ, I can't even remember that."

I looked at the display on the dash. "Three-quarters of a tank."

"Enough to get us to California, in this car. Let's run." She giggled.

I touched the back of her neck. At first she stiffened, but then her skin warmed. She straightened back from the steering wheel and turned toward me.

I turned toward her, until our faces were but a couple of inches apart.

Our ghosts came then, hers and mine.

I laughed, sort of. She laughed, sort of. I got out, and we switched places, and I sped us west onto the expressway, away from the dunes and away from the heat of an instant, momentarily as giddy as fools.

I got off at the first exit on the Illinois Tollway and pulled into a parking lot in front of a church. She had a flashlight and tissues. We went through Andrew Fill's wallet on the hood of her car, extracting its few contents carefully, as though each had been coated with anthrax. He had a Visa; a membership card to the East Bank Club, a high-end fitness center in Chicago; the Illinois driver's license; two twenties and two singles; a State Farm Insurance card showing he drove a Volvo; and one scrap of paper with a phone number written on it. It was George Koros's number. I ripped it up and scattered the pieces.

I put the cards and the driver's license back in the wallet and tossed it into the bushes. The forty-two dollars got walked to the mailbox in the door of the church. Then I rubbed my hands furiously on the grass, thinking for an instant of the day I'd met Jennifer Gale, and the agent who'd palmed Elvis Derbil's head. He'd been desperate to do what I was now doing. Except he was trying to rid his hands of coconut hair spray. I was trying to rub away death.

When there was nothing more to rub off but skin, I drove us back onto the Tollway.

"His car should have been at his trailer," she said.

"It would have attracted too much attention, sitting idle. His killer took it, abandoned it elsewhere so it wouldn't attract attention, sitting there unused."

"You'll call Plinnit?" She was teasing, settling us down.

"He'll be delighted I'm still venturing where I don't belong."

"You do that, don't you?"

I wondered whether she was thinking about me, in Fill's trailer, or us, later, in that one supercharged moment at the side of the road.

I decided I was better off not wondering about anything, for a time.

A SMALL WHITE Toyota was idling with its parking lights on in front of the turret. This Toyota was much older, and not nearly as environmentally correct as Jennifer's. I knew it, of course, like I knew the short dark hair, and then the eyes and the lips on the head that turned around to look at the back window at the approaching headlamps.

"I'll call you tomorrow," I said, pulling the Prius to a stop well short of the white Toyota.

"We're still a hundred feet away," Jennifer said.

"Close enough," I said.

I got out; Jennifer slid over and made a U-turn to go back down the short road.

I watched her taillights turn onto Thompson Avenue as I walked to the white car.

Amanda cut the engine and hand-cranked down the window on the driver's side. I liked that she kept the old crank-window Toyota. It was a remnant of her former life.

"You're here," I said.

"I didn't even think the car would start, it's been so long." She dabbed at her eyes with a tissue. "I've been sitting here for two hours, feeling bad about my father, you, Richard, me, getting sidetracked, charities, what I've given, what my father took." She tried a smile. "The damned publicity is probably going to wreck everything I maybe didn't want to do anyway."

I reached in and touched her cheek to stop the torrent of words. "Come in. We can have coffee and Ho Hos."

"I don't know that I should," she said, more slowly.

"I have Cheerios, if you prefer," I said, cracking wise as cheerily as I could, so soon after picking the pocket of a dead man.

"I didn't mean that."

"Why did you drive out?"

"You weren't answering your phones." She was looking ahead, at the great stone shadow that was city hall. "And when I got here, I saw your Jeep parked up on your lawn…"

"You shouldn't have worried."

"I didn't. I saw the fire lane sign, knew that parking on the lawn was your way of dealing with that."

"I am resourceful," I said.

"I was the one who told Sweetie about you in the first place, and now—"

"Only because she asked about me, when she began checking you out." I opened her door. "Cheerios are good. They lower cholesterol."

The skin around her eyes crinkled. Not a lot, but enough. "What girl could refuse such an enticement?"

Inside the turret, she stopped in mock amazement. "Same plastic chairs, same table saw. Why, this place looks no different than the last time I was here."

"Which was months ago."

She turned, surprised.

"Really, it's been that long," I said. "Anyway, the work has gone on upstairs."

Up in the kitchen, she went to touch one of the cabinets I'd built. "You do have a talent, Dek." Then she put a finger on the table I'd fashioned from scrap plywood, and sat on one of the curb-treasure lawn chairs I'd dragged home a dozen garbage days before. "But your furnishing skills…"

I went to make coffee.

"What about those Cheerios?" she asked, when I set down our mugs.

I reached behind me for the box.

"Milk?" she asked.

"I don't have any milk."

"Then what do you do with the Cheerios?"

"You'll notice the box has not been opened. Just looking at the cholesterol claims on the box while I eat breakfast makes me feel healthy."

"What have you been eating for breakfast?"

"Ho Hos lately, but I'll move on."

"I remember."

For a time, we talked about my rehabbing the turret, because that was safe.

"I'm still hoping my zoning will get changed," I said.

"When Elvis Derbil goes to prison?"

"Jennifer thinks that's a long way off."

"Jennifer?"

"Jennifer Gale. I told you about her," I said. "She just dropped me off. She got interested in Rivertown because of Elvis, and wanted to do a story on my zoning. I didn't want any press…" I slowed down. I was talking too much, and too fast. "I cut a deal with her. No references to you or to your father."

"It's all right, Dek. That night at Rokie's, you told me you met her."

"Yes. She finds this small, surviving bastion of old-time, iron-fisted corrup—"

"You've become friends?"

"I'm a source." Everything that was spilling out of my mouth was still coming out too frothy, too light. Too forced. "She can do me a lot of good, if she gets my zoning changed."

"That's not her main interest, though, is it, Dek?"

"Sweetie Fairbairn is every reporter's interest, right now," I said, not pausing to wonder what Amanda really meant, "but later, a little sunlight on Rivertown could lead to better times for me." I took a sip of coffee, and a bigger step. "You mentioned a Richard, out in the car."

She looked away, at the cabinets above where a stove would one day go. "Richard's someone I've met."

"You've become friends?" Only when the words were out did I realize my words mimicked hers.

"He attends the same functions I do, serves on the same boards. He's third-generation money, like me. His father founded Illinois General Insurance."

"And he's president of his own commodities trading firm," I said.

She raised an eyebrow.

"Your pictures have been in the paper, Amanda. Together."

"Dek, we haven't…"

"He's polished, successful; he understands your world. He's not some goof huddled in a turret."

She set down her coffee, looked at something, or nothing, across the hall. "Who could have known?" she asked softly.

"You mean Sweetie Fairbairn, or something more?"

"I think Sweetie Fairbairn, for now." She checked her watch, suddenly brisk. "Meeting, tomorrow morning at seven."

We went down the stairs. Every step rang the old wrought iron like a knell for the dead, or maybe for us. I didn't know.

Outside, I held her door. She looked up from inside the car. "Who's going to come out of this all right, Dek?"

I didn't answer. I didn't know.

THIRTY

THE STENCH OF Andrew Fill's tin trailer was thick in my nose when I woke in the dark the next morning. I told myself the stench wasn't real anymore.

The flies, though, had been real. As had the money.

I took coffee up to the roof to tell myself that again, and to reason with the stars.

It had been the flies and the money that had awakened me. That's what the night had distilled everything into: flies and money. There'd been too many flies, working too long, in Andrew Fill's trailer. There'd been too much money, an embezzled half-million dollars, that seemed to have been nowhere in his life.

Too many flies; too much money.

I looked out at Rivertown in the dark, but I was seeing the inside of a stinking trailer. Andrew Fill would have ripened fast, in the heat of that trailer. He would have drawn hundreds of flies the first day, then hundreds and hundreds more as the days went on. By the fast glance I'd managed at the rough gouges in his face, the flies had been excavating for quite some time. It would have taken them weeks to get that deep into his skin.

He'd been dead quite a while.

Then there was the money. According to George Koros, Fill had begun paying it back. I couldn't understand the time repayment plan; Fill should have paid it all back in one lump, been done with the fear of being prosecuted. Or he should have run. A half-million dollars would have taken him thousands of miles farther, to better destinations than a tin trailer in the muck back of the dunes.

He hadn't paid it all back, though, and he hadn't run. Because Andrew Fill had been killed right after he'd been fired by Sweetie Fairbairn, well before James Stitts got his safety rope cut. He hadn't been alive to mastermind anything against Sweetie Fairbairn.

Too many flies; too much money.

After the sun had sufficiently lit the horizon, I called Jennifer Gale.

"Have you slept?" she asked, sounding like she hadn't.

"I've been up for a time, ruminating."

"Ruminating over what?"

"Flies and money."

"Delightful. We need to talk."

"I know. It's been one of the things I've been ruminating about."

"We have to tell the police we discovered Andrew Fill's body. It isn't right, him just lying there, in his trailer, being eaten by those—"

"Out of such horror has come a plan," I interrupted.

"What plan?"

I told her, way too spontaneously, that I'd tell her over breakfast.

She said she had to drop something off for her mother. We agreed to meet at Galecki's, behind the wall of ketchup.

I GOT TO the diner first. Mama remembered me and escorted me to the booth behind the red bottles, then came back with two cups of coffee and slid in across the booth.

She pushed one cup across the table. "How rich is your girlfriend?"

I looked at her face. Not one of her wrinkles was stretching up into a smile.

"She's my ex-wife."

"How rich?"

"She'll inherit tens of millions."

"Tens of millions, whoa boy," she said, smacking her lips. "And you, you got big dough, too?"

I shook my head. "Your daughter makes more in a week than I made all of last year."

Her face tensed. "How you know what Jenny makes in a week? You a goldbrick or something?"

"I think the term is 'gold digger,' but no, I'm not. It's just that I make very little money."

"You happy making no money?"

I laughed. "No."

"You happy Jenny makes good money?"

"Not my business."

"Not now, maybe."

"Not ever."

She studied me over the steam of the coffee, decided I was probably telling the truth, and grinned. "You poor boy, but good boy, huh?"

"The best."

She nodded, unsure, and pushed herself out of the booth. Jennifer arrived five minutes later.

"Your mother and I had a short, but efficient, chat."

She groaned. "About?"

"Small stuff, like how much money my ex-wife has."

"I'm sorry, Dek. My mom…"

"I told her Amanda will inherit tens of millions. Your mother lost interest in me when I told her I didn't have that kind of money."

"Speaking of Ms. Phelps, how was your evening after I dropped you off?"

"You knew that was Amanda, waiting in that car?"

"Easy guess. She looms large in your life. More interesting, I've never heard you refer to her as your ex-wife, until just now. I'm thinking something, more final than you wanted, happened last night."

I shouldn't have been surprised. Jennifer Gale had antennae like NASA. For sure, she'd inherited her mother's directness.

"It's..." I let the thought die away, unformed.

"That complicated?"

"She's a wonderful person, orbiting in a very public executive suite, trying to do real good. The newness of it is a strain."

"And you?"

"The oldness of me is a strain, too. I keep complicating her life. My new notoriety has brought forth my old notoriety. It's affecting what she's trying to do."

A waitress came, and we ordered cheese omelets.

"I think it's time you called me Jenny. It's who I am."

"Why the change? 'Jenny Galecki' is certainly not too ethnic for media in a Polish town like Chicago."

"It seemed too ethnic for a national post." She stirred her coffee. "Or so I thought when I got into this business. My next step was going to be a local anchor slot, then on to national fame. 'Jennifer Gale' sounded so much more cosmopolitan."

"Is that still the dream?"

"Not so much. For a national slot, I should have been overseas the past few years. After my husband..." She took a sip of coffee, set down the cup. "Look, Dek, I still want a story, a big story, but not at the expense of leaving that poor man—"

"I know; we left Andrew Fill in a place where he shouldn't be. My priority still has to be helping Sweetie Fairbairn. There are unsolved murders: James Stitts, Robert Norton, maybe even Sweetie herself."

"And Andrew Fill."

"I think he was first."

"What?"

"Perhaps a month ago."

Her eyes were wide. "My God, he's been lying there a month? Absolutely, we must go to the cops."

"I could tell you you'll get in trouble with your station. You were there when I discovered Andrew. You went along with my not reporting it, at least for the night. I could try to convince you all that will play hell with your reputation, if it doesn't get you fired."

She nodded. "I thought about that—but a man lying there, dead, for months…"

Our omelets came. She pushed hers aside.

"More important, more selfish, going to Plinnit now will stop me cold," I went on. "He won't accept my showing up at another murder site. I was at Sweetie's penthouse, the night the guard was killed. I was at Fill's apartment, after he'd gone missing. Now, I'm at Fill's trailer, with his corpse inside?"

"You said Fill's been dead for a month. Duggan can corroborate you were hired two weeks afterward."

"You said this is a heater case. Plinnit will arrest me, just to play to the media."

"That will stop the investigation? You're that important?"

"You think the police are making any progress?"

"No."

"Remember Fill's wallet? Neat and orderly; nothing that shouldn't be there?"

"Money, driver's license, Visa, insurance, and health club cards."

"And one scrap of paper with George Koros's phone number on it."

"It was Koros who pointed you to Andrew Fill," she said, understanding.

"Everything I learned, I got from Koros."

"Truths, or lies," she said.

"Koros knows a lot more than he's been saying. I want to take a run at him, see what I can shake loose. I need you to go along with me on that."

"Because no one else is doing anything?"

"Because I don't know what else to do."

THIRTY-ONE

I SHOWED UP at Koros's office unannounced. Smiling for the camera behind the hanging plant, I pressed the buzzer next to the door to the inner office. Neither the smile nor the buzzer got a response. I gave the button another quick tap. There was still no answer. Given that the outer door was open, I figured Koros was in, but perhaps in conference with a client.

I sat down, in good view of the camera, and leafed through one of the *Forbes* magazines on the table. It featured a ranking of the world's wealthiest people. Disappointingly, none had made their fortunes rehabbing turrets.

After fifteen minutes, I got up and pushed the buzzer again. This time I leaned against it for a full ten seconds, all the while smiling for the camera behind the plant.

It worked. Koros slipped out, tugging the door closed behind him. I'd been right. He'd been in conference.

In spite of the fact that it had taken him fifteen minutes to open the door, he acted pleased to see me. "Thank you so much for stopping by, Mr. Elstrom. I was going to call you. I owe you an apology. I should have called you once Sweetie disappeared, to offer help in anything you're doing to find her."

"Really? What's prompted this?"

"The police. Lieutenant Plinnit assures me she is their top priority, but they're making no progress."

"I don't see how I can do any better, Mr. Koros."

"I have a proposal. I imagine you're somewhat limited

in terms of resources, now that Sweetie has disappeared. You might still have a little of her retainer left, but I want you to start charging all your time and expenses directly to me." His eyes were unblinking. "No expenditure questioned, Mr. Elstrom. I will pay whatever it takes to secure Sweetie's safe, immediate return."

"She ran, Mr. Koros. Even if I did find her—and I have no idea where to look—there's nothing to suggest she'll come back willingly."

"Then let us at least satisfy ourselves that she is all right. She must have been frightened out of her mind. She probably still is. We must locate her before whoever killed her bodyguard does."

"I wouldn't know where to start."

"Stay with Andrew Fill. Perhaps he does know something."

I watched his unblinking eyes. They betrayed nothing.

"I've run down Andrew Fill as far as I can," I said. It was true enough.

He took a piece of paper from his shirt pocket. "Andrew Fill's address in Indiana."

I looked at it. It was the address of the trailer park.

"This is better given to the police."

"I'd like you to check it out. At my expense, as I said." He made a tent of the fingers of both hands. "As the newspapers this morning have informed us, Sweetie Fairbairn is no longer a woman of unlimited means. Not even very wealthy, I would imagine. Now that it appears she's given away most of what she had, the half million Andrew is to repay may prove to be vital to her future well-being."

"Why would she give away the last of her money?"

"Severe stress, obviously. She's no longer thinking rationally. I'll pay, Mr. Elstrom. You must find her, and quickly."

"Any idea where she was from?"

"I don't know. She was very secretive about that. I wondered if she'd been abused as a child, or something. I do recall her mentioning something about growing up in California, or Oregon." He shrugged. "I'm sorry, Mr. Elstrom; is that important?"

"It might be a place for her to head to, a place where she'd feel safe. She could have relatives there."

"The fact that she never mentioned a hometown makes that unlikely."

"I suppose."

"You'll check out Andrew's place in Indiana?"

"For the half million?"

"Andrew is no killer, Mr. Elstrom."

I told him I'd go to Indiana the next day.

As lies went, I didn't figure mine were very big.

Especially not when my gut was thinking that Koros's were bigger.

I rode the elevator down to the lobby, went out to the sidewalk, and started down Wacker Drive. It was a fine summer day, and for a minute I stopped, to turn back and look at the great green curved glass that was Koros's building.

The lobby door opened, and a short woman came out and began hurrying off in the opposite direction. Though most of her face had been turned away, I glimpsed leathery, weathered skin, the complexion of a woman who'd long worked outdoors. Her slacks were pilled, and she wore a stained nylon Windbreaker.

Her hair, though, was a younger woman's blond. For one brief, strange instant, I took her for someone else. I thought she was Sweetie Fairbairn.

Too much Sweetie Fairbairn on the brain, I thought, as I walked down to get the Jeep.

I LET THE day manager of the Wilbur Wright think I was part of Sweetie's staff. The keys I'd picked up off Sweetie's carpet the day I'd found her kneeling over the dead guard helped.

"The police just released the penthouse as a crime scene," he said, sniffing as I unlocked the elevator with her keys. "That ghastly yellow police tape across this was unnerving everyone." The doors closed on his angst, and I rode up silently, alone. The elevator seemed especially hushed as it opened into Sweetie Fairbairn's penthouse.

The foyer, windowless, was dark, and though it had only been three days since Robert Norton had been killed, the penthouse smelled like it had been shut up for years. I wondered if that's what happened when a place that was used to fresh flowers suddenly went dead.

I turned on every light I passed, before my mind could make menacing shapes out of the long late-afternoon shadows. Other than the once pristine, soft white carpet, ruined now by blood dried to a dark brown stain, the penthouse appeared to be immaculate. The magazines on the coffee tables in the living room were neatly fanned; the occasional chairs had been precisely aligned. Every dish in the kitchen had been washed and put away. The bathrooms looked freshly cleaned. The guest bedrooms were neat.

Come home, Sweetie Fairbairn; your penthouse awaits. Immaculately.

Except for all that blood dried on your floor.

I spent almost an hour in her bedroom, a cheerful place of pinks and beiges. It was where I'd sent her after I discovered her with her guard.

There were no gaps in the clothes hanging in the closets, nor did any of the dressers look to have been rustled by Sweetie hurriedly packing. Her decision to vanish had been made on the spur of the moment. She'd taken nothing, other than her checkbook and the determination to give away everything she had.

The sun was almost down when I went into the room I'd saved for last. Sweetie's private study, her Shangri-La, looked as it had the night of her party, when she and I had gone for what I assumed to be a chat about the strength of my grasp on Amanda's life.

The papers in the file cabinet and desk had been haphazardly jammed in, as though they'd been pawed through, by the police, or perhaps by Sweetie's own sloppiness. As with so many things about Sweetie Fairbairn, I might never know.

I studied the appointment calendar tacked to the corkboard. Most of the days of the months ahead had been penciled in with names and times. I felt a small chill. The annotations no longer looked like reminders of meetings, appointments, and parties, but rather, the futile scratchings of a future lost by someone doomed.

I looked at the picture of the weathered covered bridge tacked next to the calendar. I'd liked Sweetie Fairbairn for that worn old postcard, like I'd liked her for setting out Velveeta for a bunch of swells. Now it felt like one more thing I'd never get to ask her about.

I left Sweetie's penthouse, having learned nothing of where she might have gone.

Or whether she was anywhere, anymore.

THIRTY-TWO

BLACK CLOUDS RISING from an unmuffled exhaust drew me to the window the next morning. Benny Fittle's rusting Maverick was parked on the street with its door sagging open. Benny, freshly talcumed with the day's new sugar, stood on my lawn, next to the Jeep, writing a ticket.

"No parking on the grass, Mr. Elstrom," he said when I charged out.

"I can't park on the street. According to you people, I live on a fire lane."

"You could park across Thompson, like I told you."

"That's a half mile away."

Parking tickets are a hundred dollars in Rivertown, unless they're paid by something other than cash, in which case they cost more. I got in the Jeep. "I'm moving it, Benny. Put the book away."

I twisted the key. Got nothing. The battery had died in the night.

Benny nudged his tongue out and resumed writing. "Got to write you, Mr. Elstrom. Thing's got to get off the grass."

I had an inspiration. "Thing's not supposed to move right now, Benny. It's in its other mode."

He looked up, brow wrinkled, his brain taxed by thought. "Whaddaya mean, other mode?"

I got out of the Jeep. "When it is on the grass, this is no longer a vehicle. It is in its lawn ornament mode."

By the confusion clouding his face, I worried that

"mode" meant nothing to Benny except when ordering ice cream to top a slice of pie.

Benny Fittle, though, surprised me. "You mean like one of those wheelbarrow planters?"

I beamed at his brilliance. "Exactly. The Jeep, when on the lawn, becomes a wheeled device just like a wheelbarrow planter."

"I don't see no flowers."

"They'll be here today."

"Mode or no mode, there's no flowers. I got to write you, Mr. Elstrom."

"The flowers are on their way, honest."

He put the ticket pad back into his pocket. "Only until this afternoon," he said and walked across the street to the dark cloud of his idling Maverick.

I didn't kid myself into thinking he'd taken pity on me. Hunger had drawn him back to his car.

THERE ARE NO auto parts stores in Rivertown, though parts get distributed from there every night. Rumor has it that another of the mayor's nephews—a cousin to Elvis, the salad oil king—runs the town's most profitable car theft and stripping operation out of an old factory building he bought at foreclosure a few years before. Those parts, though, are not available at retail; they get shipped out of town fast, in unmarked trucks.

I walked over to Jiffy Lube. They were out of batteries that would fit the Jeep, and wouldn't have one for two days. They suggested an auto parts store four miles east, in Chicago. I went back to the turret and started calling gas stations that were close enough to walk to. None carried batteries.

In the middle of it all, George Koros phoned. "You're going to Andrew's place in Indiana? It's our only lead."

He was speaking too insistently, like a man on the verge of panic.

"I'm on my way there now." I couldn't tell Koros I'd already been to Fill's trailer, and seen flies.

"Where are you, exactly?"

"Route 12. Just a few miles away, I guess."

"I don't hear a car engine."

"I keep it well tuned."

"Sweetie's future could depend on that money, Elstrom." He hung up.

By noon, I was resigned to that parts store four miles into Chicago. I called Leo's cell phone. "I need a ride."

"No problem, so long as you're in Manhattan."

"Manhattan, New York City?"

"Of course, New York City, you boor."

I told him he was worthless as a friend. He told me I was a leech, too cheap to hire a cab. We hung up on each other simultaneously, each satisfied with the depth of the sentiments that had been exchanged.

I took the cab. Round-trip, including the wait time while I was inside the parts store buying the battery, cost me fifty bucks. Adding in the battery, I'd run up a hundred-and-forty-dollar morning.

Which then bloomed to a hundred and seventy dollars, throwing in the cost of the flats of flowers that I went to buy after I installed the battery. My cell phone rang just as I got back to the turret.

I figured it was Koros again. I figured wrong. It was Jenny.

"An odd little item just came in," she said. "Based on an anonymous tip, police went to a trailer park outside of Michigan City, Indiana. They found a small house trailer on fire. Want to guess what they're looking at inside?"

I told her about Koros hiring me to find Andrew Fill. "He thinks I'm there now."

"Right now, knocking on that same door?"

"He set me up to get found near a burning corpse."

"Why?"

"I can't wait to hear his reason."

I told her I was going to stay at the turret, where anybody at all could notice that I was nowhere near Indiana.

George Koros had become a very interesting man.

THEY CAME FOR me early that evening, Plinnit and the gray-haired, gray-eyed man.

"What the hell are you doing?" Plinnit asked, getting out of the car.

"Sprinkling my lawn ornament." I stepped back from the Jeep, satisfied. I'd used scraps of wood to build racks for the hood, bumpers, and spare tire in back. They held flowers, tall, flashy flowers. They transformed the Jeep.

"You can't drive it like that," the lieutenant said.

"All I need to do is park it like that." I pointed to the FIRE LANE sign. "It's a matter of a hundred-dollar parking ticket or thirty bucks' worth of plants. There are no other options in Rivertown."

Plinnit nodded like that made sense and said, "Catch the news today?"

"I've been too busy gardening."

"Want to take a drive?" Plinnit asked.

"Andrew Fill's apartment again?" I asked, because I hoped that would sound reasonable.

"Why would you mention him?"

"It's where you always take me."

I coiled the hose, locked the timbered door, and got in their car.

We talked of flowers and fire lanes until the gray-haired, gray-eyed man drove us onto the Tollway, eastbound.

"This is the wrong way to Fill's apartment," I observed, sociably.

Plinnit turned around from the front seat. "Want to get out? We have no right to insist that you join us."

"I'll ride."

"When's the last time you saw Andrew Fill?"

"I've never met the man. George Koros told me Fill had a cottage in the Indiana dunes. He gave me the address and asked me to nose around, talk to his neighbors. He told me it was important that I get on it right away—today, in fact."

"Because Fill might know something about Sweetie Fairbairn's disappearance?"

"That's what Koros thinks."

"But you didn't go to Indiana?"

"My battery died. I blew most of the day getting a new one and then, as you saw, gardening."

"I don't suppose you have proof of that?"

I fished in my wallet and handed forward the receipt from the auto parts store.

"Someone else could have bought you the battery," he said, studying the receipt.

"That would have been delightful," I said.

Plinnit nodded, handed it back.

We crossed into Indiana in silence.

THIRTY-THREE

"I THOUGHT WE were going to Andrew Fill's cottage," I said, as the gray man pulled to a stop in front of an Indiana State Police station.

"This is close," Plinnit said, getting out.

The station house was small, dark brick, and had white-painted windows. Three police cars, a red van, and an old tan Ford Taurus were parked in front. The tan Taurus looked vaguely familiar. Then again, I supposed the world was filled with tan sedans.

A sergeant escorted us down a short hall cramped by scarred wood benches that lined both sides. The potentially androgynous bike rider from Lake Vista Estates sat on one of them, sipping Pepsi from a two-liter bottle.

"Excuse me, sir," the sergeant said to the bike rider.

With that, two confirmations were offered up. The first was that the rider was indeed a man—a fact that, in fairness, I'd pretty much assumed two days before.

The second was more troublesome. I'd been brought to Indiana to be shown to the bike rider. The little one-perp parade I was starring in was a lineup, without the bother of rounding up look-alikes. It had the potential of being one hundred percent effective. There was no way the bike rider could fail to remember me being at Andrew Fill's trailer.

The bike rider separated his head from the Pepsi and looked up. Nothing showed on his face before he dropped his mouth to the Pepsi again.

At least not yet. He could have been told to show nothing.

The sergeant, Plinnit, and the gray-haired man escorted me into a room with a yellow Formica table and four chairs. I watch television. I know those rooms are supposed to have two-way mirrors, but this one didn't.

"Why don't you have a two-way mirror?" I asked. "Budget cuts?"

Plinnit frowned and leaned back in his chair. "Sergeant Colfax here has some questions for you."

"First off, you have the right to an attorney," Colfax said.

"He has a high-priced big-gun lawyer in Chicago," Plinnit said.

"Impressive. You want to call him?" Colfax gave me a minute to think as he made a show of studying my T-shirt and jeans. The bits of old paint and caulk were still dirty and damp from the gardening I'd done on my Jeep.

"Am I being charged with something?"

"Not at the moment."

"Then I don't need a lawyer," I said.

"We've been informed you came to Mr. Andrew Fill's residence today," Colfax said.

"You were misinformed. Car trouble kept me mostly at home today."

Colfax looked over at Plinnit.

Plinnit shrugged. "On the way here, we learned he bought a battery in Chicago sometime after noon. Then, it appears, he spent the rest of the day planting flowers on his Jeep."

Colfax didn't understand. "In his Jeep? He went somewhere, in a Jeep, to plant flowers?"

Plinnit spoke slowly. "No. *On his Jeep.* He spent the rest of the day decorating his vehicle with flowers."

"You some sort of hippie?" Colfax asked me, distaste curling his lip.

"Power to the people, right on," I said, recalling a line from an old Woodstock documentary. Power, too, to the little man sucking Pepsi down the hall, a ticking bomb—but I didn't say that.

"A smart-ass?" Colfax asked Plinnit.

Plinnit grinned. "Oh my, yes."

Colfax turned back to me. "Tell me about Andrew Fill."

"George Koros, Sweetie Fairbairn's employee, hired me to find him. Koros thinks Fill knows something about Sweetie's disappearance, and told me Fill has a cottage near here. He wanted me to come out today, to interview Fill, but my battery died."

"And this evening, you rode with these gentlemen all the way here without asking why?"

"When the good lieutenant here stopped by, suggesting a ride, I figured I'd get new information."

Colfax looked at Plinnit and the gray man. "Why doesn't this man Koros work with you, instead of this jerk?"

I answered for the detectives. "Mr. Koros thinks the police are spending too much time driving aimlessly, from state to state, instead of digging in to accomplish something."

At that, Mr. Gray sat up straighter in his chair, but Plinnit stayed leaned back in his chair, grinning.

Colfax's next question was predictable. "You know Andrew Fill?"

"We've never met. As I'm sure Lieutenant Plinnit has told you, the closest I got was to enter Fill's apartment through an open door, illegally. I'm interested in talking to Fill, about whether he had motive to harm Sweetie Fairbairn."

Colfax stared at me for an uncomfortable few seconds, then stood up and went out to the hall. I could hear him whispering to someone, but not what they were saying.

After a minute, he came back. "Thank you, Mr. Elstrom," he said, because apparently there was nothing else he could say.

"My turn," I said, because it was expected. "Why was I brought here?"

Colfax ignored me, thanked Plinnit, and then led us out into the hall. The bike rider still sat on the bench, sipping Diet Pepsi.

Colfax gave it a last shot. "Excuse me, sir," he said to the man.

The little man looked up. Colfax nodded toward me.

Again the Pepsi was lowered. This time the rider stood up to what was barely four and a half feet. He looked squarely into my eyes.

"Nope," he said, after a long minute, and took another pull at the Pepsi.

"Why the short guy?" I asked Plinnit, when we got outside.

"He collects cans for recycling money, sleeps in his car. Colfax was hoping he'd seen someone out by the trailer park."

"Seen me?"

"That was the hope," he said.

"Why?" I asked, to further the charade. No one had yet mentioned that Andrew Fill was dead.

Plinnit didn't answer. No matter.

It had been the best fifty dollars I'd ever spent.

WE DROVE BACK pretty much as we'd come—in complete silence. I tried questions about Sweetie Fairbairn's disappearance and Norton's murder from the backseat, but those were met with grunts. Asking about Andrew Fill didn't even get that.

When Mr. Gray pulled up in front of the turret, Plinnit got out with me. "You keep popping up, Elstrom," he said.

"Like blossoms in summer?" I asked, gesturing at the Jeep horticulturally.

"Who'd call us anonymously, to say you were in Indiana today?"

"You won't even tell me why that matters."

"Andrew Fill was found burned to death, in a trailer, not far from that police station."

"Then someone wants me blamed for that."

"Who?"

"George Koros pointed me toward Andrew Fill. He insisted I go to Indiana today."

"You don't like Koros?" he asked.

"I don't understand his relationship with Sweetie Fairbairn."

"That's it?"

"For now."

He turned to get back in the car.

"Any idea where Sweetie Fairbairn comes from?" I asked.

"Hometown-wise, growing-up-wise?"

"Yes."

"We haven't focused on that."

"That's it?" I asked, when he said nothing more.

He smiled. "For now."

IT WAS TOO late to see if Jenny was reporting, but the ten o'clock broadcasts had just begun. Channel 5's anchor, a smiley fellow with shellacked hair, led with the big news from Indiana: "A tantalizing new lead may have arisen in the missing Sweetie Fairbairn case. Acting on a tip, Indiana police today discovered Andrew Fill, a onetime employee of Ms. Fairbairn's and someone long active in

the arts in Chicago, dead in a house trailer fire. Fill was
the director..."

I switched stations. Channel 2 was saying, "Andrew
Fill, former head of the Midwest Arts Symposium, was
found brutally..."

I turned off the little television, made tea, and took it
up to the roof.

Rivertown was in its own full fire. Neon flashed up and
down Thompson Avenue. Mixed in the usual cacophony of
tonk tunes and the hysterical shrieks of lubricated people
having Just Plain Fun were the rips and flashes of drunks
getting a jump on the Fourth of July. Short bursts of fire-
crackers and cherry bombs were going off across the spit
of land, sights and sounds of war on a bawdy street.

As I watched the tiny explosions, I let my mind nibble
at the probability that George Koros was also trying to lay
Sweetie Fairbairn's disappearance, and maybe Norton's
murder, on me. He'd tried to send me to Indiana, to get
caught sniffing around Andrew Fill's trailer at the same
time he'd tipped the police that I'd be there. He'd meant
for me and the cops to collide, leading to more suspicions.

What I couldn't understand was how that would benefit him.

Or how I could nail him for it.

I drank my tea, hummed along too loudly with the
music from the tonks, and thought. By three in the morning, when the tonks quit serenading the night, when the
last of the hookers had moaned and the last of the johns
and the cherry bombs had exploded, I was sure of only a
fraction of it.

The motive had to be money, as it so often is when
people kill. Sweetie Fairbairn was a financial wellspring,
Koros was a financial guy, and Andrew Fill was a sap.
Koros worked Andrew Fill, except he worked him dead.

He killed him, then manipulated him, missing, to take the blame for embezzling a half-million dollars.

None of that, though, explained killing James Stitts, or Robert Norton, or why Koros told me Fill had been paying the stolen money back.

None of it explained why Sweetie Fairbairn had run, either.

The tea had gone vile, and I'd gone cold. I climbed the ladders down to the fifth floor, then to the fourth. It was as I was going down the stairs to the third floor that I heard the noise from my would-be office on the second.

It was my cell phone, vibrating itself into a frenzy on the card table. I thumbed in the code, and listened.

"Mr. Elstrom." George Koros sounded panicked. "Andrew Fill is dead. It's on the radio. Please call me."

It could have been a warning, meant to stop me from going those last miles to Andrew Fill's place. Certainly, it didn't sound like a message from a cunning killer.

That blew up what little fancy thinking I'd done up on the roof, as surely as the drunks along Thompson Avenue had blown up the night.

THIRTY-FOUR

"INTERESTING MESSAGE YOU left yesterday, Mr. Koros," I said, when I called him the next morning. It was a new day for everyone, and I wanted to begin mine by setting his on edge.

"I heard about Andrew on the midnight news, and realized I'd sent you into a murder investigation." He paused for a deep breath. "Recovering what's left of Sweetie's money—money she'll need to get her head fixed, money she'll need for her defense—that was my priority. Now, with Andrew dead, we'll never find the money…"

"You're still thinking Ms. Fairbairn is sick?"

"Why else would she behave as she has? I don't know what happened to Andrew; the radio said there was a fire of some sort. Sweetie's guard sure didn't shoot himself, and she sure as hell wouldn't have given away all her money if she were thinking right. She's sick."

"You're thinking she did all that?"

"I need to get her into a treatment facility. The right doctors will make sure she stays there, instead of standing trial."

"Only if we find her."

"She'll surface when she's ready. She's tough; she's safe."

"Some would say you could have taken that half million, George."

His voice quivered, maybe from anger, maybe from fear. "Me?"

"Sure. You said yourself you managed the Symposium's checking account. You were in a position to withdraw money."

For a moment he was silent. "You're right," he said finally. "I had that responsibility."

"I'm going to keep looking for her, George."

"It'll be a waste of time."

"I'll stay in touch."

He took another moment, then said, "All right. I'm going to messenger over a corporate Visa card for you. Be prudent with it, Mr. Elstrom, but use it to find her."

I hung up without saying that using his credit card would pinpoint exactly where I was, and from that, he would know what I was doing.

I figured he already knew that.

I CALLED JENNY. "Let me tell you about my second trip to Indiana," I said, and did.

"You're lucky that little man on the bicycle didn't put the finger on you," she said when I was done.

"He saw me as an innocent man."

"He saw you as the guy who gave him fifty bucks to keep his mouth shut. That's a lot of recycled cans."

I asked her to check out Sweetie's life before she came to Chicago.

"How far back do you want me to go?"

"The day she was born. She might have gone back to one of the places she's been."

"You still think George Koros has a secret?"

"I still think he has a thousand of them."

I CALLED THE Bohemian next. "Can you put me in touch with Silas Fairbairn's closest friend?"

"Have you consulted your lawyer, the esteemed John

Peet, about whether it's wise for you to continue nosing around Sweetie Fairbairn's life?"

"She's still my client. She's still missing."

"You're still the object of police interest, not to mention press scrutiny."

"I can't sit back, waiting for her to reappear on her own."

"Big doubt, now?"

"I no longer think she's free to come back."

THIRTY-FIVE

THE BOHEMIAN HAD asked for a day but only took an hour. "Gillman Tripp was Silas Fairbairn's most frequent golf partner. He'll see you midafternoon, in the bar at the Arrow Way Golf Club. He's wearing yellow slacks and a white shirt."

I got to the Arrow Way at three o'clock. It was tucked down a long private drive lined with gnarled, ancient evergreen trees. The gentlemen moving slowly to and from the Cadillacs and Mercedeses in the parking lot were gnarled and ancient, too. With its aged membership and total seclusion, Arrow Way looked to offer a place where rich old men could play golf without wearing pants, either from preference or forgetfulness, and no one else would see well enough to mind.

The bar was at the back of the low brick clubhouse. There wasn't a dark hair on any of the men, but all of them appeared to be wearing pants. Three of them, in particular, were wearing yellow pants, with white shirts. One, sitting at a table by himself, waved me over.

"Mr. Elstrom? Gillman Tripp." We shook hands, and I sat down.

I guessed he was well past eighty, but there was no sallowness to his skin. It was browned from the sun, and reddened on the nose and cheeks from what I imagined was a fourth or fifth gin and tonic.

"Like a drink?" he asked.

"Just a Coke."

He called a waitress over and ordered my Coke and another reddener for himself.

"Anton Chernak told me you're helping to look for Sweetie Fairbairn?"

"I am."

"You're the one whose name was in the paper? The one who found her with that dead guard?"

"My name was in the paper, yes."

He leaned forward to study my shirt. I realized I should have worn the good one the Bohemian bought me. "How the hell can you afford John Peet?"

"I suspect he's praying my innocence will minimize his time." Gillman Trip barked out a laugh, leaned back, and said, "What can I tell you?"

"Where is Sweetie Fairbairn from?"

He laughed again, all gin, tonic, and mirth. "We all wondered about that, but none of us ever found out. All I know is Silas brought her home after a visit to one of his factories."

"Do you remember which factory?"

"I do not. What I remember was thinking this was no chickadee. Sweetie was well into her forties at that time. That can be a desperate age for a certain kind of woman without means. I was convinced that Silas had bit it this time, for sure."

"She acted like a hustler?"

"No. It's just that Silas was a very wealthy man, smart in the ways of manufacturing, utterly obtuse in the ways of women. It was natural to conclude he'd fallen as easy prey."

Our drinks came. His hand was steady on the new glass as he raised it to his lips. After a sip and a smile, he continued.

"I was wrong, of course. We all were. Sweetie adored Silas, and he adored her. I got the impression he'd been pursuing her for quite some time, and that she'd only reluctantly agreed to marry him."

"What made you think she was reluctant?"

"In the beginning she was…she was…" He stopped to fuel his memory with another sip at the gin. "Nervous. That's the right word: nervous."

"Nervous, how?"

"When we were out to dinner, those first times, she was pleasant enough, a real charming lady, but she was always looking around, like she was afraid someone would come up to her to tell her she didn't belong. It was understandable. A girl from the sticks, a factory-working girl, gets swept off her feet by a rich industrialist. No matter that she's older and has solid values, she's entered a world where she doesn't belong." He sighed. "At least, that's the way I saw it, in the beginning."

"You changed your mind?"

"I began to consider the possibility that something else was causing her nervousness. She was always guarded, careful to not say much about herself. Silas was evasive about her as well. Her nervousness settled down, after a few months, but a little of that evasiveness always remained, in both of them."

"I don't suppose you ever caught a hint of her maiden name?"

He smiled. "I never got a hint about her real first name, either."

I wished for a small board at that instant, something to strike the side of my thick, unthinking head. "'Sweetie' was just a nickname?"

He gave me a pitying look and said, as though to a child, "No mother names her kid 'Sweetie.' It was what Silas called her, and that was good enough for us."

He had another gin and tonic, I had another Coke, and

we went over all of it again, but he'd gotten it all out the first time. There'd never been much to know about Sweetie Fairbairn.

I CALLED THE Bohemian from the Arrow Way parking lot.

"You had a productive conversation with Gillman Tripp?" he asked.

"Yes, but it's led to more questions. Can you find out the factories Silas Fairbairn owned?"

"There weren't very many, as I recall. They made wiring harnesses for cars and trucks. Hold on."

He came back in five minutes. "Only three plants, Vlodek. One in Florida, one in Tennessee, and one in Missouri." He named towns I'd never heard of. "Rural operations. Cheap labor. Farm wives, mostly, pulling wires around posts nailed to big sheets of plywood. Silas sold them the year before he died."

"Are they still in operation?"

"I have no idea. You can call to verify that."

"Thank you."

"Stay out of the news, Vlodek."

I CALLED JENNY when I got back to the turret.

"Nothing yet on her background, Dek. I spent two hours online at the newspaper archives, and then I called around to the people who used to do celebrity columns when newspapers still had money for such things. Everybody on the social ladder in Chicago knows her, but nobody seems to know about her, at least not of her life before she married Silas. That's unusual, for someone as prominent as Sweetie Fairbairn."

"One of Silas's old golfing buddies originally thought she might have been embarrassed over her origins."

"Originally?"

"He came around to another conclusion."

"That she deliberately obscured her past?"

"Bingo," I said.

THIRTY-SIX

BEFORE I'D GONE to bed the previous night, the Internet told me that all three Fairbairn Wire and Cable assembly plants were still making wiring harnesses for automobiles, trucks, and appliances.

By ten o'clock the next morning, a FedEx driver had delivered an overnight envelope containing the Visa card George Koros said he'd send along.

By twelve o'clock, I knew, from the telephone, that none of the Fairbairn plants was big enough to have a full-fledged human resources department, that each relied on a single clerk to do the personnel work. None of the three clerks had been working for Fairbairn Wire back when Sweetie might have been there, which I guessed was at least ten years before, but each of the clerks had just learned, through the twin miracles of gossip grapevines and cable television news, that Silas's widow had disappeared, up in Chicago, following the murder of her bodyguard. None of the clerks had ever heard of Silas befriending any woman in their plant, and each supposed that if such a thing had happened, everyone in town would have known about one of their own striking it rich.

So, by noon, I was done, smacked flat against a dead end.

And I was out of Ho Hos.

The Ho Hos I could do something about. I went outside and took the wood trays of flowers off the Jeep's hood, top, and spare tire. Using the flowers to convert the Jeep into a multitiered lawn planter had worked so far—Benny Fittle had issued me no tickets—but the victory was temporary; a lizard was surely at work drafting a new lawn decoration code, specifically prohibiting the use of red Jeeps. For now, though, my potted, planted Jeep represented a victory and, as such, deserved to be celebrated. With Ho Hos.

I headed east, toward the supermarket, but then responsibility slapped a sudden, shocking hand against me and forced me to do something I hadn't done in a month. I took a hard left turn and bobbed onto the cratered parking lot of the Rivertown Health Center. Dropping the transmission into first gear, as one would to navigate the surface of the moon, I eased the Jeep over the potholes to my usual spot next to the doorless Buick that had rested there for decades. There would be Ho Hos—but first there must be exercise.

It was midday. There were still a few hours before the thumpers, Rivertown's least-evolved grade of criminal, would arrive. Delinquents from the high schools, and in some cases the grammar schools, thumpers were trainees, interns of a sort. They came to the health center parking lot to study at the studded boots of the more hardened scumbags who congregated at dusk to sell their powders, plan their burglaries, and decide which automobiles might offer the most reward from disassembly that night.

I made sure both of the Jeep's doors were unlocked, so that even the most untutored of an early-bird hoodlum could see that the radio had already been ripped out, grabbed the gym bag I keep in the backseat, and went in.

I changed into my gym duds under the supposedly dozing eye of the locker room attendant. I never bring a lock to dull his bolt cutters, and always take my wallet and keys with me. Still, I'm sure he always does a fast search of my locker before he returns to his nap, if only as a matter of self-respect.

Frankie was roosting on a broken exercise cycle up-stairs, regaling Dusty, Nick, and the other retirees with the same jokes he'd been telling since the factories used to pulse in Rivertown. Dusty, Nick, and the others never waited for Frankie's last line to begin laughing. They knew the jokes. What counted were the words and the laughs from their pasts, reminders of times when their knees were steady and the backs of their hands hadn't yet darkened from enlarging veins and spreading spots of brown. They waved me over. I shook my head. I had to run.

I'd built up a high sweat when, thirty minutes later, my cell phone rang. It was Miss Logsdon, one of the person-nel clerks I'd talked to earlier that day. She worked at the Fairbairn assembly plant in Whitaker Springs, Missouri.

"I believe I've found someone you might be interested in speaking with, Mr. Elstrom. One of our longer-term employees told me of a woman who used to work here a number of years ago. Her name is Linda Coombs."

I leaned against a wall, trying to not pant like a St. Bernard. "She remembers someone Silas Fairbairn had a relationship with?"

"Unfortunately, I don't know what Ms. Coombs remem-bers. All our employee remembers is that Linda Coombs once said that Silas Fairbairn was involved with a woman from Whitaker Springs. Our employee doesn't think the woman's name was Sweetie, though."

"Do you have a phone number for Linda Coombs?"

"Ms. Coombs has no phone, and lives on the outskirts of town. I don't have the names of any of her neighbors, and I don't want to intrude on anyone's privacy. I'm afraid you'll have to arrange a visit if you want your questions answered."

I thanked her and hung up. My breathing had slowed. Certainly, the news justified suspension of any further exercise. I headed for the showers, my mind firing thoughts of an airplane trip and an expedition-sized bag of Ho Hos.

I CALLED THE bankcard company from the turret, to activate Koros's Visa, and the nice lady asked if I wanted to activate the ATM feature as well. I said you betcha, real fast, and logged on to their Web site to provide a PIN. Two hours later, just to be confusing, I'd stopped at four ATMs on my way to Midway Airport and withdrawn the two-thousand-dollar maximum that was available for the month. Koros would get receipts, and an accurate accounting of my expenses, but he wasn't going to find out where I was searching for Sweetie Fairbairn until I'd finished.

I caught a last-minute flight to Kansas City. In Missouri, I rented a tiny Ford, pointed it southwest, and got to Whitaker Springs at dusk.

The town looked about as I'd expected—three blocks of tired storefronts, half of which were empty. A drive-in called the Dairy Delight stood in the middle of the middle block. Three older men wearing overalls sat outside on a picnic bench, eating sundaes. I pulled over and powered down the window.

"Is there a motel in this town?"

One man nodded. "Marge's," he said, "right around the next corner." He said it would be a fine place to spend an evening or two. In fact, he added, he said he could guarantee it, since Marge herself was his cousin on his mother's side of the family.

Marge's Stop and Rest was a single-story white building with a vacancy sign in the window and nothing parked in its lot. Marge Herself told me I could have my pick of rooms, as they had vacancies at the moment. And, she added demurely, a very select number of those very rooms had original marine art, painted directly on the walls by her Daughter Herself. If that sounded appealing, she especially recommended the room next door to the office.

I've never been one to turn away from free art, nor had I ever thought that art in a motel room mattered, one way or another. I was wrong. As soon as I stepped into my room, I realized I'd rather be bunking with Norman and what was left of his mother at the Bates Motel. The original art on my wall consisted of octopuses, dolphins, and a bloated manatee, painted in what Daughter Herself must have imagined to be playful poses. They were not. The sea creatures were all frozen in contortion, their eyes bulging as though they were suffering the last spasms of painful deaths.

Even worse than their popping eyes were their teeth. Either Daughter Herself did not know what was in the mouths of octopuses, dolphins, and manatees, or she had issues that demanded psychiatry. For instead of teeth, she'd given her sea creatures long, saw-toothed fangs, and tinted them in varying shades of pink, as though blood were washing from them as they writhed away their last seconds.

It was art to induce nightmares. I threw my duffel on the bed and went out.

By now the sky and most everything along Main Street were dark. I walked down to the Dairy Delight and told the young girl behind the window that I'd like to be delighted. When that dropped a blank veil over her features, I told her I'd have two cheeseburgers, an order of fries, and a cherry Coke. She smiled with relief.

The three men eating sundaes I'd seen earlier were gone. Every table was now filled with the youth of Whitaker Springs, set frantically alive by the smells, sounds, and possibilities of a midwest midsummer night. It would be no place to savor fine cuisine. Yet I dared not bring the food back to my room, for fear that the smells and sounds of me eating would excite the pained painted creatures and draw them from the walls.

I went down to the end of the block, to a bench in front of a vacant hardware store that had a sheriff's foreclosure notice in its window. I sat and ate and watched boys, in old cars with new, big-pipe exhausts, rumble back and forth past the Dairy Delight. Whitaker Springs seemed as good a place as any to while away a summer night. And I supposed it could have been as good a place as any for a woman to meet a rich man who'd buy her a new life in a big city.

THIRTY-SEVEN

"SLEEP WELL, MR. ELSTROM?" Marge Herself asked when I came into the motel office the next morning, looking for coffee. She stood illuminated in the sunlight coming in through the window. I hoped she wouldn't open her mouth to give me a full smile; I was afraid I'd see pink on her teeth.

"Very well." There was no need to say that I'd mumbled a few incantations before I'd climbed into bed, or that I'd thought to leave the bathroom light on all night.

She nodded her head in short little bobs, prompting me to go on.

"Your daughter certainly has a knack for painting things in new ways," I said, pouring coffee into a foam cup.

Her face flushed with pride. I took my coffee out to the micro-Ford before she could offer a tour of the galleries in the other rooms.

MISS LOGSDON AT the Fairbairn plant had given me good directions. I got to Linda Coombs's place in just a few minutes.

It had been years since the house had been touched with paint and brush, but the windows were clean, and the yard had been carefully mowed. I parked on what was left of the asphalt drive and walked up. A gray-haired woman opened the door a crack.

"Ms. Linda Coombs?"

She nodded.

"My name's Elstrom. I was told you might have worked with the woman who became Silas Fairbairn's wife."

"Now why in the hell would someone tell you that?"

"Because Sweetie Fairbairn has gone missing."

"That's the name: 'Sweetie'?"

"May I come in?"

"You may not. I'll come out."

Come out she did, in worn jeans, a man's red knit shirt, and lavender flip-flops.

I handed her a photo of Sweetie Fairbairn I'd printed off the Internet. "Do you know her?"

She held it out and studied it for a long minute. Then she nodded. "Older, but yeah."

"What do you know about her?"

"First thing you got to know, mister, is I'm broke. Damned broke. Second thing is I know that any woman who married Silas Fairbairn isn't broke. Third thing, anybody who is sent looking for her must be getting paid, and isn't broke, either." She stopped, so I could consider the meaning of her words.

I gave her a twenty-dollar bill. "Another will follow when we're done, if your information goes beyond what I already know." I knew nothing about Sweetie's background, but I didn't want the woman to start lying for money.

She put the twenty in her jeans. "First off, Kathy didn't work at the plant. She waitressed at a diner that used to be in town. My sister and I ate there ham night, which was Tuesdays. That's how we got to know her. We liked the ham."

"Do you remember Kathy's last name?"

"Don't know that I ever knew it. Kathy wasn't much for talking, at least not at first. Nervous, rabbitty-like, she was always looking out the front window like she was expecting bad news. Cautious with the customers, too; took our orders, hustled them back, so she wouldn't have to talk again until the food came out. But over time, she relaxed a bit, leastways around Agnes and me, and took to jawing with us when nothing else demanded her attention. We got to be quite conversational, if not friends exactly, those Tuesday nights."

"Silas Fairbairn would come to the diner?"

"No sir, not Mr. Fairbairn, least not so I ever saw. He used to come to town once every month or so, meet with the people at the plant. Usually, he'd stay over one night, sometimes two, probably ate with the big shots somewheres away. There wasn't much going on in Whitaker Springs, cuisine-wise, then as now."

She made a small laugh at that and went on. "Twice, maybe three times, me and Agnes, leaving as we did at closing time, noticed somebody sitting in a car a few stores down. Anybody waiting for anything in this town, especially in the dark, was cause for our curiosity. We got interested in who was sitting in that car. So one night, instead of heading right home after our dinner, we ducked between two buildings and waited. Ten, fifteen minutes later, out came Kathy, and got into that waiting car. As it passed under the streetlight, we could see who was driving. Could have knocked me over with a pincushion. It was Mr. Silas Fairbairn himself."

"You ever learn where they went?"

She winked, made a circle with her left thumb and forefinger, and put her right forefinger through it. "A rich man on the road's got needs, same as any man. I figured they were off to the woods or something, to take care of things."

"Kathy ever say anything about him?"

"She was supposed to announce she was screwing some rich guy, maybe for money?"

"How long did this go on?"

"Most likely until she left, a few months later. Up and out without so much as a see-you-later, the woman who owned the diner said. No one knew where she took off to."

"But you did? Or at least who she went with?"

"No. I never did connect her leaving to Mr. Fairbairn."

"You never tried to find out?"

"She was gone; we were here. End of story."

"Did she ever say where she was from?"

Linda Coombs paused, looking down the ruts at the tiny Ford I'd driven up in.

"That ain't yours, is it?"

"It's a rental."

"How much?"

"Fifty bucks, with taxes." I didn't tell her that was a day rate, worried she'd think I was an idiot.

It didn't work. "I'll need a total of fifty before I say anything more."

I handed her a ten and another twenty. "Where was she from?"

"She never said direct, but she implied it was the same kind of rinky-dink town as Whitaker Springs, except hers was up somewhere on the Mississippi River, in Minnesota or Wisconsin. Biggest thing in town was a statue of an Indian, Chief Runamuck, or Whackamock, or some damned thing. They lit it up all to hell at dusk. Folks came up to it most nights, leastways in the summer, because they didn't have anything else to do." She laughed. "We ever build such a thing around here, folks will go to that nights, too."

I CALLED LEO's cell phone.

"Are you at home?" I asked. An electric bass thumped in his background.

"Of course." His voice was barely audible above the bass.

"That noise?"

"Ma and her friends."

I checked my watch. It was ten o'clock. "They're doing mornings now?"

"Mrs. Roshiska bought a shoe box full of videos after bingo. They started at one in the morning. I've been in here all night."

The electric bass thumped faster. "You're in your office?"

"Ma had the guy who's doing the basement put in a door. A thick door. It didn't help." He dropped his voice. "Did you hear that?"

"All I can hear is bass."

"There it is again. Hear it?"

"What are you talking about?"

"Things, hitting my new door."

"Leo, you need to get some sleep."

"Ma says I can't come out once they've started exercising."

"But it's been nine hours."

"They take breaks, for vodka."

"Go see Endora at the Newberry. Have lunch in the park across the street."

"I told you: Ma says once they start up, I have to stay in until they're done." His voice dropped again. He was struggling for control. "I'm afraid."

"Of what?"

"Of the future."

"You need to sleep. But first, I need you to do something for me."

"Anything. Anything, so long as it keeps me from wondering what Ma, the other ladies, Mrs. Roshiska, leaning on her walker..."

I told him to find a town in Wisconsin or Minnesota,

near the Mississippi River, that had a statue of an Indian chief. "Womack, or someone like that."

"I'll do it, right now. Just please, please, stay on the line. I need someone to talk to."

I couldn't hear him tapping on his keyboard, for the pounding of the bass, but he was back on the line in two minutes. "Chief Winnemac. Hadlow, Minnesota. Just west of the Mississippi River."

He begged me to stay on the line, but there was no time.

THIRTY-EIGHT

THINGS WENT SMOOTHLY, for much of the rest of the day.

My one-way flight to Minneapolis got in at seven fifteen, right on time. I rented a tiny, squared-off Chevrolet, cheap, from Swifty's Rent-a-Car, just off the airport grounds. I'd never heard of Swifty's, and the car looked like a delivery van left too long in a dryer, but the price was right, thirty a day. For most of the forty miles southeast to Hadlow, things were fine.

Then, at dusk, I came up on a man driving a pickup truck with its headlights off. He was pulling a stake trailer, also unlit, filled with pigs.

The man and the pigs seemed content to move along at fifteen miles an hour. I was not. I was in a hurry to find a place to stay in Hadlow, have dinner, and be set to start prowling what I hoped was Sweetie Fairbairn's hometown first thing the next morning.

I put on my turn signal and pulled out on the left, to pass.

The farmer, without signaling, chose that exact moment to turn left.

As did his trailer. As did his pigs.

I T-boned the moron, slammed right into the side of his truck. The impact sent me off the road, upright, down into a ditch.

His truck also managed to stay upright, down in the ditch, ahead of me. Not so his trailer. Not so his pigs.

The trailer had twisted over, onto its side, splintering

its stubby wood fence. Amid great squeals of terror, or perhaps enthusiasm, the pigs exited and took off across the field.

"Son of a bitch," the livestock owner shouted and started to run after his pigs.

"Son of a bitch," I echoed, thoroughly caught up in the drama of the moment.

After two hundred yards, the man realized the futility of chasing his bacon across the field, and he came back. Furious.

"Didn't you see I was turning?" he demanded.

"Didn't you see I was already in the other lane, with my lights on, about to pass you?"

So it went for another minute or two, until we both got on our cell phones. He called a friend of his who had a brother. They each had tow trucks. I called Swifty's Rent-a-Car.

"You waived our insurance," the unruffled female voice said around the gum she was chewing. "It's your responsibility to have our vehicle towed to our nearest service center. They'll provide an estimate of repairs."

"Where are your service centers?"

"There's only the one, at the airport in Minneapolis where you rented the car."

I told her getting towed there would cost a fortune.

"You should have thought of that before you declined our insurance." I heard her type on her computer. "Meanwhile," she said, "we've placed a ten-thousand-dollar charge on your credit card. That will be reversed once the car has been repaired, at your, or your insurance company's, expense. Thank you for using Swifty's Rent-a-Car."

I was about to wish her good luck, because my credit card has a five-hundred-dollar limit, when I remembered

I'd given the Swifty's agent Koros's plastic to use for a security imprint.

It didn't matter. The gum-chewing Swifty girl had already hung up on me.

The two tow trucks came. The driver of the one that pulled my Chevy up from the ditch asked me where I was headed.

"Hadlow," I said.

"Good enough. Ralph's got a service station there. He can look at your car."

"It's a rental," I said, without knowing why.

"Even better. Rental companies take care of everything. They'll get you a new car delivered pronto."

"I used Swifty's Rent-a-Car."

"Never heard of them."

"They're cheap," I said, finding no comfort in that at all.

We clattered southeast along two-lane blacktop in almost total darkness for forty-five minutes. Then, topping a hill, I saw a round yellow light, disembodied and hovering, high in the distance.

"Do you see that?" I asked, leaning closer to the windshield.

He laughed. "UFO?"

"What is it?"

"Chief Winnemac," he said, "or at least his big cement head. The rest of him is obscured by the tree line."

"How tall is the statue?"

"Fifty-some feet, but being high on the bluffs over the Mississippi River, he appears much taller. He looks over everything for miles around."

"Including Hadlow?" I asked, mostly to make conversation.

"Especially Hadlow, because of the way the river bends."

Ten minutes later, our headlamps picked up a scalloped

beige sign announcing that the chamber of commerce wanted to welcome us to Hadlow, Minnesota. For good measure, they'd cut a profile of Winnemac at the top of the sign, implying his delight as well.

As we drove through town, I imagined the chamber of commerce would delight in welcoming anyone. The description Kathy had given Linda Coombs had been accurate. Hadlow was just another tiny, fading town: two blocks of storefronts, some twitching, some long dead; a grain elevator, missing clapboards, peeling paint, but seemingly still operating; four taverns shining small neon beer signs at the darkness; and one gas station.

It looked like it had been a fine place to leave for decades.

Ralph's service station, by its fading red and yellow colors, appeared to have once been a Shell franchise. Now it sprouted no name or logo at all.

"End of the line," the tow driver said. Once he pocketed two hundred of George Koros's dollars, he dropped the Chevy. By now, I'd run through more than half of the ATM cash.

A man in overalls came out of one of the service bays as the tow truck pulled away, and eyed the unhealthy way the Chevy's front wheel was canted out. "Animal or metal?" he asked.

"A bit of both. A man and his pigs turned in front of me."

"Won't be able to look at it until morning."

"Is there a place to stay in town?"

"Five miles south. Place used to be an Econo Lodge before the economy tanked."

"Have you got a car I can rent?"

He started to shake his head no, then stopped as though lightning had charged his skull. He wet his lips and pointed to a flatbed truck, parked next to a tow truck at the side of the station. It had been red and yellow once, too. Now it was mostly gray, where the paint had weathered off, exposing the primer.

"That's what I got to rent. Fifty bucks a day."

I told myself that, should I lose my mind, I could buy pigs, and use the truck to take them for picnics in the countryside. I also told myself that the truck was all that was available.

In the sky, in the distance, the yellow-headed Winnemac appeared to grin. I peeled off another hundred of my rapidly dwindling dollars.

The truck cab had an authentic working smell to it, a mixed bouquet of gasoline, grease, and sweat. I rolled the windows down to draw in the night air as I drove the five miles to the motel.

As Ralph had said, the place had recently been an Econo Lodge. The outdoor signs were gone, but the name was still stenciled on a canvas laundry hamper left outside a service door. I hoped that meant the place still sported beige walls, safe and free of depictions of creatures wanting to bite in the night.

My room was blessedly bland, beige and more beige. I took a long shower, had a few Ho Hos for dinner, and slipped into bed. As I lay in the darkness, drapes pulled tight against the bright concrete eyes of Winnemac, my mind stabbed me with the thought that this trip was a waste of time. Sweetie would not have come back to a place like Hadlow. It was too small in which to hide.

I pushed the thought away. Anyone could hide anywhere.

Except perhaps Winnemac.

THIRTY-NINE

THE NEXT MORNING, the desk clerk at the used-to-be Econo Lodge told me, with some pride, that the high school served a dozen local communities. His pride was justified. The high school was big. Because it was summer, only a few cars were parked in the lot.

"You say you're looking for a woman who may have attended this school over forty years ago?" the stern-faced woman in the administration office asked.

"Yes, ma'am."

"You don't know her real name, or a maiden name?"

"No, ma'am."

"Yet you think you would recognize her in a yearbook photo?"

"Yes, ma'am."

"And you think she'd look the same, after forty years?"

"Close enough, I hope, ma'am."

My side of the dialogue had been defensive right from the start. Being in a high school brought back memories of my own encounters with stern-faced administrators, and that triggered old instincts to provide short, nonincriminating answers.

"This is an insurance issue?" she asked. I'd given her one of my cards.

"A routine matter of an estate not being closed out. The company wants to make the payout but can't locate all the beneficiaries. We're hoping one or two might still be in this area."

She wrote something on a small piece of paper and handed it to me. "Our librarian is in today, preparing for the new year. She'll show you to the yearbooks."

"Thank you."

"Young man?"

I stopped at the door. "Ma'am?"

"See that you move quietly through the halls."

"Yes, ma'am."

As I walked down the hall, I looked at the slip of paper she'd given me. It was a hall pass. I wanted to laugh, loudly—school was out for the summer—but I was too old.

THE LIBRARIAN WORE faded jeans and a blue chambray shirt with rolled-up sleeves. Obviously, she'd come to school that day to sort and lift, and was not pleased with my intrusion. She put me in a small room, came back with the books I'd asked for, and told me she was very busy.

Looking for her family, I'd requested the six yearbooks around the year I estimated Sweetie would have graduated, if she'd been truthful about being fifty-eight. I began with the oldest book, going through the pictures of the graduating seniors because those photos were the largest. None resembled Sweetie Fairbairn.

I was almost through the senior photos in the next book when one stopped me. It wasn't Sweetie; it was a blond girl with a sunny smile who'd been active, for her first three years in high school, on the girls' cross-country team, the debate society, and the Future Farmers of America.

I stared at the picture, but I didn't need to. I knew that blond girl. I'd gotten a glimpse of her when she was much, much older, after her skin had gone leathery from too much exposure to the sun. I'd seen her coming out of George Koros's building.

She'd been why Koros hadn't let me into his private

office. She'd been hiding in there while Koros and I talked in his anteroom.

She wasn't Sweetie Fairbairn, not quite—but she was very close.

The yearbook said her name was Darlene Taylor.

I flipped back to the book's index. There was another Taylor listed. Rosemary. I turned to her homeroom photo.

Sweetie Fairbairn looked back at me from forty-two years before. She was a pretty girl, with happy eyes and a good smile. The girls—Darlene, a senior; Rosemary, a junior—were sisters.

I thumbed backward through the senior photo pages again, idling, not ready yet to think about what her sister Darlene's presence in Chicago might mean about Sweetie's disappearance.

This time my eye was stopped by another senior photograph, a boy's. I'd not been looking at boys, but this one, in Darlene's senior class, caught my eye because he had slicked-back hair that reminded me of Elvis Derbil's. The boy's name was Korozakis. There was no mistaking the wide Greek face. I knew that face.

George Koros.

Darlene Taylor, her sister Rosemary, and George Koros. All together in Hadlow, Minnesota.

I leaned back, shut my eyes.

Sweetie Fairbairn and George Koros had been lying to me since the beginning.

I wondered how I could find out why.

FORTY

THE LIBRARIAN MADE me photocopies of the yearbook pages. The stern-faced administrator pursed her lips at my foolishness when I came back to show them to her. "Going back four decades? None of us is that old, Mr. Elstrom. Myself, I've only been here ten years."

"Would you mind taking a look anyhow? Then I'll be on my way."

It was incentive enough. She took the three photocopies I was holding out and glanced at the one on top.

"Never seen him," she said.

"There are two more pictures."

She looked at the second copy. "No, never…" She stopped, moved the picture a few inches farther from her eyes. "I'll be darned. Darlene."

"Darlene Taylor," I said.

"Darlene Taylor, of course. I had no idea she'd been such a pretty thing."

"How about the last photo?"

She studied the third sheet. "Obviously Darlene's sister, almost close enough to be her twin, but I've never heard of her."

"You know Darlene?"

"She works here. Janitorial."

"Here? Like right now?"

"Not summers. Darlene is part of the night crew that works during the school year."

"Can you tell me where she lives?"

"Against policy."

"Can you think of anyone who would have known Rosemary?"

"This is an insurance matter?"

"A small family policy. We need to locate both sisters."

"There's Miss Mason. She used to teach English, all four grades. Last I heard, she's at the assisted living facility. It's not more than ten miles from here."

Actually, it was fourteen miles, but I resisted the urge to call the administrator and correct her with a strong "No, ma'am." It was enough to know she was wrong. Besides, I was afraid of being summoned back; I'd snuck away without turning in my hall pass.

The assisted living facility was sided with cedar, old and grayed out. Miss Mason was old, too, but not grayed out. Her hair was dyed a vibrant brown, and her lipstick was bright. She did not live there, she said pointedly; she was the facility's activities director. We sat in one corner of a large visiting room, filled with comfortable-looking sofas and chairs. The furniture looked unused.

"I taught them all, Mr. Elstrom—Darlene and Rosemary, even Georgie, though he wasn't there the whole year, of course." She handed back the photocopies. "I expect lots of folks remember them, at least those of us of a certain age."

"I'm not following, Miss Mason."

"The incident, the filling station?"

I shook my head.

"Forgive me, Mr. Elstrom. I thought you were here about that old case. Exactly why have you come?"

"I'm trying to locate Rosemary Taylor."

"About what?"

"An insurance matter."

"I would have thought those folks, the Taylors, were

too poor for any kind of insurance." She sighed. "I can't help you. Rosemary left Hadlow right after her junior year. Caused a lot of talk, because it was just a couple of months after the incident."

"The incident?" She'd said it twice now.

"The service station out by the river was robbed that April. A young attendant was shot several times, gut shot, and died of his wounds. There were no eyewitnesses, but several people reported seeing Darlene and Rosemary riding with Georgie in his convertible, out in that direction that afternoon."

"They were suspected?"

"Certainly not by right-thinking people. Georgie was always driving Darlene around in that flashy car. That day, they brought Rosemary along and were out by the river, was all." She thought for a moment, then said, "That convertible didn't help."

"What do you mean?"

"Georgie was new to town. Greek. His father was sent here to close down the paper mill, lay off the people, sell off the equipment. Took a long damned time for that mill to die, longer still for its guts to be pulled out and sold. Meanwhile, there was Georgie, a real smoothie—I expect he got his way with Darlene, that spring—breezing about in his father's flashy convertible. It struck people wrong, driving a car like that when folks were losing their jobs. Anyway, a lot of people didn't much mind when Georgie was sent away."

"After the incident?"

"Just days afterward, if memory serves. His parents said they wanted him to finish up at some fancy college prep school, to better his chances of getting into a good university, but there was talk that he was sent away because of the incident."

I pointed to Koros's yearbook photo, lying on the coffee table. "That shows him as graduating from here."

"He never finished. Yearbooks get printed weeks before the end of the school year."

"Rosemary left at the end of that same school year?"

She nodded. "First Georgie, then Rosemary."

"Why did Rosemary leave?"

"No reason to stay, I expect. She was a moony girl."

"Moony?"

"A delightful child, but a dreamer. Her head was filled with fanciful thoughts of elegant lives in elegant cities. There was nothing like that in Hadlow."

"What about Darlene?"

"She was the dutiful one. She kept on at the family place, after the mother died, and after Rosemary took off. Of course, Alta was still alive then."

"Alta?"

"The third girl; Darlene and Rosemary's younger sister."

"I didn't think to look in the yearbooks for a third sister," I said.

"Oh, no; Alta wouldn't be in any of the yearbooks. She quit going to school in seventh or eighth grade, around the time the father took off. Hard luck all around, in that family." She leaned forward. "Insurance money would sure help Darlene. She stayed on after Alta died, though I'll never understand why. She should have left. She was a pretty, bright girl. She could have fashioned a better life for herself, somewhere else."

"Alta died?"

"I told you: hard luck all around in that family, especially that year."

"When did Alta die?"

"September, three months after Rosemary took off." She pursed her lips, thinking back. "Their mother died the winter before. There was talk about sending the girls—remember there were three of them, with Alta being disabled in some fashion—to state care, but Darlene, being the oldest, fought that. She said she could manage the family." She reached for the yearbook copies and held one up. "Yes, see here? Darlene was an active girl during her first three years of high school, but senior year, she did nothing. She dropped out of everything to keep that family going."

"By then the father was gone."

"Long gone, the bastard. Hand it to Darlene, she was tenacious. After the mother passed, she and Rosemary alternated the days they went to school, so that one was always home with Alta. But the impact was hardest on Darlene. She was the oldest."

"Alta was disabled?"

"Mental or physical, no one quite knew what she suffered from. She contracted something and after that was never seen. Folks supposed Martha Taylor, the mother, thought it inappropriate to put her youngest child on display. Things were like that, then."

"What did Alta die of?"

"A virus, I think. Anyway, folks expected that would be the last straw for Darlene, but she stayed on, cleaning at the school, and farming some. It must be difficult, being out there all alone. Of course, she doesn't really farm, just tends a plot for her own needs. She has a man stop by, now and again, I hear, to help with the heavier chores."

"Does Rosemary ever come back?"

"Oh, how I wish she would. She was charming, utterly charming. She had such—" She stopped, hunting for the right word. "Hope," she said finally. "Rosemary had such hope. It came through so strong in her stories."

"Stories?"

"She was always writing stories, and not just for my

English class, either. They were romantic, and tragic, but underlying, there was always hope. She wrote a whole novel, her junior year. It was about a man who entertained kids, I think. Got a mention in the local paper for that, and the school mimeographed a bunch of copies, thinking it would inspire other students to take up writing. It's not that the writing was particularly good; it was her tenacity that made the impression, her willingness to write such a long thing. Then, as now, young people were not known for their powers of concentration."

Something faint nagged at the back of my gut. "A story about a man who entertained kids?" I asked, hoping I sounded merely conversational.

"I think he got killed, toward the end of the story. Romance, tragedy, and hope. Young Miss Rosemary's heroine rose above the tragedy, and went on to work with ill children."

"How did he entertain the kids?"

"Well, I don't quite remember—"

"With balloons? Did the man entertain children with balloons?"

"It's been years since I looked at it—"

"You have a copy?"

Her eyes narrowed, seeing through the lies I had told. "What are you after, Mr. Elstrom?"

"Do you still have the story?"

"Somewhere, I suppose."

"I need to see it."

"Why on earth would you want to?"

I couldn't lie anymore. "Something more than idle curiosity."

She folded her hands in her lap. "Best you ask Darlene about these things—and that insurance you say you're here about."

She gave me directions to the Taylor place, and I walked out into the sunshine. It took some time to put the key in the ignition, because I had to sit for a while, in that truck cab that smelled of grease and gasoline and sweat, and think about the death of a gas station attendant, and the death of a clown…and wonder what might have been set in motion over forty years before.

FORTY-ONE

I FOLLOWED A road that had once been gravel but was now worn to rutted brown clay, flecked only faintly with the gray of a last few embedded stones. I passed no houses. It was empty country.

The Taylor place was four miles outside of Hadlow, a leaning cottage stuck on more hard brown ground, surrounded by once-cleared fields that were now thick with thin, spindly trees. Whatever Darlene Taylor had grown in the small plots had curled up and died, giving way to weeds.

Weeds, and perhaps a twisted idea of how words of romance and murder and a clown, written by a high school girl long before, could be used for blackmail.

The house appeared deserted. A piece of cardboard had been taped inside to cover a shattered front window. The screen door was canted outward, about to fall off its hinges. The place looked as it should, if Darlene Taylor had abandoned it to come to Chicago.

Except for the weeds in the front. Someone had trampled them recently, walking up to the house. They were only now beginning to spring back up.

I left the truck on the road and came up on foot. I knocked on the door, waited, knocked again. No one answered.

I tried the handle. The front door was locked tight, and all the windows looked to be latched. All but the one covered by cardboard.

I walked around to the back. An old water pump stuck up out of the ground, five yards from the house. An outhouse stood fifty feet past that, near a sparse copse of trees. It leaned in the same direction as the cottage.

The rear door was locked, too.

I rubbed a window made filthy by blown dirt and pressed my face against it. I was looking across a kitchen sink, at a plate of beans, half eaten, set on a porcelain-topped table. The beans looked fresh, not dried or discolored. A smear of gravy beneath them glistened in the sunlight coming in diffused through the window.

I watched the beans. Things moved across them, like they'd moved across the corpse of Andrew Fill.

Flies.

I went back to the truck and drove away.

I'd come back after dark, to see if Darlene Taylor had come home.

THE LITTLE RENTAL Chevrolet sat in front of Ralph's service station, its driver's side front wheel bent at exactly the same angle as the night before. Hearing the familiar sounds of his truck clattering up to its rightful home, Ralph came out of the bowels of his station, wiping his hands, and struck a pose in front of the wounded Chevrolet like he was studying sculpture.

"I've been thinking on this all morning," he said. "I'm not sure if I can make it drivable."

I squeezed the last of Koros's cash in my pocket, sensing Ralph was about to squeeze me. "What will make you sure?"

"I'll have to start pulling off parts. It'll take days, and big money."

"We'd better tow it, then."

"Where to?"

"The rental place in Minneapolis."

His voice brightened. "That's a long, long ways."

I gripped the cash in my pocket tighter. "How much?"

"I'd have to think on that."

I knew what he had to think about. He had to guess how much I was clutching in my pocket, and what he could rationalize that into, in per-mile towing charges.

"Let me know, Ralph," I said, hoping he couldn't hear the defeat in my voice. I went back to the smells of grease and gas and sweat percolating in the cab of his truck.

I HAD THE afternoon and early evening to kill. I decided to begin by stabbing at it with a plastic knife and fork. I pulled into the parking lot of a fast food place at the edge of town called the Would You? and ordered the chicken basket.

It was after lunchtime. There were no teenagers loitering in front. There had been, though—years and years of them, judging by the carvings on the wood planks of the picnic tables. Love had been memorialized there, in initials filled with chicken and burger grease sure to protect it from the harsh Minnesota winters, likely to last longer than the love itself.

I would have bet most towns had such hieroglyphs. My town, Rivertown, certainly did, though instead of being carved into tables, ours were cut into the sides of Kutz's Wienie Wagon, a wood-slatted trailer that had been pulled beneath one of the overpasses when FDR was president and left to sink on deflating tires. My own initials were there, paired with a girl's, inside a heart. Years later, she'd come back to cut another heart, larger, to surround the first one. It had taken me too long to learn about that second heart.

My chicken—a leg, a thigh, and a breast—came with a biscuit and french fries, enough goodness to clog even the most elastic of arteries. As I ate, I studied the carvings on the table, wondering if Rosemary Taylor's initials had been carved at the Would You? Or whether the tables from her high school days had been discarded, their initials lost, and the whole process begun all over again.

The chicken, biscuit, and fries were excellent. When I turned in my tray, I was tempted to tell the young lady behind the Would You?'s grease-smeared glass that I would again, if allowed. I didn't, because I worried she'd misinterpret my play on the name of the place and call the police.

I walked to the truck, leaned against its fender. It wasn't hard to see Georgie Korozakis, cocky and young, breezing along that Main Street in his father's convertible, with Darlene Taylor nestled beside him, her blond hair blowing back, both of them laughing at the wind and the notion of ever growing old.

I called Amanda. Her secretary told me she was out at a luncheon and wasn't expected back until much, much later. I didn't want to wonder if that was true.

Leo didn't answer his cell phone. He was probably in a meeting somewhere.

I called Jennifer Gale. She sounded glad to hear from me.

"Want to have dinner after the news tonight?" she asked. "I can tell you how I've struck out, trying to trace Sweetie Fairbairn's background."

"I'm in Hadlow, Minnesota. I got into an altercation with a truckload of pigs."

"Are you all right?"

"I am. The farmer who caused the accident is angry, as will be George Koros when he finds out his credit card is being charged ten grand against car repairs. The pigs, though, appeared to be ecstatic. They took off across a field and might now be in Mexico."

"Why are you in Hadlow?"

"I got a lead into Sweetie Fairbairn's background."

"I thought you were going to keep me current on all this."

"That's what I'm doing. Things have happened so fast there wasn't time."

"Did she come from Hadlow?"

"You're not going to broadcast this yet, right?"

"Right."

"Sweetie came from here. So did her sister, a woman who I saw at George Koros's building. So did George Koros."

"All three of them?" She inhaled sharply. "Big news, Dek Elstrom."

"Indeed."

"When can I use this stuff?"

"When I'm sure none of it incriminates the missing Ms. Fairbairn."

I told her I'd check in with her when I learned something new.

I didn't say that hearing her voice made me feel not so alone.

FORTY-TWO

THE MOON WAS a thin sliver in the sky. There were no head-lamps moving in either direction; no house lights lit the fields. Not even Winnemac showed his spotlit head. I was alone in that black part of Minnesota.

Still, I cut the headlamps a half mile before the cottage and coasted to a stop. I wanted to come up to the Taylor house on foot. In case Darlene had returned to finish her beans.

There was just enough moonlight to show me the edge of the road. My feet made no noise as I hurried along the hard clay.

Then there was a light, off the road ahead, to the right.

It was faint and flickering, barely visible in the darkness. I moved forward slowly until suddenly the light disappeared.

I'd gotten to the front of the Taylor cottage. The light was flickering from the back, and was now blocked by the front of the house. It was candlelight I'd seen; the house didn't have electricity.

The realization tingled at the back of my neck. I didn't want to wonder what such a hellishly poor place had done to Darlene Taylor, living out her nights in such blackness, so far out of town, and so alone. With only a candle to keep away the dark.

There was no car on the rutted drive. Whoever was in that cottage had been brought there, or had come up as I had, on foot.

I crouched down and moved around the side of the house to the back. I remembered the three windows. The dim, flickering glow was coming from the middle of them. The kitchen window.

The kitchen window I'd rubbed, to see through. Whoever was inside would know someone had been there.

That couldn't be helped now. I stayed low as I passed beneath the first window. At the one in the middle, I eased up slowly for a look.

The plate of beans was still on the porcelain-topped table, but now the stub of a candle, guttering, had been stuck in the center of it.

Something rustled low, ten, twenty feet away.

In that instant, I understood. A candle stuck in a plate of beans, not for a light but as a beacon, to draw someone who should not be there.

I caught my breath and turned.

A flash lit the darkness, followed by an explosion. My right side went hot. I'd been shot.

I turned, to run. The wound in my side had a thousand tentacles, each one clutching a dagger. Pain in my legs now, pain in my arms; too much pain to run. I fell.

Then he was on me. His boots kicked at my arms and my head. I rolled onto my right side, trying to protect the wound. He kept kicking, again and again. I raised my left arm, to fight off the blows. He kicked it down and danced back, a black shape crouched against the charcoal sky.

I rolled away, somehow got to my feet. He came at me low, breathing heavily. He was tiring. I slapped out with my left hand, hit his head, caught his hair. It was oily, greasy, and long. My right side was on fire, but there'd be more pain, more bullets, if I let go. Death would come.

He thrashed away.

I turned, to run. It was all I could do.

His hands were too fast. He caught me around the waist. The hard metal of the handgun beat at the wound on my right side, once, and again.

Enraged at the pain, at the life that was leaking out of me, I beat at the side of his face with my left fist. Something crunched. Maybe his nose, or his cheek. He screamed. It was the loud wail of an animal. I swung at the sound of him. He moaned. His hands let go. He fell.

He still had the gun.

Hugging my right arm against the blood at my side, I began to run. Each footfall sent an iron rod of fire into my right side. I wanted to scream at the jarring and the pain, but to cry out would draw him right to me in the dark. My only chance was to reach the trees back of the fields before he recovered enough to come after me.

After a minute, after an hour—time was lost; there was only pain—I found a tree, then another. I was in the woods. I clutched at their thin, spindly shapes, one to the next, finding my way deeper into the woods with my good left arm.

The darkness would hide me, if I stayed quiet.

I heard something, stopped and held my breath. He was thrashing nearby, loud. I tugged off my belt and cinched it around my left hand, metal buckle dangling a foot at the end. It was the only weapon I had.

His footfalls faded, and then they were gone. I started up again, careful to feel ahead of me for the next tree. He could have stopped, to strain for the sound of me.

Each step was a new hammer blow to the wet wound in my side. Pain was good, I had to believe. Pain would keep me moving. I would live if I could do the pain.

A tree root seized my foot, and I fell hard to the ground. Panicked, I lurched up. He'd heard me now. I started to run, hit a tree, went down. I bit at my lip until I could taste blood, but I made no noise. I got up, went forward.

A hundred more times I fell, got up, and fell again. Then I had no strength to get up anymore. My whole right side was drenched, wet down to my shoes. Maybe there was no more blood. It was all right. I would lie still, and the darkness would keep me.

SOMEONE CAME, AND took my good left hand. I had no strength; I could only breathe. My arm jerked, there was an explosion—and then the person went away without helping me at all. I wondered if I'd been shot again, and was supposed to bleed to death, in those black woods.

I had the thought that I should laugh.

Surely there was no more blood.

FORTY-THREE

SOMETHING SMALL DRAGGED itself across the skin of my hand.

I blinked my eyes until they'd cleared enough to see a fuzzy rectangle of light high up, past my feet. I blinked some more. Hospital light. Hospital bed.

A technician was swabbing my left hand. She finished and stepped away.

"What's that for?" I asked, through a mouth full of cotton.

A different woman came to stand next to my neck. "Gunshot residue," she said.

"Then swab my side. That's where the bullet went in."

"You're damned lucky, Vlodek Elstrom, you didn't put that bullet into your heart."

I strained to look up at her, but her face was a blurred circle in the glare of another fluorescent fixture, this one mounted right above my head.

She moved back so I could see her. She was attractive, in her early forties, Nordic blond and blue-eyed. She wore a tan uniform shirt, dark green trousers, and a black leather gun belt.

"You're a cop?"

"Of course I'm a cop. We get called on gunshot wounds, even if they are self-inflicted."

"I didn't shoot myself, damn it." I grabbed the bed rail with my left hand, to pull myself up, but my foot tugged

back from the end of the bed. "You cuff suicides up here?"
I said.

"When requested."

"I didn't put a bullet anywhere. It was put into me."

"By who?"

"I don't know."

"Would you like a lawyer?"

"I want to speak to your superior."

"I am the superior. I'm the sheriff, Ellie Ball. I'm also
the newest friend of a Lieutenant Plinnit, down in Chicago. He responded right away to the inquiry I sent. He's
quite interested in your, ah, accident, and is on his way
up here."

It explained why I was cuffed to the bed frame. Plinnit.

"It was no accident. It was no suicide. I was shot."

"Mind if I record this?" She pulled a bed tray over and
set a small recorder on it.

I rattled the cuff chain with my left foot. "Obviously,
you can do whatever you please."

She spoke the date and then the time—5:15 p.m.; I'd
lost almost the whole day—named the hospital, and identified a deputy, standing against the wall, as a witness to
the proceedings. "Mr. Elstrom has consented to this interview without presence of counsel to represent him," she
said to the recorder. "Right, Mr. Elstrom?"

"Why is this necessary?"

"Lieutenant Plinnit asked that your statement be taken
promptly. He said he was worried you'd find another gun
and finish the job."

"How did you find me?"

"One of our locals was driving by at daybreak, and recognized Ralph's truck parked out in the middle of nowhere.

He couldn't find Ralph, but he did hear you, moaning, not far off the road."

Even through the drugs, I had an inspiration. "I'll bet you didn't find the gun."

"Actually we did, right where you dropped it. We're testing it now."

"So you're arresting me for attempted murder on my-self?"

"I'm merely taking a statement, Mr. Elstrom."

"Then remove the cuff."

"You're being held as a courtesy to Lieutenant Plinnit. He said he wants to arrest you. He'll detail his charges against you when he arrives tomorrow morning."

"What charges?"

"Suspicion of murder."

"Who got killed?"

"You can ask the lieutenant."

"I need to call my attorney."

Ellie Ball and her deputy left the room.

I called Leo's cell phone. "Where are you?" I asked when he clicked on. Loud accordion music was playing at his end.

"I just got home from Los Angeles. Ma has the stereo guy over. He's setting up huge television speakers in the basement. I want to cry."

"I'm in Hadlow, Minnesota."

"Doesn't sound as good as L.A."

"I've been shot, and I am leg-cuffed to a hospital bed."

"Definitely not as good as L.A., though I hear those movie star types go for cuffs."

"I'm serious."

"You're not."

I gave him a one-minute summary.

"I don't understand," he said.

"Neither do I, but I'm medicated and in deep shit."

He said he was on his way back to the airport.

"No surprise, Mr. Elstrom," Sheriff Ellie Ball said when she came back in. "You had residue on your left hand."

"I fired no—" I stopped, remembering the touch of someone's hand as I lay on the ground in the woods. I remembered the explosion.

Someone had fitted my hand to a gun—and fired.

"Son of a bitch," I said.

"I thought you'd say something like that," she said. "What were you doing in those woods? Nearest house is a half mile away."

I'd stumbled far enough from the shack for her not to make the connection. She would, though, when she learned I was in Hadlow tracking Darlene Taylor, and I had no doubt that she'd find that out. Hadlow was a small town.

"I'll wait for Plinnit," I said.

She clicked off her recorder and headed for the door.

"By the way, Chief...?" I said. My pain medication was wearing off.

"It's Sheriff," she said. "Sheriff Ellie Ball."

"By the way, Chief. Something you've neglected: I'm right-handed."

My pain meds were in full retreat now, chased away by the hot fire from the hole in my side.

"So what?"

I wanted to scream for a nurse, but first I wanted to scream at the sheriff.

"I want you to ponder how the hell I got gunshot residue on my left hand when I'm right-handed."

"Oh, I thought of that, Elstrom. I'll consider it again,

and out loud, if you'd like. You had to use your left hand, if your intent was to wound your right side."

"Where's the sense in that?"

"To make it look like you didn't shoot yourself. I'll tell the nurse you might need a pill," she said and walked out.

FORTY-FOUR

A RIOT OF color moved next to me, no doubt a cheery nurse in a cheery tunic. I rubbed at my eyes, to see through the fog of drugs they'd used to quiet me for the night.

"Morning, Killer," Leo said.

His shirt was brighter than the blue of any sky, except in those spots where it was orange, or red, or green, or pink. A riot of color, for sure—and of relief.

"They've cuffed me to the bed, Leo."

"At the direction of Lieutenant Plinnit, who is outside, dying to talk to you."

"You've kept him away?"

"I told him I'm here because John Peet is addressing the Supreme Court."

"Dressed like that? You, a lawyer?"

"I never used the *L* word. I merely said I was representing you. As far as the clothes, I implied I practice in Miami."

"Practice?" I repeated, not understanding because there was still a residue of drugs. "In Miami?"

He stepped back and did part of a dance thrust. "Samba," he said.

I would have laughed at the nonsense of it, but that would have hurt.

"Anything you want to tell me, before I let Plinnit in?" he said.

"I'll fill you in later, when we're away from here."

He left the side of the bed and came back with Plinnit.

"Killer, Lieutenant Plinnit is here," Leo announced.

"Your smart-assed tone isn't helping your client, Mr. Brumsky," Plinnit said.

"Why the cuffs, Plinnit?" I asked.

"Suspicion of murder."

"That's what the sheriff said. Still Robert Norton, the guard? Or are you still flailing away at Andrew Fill?"

He held up a small plastic evidence bag. Inside was a spent bullet. "The sheriff just gave me this. They dug it out of your side. It matches the gun that fell from your hand."

"Why would I go off and shoot myself in some remote woods?"

"Remorse. You crawled there to die a sorry death, after you shot yourself. And it wasn't just any old remote woods. Sheriff Ball found blood at a small farm nearby, owned by a woman named Darlene Taylor. We're hopeful it's your blood, like we're hopeful this bullet will match two we recovered from behind the left ear of one George Koros, late of Chicago, Illin—"

"Koros is dead?" I struggled to sit up. A chained left foot and a shot right side brought me down, fast.

"Two shots to the back of his head, as you well know. Cleaning staff found him facedown at his desk."

"I killed Koros, then came up here to shoot myself?"

Plinnit nodded too happily. "Fits together nicely, doesn't it?"

"It's crap."

"It's enough to hold you for some time. If you've got other thoughts, tell me now."

"When was Koros killed?"

"The ME hasn't issued his final report, but it was the day before yesterday. We've been looking for you ever since. Your ex-wife said she didn't know where you were."

"I was here, in Hadlow."

"Beyond you possessing the gun we think killed George Koros, we found a credit card statement lying next to his head," he said, ignoring my alibi. "He'd pulled it off his online account. It shows you've been making substantial cash withdrawals against his card."

"He sent me that card. I used it for traveling cash, to get to Missouri, then up here."

"To find Sweetie Fairbairn?"

"Yes."

Plinnit wasn't taking notes. He knew I didn't kill George Koros.

"So what have you found?" he asked.

"A concrete Indian chief."

He frowned.

"And, of course, someone with a gun," I added.

"Rosemary Taylor's sister's cottage is what you found, Elstrom. Remember Rosemary Taylor, the girl who became Sweetie Fairbairn?"

"The truck," I said. "Ellie Ball told you about the truck."

"Uh-huh, and the copies of yearbook photographs she found in it. She contacted the high school. They said you'd stopped by. I looked at the photos. Sweetie Fairbairn, in high school, looked back."

"Sweetie Fairbairn hasn't been here for a long, long time."

"Are you saying Darlene Taylor shot you and then beat you? A woman who, by most accounts, is small of stature and around sixty years old?"

When I didn't respond, Leo said, "Dek's never been good with women of any age, Lieutenant."

Plinnit kept his eyes on me. "Did Darlene Taylor shoot you, Elstrom?"

"I can't imagine."

"For getting wise to her and Koros's extortion of Sweetie Fairbairn?"

He'd learned a lot, none of which pointed to any wrongdoing by Sweetie Fairbairn. It was time to tell him more.

"That, and their murders of Andrew Fill and Robert Norton," I said.

I told him I suspected that somehow Koros had discovered his old high school friend, Rosemary Taylor, living as Sweetie Fairbairn at the end of a rainbow in Chicago; that he convinced her to set him up with a monthly retainer and a fancy office on Wacker Drive; and that at some point, that hadn't been enough. He killed Andrew Fill for a half-million dollars, but that wasn't enough, either, not when there was so much more. So he brought down Sweetie's struggling sister, Darlene, to help him with a crafty extortion plot, probably centered around getting Sweetie blamed for Fill's and Norton's deaths. She outfoxed them, though. She ran, but not before giving away most, if not all, of her money. It killed the plan. Darlene murdered Koros so there'd be no remaining witness to their plot, and ran back up to Hadlow to resume life in the slow lane, at least until she could ease away with what was left of the half million Koros had embezzled from the Midwest Arts Symposium.

The only things I left out were the clown and the woman in the limo who'd hired him. Those pointed too directly at Sweetie Fairbairn.

"Slinking back here, hoping nobody knew she'd even been away, she got a bonus: you, peeking in her kitchen window?" Plinnit asked when I was done.

"Why not? Koros had told her I'd been sniffing around. I was a loose end. She shot me, and tried to make it look like a self-inflicted wound. She figured on me bleeding out in the woods, perhaps clutching the gun that killed Koros."

"You really think it was Darlene Taylor, a short, sixty-year-old woman, who shot and kicked the crap out of you in the woods?"

"She could have had help. There could have been two people."

"Can you prove any of this?"

"Not a bit."

"All I'm certain of is that you keep popping up where you shouldn't be." He treated himself to a false laugh. "Even up here, first thing you did was find the wrong side of the road, to run down a truckload of pigs."

"You know I didn't kill anybody. Not Andrew Fill, not Robert Norton, not George Koros."

"Here's all I need to prove for now, Elstrom: You were up here, with what we both believe is the weapon used to kill George Koros."

"I have no motive."

"He found out you were tapping his charge account. He got mad, said he was going to report you to the police."

"Cash for airplane tickets."

"Plus another ten grand for crashing your rental car. People get killed every day for a lot less."

"Bullshit, Plinnit."

"That's what I think, too." He started for the door. "Until I think otherwise, you and the bed are chained." He walked out of the room.

FORTY-FIVE

ELLIE BALL CAME to my room three hours after Plinnit left.

"You are?" she asked Leo, frowning at his outlandish blue rayon shirt.

He got up from the chair in the corner, not that it made much difference, height-wise.

"Mr. Elstrom's adviser."

"Not his lawyer, as you told Lieutenant Plinnit?"

"I said only that I was Mr. Elstrom's representative, Madame Law Woman. I never directly lie to the police."

She turned to me. "He must sit in with us?"

"Yes."

She came to the side of the bed, unlocked my leg, and set the cuffs next to the chair she took. "I've spent quite a bit of time with Lieutenant Plinnit. He just got confirmation from his medical examiner: George Koros was killed when you were up here. That made him angry. He is on his way back to Chicago."

"I'm free to go?"

"Depends on your doctors—and on me."

"You?"

"I can think of charges: unlawful possession of a firearm, trespass at the Taylor place, and," she said, smiling just a little, "there's still the matter of your run-in with those pigs, even though it's not my county."

Leo spoke. "What about the attempted murder of Dek, here?"

She lowered her eyes to the shirt drooping on him. "How do you keep that so bright?"

He smiled, bisecting his pale, narrow, bald head with perfectly white teeth. "Plant food."

"Who shot you?" she asked me.

"George Koros's killer."

"Don't evade."

"There's only one person left with motive: Darlene Taylor."

"A sixty-year-old woman shot and beat you?"

"The only thing I'm sure of is that Darlene's involved deeply in this thing. Down in Chicago, she must have seen, like the cops would see, that I'd pulled cash from Koros's credit card account. She knew I was on the move, tracking her sister. She also knew those withdrawals could point to me as Koros's killer. She came back up here, hoping no one knew she had ever left. As I told Plinnit, I think she brought back a substantial amount of money that Koros had embezzled from Sweetie Fairbairn. I think she intended to wait things out a bit, maybe until I was arrested, before disappearing from Hadlow permanently."

"Except you showed up at her place?"

"It must have been a shock, learning I was sniffing around her property, but then she saw I could be a bonus. She could shoot me with the gun that killed Koros, fire another round with my hand on it to put my prints on the handle, and leave me to bleed out in the woods. My death would look like a suicide, perhaps an act of remorse after killing Koros. The problem was, she couldn't know that I'd already been up here for a while, and could prove I wasn't in Chicago when Koros got shot. The finger's going to come back to point at her. You've got to be vigilant. If she learns I have an alibi, she'll run, if she hasn't already."

"She killed her sister's guard and George Korozakis?" she asked. "Rosemary, too?"

"I'm hoping Sweetie's alive, and running."

She said nothing for a moment. Then, "If you're right, it's a tragedy, all around. Folks say Georgie Korozakis and Darlene Taylor were quite an item, once upon a time."

"Things can change people. Like the incident."

A hardness flashed across her face, and then it was gone. "So you're saying their romance got rekindled, all these years later?"

"For the love of money, this time."

"I suppose." Ellie Ball looked at the door. She was ready to leave. To be done with me.

"You know what I can't figure, Sheriff?"

"What's that?"

"Whether any of this ties back to that incident, when they were kids."

I was right. Her face tensed again at the second mention of the incident. She stood up and started toward the door. "Have a safe journey back to Chicago, Mr. Elstrom."

I'd struck a nerve with that random question about something that had happened long ago.

"Any thoughts as to why Darlene Taylor hung around that shack all those years, living in such squalor?" I asked her back.

"The doctor is going to release you today," she said, without turning around. "Lieutenant Plinnit said he'd be happy to arrest you down in Chicago, if I don't decide to charge you with something up here first. Best you leave town before I change my mind."

"Haven't you ever been curious why Darlene stayed on,

after her sister Alta died? Don't you want to know why someone would live out in that shack, for forty years?"

"There's those of us who love Hadlow," she said and stepped out into the hall.

FORTY-SIX

I'D HAD MUCH time to think, and to imagine, chained to my hospital bed.

Motives I understood. It was money, for Darlene and Koros. It was money, too, with Sweetie. She threw it away as she ran, to stop the killing.

Means, though, troubled me. I didn't understand the clown.

I called Miss Mason from my wheelchair, out front, while a nurse assistant and I waited for Leo to bring around faster transportation.

"Did you talk to Darlene?" Miss Mason asked.

"I didn't find her at home."

"I heard you got shot."

"Yes." News like that would have traveled fast across Hadlow. "I'm still interested in that story Rosemary Taylor wrote in high school."

"I found it, and read it again, last evening. Quite remarkable."

"About a man who entertained kids."

"Yes."

"The man was a clown, wasn't he? And he fell off a roof?" It was one of the things I'd become certain about, chained to my bed. Young Rosemary Taylor had written about a clown who'd gone off a roof.

"How did you know?"

"I'd really like to read it," I said.

"So you said earlier. You also said you're here on an insurance matter."

"I can't tell you what I'm working on."

"Is Rosemary in trouble?"

"Yes."

"Would the manuscript help or hurt her?"

"I don't know."

For a moment, there was only silence. Then she said, "I'm on my way out. I will leave it in an envelope outside my front door at home. I would like it returned tomorrow." She gave me directions and hung up.

A blue Chrysler minivan pulled up under the canopy. The nurse's aide started pushing me toward the curb, having recognized Leo. I hadn't, not at first, not in such a vehicle. I told her I could manage by myself, and pretty much did, though there were moments when all three of us held our breaths.

"What were you doing, jabbing the sheriff about that long-ago murder?" Leo asked after I eased in. It was the first time we'd been alone since my chat with Ellie Ball.

"For a guy whose regular ride is a Porsche, your idea of a fun vacation rental is perverted."

"Don't sidestep. Though for your information, I thought you might need to be carted horizontally back to Rivertown, especially if you'd ceased breathing. Hence, the minivan. What was that with the sheriff?"

"As you said, I was jabbing, and doing it blindly. Motive, for Koros and Darlene, I can understand: control of Sweetie's millions. What I can't quite figure is means. What did they have on Sweetie Fairbairn, and how did they use it?"

"Something to do with that clown's death."

"That I think I'm about to understand. That can't be all of it, though. There's that gas station killing, and how

Georgie Korozakis left right after, and then Sweetie, at the end of the school year."

A smile played on his lips. "Shall I start this fine vehicle, drive us back to the motel, then on to the airport? Or do you think driving down to Chicago would be easier?"

"Driving will be easier on me, physically," I said, adding slowly, "We'll get back in the wee hours."

"Yes."

"About the time Ma will be firing up her new speakers."

There was silence. Then he said, "I'm being played. You're going to suggest an alternative?"

"More of a diversion." I signaled for him to start up.

MISS MASON'S HOUSE wasn't far. An envelope was leaned against the front door, as she'd promised.

"What's this?" Leo asked, after he'd retrieved it.

"Confirmation, I think."

We stayed in the driveway while I fanned the manuscript. It was thin, mimeographed in faint blue ink, and less than a hundred pages. I found what I'd expected quickly.

"Now what?" he asked, when I set the manuscript on my lap.

"Now, a return."

Leo nodded like he'd been given a choice.

"JUST A QUICK drive-by, to see if she's home," I said, when we were a mile away. It was an hour before sunset.

"You're crazy."

"Nobody's said she's been around."

"Darlene's around. Touch your shot flesh if you don't believe."

"She's not being smart. She should be here, acting innocent, visibly renewing her vows of poverty until it's safe to take off with the half million."

"Unless she doesn't want to be questioned, a frail sixty-year-old, for beating the crap out of you."

"There is that, yes."

We got to the cottage. There was no car parked in front.

"She could still be home," Leo said uncertainly. "With another gun."

He was nervous. So was I.

He pulled to a stop. I opened the car door.

"What the hell, Dek?"

I eased onto my feet. It was like standing in a rowboat, in a squall. I hung on to the outside rearview mirror.

He killed the engine, got out, and came around. "Didn't I just remind you that you got shot here?"

"The memory is fresh." So was the pain in my side. I started walking up to the cottage.

"Not to mention beaten, by that frail, older...?" He let the insinuation dangle.

"I believe I'm not the only one troubled by older women," I said, dangling my own insinuation next to his.

He sighed, a fine confirmation that he was thinking about his mother and her friends, all of whom were no doubt jiving in the bungalow basement at that very moment.

He followed me to the door. I knocked. Then I banged.

No one answered. I tried the handle. It was locked.

"Maybe she went to town, to buy another gun," Leo offered.

"Plan B," I said.

"That would be?"

"You going through a window, to unlock the door."

"Into a creepy cottage, to be confronted by a madwoman with a gun?"

"Just to see if she's packed up and left for good."

"Why pack? She's got half a million dollars to buy new things."

"She's not home. Let's at least look."

"What if she comes home? She'll call the cops."

"No; she'll shoot us with that new gun you said she's buying. Best to hustle, Leo." I pointed to the window covered by taped cardboard.

He went over to it. Sun rotted and soggy, it fell inward with a faint push. He hoisted himself up and dropped into the blackness behind it.

I waited by the front door, feeling every beat of my heart grind into the torn flesh at my ribs. The sun was setting. The road and the fields around the house were getting darker. I didn't want to be there; I didn't want to see a pair of headlights working their way down the road toward the cottage.

The lock on the front door clicked, and the door swung open. Foul air came out.

"Jeez, Dek, it's bad in here," Leo said from inside the gloom.

Memories of Andrew Fill in his trailer came back. "Bad housekeeping bad?"

"I hope."

I hobbled in, and he shut the door. "What are we looking for?" he asked.

"Fast enlightenment," I said. The dark house seemed to be darkening by the second.

"Shit," he said and went to the back.

The tiny front room was a mess. Soiled plates, crusted with ancient food, were stacked on an end table. One leg had broken off the couch and been replaced with a split piece of a log. Stubs of candles were everywhere, stuck to mismatched saucers and one in a ridiculous plated candelabra.

A hundred *People* magazines, years of peeks at the lives of the rich and famous, lay in a spilled-over pile in the corner. I wondered if Darlene had been able to look at them after Koros sent word that her own sister Rosemary was living such a life high in a penthouse in Chicago.

It was a place to go mad, that cottage without plumbing or electricity. A place to get out of before Darlene came rolling up the road.

"Anything, Leo?" I called toward the back of the house.

He came out in the hall. "Two bedrooms. Two closets. Two sets of clothes, one adult's, one kid's."

"Kid's clothes? You're sure?"

"Teenager's, thirteen maybe. Jeans, knit shirts, flannel shirts."

"Old clothes?"

"One pair of jeans looked new."

"There's nothing to be learned here."

He was in the living room, by the front door, in an instant.

For sure, it was a place to go mad—and it had gotten way too dark.

FORTY-SEVEN

WE SAT ON the side of the Would You? at the table farthest from the high school hormones firing under the yellow bug lights in front. Leo had taken our empty chicken baskets back up to the counter and come back with new Cokes, and for another half hour we'd traded Miss Mason's mimeographed pages back and forth.

"Damning stuff for Sweetie Fairbairn, I suppose, if this got out," Leo said, looking up from what young Rosemary Taylor called *Hunting Will Slater*.

He read the key paragraphs aloud. "*Will Slater leaned forward over the edge of the roof. Down below the children yelled in excited exuberance. One by one, Will began unleashing his balloons into the Wedgwood blue sky, sending them soaring weightlessly, freely forever, into the cloudless heavens. Transfixed, the boys and girls laughed excitedly at the soaring balloons and at Will Slater, the leaning man handsome even under clown makeup. For from below, he seemed to be leaning almost straight out from the edge of the building, godlike, weightless, and so manly. Samantha laughed, too, excitedly and exuberantly, caught up in the adoring enthusiasm of all the children around her, their zest for laughter and excitement. And her love.*"

He took a sip of Coke and went on. "*Suddenly something changed. Will Slater's voice, that wonderful, deep baritone, called out, higher in pitch than Samantha had ever heard it. The children sensed it immediately, and stopped their laughing. It was a note of fear from the throat of a man who was never afraid. And then, as she watched, the man she loved, handsome and youthful, the safety rope that Will Slater had always told her he checked and double-checked, let go suddenly, and Will Slater fell over the edge of the building, his safety rope now horribly unhooked, to the certainty of death below."*

He set the sheets on the table. "Thus he became a dead hunk of a clown. A tragic romance, written by a high school girl."

"A script for murder, written by a high school girl."

"Used to kill a clown and then prime Sweetie for black-mail?" He arched his formidable eyebrows. "That's too extreme. Why risk an actual murder? Koros or Darlene could have simply mailed a copy of the old manuscript to Sweetie, along with a specific threat: 'Pay up or we'll kill a clown. We'll send your old story to the newspapers and you'll be blamed.' Sweetie could have just laughed. A story she wrote in high school doesn't make her a murderer forty years later. No, Dek; it's too extreme."

"By then, things were extreme. Koros had already killed Andrew Fill, to make sure the fall guy for the embezzled Symposium's half million could never return to tell the truth about who really took the money. I think his initial plan was simply to bury Fill in the muck behind the dunes, let people think Fill absconded with the dough."

"Then big greed reared its head? Koros changed his mind, decided to keep the corpse around to get Sweetie blamed for Fill's murder?"

"Why settle for a measly half million when there were so many millions more? The corpse could be useful, if it were found with something of Sweetie's—perhaps just a hair—on it. Sweetie had motive: Fill had shamed her, em-bezzled from her. Getting the money back wasn't enough for her; he had to die. The police would buy it."

"So he kept Fill in the trailer, ripening, while he for-mulated a new plan?"

"Koros remembered his old high school love, and how closely the two sisters had resembled each other. He looked her up, and found her ripening, too, on the old Taylor homestead—and he saw, with extreme delight, that Dar-lene could still pass for her sister, at least from a distance. She must have gone nuts when he told her Rosemary was living the good life in Chicago."

"And one of them remembered this?" He tapped the pages on the table.

"Getting blamed for the clown's death, on top of Fill's, could be enough to get Sweetie to run. Koros could then loot her estate at his leisure. It was perfect. Sweetie would be blamed for taking all her millions with her." I picked the title page from the pile of papers and held it up. "Even the pseudonym Rosemary used—"

"'*Hunting Will Slater*,'" Leo read aloud, "'by Sweetie Rose.' Sweetie Rose, Sweetie Fairbairn. I don't know. It still sounds too circumstantial."

"Combine it with Stitts's widow recalling it was a woman in a limo who'd hired her husband to dance on a roof, and throw in the killing of her guard. Who wouldn't run, Leo?"

"Why didn't Sweetie hire some high-priced lawyer to pick apart what still seems like an awfully circumstan-tial case?"

"I think there's more I can't see."

"Why did Koros tell Sweetie that Fill had begun to pay back the embezzled funds?"

"That's easier to understand. Koros needed time to ready his new plan."

"To keep anyone from nosing around?"

"Sweetie could have changed her mind about not prosecuting Fill. Or maybe one of Sweetie's fellow board members at the Symposium might want an investigation. Saying that Fill was paying back shut all that down. The money was being repaid, end of story."

"Shut you down, too, after you wandered into the investigation?"

"I was an added complication, a sign that Sweetie wasn't about to run. That's when they killed the guard, to put more pressure on her. They figured right, and they figured wrong. They sent Sweetie running, all right, but she gave away her money on her way out of the penthouse. In an instant, everything got ruined. Also, there was still Andrew, spoiling in his trailer, yet to be found. Sooner or later, someone in that trailer park was going to get a whiff, and maybe things wouldn't point only to Sweetie Fairbairn. They had to cover their tracks. That's why they torched the trailer, to destroy Fill's body."

"A murder they tried to get you blamed for."

"They must have worried I'd learned too much. It was either Koros or Darlene who tipped the police that I'd be coming to the trailer."

"They had to shift gears, though, when you didn't show."

"One of them was watching me in Rivertown while the other was in Indiana, torching Fill's trailer. When they realized I wasn't going to come to the trailer, Koros backpedaled, calling me to pretend surprise that Fill's trailer had been burned, and apologizing for insisting that I go."

"OK," he said. "I'll buy that Koros was an evil mastermind, that he found Darlene rotting in that shack with no electricity, no indoor plumbing, doing nighttime cleanup at the high school for subsistence wages, and stoked a big rage by telling her Sweetie was living rich in Chicago. I'll buy that it was Darlene in the limo, trying to be seen as Sweetie hiring the clown. I'll buy that it was Darlene or Koros who cut the rope, and who later killed Sweetie's guard, to induce Sweetie to run, and run fast."

He paused and offered up a smile.

I recognized the smile. He'd found a fatal flaw in my reasoning. He usually did.

"Nice and tidy thinking," I ventured, but it was tentative.

His eyes glistened; his smile widened. "I'll even accept that it was a sixty-year-old woman you were wrestling with, on that dirt farm."

"We weren't wrestling. She'd shot me. Once I was down, she mostly kicked." I arched my own eyebrows, desperate for a retort. "Surely you know older ladies who can kick?"

"Alas, yes," he said, unfazed, "but that is irrelevant to the major flaws in your reasoning." His straw slurped at the bottom of his cup. "Most likely, Sweetie Fairbairn is simply running from her own crimes. She could have killed Andrew Fill for stealing money from her. She could have killed the clown, to act out her own long-festering fantasies. She could have killed her guard because he'd heard something about her misdeeds. She could have killed George Koros because he got wise to what she'd done. As for her giving away all that money, on her way out the door, remember that no one yet knows how much money she had in the first place. For all the money she gave away, she might have taken plenty more with her, to use to stay invisible for the rest of her life."

He leaned across the table as much as his height would allow. "That said, do you know what really knocks the hell out of your theories?"

I knew what he was going to say. I had considered it as I lay in the hospital.

I spoke fast, to beat him to it. "Koros and Darlene didn't

have to kill all those people to get at Sweetie's money. They only had to kill one person: Sweetie Fairbairn herself. Darlene was Sweetie's closest surviving relative. Even with a will cutting her out, she could make claim against at least some of those millions."

He smiled and stood up, happy that I'd seen his logic, and helped me to my feet. We started toward the rental van.

I looked past him, at the high school kids circling each other at the front of the Would You? Boys, shaggy and scruffy, too cool to comb; girls, studiedly casual, too eager to not be eager. All of them were full of themselves, full to bursting, full of the night. It seemed like a thousand years since I'd felt a summer's evening that way—the heat, the musk, that special young lust for almost everything.

Then I saw the sheriff's cruiser, parked a bit too far down the block.

"We'll start for Chicago first thing in the morning?" Leo asked, still strutting brain-wise, as we got in the van.

I didn't answer. He drove us away in silence, enjoying his crafty refutation of my theories about Sweetie Fairbairn. I watched the outside mirror. After a mile I was sure.

"Sweetie Fairbairn was a philanthropist," I said. "She'd have had an ironclad will, leaving money only to those charities she believed in, not to some sister she hadn't had contact with in forty years."

He groaned.

"We're of interest here," I said.

"What are you talking about?"

"Those headlamps following us."

He checked the rearview.

"They belong to the sheriff's car that was parked down

the street from the Would You? Ellie Ball wants to know
what we're up to."

    "Which means?"

    "Tomorrow, we ask her why."

FORTY-EIGHT

THE NEXT MORNING, a sheriff's car was parked right in front of my door when I stepped out with thin, room-brewed coffee to smell the day.

"Mr. Elstrom?" the deputy asked, getting out. "The sheriff would like you to come to her office."

"Come, or be brought?"

He shrugged.

I said we'd be there in an hour, and went to knock on Leo's door.

"BEEN OUT TO the Taylor place recently?" Sheriff Ball asked as Leo and I sat down.

Her office had a glass-topped table, four chairs, and a window that looked out over a small parking lot. She'd decorated her walls with photos of uniformed officers. Some of the photos were old, yellowed with age.

"Yesterday evening," I said.

"Both of you?"

"Just me."

"In spite of just being shot, you felt well enough to drive?"

"Piece of cake."

"What were you doing out there?"

"Wondering, like you, if Darlene was around, and whether there was anything out there that might incriminate her in her sister's disappearance."

"And in your shooting?"

"That's of some interest, yes."

"You smashed your way in?" She turned to look at the purple iridescence, spotted here and there with shell shapes of orange and light blue that, today, was Leo.

Leo smiled.

"Nah," I said. "I just pushed some cardboard back from an unlocked window."

"You then crawled through, twisting your wounded side?" Ellie Ball asked.

"I'm agile, even in pain."

She let the lie go. "What did you find?"

"Gossip magazines and adult clothes—and kid clothes, for someone twelve, fourteen years old."

"Alta's clothes," she said.

"After all this time?"

"I've heard Darlene never got over her sister's death," she said.

"The mother died earlier that year?"

"January or February. Though she was only a senior in high school, Darlene was quite fierce about keeping the family together. She and Rosemary, a junior at the time, alternated days, so one would always be home with Alta."

"What was wrong with Alta, that she needed constant care?"

"She was a high-tempered girl, small physically, but very intelligent. Did well in the primary grades. Then, around junior high, she contracted a virus that apparently caused some damage. They pulled her out of school, and that was the last folks saw of Alta Taylor."

"After high school, Darlene worked janitorial at night?"

"Also so she could be home days, to take care of Alta."

"What did the mother die of?"

"Fell and hit her head. Where's this going, Mr. Elstom?"

"Why did you pull us in here?"

"I'm always interested in trespassers."

"There was an autopsy for the mother?"

"Why would you ask that?"

"Isn't an autopsy expected, in cases of questionable death?"

"Nothing about it was questionable. Darlene saw her mother fall. Besides, we were poor rural, then as now. No money laying around for an unnecessary autopsy."

"No autopsy for Alta, either?"

"No mystery there, either."

"What did she die of?"

"Sickness of some sort."

"A lot happened to the Taylor family that year," I said. "The mother dies early, in January or February. In April, a gas station attendant gets killed—"

Sheriff Ellie Ball's eyes flashed. "Wait just a damned minute. How does that fit in?"

"Both Darlene and Rosemary were seen near the gas station that day."

"With Georgie Korozakis, riding around in his convertible. They were kids, out joyriding. Nothing more."

I went on. "Then Rosemary Taylor takes off, in June. Alta dies three months later. Tell me, Sheriff, have things happened that fast to other families in Hadlow?"

Ellie Ball glared at me, said nothing.

"What did Alta Taylor die of, exactly?"

"You're asking whether Darlene murdered Alta?" Her words came out exaggeratedly slow, weighted with fury.

"Whether Darlene murdered the mother, as well." I tried to smile sweetly.

She stared at me for a long moment. Then she reached for her phone and tapped three digits.

"This is Ellie. Could you look up Alta Taylor's cause of death?" We waited in silence for longer than we should have until, finally, the sheriff nodded and hung up. "Alta Taylor died September third."

"Cause of death?"

"She's working on that."

For a time, Leo's insanely purple shirt was the loudest thing in the room. Then Sheriff Ball said, "I might have to call you later with Alta's cause of death."

I stayed in my chair. "Why did Georgie Korozakis get sent away from here, with just a few weeks to go before he was to graduate?"

"Sent away? I heard his parents thought he'd have a better chance at a good college if he graduated from a higher-ranked high school than ours."

She'd spoken in a monotone, as if she were offering up the words from practice rather than any new consideration of my question. Ellie Ball had already thought about Georgie Korozakis, plenty. Like she'd already thought about the Taylor girls, plenty. About how they all fit into that incident at the gas station.

She glanced at the telephone, as though willing it to ring with the answer about Alta's cause of death. Then she looked at her watch. "My, the time," she said.

"Tell me it's time to let me go through the file on that gas station robbery, so we can be on our way."

She raised her eyes, and surprised me. She smiled.

FORTY-NINE

SHE WALKED US to a small interview room. The walls were the green of dying plants; the chairs, the pink of red plastic rubbed too many times with bleach. The ceiling tiles were yellowed, from when smoking had been allowed. I might have confessed to something, too, if I were interrogated in that room.

She came back five minutes later and set a worn large brown tie-envelope down on the scarred wood table. "It won't take you long to see there's nothing in here," she said.

"There were never any suspects, never any leads?"

"The gas station was kind of remote."

"Or never any real investigation?"

"The sheriff did what he could."

"You know this?"

"You'd do well to remember I'm being hospitable, Mr. Elstrom. I could make you file a Freedom of Information Act request for this material. Given your social skills, processing your request could take weeks, months, or perhaps years." She left the room.

"You found a nerve," Leo said.

I lowered myself onto a chair and undid the tie on the envelope.

Ellie Ball's assessment of its contents had been right. There wasn't much inside, just three thin manila file folders, a blue wire-bound notebook, and a plastic sandwich bag containing two spent bullets.

"Though the station is old, we should assume this room is bugged," I said, reaching for the notebook.

Leo laughed, taking a file. "Nuts. I was hoping to say something of interest."

The notebook contained Sheriff Roy Lishkin's record of his investigation. The first page summarized the details, such as they were: Willie Dean, age twenty-four, had worked at the gas station, three miles east of Hadlow, for two years. According to the station's owner, Willie was a reliable employee, a competent mechanic, and as honest as the day was long. The station's owner could not imagine Willie having an enemy, certainly not one who would shoot him in the stomach.

Lishkin's notes made it clear, based on the fact that the station's cash drawer, beneath the counter, had been emptied, that Willie had been killed in the course of a robbery.

The next two pages recorded his interviews with eight individuals who lived out near the gas station. Five had not seen or heard anything. Each of the remaining three remembered seeing the Taylor girls breezing along with Georgie Korozakis in his convertible, the day of the robbery. All three had known the Taylor girls since they were little. None thought it remotely possible they could have had anything to do with the murder.

"You'll find the files interesting," Leo said when I looked up after reading Lishkin's notes a second time. He pushed them across, and I gave him the notebook.

A name had been written on each of the three file folders: George Korozakis, Darlene Taylor, Rosemary Taylor. Inside each file was a single piece of paper, apparently torn from the wire-bound notebook. Lishkin had intended to maintain a light surveillance on each of the three teenagers in the weeks and months following the killing.

Georgie Korozakis's sheet began with the date he left

Hadlow, four days after the killing. According to Lishkin, he enrolled in a prep school in Connecticut. Georgie
graduated two months later, remained in Connecticut for
the summer to work as a clerk in a Woolworth's, and left
at the end of August for a college I'd never heard of in Ver-
mont. No entries followed after that.

Darlene Taylor's sheet had only one entry: "Remains
in Hadlow."

Rosemary's lone entry was just a few words longer:
"Left Hadlow, following graduation, June 12. Per SP, no
DL. Whereabouts unknown."

"'Per SP, no DL,'" I read aloud, from Rosemary's sheet.
"Per state police, no driver's license. He tried to track her,
but couldn't."

"She must have started using aliases right away," Leo
said.

"Not only did Sheriff Lishkin not have other suspects,
it looks like he gave up tracking Georgie, and trying to
find Rosemary, by the end of August."

"Certainly by September third?"

"The day Alta died."

His twin caterpillar eyebrows rose up on his bald head.
"Not very tenacious, the sheriff?"

"Or by then, he'd learned all he needed to know."

I picked up the small bag containing the two spent bullets. They looked almost pristine, not at all damaged by
their business of killing a young gas station attendant.

For a moment, I let my fingers linger on the wire tie
that kept the little bag closed, wondering if anyone would
notice whether one of the two was missing. I pushed the
thought away; I had no gun to compare them to. I put
the bag, its contents intact, back into the large envelope
with the wire-bound notebook and the three thin manila
file folders.

That the Taylor girls and Georgie Korozakis had been near the gas station quite naturally interested Sheriff Lishkin.

What interested me was all the blank pages in the wire-bound notebook…and why Sheriff Lishkin hadn't used one of them to write down the one question that must have haunted him to his death.

FIFTY

"SHERIFF LISHKIN HAD DOUBTS," I said from Ellie Ball's office doorway.

She leaned back in her chair, trying to paste surprise onto her face. It was a faint fit. "Doubts?"

"Have you gone through that material?"

"There's nothing there."

"That says plenty. Perhaps Sheriff Lishkin's search naturally narrowed to the link between Darlene Taylor and Georgie Korozakis and the gas station robbery—"

"And Rosemary?" she interrupted. "Don't forget your Sweetie Fairbairn."

"He quit investigating by September. That's too soon to give up on a murder investigation."

"Roy Lishkin was a very thorough man. He did what he could, I'm sure."

"It must have driven him crazy, not solving that case," I said.

"What more do you want, Mr. Elstrom?"

Leo moved past me, gently dropped the file envelope on her desk, and retreated back out of the office.

"Who's still around that can tell me about Alta Taylor?"

"Alta?" She almost spat the word.

"Who knew her? Who knew what kind of shape she was in?"

"That can't matter now."

"It does when you can't tell me what killed her. Was

she able to get around by herself? Could she feed herself? Could she bathe? Why did Darlene and Rosemary have to alternate staying home, so that one was always with Alta?"

"Alta's been dead over forty years. No one's left who knew her, except Darlene, and Rosemary."

"A doctor, then, or a dentist. Someone had to know her."

"They're all dead. Her mother kept her home. Alta died unknown, save to her mother and the girls."

"You'll never find Alta's death certificate, will you?"

"You'll be leaving now, Mr. Elstrom," Ellie Ball said.

"There is still the matter of my getting shot, Sheriff. How is your investigation of that coming?"

"We're on the lookout."

"Like Roy Lishkin was on the lookout?"

"We're looking for anything that might suggest your wounds were not self-inflicted."

"You know I didn't shoot myself." I turned to leave, slowly, so as not to excite the holes in my side, but one last fury had to get out. "What happened to the gun?"

Her eyes looked past me, at the purple that was Leo, but I had the feeling she wasn't seeing him, either. Something had changed on her face.

"The gun?" she asked, in a flat voice. "Plinnit took test fires back to Chicago, to compare with what they extracted from Georgie Korozakis. We've kept the gun here."

"I meant the gun that killed the gas station attendant."

"I don't know," she said.

"It was never found?"

"I just told you: I don't know what happened to that gun."

"There's no mention of it in Sheriff Lishkin's notes. That's odd."

She tried a smile. "Take care, Mr. Elstrom."

"WHAT JUST HAPPENED?" Leo said, checking the rearview mirror for perhaps the tenth time. He'd not said a word until we were a solid mile from Ellie Ball's office.

"Which part?"

"For openers, beating on her about the gun used in the gas station robbery. That it was never recovered is understandable. The killer would have taken it with him."

"I think it's resurfaced."

"Where?"

"In my hand."

He hit the brakes, skidding to a stop, and turned to look at me. "You think that was the same gun that killed that gas station guy?"

"Just a hunch. That little bag in the evidence envelope contained two spent rounds. They looked like the one Plinnit said was dug out of my side."

"How many times have you examined a bullet?"

"None."

"How many times have you even held a bullet?"

"You mean other than the two in the plastic bag, just a few minutes ago?"

"Don't obfuscate."

"That would be none, as well."

"So much for your ballistic expertise."

"It's an intriguing possibility."

"That the same gun did the gas station attendant, Koros, and you? Darlene Taylor was the shooter, all three times?"

"Why not?"

"Again I ask: She's the one who shot you and then beat you up? That sixty-year-old woman?"

"Maybe she hired someone to shoot me."

"Please, don't tell me it could have been the handyman who occasionally came around to help with chores. Like, 'Joe, today I want you to do some weeding, mend the screen door, shoot Dek Elstrom, and then beat him half to death'?"

"What's the bigger question, Leo?"

He paused, thinking. It always drove him nuts when I saw something he missed.

"Is it real big?" he asked, watching my face carefully.

"Huge."

"Damn it. I know it has to do with Alta Taylor," he said, "because you pressed the sheriff so hard about her." Finally, he scratched his cheek, a sure sign of surrender. "Shit, I don't know."

"One of the Taylor girls, either Darlene or Rosemary, always made sure to be home with Alta."

"Ellie Ball made a point of that."

"Alta couldn't be left home alone."

Leo's pale face darkened with what I hoped was embarrassment. "Roy Lishkin interviewed three people who saw both Darlene and Rosemary out driving with Georgie Korozakis that day. Both girls shouldn't have been out driving. One of them was supposed to be home with Alta."

"Bingo."

"Unless Alta was in the car that day," he said fast, so I couldn't.

"Bingo."

"But nobody saw Alta. And why was that, the uncharacteristically slowed but inevitably brilliant Brumsky asks? Because they kept her down, in the backseat of that car. And why was that, the brilliant Brumsky considers, at warp speed? Because she was the shooter," he yelled, "and the two girls figured that if no one could place her at the scene, she'd never get charged."

I nodded, because saying "Bingo" again would have been superfluous.

FIFTY-ONE

"Isn't it a little early for indigestion?" I said. Leo had slowed, approaching the Would You?

"It's almost eleven o'clock, it's the only restaurant in town, and we need sustenance for our journey back to Rivertown."

By now we were creeping forward at five miles an hour.

"Look at that couple enjoying their chicken baskets," he said. "They're in their late seventies, at least. Do they look indigested?"

They didn't, but they did look like something else: history.

"Turn in," I said.

Leo swung a fast right into the parking lot, slammed on the brakes, and was scuttling to the order window before I could change my mind. I eased out and hobbled over to the couple.

"Arthritis?" the woman asked, noticing the gingerly way I'd walked up.

"Hunting," I said. "You folks live here long?"

"Seventy-four years for me, seventy-five for Clarence."

"Seventy-four for me, same as you," Clarence corrected. "I'm only three months older."

"I was rounding," she said.

"Both of you would remember the Taylor girls, then," I said.

"Darlene and Rosemary, real lookers," Clarence said.

"Why would you want to know about them?" the wife asked.

"An insurance policy was taken out on the three of them, when they were children."

"Three of them?" the husband asked, looking confused.

"Alta, Clarence. Remember, there was Alta."

He nodded. "The one that never came to town."

"Darlene's still around," the wife said. "You can talk to her direct. Rosemary, though, took off when she was still in high school."

"So I was told," I said. "Following some trouble at a gas station, or something."

"Nothing to do with those girls," Clarence said.

"A killing," his wife said to me. "Folks saw them nearby."

"There was a boy with them," Clarence said.

"Folks wondered if the sheriff thought the three were involved," the woman said.

"Baloney," said Clarence.

"Darlene and Rosemary were real nice girls," said the wife.

"That boy left the summer after the incident," Clarence said. "What the hell was his name?"

"He didn't wait until summer, Clarence. He left just a few days afterward."

"What the hell was his name?" the old man repeated.

"Georgie Korozakis," his wife said. "He was sweet on the older girl, Darlene."

"Did you think the Taylor girls were involved?" I asked.

"Only busybodies thought that. Nobody with a brain," Clarence said.

"How about Sheriff Lishkin?"

"He didn't, either," Clarence said.

"You go ask Ellie about that," his wife said to him. "You go ask her how he spent every day that summer."

"Ellie Ball, the sheriff?" I asked.

"Ellie Ball, Roy Lishkin's granddaughter," Clarence said. He looked at his wife. "I'll bet she'll say Roy never believed those girls had anything to do with that shooting. As for that boy…"

"Georgie Korozakis," his wife said.

"Moonstuck on Darlene was all he was ever guilty of. She was a looker, that Darlene."

"An attractive girl," his wife agreed.

"Great body. Damned shame, the way those looks got washed away, living out on that farm," Clarence said. "Even cutting it back, the way they had to after Herb took off, it's still too much ground to take care of for one woman."

"Still, they were better off with him gone," the wife said.

"Wasn't much of a farmer," Clarence said. "Drinking, now, that Herb could do. And he got mean doing it, every time."

"Obsessed, he was, for a time," the woman said.

"Herb Taylor?" her husband asked.

"No; Roy Lishkin. Like I said, he was out to the Taylor place every day that summer," the wife said.

"What about Alta?" I asked.

Clarence pursed his lips at the recollection. "No one ever did see much of her, after she grew some. Not that folks had cause to drive out that way. Only thing out there was the Taylor farm, and it had gone to hell even when Herb was around. No one ever went visiting there."

"Except Roy Lishkin," his wife said, "every day, the summer of the incident."

"Baloney. You heard all that from people who knew nothing," Clarence said.

"No one saw Alta that summer?" I asked.

"No one had seen Alta for any summer, in quite some time," said the wife. "The girl had some sort of breakdown, and Martha kept her sheltered. Some said her condition was the last straw for Herb, chased him away."

"Martha had a condition?" her husband asked.

"Alta," his wife corrected.

"Alta died, that same summer," I said.

"Scarlet fever," said Clarence.

"Pneumonia," said his wife.

"Scarlet fever," the old man said again.

"Best I can say: Go see Darlene," the old woman said.

"Baloney business, all of that," Clarence said.

I left them to their facts and went to where Leo was sitting.

"What are those?" I pointed to the breaded clumps lying next to the chicken in the baskets he'd bought.

"Fried jalapeño cheese broccoli florets. Healthy."

"Healthy how?"

"Broccoli's good for you."

"Deep fried?"

"Broccoli's broccoli."

"What about the jalapeño part?"

"For the sinuses."

"Baloney," I said, because the word was still ringing in my head.

FIFTY-TWO

FIVE MINUTES AWAY from the Would You? Leo cracked wise in what he regarded as a great Humphrey Bogart voice, "We've picked up a tail." His Bogart was nervous.

I checked the outside mirror, saw the cruiser. "One of Ellie Ball's deputies again, and not too subtle this time. He's staying close."

"*Por qué*?" he asked, slipping his Bogart into Spanish for no appropriate reason.

"Intimidation. We're not being tailed; we're being nudged, out of town."

"*Por qué*?"

"Because she's afraid we'll stumble into something she does not want stumbled into."

"What could that be?" he asked, blessedly back in English.

"The incident. I think it figures into everything I'm looking at."

"What are you looking at?"

"I have no idea. I want to see if any of the people who saw the kids out by the gas station are still around."

"Then we're out of here?"

"Anxious to get home, are you?"

"Ambivalent. Ma will be dancing the night away with her friends. On the other hand, if I stay up here with you, I might get shot."

"It's a toss-up," I agreed.

AT THE MOTEL, I gave Leo the names I'd written down at the sheriff's office, and he headed off to question the desk clerk. I went into my room, to the phone book and directory assistance.

It was short work. Only one of the three names had a working phone number.

Before I could call, Leo came back with the news that the desk clerk didn't recognize any of the names. He also brought back three Cokes. He gave one to me, went out to pass another in through the deputy's car window, and leaned against the cruiser's door. Leo is like that; he makes people comfortable with him in seconds. In no time at all, he'd have the cop talking about something that might be useful.

The only active name answered her phone on the third ring. I played it straight up, introducing myself and saying I was interested in the gas station killing forty years before.

"My word, I thought that was talked out years ago," she said.

"I'm particularly interested in your conversation with Sheriff Lishkin."

"You mean when I said I'd have no part trying to railroad the poor Taylor girls and that Georgie Korozakis?"

"Actually, his notes didn't mention that."

"Good thing, but he wasn't going to do that, anyway. He was just looking for the truth."

"You're sure you saw both Darlene and Rosemary in the car?"

"They were good kids, the Taylor girls. You'd see Darlene everywhere with that boy, Georgie, racing around in his convertible, laughing, sucking up life. Big car, it was. A Chevy Impala, white, I think. My husband always wanted one just like it."

"There were three of them, out that afternoon?"

"That's what made it memorable, that and their faces. Every other time, it was just Georgie and Darlene, all the time laughing, stuck on each other."

"Their faces?"

"They looked scared to death. Georgie's hands were tight on the wheel; I could see his knuckles popping, white as the color of his car. Darlene was up front, riding shotgun like always, but there was no giggling for her, not that day. She was staring straight ahead like she was willing the road to swallow her up. Rosemary was in back, hunching down toward one side, like she was holding at her stomach. Sick, maybe."

"You told Lishkin they were driving away from the gas station?"

"All I said was they were out this way, and they were not exhibiting their normal demeanors." She breathed heavily into the phone. "No way those kids did any killing. I didn't know Georgie—he'd only been in town for a short time—but everyone said he was real mild-mannered, no burden to his teachers or to his parents."

"Darlene?"

"Sweet-tempered girl full of spunk, an asset to her mother and that disadvantaged sister."

"That was Alta?"

"A problem child. Mean-spirited, some said. Not similar in appearance or demeanor to the older two girls. People wondered about that."

"Wondered, how?"

"There was talk. Always is, in a town like this. Martha Taylor and Roy Lishkin went way back, to when they were kids. People wondered about Alta, is all."

"There was talk that Alta was Roy Lishkin's child?"

"Bothersome talk, was all it ever amounted to. Gossip. Some said that's why Herb left, that he found out. Theory was, that's why the child acted up, that she'd found out as well. Martha used to bring her to town, but then she quit that when the girl started getting out of hand." She stopped for a minute, then continued in a softer voice. "Darlene was an angel. She helped her mother with everything around that dust patch of a farm, and that included Alta. When Martha died, Darlene took charge right off, taking care of the two other girls."

"What about Rosemary?"

"Always dreaming, head in a book. Even wrote one. A thin thing, but the folks at the high school made a fuss over it. There were mimeographs of it all over town. I tried reading it. Tacky thing, as I recall. I don't expect she was of much help around that place, spending her time on such foolishness. Didn't surprise me one bit when she took off, leaving Darlene stuck to that place and that poor, agitated child."

"Did you think those kids happened upon the scene at that gas station?"

"Meaning, did they stop for gas, see the blood and the body? Then take off, because they were scared they'd be blamed? Bless you, sir."

"For what?"

"For seeing that as a distinct possibility. That's just what I told Roy Lishkin."

"He didn't write that down, either. He just noted it was a robbery gone bad."

"You must be mistaken. He knew it was no robbery, gone bad or otherwise."

"There was cash in the register?"

"There was no register, just a drawer beneath the counter. Anyone going out there to rob the place would have robbed the place, know what I mean?"

"You're sure the cash drawer wasn't emptied?"

"Darned sure. My cousin's husband owned that gas station. He told Sheriff Roy he lost a fine young employee, but no cash."

Roy Lishkin's notes were wrong, saying that the cash drawer was empty.

Deliberately wrong.

FIFTY-THREE

AN EXPLOSION, SET off on my way out of town, seemed appropriate.

I called Ellie Ball. "Have you located Alta Taylor's death certificate?"

"It was pneumonia, just like I said."

"You found the death certificate?"

"You're leaving?"

"How can I find Alta's birth certificate?"

"Why would you want that?"

"There are rumors about her paternity."

It was enough. She hung up.

I stepped outside. Leo was still leaning against the cruiser, but the radio inside was crackling to life and the deputy was powering up his window as he reached for his handset. I assumed Ellie Ball was calling to find out what I was up to.

"Let's pack up, we're leaving," I said to Leo.

"Leaving, like in finally going back to Rivertown leaving?"

"I've become something of an issue here," I said, with what I thought was refined understatement.

"We're still driving?"

I nodded again. Leo's smile showed relief. Driving would take longer, and that was a real incentive when one's septuagenarian mother and her friends were seeking youth in one's basement.

"See you in twenty minutes," he said and darted into his room.

He came out in ten, grinning when he saw me already sitting in the minivan's passenger's seat. He threw his bag in, didn't bother to ask if I needed a loan to pay for my room, and beat it down to the office to settle both our bills.

Five minutes later, we were headed toward Hadlow with the deputy tailgating a hundred feet behind, murmuring into his handset.

"I have news," Leo said.

"So do I. You won't believe—"

Leo held up his hand for silence. "Mine is huge."

"Then continue."

"Apparently, reclusive Darlene isn't so lonely after all. Our friend behind us"—he cocked a thumb back at the trailing deputy—"normally works the overnight shift. He said he sees Darlene driving around in the middle of the night, always with the same guy."

"She works the night shift at the high school. She's sharing a ride home with a co-worker."

"Nope," he said. "They're out much later than that. Three or four in the morning is when he sees them. The guy is doing the driving, though they're always in her old Taurus. It's quite the joke at the sheriff's station, her sneaking around, doing some guy on the back roads, and in her own car, no less. They're hoping to spot the car weaving or something, so they can pull them over and find out who the mystery man is."

"Mystery man," I said.

"Don't you see? That must have been who took you down behind the Taylor place. You owe me, big-time. No one can say you got rolled and shot by a sixty-year-old woman. I've found you a stronger culprit—a *manly* culprit."

I supposed it was a relief, though it needed more thought.

We came to Hadlow, and Ralph's defrocked Shell station, and there was no time to talk more.

Ralph said he'd been mulling on it for the past two days, and decided he'd need nine hundred dollars to flatbed the rental Chevy to Swifty's at the Minneapolis airport.

I opened my wallet, fanned it open to show I was removing all the bills, and counted them out. I had six hundred and forty-one of George Koros's dollars left. I took out the change from my pants pocket. Seventy-eight cents.

I put all of it in my left hand. "For the balance of the truck rental and the tow to Minneapolis."

"What about the charge for me to be driven out to pick up my truck you abandoned?"

"Included," I said.

He looked at me, looked at the money, and after the briefest of hesitations took it all. He must have decided it would be a lifetime until another guy who couldn't navigate around a truckload of pigs came along.

"Now your news," Leo said, as we headed toward the interstate.

I told him what the woman who'd seen Georgie and two Taylor girls speeding away from the gas station had said.

"From that you inferred that Sheriff Lishkin covered up the whole thing, because Alta was his daughter?" he said.

"He must have figured out what went down at the gas station fairly quickly—either by Alta's behavior or Darlene telling him—and that it wasn't a premeditated crime. Somebody, likely Georgie, brought along a pistol, maybe for target shooting. Alta got her hands on it and blew away the gas station attendant. Lishkin had witnesses who'd seen Georgie and the two girls out in the car, near the gas station. He also knew Alta was never left alone. He had to figure Alta was along for the ride, even though no one saw her in the car. The best Lishkin could do, afterward, was drive out to the Taylor place every chance he got, to make sure Darlene had Alta under control. Then Alta died."

"Of pneumonia, or of Darlene?"

"The answer to that is buried at the cemetery, along with the DNA that would tell us whose daughter Alta really was."

"So there was nothing left for Lishkin to do but make up a scant little report about the crime being a robbery, and file it away to confuse anybody who might read it years later?"

"Alta was dead. Case closed."

We came to an intersection, empty of everything except weeds. I told Leo to pull over. Behind us, the deputy sheriff stopped. I could only imagine what he was saying on his radio.

"What's up?" Leo asked.

I pointed across the street, at a barren plot of ground partially covered by stained concrete slabs. "That's where the gas station was," I said. "Seems like there ought to be a marker, something to signify that lives got lost there, one day in April, over forty years ago."

"Lives? More than one?"

"An arts symposium director, a clown, a bodyguard."

"And a man who was once a boy with a convertible?"

"Absolutely. He was a victim, too."

"At least now we know what he had on Sweetie Fairbairn."

"Accomplice murder. Technically, she was guilty, like Darlene, like Koros himself. A retainer and rent on a fancy office must have seemed like a bargain to keep Koros's mouth shut."

I leaned forward to look up. Chief Winnemac's immense shoulders and head loomed high above the tree line.

His back was toward us; he was looking toward the river. My head felt immense and heavy and full of concrete, too. I leaned back on the seat. I was exhausted by the weight of all the ruin that had been set into motion at that corner.

Leo put the car into gear. "You're done?" he asked, as he started us away.

"By now, Plinnit has put out alerts on Darlene for the murder of George Koros. It's in his hands."

"What about the murder of that kid at the gas station, back in the day?"

"I'm not going to say anything about that. Too many lies, too old to unravel."

"Ellie Ball's not going to bring it up, not with her grandfather so involved," he said.

We came to the interstate. "Cop's gone," Leo said, checking the rearview as we drove onto the entrance ramp.

It felt good, riding on something solid, going in a certain direction.

I looked back. The tall pines along the road had already obscured where we'd just been.

I so wanted to believe that.

FIFTY-FOUR

My CELL PHONE woke me. I'd slept through half of Wisconsin.

"What's shaking?" Jenny Galecki asked.

"I'm headed back to Chicago."

"Wounded, I just heard."

"How did you hear?"

"Sources. How are you feeling?"

Her source had to be Plinnit. I didn't know whether he was using her or she was using him. Most likely it was mutual.

"I'm feeling sharp enough to fence with you about releasing what I know," I said cleverly.

"Everybody's got the story: The police are looking for Darlene Taylor, Sweetie Fairbairn's sister. Apparently, she's no longer at home in Minnesota. I'm guessing you probably knew that first."

Definitely her source was Plinnit.

"How's your investigation into Rivertown citizen boards?" I asked, to change the subject.

"I'll drop by tonight, after the broadcast."

She gave me enough time to say no to that. When I didn't, she said, "Until tonight," and hung up.

"Where does she fit?" Leo asked the instant I clicked off.

"Who?" I asked, sounding dumber than an iron bar.

"The lovely, ambitious, and potentially man-eating Jennifer Gale? Or, as you now call her, Jenny."

"Beats me, Leo."

He looked over at me. "No, I meant how does she fit into this case?"

"She's already cultivated Plinnit as a source, though she said everyone in Chicago now knows the police are looking for Darlene."

"You going to tell her about the gas station?"

"I won't have to. The old story will blow wide open when the press digs into Darlene's background. Young Rosemary's presence in that car, at that gas station, will come with it."

"It would be tough to prove anything about that," he said.

"I'll bet that's not what Darlene and Koros passed on. I'll bet they got word to her that they could alibi each other, and make Sweetie the shooter."

"Another reason to run?"

"On top of being blamed for everything else? I'd have run, too."

We fell silent then, each of us content to watch the white road-dividing stripes slip under the front of the minivan. I imagined he was ready, like me, to let everything we'd learned slip away as well.

After a half hour, though, Leo had a question. "Did you deliberately forget to swing by and return Rosemary's manuscript to that retired lady?"

"What I heard," I said, "was those mimeographs were all over town, back in the day. If none survived, other than the one Koros must have had, and the one I forgot to return, well…" He couldn't see me smiling because, by now, it was dark.

"Isn't that suppression of evidence?" he asked, in his most sanctimonious voice. "After all, that manuscript could incriminate your client."

"Damn," I said, thinking of matches and a small fire.

I slept, on and off, for the next hours as we drove south through Wisconsin. Sometime around Rockford, Illinois, I remember waking up, and Leo asking if I was sure I could negotiate the turret by myself. He said he'd be happy to stay over.

I told him all I needed was Ho Hos, and I had plenty of those.

I didn't tell him that Jennifer Gale had said she'd stop by.

IT WAS TEN thirty when we got to Rivertown. As we turned off Thompson Avenue, Leo said he'd drive to the airport the next day to turn in the minivan and get my Jeep. I told him I felt well enough to drive the Jeep now. He told me no one should ever feel well enough to drive my Jeep. There was logic to that. I gave him my keys.

He stopped the van halfway through the turn to the turret and turned on the high beams. The headlamps lit up the corner of the spit of land, and the turret beyond.

"Jenny's Prius," I said, of the car parked in front of the turret. "She said she was going to——"

"No. This side of the turret, back toward the river."

I saw it, something small and shiny, glinting in the headlamps, lying on the ground. He eased the van forward.

"My blue plastic tarp," I said. "It's supposed to be covering the ladders around back."

Leo stopped the van. "Look at the turret door."

Even from a distance, I could see the long scratches around the lock, fresh and white against the dark wood. They looked like claw marks made by an animal.

"Someone was anxious to pay me a visit," I said.

"Let's call the cops."

I looked at Jenny's Prius. "In a moment."

He pulled forward another twenty feet, angling the van to best shine the high beams on the tarp. I was just reaching for the door handle when his hand shot out and grabbed the back of my shirt collar.

"No," he said.

The shiny plastic hadn't been laid out flat on the ground. It was covering something. Something mounded.

I pushed his hand away, opened the door, and slid off the seat to stand on the ground. For a second, I teetered from the pain, and from what I knew, in my gut, was under the tarp.

"I'm calling the cops," Leo's voice said, from far away.

I headed for the tarp. There was no doubt what the shape was, covered up.

My right side was throbbing around the stitches. I moved slowly, suddenly in no hurry to see what was under that tarp.

I bent down, pulled back a corner.

I saw a woman's naked foot.

FIFTY-FIVE

A NEW PAIR of high bright headlamps angled onto me.

"Stop!" a cigarette-roughened voice yelled.

"I need to see." I tried to shout, but it hurt my side. I started toward the opposite end of the tarp. The head end.

"Hey, I was the one who called," Leo yelled.

"Damn it, step away!" Cigarette Voice called out.

Car doors slammed. Two long shadows came running up. A hard hand clamped the back of my neck.

"That's far enough," the second voice said, next to me. Rivertown uniforms, the cops Leo had called.

"Your hands," the cop with his hand on my neck said. "Show me your hands."

I turned toward him, hands out, so he could see they were empty.

"We're the ones who called," I said, dumbly mimicking Leo. It was all I could think to say.

The second cop's hand relaxed on my neck as the cigarette-voiced cop moved around the tarp. He knelt at the head end and pulled back the corner.

The body lay facedown, its hair white and colorless in the glare of the headlamps. It could have been blond.

For sure, it wasn't dark, it wasn't lustrous. It wasn't Jenny.

Air came into my lungs then, sweet and cool in the summer night.

"Female. Older. Dead," the kneeling cop said in his cigarette voice.

"Who is it?" Jenny said, behind us.

The cop's hand on my neck fell away. I turned with him. She stood ten feet back, a dark shape in the white glare of the headlights.

"You are?" Cigarette Voice asked, looking up.

"The reporter broad that's been rousting Mr. Derbil," the cop next to me said. "What are you doing here, lady?"

"I was driving by, and thought I'd take another look at city hall. Marvelous architecture. Spur-of-the-moment thing. Then I saw you come up."

Both of the uniforms must have recognized a lie, but they were smart enough to not antagonize her. She was the fire under one of their own, Elvis Derbil.

"There's no story for you here," the cop next to me said. "Please wait out by the street."

Another car pulled up. Jenny turned and started walking toward Leo. I took a step to join them.

"Not you. You stay," the kneeling cop said, standing up.

Two Rivertown detectives got out of the car and came over.

"Quite a party you guys are having," one of them said, staring at the shape beneath the tarp. He had whiskey on his breath, and a soft slur to his words. He'd been enjoying an evening of free fuel at one of the tonks along Thompson Avenue. "Who's the stiff?"

The smoker cop bent and pulled back the tarp.

I had to look for a number of seconds, to be sure.

"Darlene Taylor, I think," I heard myself say.

"You kill her?" one of the detectives, probably the sharpest, asked.

"Sure. Then I covered her up on my property so there would be no doubt, and called you guys to arrest me."

"Wiseass," Cigarette Voice said.

"You need to call Lieutenant Plinnit of the Chicago police," I said. "He's got a bulletin out on her."

"For what?"

"Call Plinnit. You're going to want to hand off this crime scene before an army of reporters gets here."

As though on cue, Jenny's Channel 8 News van rolled up and stopped. She must have called her station before she'd approached the tarp.

"You got a number for this Plinnit?" the detective asked quickly.

"Ms. Gale over there does," I said.

He walked back to the street.

Cigarette Voice covered up Darlene, and then nobody moved. We stood, the Rivertown uniforms and one detective and me, white as plaster statues in the headlamp beams shining on us from the street, while the other detective talked to Jenny.

The same bearded, burly cameraman I'd seen the day Elvis was arrested got out of the news van. The detectives glared at him.

I looked down at the ground. Almost everything I'd come to believe about Sweetie Fairbairn lay dead under the shiny blue tarp just inches from my feet.

Plinnit arrived, too quickly for him to be responding to the Rivertown detective's call. Jenny must have called him, too, after she'd called her newsroom.

Plinnit had brought a van and two evidence technicians from the Cook County Sheriff's Office. The evidence team looked at us, standing around the blue tarp, mucking up the crime scene, and told us to move away, fast.

As I walked toward the street, someone moving well behind the small throng of people caught my eye. I thought I recognized the man's skulking gait as Elvis Derbil's, but his being around city hall so close to midnight didn't make sense.

By now, Jenny had gone to talk with her cameraman. Perhaps pointedly, perhaps not, she wasn't looking anywhere near where I'd seen Elvis. I walked over to Leo.

"Did you see the face?" he asked.

"Darlene Taylor."

"Who does that leave?"

He'd asked it rhetorically. I didn't need to answer him. We both knew Sweetie Fairbairn was the only one left.

I stayed with Leo, well back of Plinnit's crew. I looked at the river, rippling silver in the moonlight, and at the turret, blindingly white in the glare of all the lights. I did not look at Jenny, now filming with her cameraman. I did not look at the people clustered around the corpse.

After a time, a technician stood up from the body. He and Plinnit came to the street, and found me.

"At least a day," the tech was saying to Plinnit. Then, to me, "The tarp has been here?"

"Yes, covering my ladders in back."

"We'll check it for prints," the tech said to Plinnit and walked away.

Plinnit turned to me. "Popped up in the thick of it again, I see."

"This is my home. I pop up every day here, usually before dawn."

"Your local detectives said you identified her as Darlene Taylor?"

"I believe I saw that woman coming out of George Koros's building. She startled me into thinking, for an instant, that she was Sweetie Fairbairn. The family resemblance was certainly there in those yearbook photos."

"What about behind her home in Hadlow? Didn't you see her there as well, when she allegedly assaulted you?"

"It was dark."

"It's motive. She shot you; you wanted revenge."

"I just got back from Hadlow. Ellie Ball had a deputy tail us to the county line. She can verify I couldn't have gotten back here in time to kill Darlene Taylor."

"How do you know when Darlene Taylor died?" he asked, but the enthusiasm was gone from his voice. No doubt I'd disappoint him by having an alibi once again.

"There's something else." I told him about the scratches on my front door.

Plinnit left us for a moment and came back with a uniformed officer and one of the evidence techs. We walked over to the door.

"You say the scratches are new?" Plinnit asked me, looking at the marks around the handle.

"Someone wanted in."

"Me, too, now," Plinnit said.

We waited for the crime scene technician to finish pressing some sort of tape on the lock for fingerprints. When he was done, Plinnit put on fresh gloves and pressed the thumb latch. The door swung open.

"You're sure you locked it?" Plinnit asked me.

"Yes."

I reached in past him to switch on the light, then moved aside to allow Plinnit and the uniformed officer to go in first. Finding a corpse alongside the turret had whetted my appetite for caution. Considering that the killer might now be inside my turret provoked outright fear.

Jenny and her cameraman had come up to the door. "Not you," Plinnit said to them. They stepped back onto the lawn.

"Charming," the lieutenant said, of the plastic conversational grouping I'd arranged around the table saw.

"Upstairs is better." Leo had followed us in. "The lawn chairs up there are webbed."

"You live here?" Plinnit asked him, ready to throw him out. "I hang around whenever Mr. Elstrom needs protection," Leo said.

Plinnit looked at me. I nodded. It was a laugh, but it could be true enough, for that night.

"What's out of place?" Plinnit asked.

"Everything looks as I left it."

Plinnit and the uniformed officer signaled for Leo and me to wait on the first floor as they walked the second floor, and then the ones above that.

Some time later, they came down.

"We checked all five floors. Nobody's here now," Plinnit said.

The uniformed officer went out the front door. Plinnit, Leo, and I went up to the kitchen. They sat on the webbed chairs, and I made coffee as though I needed to get wired.

"Interesting coffee," Plinnit said, grimacing at his first sip.

"I get it on sale where Leo gets his shirts."

Plinnit raised his cup in a sort of vague salute to Leo. "Tastes as good as your shirts look, certainly."

"Thank you," Leo said.

"How soon will you make a positive identification?" I asked.

"I'll send photos up to your friend Ellie Ball. She'll find someone who knew Darlene Taylor."

He looked at me and waited.

After I said nothing, he said, "Any thoughts, Elstrom?"

I took another sip, pretending to consider. "You may be right. This coffee is really lousy."

"Sweetie Fairbairn," he said.

"I'm not seeing motive, Lieutenant."

"Best motive of all: self-defense," he said. "Darlene Taylor and George Koros came at Sweetie Fairbairn to bleed her dry, and they killed her guard to do it. Ms. Fairbairn could have killed Darlene to keep from getting killed herself."

"OK," I said.

"Or not OK, if Sweetie Fairbairn hired you to kill her sister," he said.

"Ask Ellie Ball, when you send up the pictures. I couldn't have been down here when Darlene was killed."

"Again: You know her time of death, how?"

"For now, I'm supposing she's been dead for some hours this evening. If I'm wrong, I've got a problem."

"Why would Sweetie Fairbairn want to lay this on you, Elstrom?"

"She didn't shoot me in Hadlow, Lieutenant. Besides, I can't see her coming out here to dump Darlene's body."

"Unless it was to set you up even more. Listen to me. You're over your head. Loyalty's OK, but you're dumb to stick to it longer than you should. You're being set up, and now you've really got something to worry about."

"I'm betting your ME will show Darlene has been dead for hours, and Mr. Brumsky will tell you I've been with him, driving down from Minnesota."

Plinnit looked over at Leo.

"Once we've negotiated an appropriate fee," Leo said to him.

Plinnit scowled. "You're missing the point," he said to me. "Big things are being dumped around you: Sweetie Fairbairn's guard, Koros and his murder weapon, now the dead Darlene Taylor. That's groundwork, Elstrom. You're being set up for a grand finale, the last big event."

"More coffee?" I asked.

"Someone didn't slip your lock for nothing, Elstrom."

"I'll look around, but I doubt anything's missing."

"He has nothing worth taking," Leo added, to be help-ful.

"Damn it, Elstrom," Plinnit said.

I knew, but I played anyway. "OK, Lieutenant; what's the next big event?"

"Your corpse, to end the show."

FIFTY-SIX

So IT WENT, until three in the morning. Plinnit never got satisfied with what I was telling him. I didn't, either. I could not figure why Darlene Taylor turned up dead behind my turret, or who could benefit from that.

Surely, after Leo and Plinnit helped me walk all five floors, I could not figure out how anyone had benefited from breaking into the turret. Nothing was missing.

Finally, we walked out into the night. By then, the Channel 8 News van and Plinnit's crew had left. Oddly, Jenny's Prius was still there, but she might have hitched a ride back to the studio with her cameraman, to process footage, or whatever newspeople did in the middle of the night.

A dark sedan also remained, parked back toward Thompson Avenue.

"My people, to keep you alive, at least until I can verify Darlene Taylor's time of death," Plinnit said.

Leo pulled a parking ticket from his windshield. "Damn it," he said.

Plinnit had gotten one, too. "What the hell is this?" he asked, ripping it from beneath his windshield wiper.

I pointed up at the sign. "Parking citation. You've parked in a fire lane."

"I'm a police officer."

"I'll call you tomorrow," Leo said.

"I'll call you tomorrow, too," Plinnit said, "after I learn your alibi doesn't check out."

"I have questions," Jenny Galecki said, stepping into the front door light.

For a moment, nobody spoke.

"Damn it to hell," Plinnit said, getting into his car and slamming his door.

"For sure, I'm calling you tomorrow," Leo said, getting into the minivan.

"This will lead our first news, at noon," Jenny said to me, the only one left.

"You've been alone out here, in the dark, all this time?"

"My cameraman just took off. We had officer Fittle to protect us."

"Still, it was dangerous to wait. Whoever killed Darlene Taylor also tried to break in here."

"Gone now?"

I nodded. "Coffee?"

"Sounds perfect."

Upstairs, my hand shook as I went to the sink to rinse the carafe. I took that to mean I'd had too much coffee and nothing more.

I set down the carafe. "We could have wine and Ho Hos instead," I said.

"Even lovelier." She sat at the plywood table.

I've had the same gallon of Gallo for years. It used to be a temptation, which is why I still keep it. It is covered with dust, untouched since the day I moved into the turret. I accept victory wherever I can find it.

I poured us each two inches of the wine, opened a fresh pack of Ho Hos, and told her everything I knew that wouldn't point at Sweetie Fairbairn.

"Not much of that is usable," she said when I'd finished.

"Everything I told you about Alta Taylor and what I think was her role at the gas station killing is conjecture.

Same with Darlene's role in the murders of Stitts, the guard, Andrew Fill, and George Koros."

"For now, I'll go with the discovery as a Jane Doe next to your turret—by you, Dek; you're the one who discovered the body. With you comes mention of Sweetie Fairbairn, because you were the one who discovered her kneeling over the guard's body. It's all part of the story."

"I understand."

"When Plinnit gets solid identification that it was Darlene, the link between her, Koros, and Sweetie Fairbairn will come out. Then the story will go back to Hadlow, and to you getting shot up there." She tried to smile. "You'll be the talk of the town."

"No Amanda," I said.

"Not from me, but somebody will connect her to you." Then she said, "Are you tired?"

"I slept half the way back from Minnesota, then drank coffee here for at least two hours. Now I've had wine and Ho Hos. I'm rested, caffeinated, and sugared enough to be awake for a month."

She held out her glass for another two inches of wine. "How about building a small fire in one of your big fireplaces?"

I could have paused to think, but I didn't. I picked up some wood scraps from the pile in the kitchen, and we walked across the hall to my office. I opened the flue for the very first time since I'd lived there. The wood was dry, and caught almost immediately. I wheeled the tilting red desk chair over to the electric blue La-Z-Boy, and for a time we sat, mismatched people in mismatched chairs, silently watching the fire.

"I can't believe you've never had a fire here," Jenny said, taking a sip of wine. "Not on the first floor, either."

"I have on the third floor."

"Ah, the bedroom." She grinned.

I added more wood.

"I'm sorry," she said. "I should have wondered whether you were saving this fireplace to use on a more special occasion."

"Finding a corpse behind one's home isn't special enough?"

"I meant with Ms...."

It was a nice thought. Although it was probably no longer relevant. I shook my head.

She looked into the fire. "My husband and I had a small cabin. Not much more than a shack, in Kentucky. No electricity, no running water, but it had a big fireplace." She turned to me and smiled. "We had great heat, he and I. We used it all the time."

"Your husband," I said.

"Afghanistan. We knew it was a gamble, but he—no, we—" She stopped, and looked away, back toward the fire, but not before I'd seen the tears in her eyes.

"No," she said, after a moment. "It was I who wanted the national stage. He wanted it because I wanted it. He got a job as an independent, got sent to Afghanistan. Road bomb."

She set down her plastic cup, still staring into the fire. After a time, she fell asleep.

I watched her, I watched the fire. Then I covered her with a blanket as she slept in my ridiculous blue chair and went upstairs to try to sleep.

FIFTY-SEVEN

I OUGHT TO have slept soundly, for eventually the coffee, the wine, the Ho Hos, and even the nerves should have worn off.

I ought to have slept soundly, for Plinnit had left behind two plainclothes officers in a dark Buick sedan, to watch the door.

I ought to have slept soundly, for I was tired, even though Jenny Galecki, a woman I liked to think I admired because I didn't want to call it anything else, was sleeping in my La-Z-Boy, just one lone, warmer floor below.

I ought to have slept, but I didn't, because I couldn't think who was left to kill Darlene Taylor, nor why she'd been dropped alongside the turret, nor why the killer had needed to get inside. It should have been enough for Darlene's murderer to drop her corpse and leave.

Unless, as Plinnit said, Darlene's killer also wanted to kill me.

I thrashed with all of it until eight in the morning, and then I got up, shaved closer than usual, and came down in better clothes than I ever wore around the turret.

She was gone. She'd left a note. "Good wine. Good fire. Great Ho Hos. J."

It was just as well. I went into the kitchen and made a pot of the marginally splendid Discount Den coffee. I wanted to take a cup up to the roof, to look at the town, but I couldn't figure out how to negotiate the ladders with my wounded side. I thought about going down to the bench by the river, to watch the flotsam bob in the water, but I'd be on view to Plinnit's plainclothesmen—and, perhaps, to whoever had left Darlene Taylor dead in my yard.

I looked out the window. No press vans had yet arrived. Jenny and Plinnit must have reached an accommodation. Apparently, Plinnit was keeping a lid on the discovery of the corpse until noon, when Jenny was set to broadcast it to the world.

I took the coffee into my office, eased aboard the La-Z-Boy, and watched the rising sun brighten the beiges, browns, and yellows of the curved block walls.

The sunlight had reached the card table I use as a desk. The table is old, something I found in someone else's trash. It is covered with a nubby gray sort of plastic that never looks good, no matter how the sun moves across it.

Something sparkled there, caught by the sun. I craned my neck to see. It was my letter opener, a cheap stainless steel thing. It lay by itself, on the center of the table. It shouldn't have been by itself.

I knew then what was gone. I knew what Darlene's killer had taken.

It was the small ring of Sweetie's keys that I'd picked up so mindlessly from the carpet the day I'd found her kneeling over the dead guard. The keys I'd never told Plinnit I'd found. The keys I'd used to get in to take another look around Sweetie's penthouse.

Only one person could have known I might even have had those keys.

The person who'd dropped them. The person who'd run away.

Sweetie Fairbairn.

FIFTY-EIGHT

THOUGH SHE COULDN'T have gotten much sleep, Jenny Galecki looked every bit a fresh, rested Jennifer Gale that afternoon. Her report led the noon broadcast, beginning with a very short video of several men leaning over the shiny blue tarp. Featured prominently in the center of the frame was me, mouth agape. I looked like someone who'd been thrown off a bus.

She reported that the dead woman had not yet been identified, but since the body had been found at the home of Vlodek Elstrom, the associate of Sweetie Fairbairn's who'd discovered her murdered bodyguard, police suspected the newest killing was also linked to Ms. Fairbairn's disappearance.

She did not say that any of that was sure to renew police interest in me as a suspect.

I called Leo and asked him to drive me to get the Jeep, pronto.

"You're not going to believe what's happening," he said.

"Jennifer Gale, on the news. I saw."

"No, I mean Ma."

"She all right?"

"She's still redecorating. As for you coming along to get the Jeep, forget it. Endora's much better company. We're leaving now."

"I insist."

"Possession is nine-tenths of the law. You gave me your keys last night, remember?"

There was no arguing with that. The day had become a game of movable keys. I told him to hurry up.

I called Plinnit's cell phone. It went right to voice mail. I left him a message, asking him to call me. Then I called his precinct.

"He's off for the long weekend," a woman, young-voiced, said.

It took me a minute to remember it was the Fourth of July. "I have to talk to him."

"He's off for the long weekend, Mr. Elstrom," she said again, this time testily. "Can someone else help you?"

"Plinnit has the background."

"He's off for—"

I stopped her third swing. "Tell Plinnit that I'm going to break into a crime scene, and maybe risk getting killed. He'll never be able to put me behind bars if I'm dead." I did not mention that Sweetie's keys were missing. It would only unnecessarily irritate him.

"Are you crazy?" the young-voiced woman asked.

"Have a great day," I said, and hung up.

Plinnit called in five minutes. "Did your sleepover end badly?"

I told him I wanted another look around Sweetie Fairbairn's penthouse.

"You want me to call the Wilbur Wright, say it's OK for you to go in?"

"Yes."

"To look for what?"

"Anything that might tell me where Sweetie Fairbairn is."

"Why now?"

"What?" I asked, confused.

"Why call now for my permission to enter Sweeetie Fairbairn's penthouse? Last time, you marched in there

alone, brazenly unlocked the elevator using keys you no
doubt merely overlooked giving to us, and rode up like
you owned the place."

I started to sputter, summoning indignation, but he cut
me off. "That video camera in the lobby we talked about,
the one that had you entering the penthouse the day Robert
Norton was killed? We can play you a more recent tape,
showing you coming back, using the keys you're pretending to be confused about, the ones that have Sweetie Fairbairn's initials on them."

"The concierge," I managed.

"Of course the concierge," he said, laughing. "He called
us as soon as you went up."

"Why didn't you come for me?"

"I had a man in the lobby by the time you came down.
He advised that you looked too stupid to be bringing anything out with you. I concurred, telling him you're too
stupid to be a killer as well."

"Thank you," I said stupidly. Then, "The keys are missing."

"That's why your visitor broke in last night?"

"I don't know."

"Tell me what else you haven't yet told me, Elstrom."

I told him about the manuscript Sweetie Fairbairn had
written in high school, and how that was meant to point
to Sweetie as having murdered James Stitts.

"Darlene Taylor and George Koros came at her quite
deliberately," I said. "They wanted her to run, and to stay
gone, so they could be thorough, and steal every nickel
she had."

I stopped then, wondering if I should tell him about the
gas station incident, and a too-fast investigation by Sheriff
Roy Lishkin, who may have been Alta's father. I decided

anything Plinnit learned about that he could get from Ellie Ball. Or from the press.

"It was Darlene under that tarp?" I asked.

"Ellie Ball confirmed it from the photo I sent her."

"Now, about my getting into Sweetie's penthouse…?"

"You still haven't told me what you hope to find."

"Whatever Darlene's killer was looking for at my place."

"Which is?"

"Some clue to where Sweetie Fairbairn ran."

"You think Darlene's killer left your turret with Sweetie's keys, and used them to get into her penthouse?"

"It's worth a look."

He stopped to think, then said, "I can't put civilians in jeopardy."

"Put a man at the Wilbur Wright, maybe even up in Sweetie's penthouse. Call the manager, or the concierge, tell him to let me in."

"How's that help me?"

"I find Sweetie, you get answers, and cooler air on the back of your neck."

"How about whatever you find you turn over to me, and I'll get my own answers from Sweetie Fairbairn?"

"I might have issues with that."

He sighed. "First I'll tell the officers I've got watching you that you're deranged. Then I'll think. Then maybe I'll call you back."

LEO PULLED THE Jeep onto the lawn an hour later. Endora had followed in the Porsche, with the top down.

"Care to come up for coffee?" I called out the second-floor window. I wanted company. I'd been counting minutes, waiting for Plinnit to call.

"You made fresh?" Leo asked, getting into the passenger's seat of his Porsche.

"I can make fresh."

"With different beans and a different pot and different water?"

"We could have Ho Hos, too."

"Jeep key's under the mat," he said, "though I can't imagine anyone stealing it."

Endora called up to add that they had plans. Obviously, Leo had poisoned her mind about my coffee.

They took off, in love with each other and, apparently, good coffee.

Across the spit of land, the dark blue Buick had been replaced by a maroon Chevrolet Impala.

More minutes, and then more hours, dragged. Then, two hours before dusk, Plinnit called and said I could go to the Wilbur Wright.

FIFTY-NINE

THE EISENHOWER EXPRESSWAY was jammed with cars jammed with people headed downtown, for beers and wienies and fireworks at the beach. My shot right side started its own fireworks early, throbbing as soon as I began working the Jeep's gears. By the time I got to Damen Avenue, the few miles of shifting from first gear to second and back to first again had enraged my side into a full fury. I got off the expressway and pulled over. The bandage around my chest was still dry, but the pain was telling me there were no long-term guarantees.

I started threading north on the side streets, but it was no better. I got stopped at almost every intersection by slow-moving clusters of people toting lawn chairs, blankets, and red coolers that looked like little white-topped coffins. Each time, I patted my shirt, feeling for wet. Each time, I heard Plinnit's voice, "Because you're dumb, Elstrom. You don't know when to give up."

Several times, I thought I spotted Plinnit's men in the maroon Chevy, trailing me. I tried to find comfort in having such protection, but with the thought came the reminder that someone might still be out there, hunting me.

Either way, it didn't matter for long. Plinnit's men finally disappeared for good into the traffic behind me, and I never did see them again.

I got to the Wilbur Wright at eight o'clock, gave my car key to the valet, and went inside.

The concierge frowned and told me the hotel manager

was shut in his office, and no, the concierge didn't know anything about any arrangement to let me into the penthouse elevator. I asked him if he might knock on the manager's door.

"Strange," the concierge said. "He almost never shuts his door. Let's wait a few moments, then I'll knock."

Someone else came up then, a hotel guest, and that returned the concierge to grinning. I walked over to the penthouse elevator, wondering if perhaps Plinnit's man had already arrived and had unlocked the door.

I pressed the button. The elevator doors slid open. Plinnit had called and instructed the manager to unlock them. I stepped in and rode up.

The empty, hushed foyer smelled faintly of old sweat. For an insane instant, it sent my mind darting back to Minnesota and the dark of a night behind Darlene Taylor's shack. The man who'd shot me had smelled of old sweat, too. I switched on a small lamp. It made the foyer brighter, but no warmer.

I called out to Plinnit's man. He didn't answer. He might have been down in the lobby, cadging a cup of coffee, or perhaps in with the manager, behind those closed doors.

I wondered if I should go back down to the lobby and try to find the cop. Sweetie's keys were in the hands of a killer; I didn't need to be banging around the penthouse without protection from one of Plinnit's men. Then I realized the cop would have cleared the place, to make sure no one was lurking.

I stepped into the living room, lit only by the sun starting its slow settle into the west. Horns had begun honking on the streets below, drivers caught in the Fourth of July crush, anxious to find a place to park before the fireworks began.

I wanted to hurry, too. I felt like an interloper, an intruder into a space that had settled itself to die. I looked into the darkness down the hall. I was going to only one room, her study. I wanted to look again at her papers and her pictures and her notes, to see if something might trigger a fast thought about where she might have run.

Even if I couldn't find a clue, I wanted a rationalization that I could give myself in the middle of the nights sure to come, that I'd searched absolutely and thoroughly, done every last thing I could to find her and warn her that whoever was coming for her might never give up.

That is, unless she'd been the one doing the killing.

Fifteen minutes was all it would take.

A car alarm went off down below, impatient, blaring eight times before it went silent. I started through the living room, careful to step around the large stain that had dried black in the middle of the room. I switched on a lamp, and another. Fifteen minutes and I could be gone.

Sweetie's study had one small window that faced west. The building next door, taller and sided with flat planes of dark glass, was a monstrous, hulking shape that blocked out everything behind it. I turned on her desk lamp and sat down.

The contents of the file drawers seemed to be in the same disarray as the last time. I pulled out a file, then another, fanning its contents before setting it on the floor. It was all charitable stuff, one folder per charity. Each file included initial request letters, her research notes and Internet investigations, and copies of her letters informing the applicants of her decision, up or down, concerning the possibility of a donation. Sweetie Fairbairn had spent thousands of hours giving hundreds of thousands of dollars away.

At some point, I thought to look at my watch. I'd lost track of the time. A whole hour had passed. I leaned back, to rub the strain from my eyes, and looked again at the calendar thumbtacked to the cheesy corkboard. June had changed to July, but there was no one now who needed to turn the page.

I remembered, then, the postcard that had been tacked next to the calendar. It showed an old covered bridge that had octagonal windows. The postcard was frayed, and riddled with punctures at the top, as though it had been taken down and studied a thousand times.

I'd liked Sweetie Fairbairn for her old postcard, like I'd liked her for her Velveeta, the night she'd brought me into her study. It showed she had roots in soil better than some fool penthouse atop an overpriced boutique hotel.

The postcard was gone. A souvenir hunter could have taken it, a cleaning person or a cop, someone wanting some last thing of Sweetie Fairbairn's.

Something stirred faintly, outside the room.

Then came the smell I'd first noticed when I'd first come in. Old sweat.

I looked toward the hall.

The barest hint of a leg was sticking out from the edge of the doorway.

SIXTY

I PUSHED AT the arms of the chair to get up. A hundred nails of pain knocked me right back. My right side had gone stiff in the hour I'd been sitting. I rocked myself forward and managed to stand.

What I'd ignored in my haste came clear in an instant.

A set of elevator doors that should have been guarded, because they were unlocked.

A cop, sent by Plinnit, who wasn't in the penthouse.

The faint, lingering smell of old sweat. That smell should have turned me around, sent me right back down in the elevator. Because I'd known that smell. It had been all over me, kicking, in back of a shack in Minnesota.

Now, he'd been heading toward the dark end of the hall. Down toward the emergency door, I hoped.

The foyer; I could get back to the foyer. Press the elevator button, step in, push another button. The doors would close. I'd be safe.

I moved slowly toward the door. One fast low dash past the kitchen, through the living room, and into the foyer, and I would be gone.

The desk lamp behind me went out. As did the glow down the hall, from the lamps I'd turned on in the living room and the foyer. Everything had gone dead.

The power had been cut, by the man who smelled of old sweat. He'd have a gun. Or a knife.

I froze. For an instant, my mind flirted with crazy hope: Surely they'd notice, downstairs. The glossy-headed con-

cierge, or the manager out now from behind his closed
door, would realize the power had been cut in the penthouse, and would ride the elevator up to investigate.

My gut twisted: No; they wouldn't notice. Sweetie's
penthouse had been dark since she ran. Same old, same
old; Sweetie's home was supposed to be dark.

I had to move. I edged into the hallway. To my left was
nothing but darkness, down the hall to the back of the
penthouse. To my right, through the hall, the living room
sofas and chairs were blurred dark shapes backlit by the
lights of the city. The man with a gun, or a knife, could
be anywhere, left or right.

Red, white, and blue stars flashed outside, lighting up
the living room. Car horns went off as another burst shot
into the sky.

It had to be now. Hugging my side, I ran through the
hall, past the kitchen, through the living room, and into
the darkness that was the foyer. I misjudged the distance,
slammed into the elevator doors. I found the button, pushed
it hard, and turned around to put my back against the door.
I'd kick at him if he came.

No sound came. No whine of a motor, no cinching of
a cable.

It couldn't be. I turned around, found the button again.
Still, no sound.

Elevators were always powered by a separate circuit.
Master switches didn't kill elevators; they killed lamps
and refrigerators and televisions. Not elevators, not ever.

Unless that damned Duggan, or some other well-meaning security son of a bitch, had installed an override that
would cut power to the elevator, a fail-safe to keep people out.

Something I'd never find, not in the dark.

I stabbed at the button again and again. Nothing.

I pulled out my cell phone. I couldn't call the front desk; I didn't know the number.

I could call 911. Except the man who smelled of old sweat would hear, and know exactly where I was. I'd be slashed or shot before the first police vehicle could get anywhere near the Wilbur Wright.

Another burst of fireworks exploded outside, these blue and orange. Chicago Bears colors, I thought to think, grasping for anything but fear.

Emergency stairs. Down the long hall. Where the bastard had to be.

Unless he was in the kitchen, or one of the bedrooms. Unless he was in the living room, only ten or twenty feet away, waiting for me to make my move.

The blues and the oranges faded and were gone. For one insane second, I wanted to shout into the darkness: There was nothing left, not for him, not for me. All that remained was old files and the dried stain of the last of the guard's life. Her money was gone. There was nothing to take, not anymore.

More fireworks would come, and I needed darkness now. I stepped gingerly out of the foyer, straining for the sound of a breath, the smell of old sweat.

A thousand yellow pinpoints fired in through the windows, lighting me up brighter than a man on fire.

I ran, clutching my side, past the kitchen on my right, the study on my left, toward the blackness at the end of the hallway. Behind me, the yellow pinpoints fell away. Again the hallway went black.

One step, another, and another, each one bringing me closer to the door, and to safety.

Something grabbed my foot, pitching me forward onto something large, bundled, and high. Pain, hot and deep, roiled up from the wound at my side. I reached out to fight the thing on the floor with my good left hand.

I touched fabric—and hair, wet, sticky hair, not moving.

Sweet Jesus, someone else was dead. Plinnit's man, had to be.

I rolled away, fighting the panic, bumped into the wall. Pushing against it, somehow I got myself up. Behind me, a new burst of fireworks exploded through the living room and into the hall, washing everything in red, soft and gauzy.

Ahead, a shape rose from a crouch.

He came low, with incredible speed, and knocked me back down onto the carpet. He had no weight; he was all fingers and long jagged nails, clawing at my skin, frantic to get at my face and neck. Lips, wet huge lips—an animal's lips—parted against the soft flesh under my chin as his teeth fought to bite into my flesh.

He smelled of oil and sweat. He smelled of death.

I pushed up with both arms. He fell back. My side ripped open, stitches tearing loose, wetting the side of my shirt with what was left of my blood.

Someone screamed. It was me.

He came again, a panther, slamming me against the wall with a soft grunt, tearing at me with his animal fingernails, biting my flesh, tasting my blood.

I kicked at the smell of him, and caught him somewhere soft. His breath came out, hot and foul, just above my head. I kicked again. He howled, and dropped onto me. I hugged his head, found a greasy ear, and tugged. He thrashed against me, working his wet jaw to find my skin with his teeth. I folded his ear into my fist, dug in my fingernails, and ripped.

He screamed.

Another starburst, blue and red and white, fired into

the hall. In the new light, I saw his eyes, wet and glinting. I knew those wet eyes.

From Hadlow…and from somewhere else.

I squeezed hard at his ear. He bucked and broke free.

The pinpoints of reds, blues, and whites began to melt.

He whimpered; his breathing, ragged, panting, was becoming fainter. He was crawling away. Suddenly, he stopped and, more horribly, started scratching at the floor. In the last light of the reds and the blues and the whites, I saw him. He was clawing at the floor, like a dog.

For what he must have dropped. His gun, or his knife.

My right side was soaked. The stitches had shredded my flesh and torn loose. I'd bleed out, if I didn't get out of there.

The last of the light dissolved. The hall went black.

Somehow I stood. Nothing mattered except getting out of there. I charged the sounds of his gasping lungs and scratching hands. I kicked blindly into the sick feral noises in the dark. My foot caught his underbelly. He howled, but still he scratched at the carpet. He'd kill me when he found it, the gun or the knife. I kicked him again. He grunted, a soft exhalation. Still he kept on, clawing at the carpet.

Fireworks, incredibly happy and purple and white, flashed from behind me, their colors soft on the grease of his hair.

He stopped his insane scratching, and with the agility of an animal, certainly nothing human, he rose. Instead of turning to charge me once again, though, he ran, a twisted wretched mass, toward the back of the penthouse. He hit something solid, there was a bang and then the squeal of unused hinges, and suddenly a long rectangle of yellow light flooded into the hallway. For an instant he teetered upright, a grotesque, misshapen figure frozen in the blinding light. Then he was gone. The door slammed shut. The hallway went dark once again.

I had nothing left. I leaned against the wall, wanting only air. My cheek was hot against the soft cool fibers of the silk wallpaper. I breathed, deeply. It was almost a miracle.

My right side was sodden. I couldn't stay. I had to get down for help.

I put a foot forward, and, leaning my left shoulder against the wall for support, I moved toward where the yellow light had been. Ten steps, nine, and I felt the cold metal of an emergency door. I pushed the panic bar and the door swung out.

Doubled over, clutching at my torn flesh, I hobbled into the harsh safe light at the top of the stairs.

SIXTY-ONE

THE EMT PROBED the sutures on my side one last time. Sounding shocked, he said they had held.

"What's all the mess, then?" Plinnit asked him.

"Some tearing, but mostly it's just leakage," the EMT said. He put a fresh bandage over the wound.

I lay on my good side, on a stretcher in the lobby of the Wilbur Wright. Well-dressed hotel guests and blue-dressed cops surrounded us. They'd just watched an ambulance take away the officer Plinnit had planted in the penthouse, the man I'd fallen over in the hall. Plinnit told me he'd been cut a dozen times and was unconscious, but was expected to live.

"Lucky for you, your assailant dropped the knife in the living room before he could then use it on you," he said.

"In the hall." I remembered how the man-animal had clawed at the carpet, frantic to find it.

"Just before the hall. We found the knife in the living room. By the blood trail, we ascertained my officer was stabbed there, then staggered down the hall, trying to get out the emergency door."

It made no sense. But I was alive.

The EMT bent and began wiping my left hand.

Plinnit froze. "What the hell are you doing?" he shouted.

"Cleaning away the blood," the EMT said. "This man used his left hand to protect himself. He might have infected cuts."

"His cuts can be tended later." Plinnit turned to a crime

scene technician. "Bag his hands until you can scrape underneath his fingernails."

An elderly lady, ten feet away, gasped at me, the killer.

The crime scene technician put paper bags onto my hands.

"I fell onto your man," I said. "Of course I'll have his blood and his skin on me."

"More interesting," Plinnit said, "we're checking my officer to see if he got your skin under his fingernails, trying to defend himself."

The elderly lady, now within six feet, gasped again.

"It was someone else, Lieutenant. Short and light, but powerful."

The elderly lady edged forward another foot. Her perfume got even closer, thick and cloying, like Elvis Derbil's coconut hairspray.

I gestured at her with my bagged hand. "I think it was her, Lieutenant."

"Asshole," the old woman said, shuffling away.

"Christ, Elstrom," Plinnit said.

"All right, Lieutenant," the EMT said. He pulled my sodden shirt down over my side and stepped back.

The crime scene technician came back with some sort of kit, removed the bags from my hands, and scraped underneath my fingernails.

When he was done, Plinnit said, "Let's go to the movies." He helped me sit up, and he and the EMT lowered me into a wheelchair. As Plinnit began pushing me into the manager's office, I saw that the wood trim around the door had been splintered.

"We had to break our way in. The day manager was unconscious, but you might already know that. Either you or someone else cracked his head open with a stapler."

The glossy-headed concierge was waiting inside the

office. He pressed the button on a small video monitor on top of a file cabinet. Plinnit stood behind me, exhaling on the top of my scalp, and we began to watch the images on the screen.

"This is our only camera," the concierge said. "It's old, not digital, and records only the people in the lobby." He fast-forwarded the security tape, turning the silver-haired, well-dressed people into jerk-legged comics, like actors in Charlie Chaplin movies.

"There," Plinnit said. "Our hero arrives."

The concierge slowed the tape. I came into the picture, pushed the elevator button, and got in.

"This is our ending point. If we can go backward from here?" Plinnit said to the concierge.

The concierge reversed the tape, again at high speed. First me, then the other Chaplin figures began speed-walking backward through the lobby, robots run amok.

"Stop there," I said, when he got to something dark, approaching the penthouse elevator.

The concierge slowed the video to regular speed. Someone in dark clothing was crossing the edge of the lobby.

"That's nobody," the concierge said, advancing the video frame by frame. "A homeless woman. She comes in to use the first-floor washroom. The manager throws her out."

"She comes in frequently?" Plinnit asked.

"Not frequently, but she's been in here before."

On the screen, the woman paused to look around, and inserted a key into the lock that opened Sweetie Fairbairn's elevator.

"Ah, hell," the concierge said.

"Freeze that," I said, as the woman again looked to the side.

The concierge pressed the remote.

Only her profile was visible, but it was enough.

"She look familiar, Lieutenant?" I asked.

Plinnit walked around my wheelchair, to stop two feet in front of the monitor. "Something about her…" He turned to look at me, confused.

"Call the Michigan City police. Ask them what they have on that person they brought in to give me a look-over."

"That guy who collected cans?" Plinnit leaned closer to the video screen. "You're saying that odd little man is masquerading now as a woman?"

"You tell me."

"But why?"

"I think he was the torch for Andrew Fill's trailer. He could have done Fill earlier, as well."

"You were there, weren't you?" he asked, his eyes hot on me. "You were in Indiana beforehand."

I said nothing.

"Michigan City called me. It took a long autopsy, but they found that Fill was dead way before the day of the fire," he said.

I could only shrug. Anything more might get me arrested for Fill's murder.

SIXTY-TWO

LEO CABBED DOWN to the Wilbur Wright, had the valet pull the Jeep around, and was behind the wheel when the concierge wheeled me out. Getting in, I saw a clumsy sort of wide strap that lay on the dashboard.

"You can wrap it around like a belt to hold your arm at your side, if movement is painful," he said.

"Where the hell would you get something that barbaric?"

"Barbaric? That was Pa's. From one of the times he fell, coming out of the tavern. He hurt his arm."

"I don't remember him hurting anything."

Leo grinned. "He never spilled a drop."

Instead of heading west toward the Eisenhower, he drove east, almost to the lake, and picked up Lake Shore Drive, southbound.

"No," I said.

He kept looking straight ahead.

"I mean it, Leo. Amanda and I, we're not, ah…" He was heading toward Amanda's condominium.

"I know you're 'not, ah…,' but from what you told me on the phone, some guy approximately half your size, and apparently a cross-dresser, keeps beating on you."

"I can take care of myself."

"Of course you can. If the killer cross-dresser comes for you again, I'm sure you can puncture his, or her, eardrums with your screaming." He slowed to turn in front of Amanda's high-rise.

She was waiting under the canopy, dressed in a glittering dark evening gown. Next to her stood one of the building's uniformed security people, and a younger, dark-haired man who had the unsmiling face of someone who was used to shooting people.

"I can do this myself," I said to Amanda after she opened my door. Getting out, I fell back against the Jeep. The young dark-haired man was at my side in an instant, and caught me before I fell to the ground.

"Of course," Amanda said, "and if you can't, Mike here"—she gestured at the unsmiling young man who was holding me up—"can throw you over his shoulders and carry you to the elevator like potatoes."

"Ex-cop?" I asked Mike.

"Current cop, moonlighting," he said.

Amanda reached to steady my elbow. "He does security for my father."

Leo had stayed behind the steering wheel.

"How are you getting back to Rivertown?" I asked him.

"In this."

"I'll be stuck here."

"In a high-security building, with extra security? Jeez, why didn't I think of that?" He grinned, ever a smartster. "Want the strap?" he asked, reaching for the top of the dashboard.

"See those stenciled initials: R.P.D.?"

He looked down at the strap now in his hands. "Yes?" he said, uncertainly.

"Rivertown Police Department. It's an old-time restraint, meant to cinch both arms tight to the torso. Supposed to work like a straitjacket, only it's cheaper. Your pa probably found it on the street, thought it might be a way of controlling you."

His grin got wider, and then he drove away.

Truth was, I didn't like the idea of being alone in the turret that evening, not with a killer loose, and me feeling like I'd dripped the last of my strength away in Sweetie Fairbairn's hallway. Then again, I didn't like the idea of being alone with Amanda, either, because I didn't want to think about what she'd been in the middle of, dressed as she was for a fine evening.

I said nothing more to any of them, and instead concentrated on beating Amanda and Mike to the lobby.

"I'm not helpless," I said, unnecessarily, as we rode up in the elevator.

"Darn tootin'," she said. "Thank you, Mike," when we got to her condominium.

"We'll be watching your door from the end of the hall, Miss Phelps."

"Thank you, Mike," I said.

"You're a real prize," he said.

"Darn tootin'," I said.

I understood the reason for her evening dress as soon as I hobbled into her apartment. She'd been hosting a dinner. The last time I'd been there, several months earlier, the living room was sparsely furnished, containing only a low magazine table and a long sofa facing a sort of gallery wall on which she'd hung her big Monet, small Picasso, and the other works that together were worth over eleven million dollars. We'd made love on that long sofa.

Now that sofa was gone. In the room was new furniture, lots of it. An elegant dining room table was set for eight, on which remained plates of half-eaten food. The place smelled of candles, hurriedly snuffed.

I resented all of it—that new decor, the fancy food, the candlelit conviviality that she could enjoy without me.

"I didn't want to come here," I said.

"So I would expect." She slid out one of the high-back

dining room chairs. When I sat down, she turned up the dining room lights and bent to peer at the scratches on my face.

"A bite?" she asked, lightly touching my neck.

"Yes."

"You look like you've just had sex with an angry woman," she said, trying to smile.

"Not yet." I could always be counted on for lame, inappropriate jokes.

She straightened up. "You can watch me clean up."

"What? No staff?"

She didn't know whether to take that as a barb or not. I wasn't even quite sure how I meant it. The Amanda I knew, or maybe the Amanda I used to know, didn't have nice furniture and elegant dinner parties, and she didn't wear fancy evening clothes. That Amanda, my Amanda, had been content with her old, long sofa, to sit and study her artworks and to make love, as though those were the only things that would ever matter.

"Actually, I did have people to serve, this evening," she said, evenly. "I asked them to leave, along with my guests, right after Leo called." She picked up two plates. Starting for the kitchen, she asked, "Does that count for anything?"

"I'm a jerk," I said.

"No lasting damage," she said, going into the kitchen. Then, in the arch, mock-bitch voice she used to use, whenever I'd tease her about owning eleven million bucks in art, she said, "Besides, the fish was quite overdone."

SIXTY-THREE

I WOKE UP to sunlight streaming in from the east, over Lake Michigan. Alone, in Amanda's guest room.

She'd put my terry robe on a chair close to the bed. That robe had survived our marriage, our estrangement, a divorce, and the beginnings of a reconciliation. I was not sure if it was surviving anything now, but I took comfort in the fact that it was still in Amanda's home. I slipped it on and crossed the room to the guest bath—with much grace and good balance, I thought, being that everything hurt.

She'd set my spare shaving kit on the vanity, another sign that my presence still survived in that otherwise redone high place. The mirror showed me a face that had been scratched raw, top to bottom, twenty times. Shaving would be out of the question for some days. I took a long, careful shower, and emerged, perfumed by her soap, robed in terry, and moved as jauntily as I could out to the living room.

Amanda and Leo were drinking coffee on the balcony. I split my face, lined as it was in red like some crazed map showing only north and south routes, into an idiot's smile.

"He returns from death," Leo said, through the screen. They both got up, made appropriate fussing gestures, and got me settled onto a chair. Amanda gave me the kind of brief peck on the top of the head one would give a visiting nephew with acne, and went inside to get me some coffee.

"I brought you clean clothes," Leo said. "Alas, they are identical to your other clothes: blue shirts and khaki pants. At least they are not bloody."

My raw face pulsed hot. "You've got to stay away from the turret. There's a killer out there, maybe still looking for me."

"A half-pint cross-dresser, smaller even than me?" he asked, laughing. "Fear not, because the turret for now is the safest place on the planet. I'd barely come to a stop in front of your abode, still mulling whether it would be better to treat you to a new image from the Discount Den"—he paused to finger the hem of the day's shirt, an atrocity of pink birds—"when, suddenly, two plainclothes cops were all over my Porsche."

"Rivertown?"

"They were Chicago cops, detailed there by Plinnit. I showed them my driver's license; they called Plinnit. He agreed I could go inside so long as one of the cops accompanied me. That guy came out shaking his head, asking over and over why your shower was hooked to a water heater with garden hoses. I told him that you'd not yet taken a course on plumbing."

"Plinnit's serious about finding who's out there, hunting." I was relieved.

"There's more. Plinnit assigned another Chicago copper, uniformed, to keep Amanda's security guys company down the hall. I think there's another one, in plainclothes, down in the lobby. You've got heavy protection, my friend."

Amanda came back with a carafe of coffee and a cup for me. "Leo and I have been sitting here, arguing over who would get the privilege of waking you, so you can call Plinnit to find out if he's learned who your man-lady enemy might be."

I took the cup Amanda filled, sipped at the coffee.

"Well?" she asked.

"I haven't finished my coffee yet," I said.

Leo shifted forward on his chair, as though to get up. "Amanda, can you help me throw him over this rail?"

"I doubt Plinnit's going to know," I said.

"They took scrapings from under your nails," Leo said. "They'll know soon."

"DNA tests are useful only if the person is already in their databases. You've been watching too much television."

"Oh no. I no longer go near television," Leo said quickly.

By the way Amanda laughed, Leo had made some sort of joke.

"What are you two talking about?" I looked back and forth, between them.

"You'll have to see for yourself, when you're better," Leo said.

"Lieutenant Plinnit is not going to get any answers about that man's identity?" Amanda asked me.

"He's somebody Darlene and Koros knew. He's probably an amateur, like them, and might not be local. For sure, the name he gave the Michigan City police won't check out."

"Amateur or not, he almost got you in Indiana," Leo said to me.

"What's he talking about?" Amanda asked me.

"My little murderous bike-riding friend had been dispatched to Indiana by Darlene and Koros, to hang out until Koros could get me to go there," I said.

"To torch the trailer with Dek near by," Leo said.

"Their plan was to get me blamed for Fill's death." I pulled the robe tighter. "We must have shocked the hell out of our little friend, when we showed up early."

"We? Who were you in Indiana with, Dek?" Amanda asked.

"Remember, that night you drove out to the turret? The news reporter who dropped me off—"

"Jennifer Gale? She keeps figuring into things, doesn't she?"

Like that silver-haired commodities fellow keeps figuring in, I wanted to say, but that was the kind of pettiness I'd slipped into, before Amanda and I divorced. I'd spent my energies looking for ways to accuse, instead of finding ways to fix.

I wasn't going there again. "I'm going to get dressed," I said, standing up.

"You don't need to explain," she said.

"I have to get on with things."

"What things?" Her eyes were intent. Her concern was real.

"Finding who's still hunting Sweetie Fairbairn."

"My God; that's for Plinnit. You're safest here."

I needed to leave. For her, and for me. I went inside, picked up the duffel Leo had brought, and got dressed. I didn't know what to do with the robe, so I left it on the bed, hoping Amanda would know.

SIXTY-FOUR

AFTER LEO DROPPED me off, I went down to sit on the bench by the Willahock. I would have preferred the isolation of my roof, for I had many nagging thoughts and I think better in thinner air, but the EMT who treated me at the Wilbur Wright told me any more trauma to my right side would put me in a hospital bed with an antibiotic drip for a week. Possessing some genius, I took that to mean I should not climb ladders.

There was also the matter of Plinnit's cops in a dark sedan. They'd followed us from Amanda's. This time, I was much more amenable to letting them keep an eye on me.

So for all sorts of good reasons, I walked my shot side down to the river, to watch the milk jugs tango with the oil containers.

I'd only been there for five minutes when I heard footsteps hurrying along the river walk, approaching the turret and city hall. No one ever walked along the river. When the developers lost interest in paying the grease it would take to develop Rivertown, the lizards lost interest in maintaining the asphalt walk. It had been a skin coat anyway, put down cheaply and hurriedly by some lizard relative with more greed than tar, and it had cracked and heaved in just a few weeks. Since I'd moved back to Rivertown, I'd never seen anyone use it.

I turned to look. Elvis Derbil, dressed in a black shirt and black, low-riding jeans, scuttled into view like one of the rats I occasionally saw moving in the bramble along-side the water.

His eyes widened when he saw me. The skin on the top of his head, already glistening from the midday heat, deepened now to an alarming red. He made a swallowing face, looked away, and hurried on toward city hall without saying a word.

These were strange days. Elvis never walked more than the few steps it took to get to one of the city's Cadillacs. Certainly, I'd never seen him walk along the river.

Except for today. Today, Elvis was walking—and sweating.

I watched him disappear past the untrimmed bushes, and let him disappear from my thoughts. Today, Elvis was irrelevant.

I looked across the water…and saw, in the sifting shadows and shapes the wind was making of the leaves, the shadow, too, of Darlene Taylor.

I wanted the simplicity of seeing her purely as a ruthless killer, but that image was being jostled by other imagined snapshots, firing fast inside my head.

I saw her on a fine autumn day, a pretty young girl with her blond hair blowing back, laughing beside Georgie Korozakis as they raced in his convertible down Main Street, Minnesota.

I saw her in late winter, after her mother died, in a shack stuck on frozen ground, determination already cutting lines into her pretty young face as she began alternating school days with Rosemary, so that someone would always be home with Alta.

I saw her in spring, on a lush afternoon gone suddenly, shockingly bad, watching horrified as Alta, crazed and screaming, fired a revolver at a gas station attendant, and sent the rest of their lives to hell.

Not quite, though. Georgie and Rosemary got to flee. Georgie, within days; Rosemary, in two short months. It was Darlene who had to remain, bound to Alta as surely as if by a chain.

I saw her that summer, struggling to remain impassive when Roy Lishkin stopped by time and again, probing, implying, maybe even saying outright he knew damned well there hadn't been just three of them in that convertible. That Alta had been along, too.

I saw her years later, after life had cut the last smile out of her face, when Georgie Korozakis called, out of the black of her past, to tell her that Rosemary, another golden girl but the one who had gotten away, had married rich and was living high above any trace of old grit in a penthouse in Chicago.

And I saw her dead beneath a blue tarp, not fifty feet from where I was now sitting.

I saw all that with clarity, in the leaves in the trees across the river. Yet when I tried to see Darlene snap, and perhaps kill Alta, or put a gun to the back of Georgie Korozakis's head so many years later, the shadows in the leaves across the river blurred. I could see her killing the clown, James Stitts. I could see her killing the guard, Robert Norton. But I couldn't see her killing those she'd once loved.

"You get attacked in Sweetie Fairbairn's penthouse and don't think to call me?" Jenny said, startling me into attempting a fast turn, which startled my newly tightened stitches into fast pain.

"It just happened last evening," I said, still turning but now more prudently.

"I know," she said, sitting beside me on the bench. She wore huge dark glasses, and the same baggy jeans and loose sweatshirt she'd worn the first time she'd come to the turret. An incognito outfit, I'd thought then. An incognito outfit, I thought now.

"You heard about me from Plinnit?"

"From a source," she said. "Actually, I heard several hours ago. You've not been answering your phone."

"So you drove out?"

"I was in the neighborhood. Our bike-riding friend attacked you?"

"I disturbed him in the penthouse. He must have been looking for a lead to Sweetie Fairbairn's whereabouts."

"Why? His employers, Koros and Darlene, are dead. Their target, Sweetie, gave away all her money, and has disappeared."

"Incriminating leftover loose ends, maybe. Otherwise, I don't know."

"There's nothing more you can do, Dek."

I looked down the river walk, toward city hall, then turned to smile at her. "You just missed Elvis Derbil."

Her face betrayed nothing behind the big sunglasses. "Besides your being beaten in her penthouse, there is other Sweetie Fairbairn news," she said. "You must promise it's not for broadcast, nor will you repeat it to anyone, nor will you even think about it unless you are in my presence—"

I tried on a grin. It hurt the road map lines on my face, but it felt good anyway. "Stop making fun of my conditions. Can't you see I'm wounded everywhere?"

She took off her sunglasses and rewarded me with mirthful eyes. "Sweetie never married Silas Fairbairn."

Across the river, the milk jugs made noise, seeming to bob faster at the news.

"What the hell?"

"I've checked everywhere, even hired a national service to double-check databases I've never heard of. Silas Fairbairn never married anyone."

I saw the future then, and I laughed, really laughed. It was worth the pain.

"Perfect," I finally managed.

"It will lead the news, along with you, tonight at six." She glowed with what was going to be a huge triumph. "They're moving me up to the dinner hour, because they're afraid someone else will find out about it."

"You're sure: Sweetie gave away millions that were never hers?"

"Just like I'm sure Silas will have more relatives than he ever knew. They'll hire lawyers to recover those millions. Can you imagine how that will look? Greedy relatives going after cancer foundations, children's hospitals, trying to take that money back? There will be no shame, not for the people after those millions."

"News at noon, six, and nine, for years to come," I said.

Her face turned serious. "Do you think Sweetie Fairbairn will ever be found, dead or alive?"

"I don't know."

"But you're done, aren't you?"

She was smart, the beautiful Jenny Galecki. More, though, she was intuitive. Enough lives had already been snuffed out. Hunting Sweetie Fairbairn, inadvertently leading others to her so that she might be prosecuted for a death long ago or those more recent, or even for giving away millions of dollars that weren't hers to give, required someone with more rectitude than I now had.

"I imagine," I said. Then, making a show of admiring her incognito outfit, I asked, "How's the salad oil investigation going?"

She smiled and put on the cover of her sunglasses. "There won't be anything on it for months."

"Or maybe for forever?"

Her head didn't move. Her sunglasses only reflected, nothing more.

"How about those citizens' committees, unknown to actual citizens, you said have been formed in Rivertown?" I asked.

"I'm sure I don't know what you mean," she said, but one pair of the faint lines at her mouth was working against a smile.

"I did tell you, did I not, that Elvis just passed by here, walking toward city hall?"

The pair of faint lines at her mouth gave way, just a little more.

It had been no coincidence that Jenny had appeared so soon after Elvis Derbil passed by, sneaking back to city hall. Elvis had become Jenny's newest source.

She stood up and kissed an uncut part of my cheek. "There'll be no sharing any of your conjecturing, on any subject, for the time being."

Her kiss stayed warm on my cheek, long after she'd driven away.

Strange days, indeed.

SIXTY-FIVE

I CALLED PLINNIT at five o'clock, because I'd gotten nowhere, spending the whole afternoon scratching at something by myself.

"Did you get your DNA results—?"

"My officer is recovering, thank you," he said, cutting me off.

"That's a relief. Did you get those DNA results?"

"The damned EMT cleaned your hands. If we get anything at all, it will be tomorrow, at the earliest. Why are you interested?"

"Naturally enough, I want to know who attacked me."

That wasn't true; I'd actually called to be certain of who had not attacked me. What had started as an idle theory around lunchtime had spent the afternoon blossoming into a bizarre almost-certainty, but I could tell Plinnit none of that.

"I'll call you when I hear," he said.

"You will?"

"Probably not." He hung up.

I called Leo. "I might need my Jeep." It was parked at his place.

"Let me look out the window… Nope, it's still there. I left the doors open, and the engine running. Someone could have taken it, I suppose, but if they did, they returned it."

He came by in fifteen minutes, but he was in his Porsche. "This way, you'll only have to drive home," he said, "and if you're willing, I can show you the basement and the television."

"Your basement? Does this have something to do with what you and Amanda were laughing about this morning, about you no longer going near television?"

"Amanda was laughing. Not me."

He wouldn't say anything more. Ten minutes later, when I'd gotten down his basement stairs, I understood.

Ma Brumsky's playroom had undergone more transformation. Plush dark red drapes covered the walls, and black tiles had been installed on the ceiling. Combined with the gold-flecked red floor I'd seen the last time, the basement had been turned into an adolescent boy's idea of a strip club.

"Exactly what goes on down here, Leo?"

"My, whatever do you mean?" he asked, feigning ignorance.

"The curtains, for starters." I walked over to touch one of the red drapes. It was made of thick velvet. "These go a long way to tart up the place."

"Ma's tastes keep evolving."

He picked up a remote control and pressed a button. The television and DVD player at the far end of the room came to life, and a significantly implanted blond woman, wearing either a black vinyl dress or black paint, appeared on the screen.

"…drive your man crazy." The blonde winked one heavily lashed eye. "Now, your first move."

She moved to a silver pole and gently began to sway against it. Soft music grew louder as she began to twirl, ever so slowly.

Leo moved to the wall and reached behind the curtain. Off went the bright yellow ceiling lights, on came a soft red glow that brought out the textures in the folds of the bloodred velvet curtains.

"Yes," the implanted woman on the video moaned. She reached behind her to undo a clasp. Definitely, it was a dress, and not paint.

"No," I said, my mind on fire with the image of Ma Brumsky and her friends, clinging to their poles, and heaving in sync with the blonde on TV.

Leo froze the image on the screen before the dress fell away.

I hugged my arms across my chest, palms at my sides. My stitches could not afford a convulsion. "Leo, they're in their late seventies…"

"Some are in their early eighties," he corrected.

I sidled up to hold on to a pole, for support. "They're widows."

"Not Mrs. Roshiska. Her husband is still breathing. With a tank, granted, but he's still breathing." He switched off the trick red lights, brought back the basic yellows.

Order was restored, at least until I noticed something half hidden under the base of the television.

"What's that?" I asked, of the spangled thing that peeked out.

He saw it, moved his foot quickly to push it all the way out of sight.

"They've got outfits, Leo?" My side was starting to pulse, as deep as Ma's exercise music.

"They quit quilting at the church. Now they make outfits."

"These outfits? Is that what you were hearing hitting your door the night I called to ask you to find a town with a statue of an Indian chief? I thought you were going nuts, but you were hearing outfits, being cast off?"

"No. I was giving in to my fears. They were merely

throwing towels. They sweat. Still, to be sure, I called Bernard—"

"Ma's friend's nephew, Bernard, the accountant? The genius that put you onto the idea of pole dancing?" I hugged my side. The stitches had been through enough.

"Bernard told me not to worry. Nothing's coming off."

"Because they can't work the clasps?"

"They use Velcro—" He stopped when he saw my face. It must have been crinkling with the pain.

"Ma says putting on beads is good," he hurried on. "Close sewing does wonders for finger dexterity, with the arthritis."

I had to look away, anywhere but at Leo or the torso frozen on the television screen. And was saved by the sight of my watch. It was almost six o'clock.

"Turn the television to Channel 8," I said, trying not to shout with relief.

He thumbed the remote, replacing the blonde with Channel 8's logo.

Jennifer Gale led the broadcast. "Vlodek Elstrom, onetime retainer of the missing Sweetie Fairbairn, was savagely beaten in Fairbairn's penthouse late yesterday. Sources say Elstrom was combing through Ms. Fairbairn's records in another attempt to determine what happened to the missing philanthropist when he was attacked. Officially, the police have offered no comment on the assault, but sources familiar with the investigation have revealed the possibility that Elstrom's attacker was caught on a video surveillance tape, and that an arrest may be forthcoming."

Jenny then dropped the bomb. "In a related development, this station has learned that the woman known as Sweetie Fairbairn was never married to Silas Fairbairn, the well-known industrialist long thought to be her husband.

This may be a huge setback for the many recipients of Ms. Fairbairn's philanthropy, because she might never have had the authority to disburse Mr. Fairbairn's millions. We'll have more on this developing story in the days to come."

Boom. She signed off.

"Holy smokes," Leo said.

"Jenny told me about it this morning."

"Sweetie Fairbairn sure wasn't what she appeared to be."

"Which leads me to an inspiration I've had." Before I could continue, the front door slammed upstairs, and the sound of heavy footfalls, accompanied by one small set of squeaking walker wheels, began crossing the floor above our heads.

Leo's eyes went wide. "They keep coming earlier, for the vodka, then for the sewing. Let me buy you dinner, Dek. Steaks, seafood, anything."

"Don't you want to hang around and learn to dance?"

"Hurry," he said, "before they start the long trek, coming down here." He moved ahead of me, to the stairs.

"I might want you to drive me back up to Hadlow," I said, not moving.

He turned to look at me, his eyes bright with anticipation. "Now? We could leave now?"

"Tomorrow afternoon. I've got to attend something in the morning."

"Tomorrow afternoon is real good," he said, going up the stairs, two at a time.

SIXTY-SIX

PLINNIT CALLED AT two the next day. By then, we'd already crossed into Wisconsin. Leo always went fast, no matter what he was driving.

"I didn't figure you'd call, Lieutenant," I said, loud enough to be heard above the clattering.

It was a lie. I most certainly was expecting his call.

"You on the road?" he asked.

"They're a mess." He didn't have to know which road I was on.

"I'm at your, ah…residence."

He must have gotten big news, if he wanted to jam it down my throat in person.

"I'm out, catching up on things," I said.

He paused, waiting for me to say where I was. When I didn't, he said, "I should wait for you?"

"I'll be home late."

"Say again? I can't hear, for the noise at your end."

"I said I'll be home late."

"If we're not in jail," Leo mouthed, next to me.

"I'd hoped we could talk in person." His disappointment sounded genuine.

"You stopped by with DNA results?"

"Only a partial profile, I'm afraid. Your hands were cleaned, of course, and there were nylon fibers under your nails as well, indicating you'd scratched at the carpet, removing more evidence." His voice brightened. "Still, there was enough to analyze."

He paused, savoring his moment. The pressure on him to find Sweetie Fairbairn must have increased tenfold since the news got out that her donating spree had been illegal. The recovery of millions of unlawfully disbursed dollars was at stake now, and Plinnit was destined to spend the rest of his career, and the years beyond, testifying in one claim trial after another.

Naturally enough, he'd want to share his pain. When the DNA results came back, he must have fairly flown out to the turret.

Except I had deprived him of satisfaction, once again. I wasn't at home.

"Who was the attacker, Lieutenant?"

"You already know."

"Let me guess: You compared what you got from my hands with the samples from Sweetie Fairbairn's toothbrush or hairbrush?"

"Sweetie Fairbairn was the one who attacked you, and you damned well know it."

Very carefully, I said nothing.

"She's playing a sick little game," Plinnit continued. "She cut my officer and attacked you. My only question is why you won't say that."

"You saw the hotel lobby video. The person who used the elevator key to the penthouse was not Sweetie Fairbairn."

"That can-collecting runt must have let her in through the emergency door. My gut tells me you're in this somehow, Elstrom. I'll be in touch," he said, hanging up.

"Plinnit's not satisfied," I said to Leo.

"The DNA was as you expected: Sweetie Fairbairn was the one who attacked you?"

"The profile was incomplete, but that's where it points."

"You might be right about this trip after all," he said,

"but I was wrong about taking this truck on the highway. I'm going deaf."

I'd been particular about what we needed. It couldn't be checked for mileage or traced, by receipt, back to either of us. That ruled out a rental. It couldn't be recognizable as belonging to either of us. That ruled out his Porsche and my Jeep. Finally, it had to haul a couple of long-handled things, which didn't rule out anything, but when I finished explaining all this to Leo, he nodded, smiled, and got the same truck from the self-storage facility we'd used to get poles for Ma and her sister strippers. With its rust, gray primer, and faded blue paint, the loaner truck was remarkably unremarkable. It was perfect.

Except it was noisy. Its panels rattled; its transmission whined. The shovel and pick I'd thrown in the back only made the din worse.

"You sure we couldn't have flown, at least partway?" Leo asked. Again.

"What's the rush? We don't want to get there before dark."

"We could have passed the time at a Burger King."

"No plane tickets, no credit card charges, no surveillance videos, no records of any kind. If I'm wrong about what we'll find, we could be committing a serious crime."

"Are you wrong?"

"No chance. Plinnit's partial DNA results just said I'm right."

That point silenced him, and he let me sleep while he drove another hundred miles. I was still exhausted. I'd been up most of the night, imagining the impossible, at least until it became so glaringly obvious.

"We just passed a sign for a cheese house," he said, when I woke up. "Next exit. Authentic Wisconsin cheddar. They might even put it on a hamburger."

"No sit-down restaurants, no lingering anywhere. Have a Ho Ho."

"We're low on gas, and I've hated Ho Hos my whole life."

"Then get something when we gas up—but remember: Use cash only, and keep your hat low."

"I should have brought my plastic glasses, the ones with the rubber nose."

"Just remember your hat."

"I suppose this all means there's no chance for the Would You? No fried jalapeño cheddar broccoli florets?"

"Are you nuts? That's the last place we can be spotted."

"Second to last," he corrected, referring to our ultimate destination.

"We'll be back in Rivertown by morning, and can eat like kings."

He cleared his throat. "Unless we're in jail."

"There's that," I agreed. "You're sure Endora will send a text when she's verified the delivery?"

He checked his phone. "Nothing yet."

He headed off the interstate, grunting as he bypassed the cheese house, and pulled into a busy-looking gas station. I slid down low on the seat as he stopped at the pump farthest from the door. He put on his glaucoma sunglasses, tied the chin strap on his straw hat, and got out. After filling the tank, he slouched in to pay for the gas. He was inside a long time.

When at last he came out, he was carrying a paper bag.

"What's in the bag?" I asked, when he got behind the wheel. It smelled wonderfully of things fried.

"I kept my hat low, like I had a scalp disease," he said.

He started the truck and drove us back onto the interstate.

"What did you bring me to eat?" I asked, sitting up now that we were safely away.

He'd set the bag on the floor where I couldn't reach it.

"Three hamburgers for me. They look good."

"How many for me?"

"I got you something even more special." He set the bag on the seat between him and the video camera, reached in, and came out clutching a package of Ho Hos.

Then he laughed and laughed.

SIXTY-SEVEN

"I DON'T LIKE hunting around in such darkness." Leo crept the truck along the deserted two-lane road. There was nothing on either side except trees.

"It's not completely dark," I said. "We have the chief."

Winnemac's cement head, lit bright, hovered above the tree line like a bodiless apparition in a horror movie. He was at least two miles away, and his unblinking concrete eyes were aimed at the river, but I felt he was watching us, angry at what we were about to do.

"Endora texted, saying it's been delivered?" It was the fourth time I'd asked. I didn't like skulking along the dark, deserted road, either.

"One hundred and fifty dollars' worth of floral wreath," he said.

"For sure, it's going to be the biggest one there. Not to mention the only one with a big blue and orange bow." Chicago Bears colors, an additional stroke of my genius, had been on my mind since the fireworks at Sweetie's penthouse. "We'll find it in a heartbeat."

"People don't set out such wreaths in the heat of July," he groused, but that was from envy of my superb idea.

The Internet driving directions I'd printed that morning said to turn right. We did, and went through more woods for another one-point-four miles.

We came to an iron arch, and he parked the truck next to a copse of trees. He shut off the lights, and we got out.

There was a full moon. We wouldn't have to risk the flashlights until we started working.

He shrugged on the backpack and took the shovel and the pick out of the truck bed. I carried the video camera.

The sign on the iron arch was readable in the moonlight. It said the cemetery grounds had been consecrated over two hundred years before. I didn't doubt it. Many of the granite markers looked to have been shifting in the ground for a long time, and now resembled loose teeth gone crooked in a shriveling old mouth.

"We don't belong here," Leo whispered.

"Piece of cake," I said.

"Piece of Ho Ho," he said, with more derision than I thought necessary.

Our feet rustled through the carpet of rotting leaves as we moved between the markers.

"There's not one wreath here, floral or otherwise," he said, when we got to the center of the cemetery.

"Got to be."

"Maybe they're going to deliver it tomorrow."

"Endora said it was delivered today."

"Wait; look there." He pointed to the far side of the cemetery. At the edge of the woods, an enormous wreath had been set up on a wire stand, though we were too far away to tell if it had a blue and orange bow.

I allowed, silently, as to how that last detail might not have been such genius anyway. The wreath looked to be the only one in the cemetery.

"No problem picking ours out," I said, before he could say anything.

"Genius, for sure," he said, as we walked to the wreath.

He set down the shovel and the pick, then took off the backpack.

I brushed away the cover of wet leaves with my foot.

The flat marble marker was tiny, barely eight inches wide, twelve inches long. I eased down to read it.

Only the name was engraved, faint in the moonlight: ALTA TAYLOR.

"We'll sweep the leaves back when we're done, the ground will settle back beneath them next winter, and no one will ever know," I said.

"More genius," he muttered.

He started digging. The ground had hardened over the forty years, making it slow work. At least a dozen times he ran into tree roots encroaching from the edge of the woods, and had to flail at them with the pick until they broke away. Finally, after three hours, he got down to where his shoulders were at ground level.

"Grave invasion is hard work," he said, taking a break.

"Technically, no," I said. "There's got to be someone buried here for it to be a grave."

"You're sure there's nobody home?"

"Just an empty coffin, filled with rocks to approximate her weight. Plinnit's DNA test proved she's alive."

"You said he sounded a little unsure."

"Sisters with the same mother but different fathers wouldn't have an exact match, but there would be some similarities. It's why the DNA from beneath my fingernails can't exactly match what they got from Sweetie's hairbrush."

"You're absolutely sure there's nobody down here?"

"Alta's alive and scratching."

He resumed digging. Twenty minutes later, at just past one thirty, his shovel rang against something metallic. He jumped back as far as he could in the small hole.

"Oh, man," he said, letting the shovel drop.

I repeated what I'd told him, driving up. A dozen times.

"Sheriff Lishkin had been pressing all summer for the

truth about what happened out at that gas station. Darlene had to pass Alta off as dead, to shut down the investigation."

"I thought you said Alta was his daughter."

"He was still sheriff. He needed to know what happened."

I shined the flashlight into the hole.

He'd uncovered a small section of mottled gray metal.

"A tin coffin?" he asked.

"Cheap. The right thing to put in the ground if all you're burying is rocks. Brush the dirt away. We'll pop the lid, make a video showing it's empty, fill the hole, and be gone."

The lid was dished inward, and corroded everywhere with splotches of rust.

"We got here just in time," Leo said, from the hole. "The lid's about to collapse."

I handed him the hammer and the pry bar, then shouldered the video camera and aimed the flashlight into the hole.

"They could say we staged this," he said.

"It's the only proof I can think of."

"Jeez, I wish I could see better," he said.

A huge burst of light hit us.

"How's this?" she asked.

SIXTY-EIGHT

"SHIT," I SAID.

"Ho Ho," Leo, the jokester, said.

"Ellie Ball," Ellie Ball said.

I turned around, raised my hand to shield my eyes from the glare of the light.

"You guys stay back a bit," she said to whoever was with her. She started moving forward, increasing the glare on my face.

I turned my back to her.

"Damn," she said, when she got up to the hole. "You slicks from Chicago are clever. That wreath business was a real special piece of work. Guy at the florist's told me it set someone back one and a half large. And that bow—blue and orange? Was that you, Elstrom? Clever again. No way your hundred-and-fifty-dollar floral wreath was going to get lost in the sea of the other hundred-and-fifty-dollar wreaths this place is always littered with. No sir; yours was going to stand out, because of that big bow. Clever again by half, though I've got to ask: Have you noticed any other wreaths here?"

She had people with her, I reminded myself. She had a gun, and they must have had guns. Behaving agreeably seemed prudent.

"No," I said.

"That could be because folks around here don't have that kind of money for floral wreaths, especially not when they'll wilt in the heat we get this time of year. Wouldn't you agree, Elstrom?"

"I know I would, Sheriff," Leo said, reaching to pull himself out of the hole.

"Stay the hell down in that hole."

"Damn it," I said. "Your problem is with me, not him."

"That's for sure."

She switched off the light, and the world blessedly went red. Until my eyes adjusted, and it changed again, to a deep blue, milky from the moonlight.

Belowground, Leo sighed with relief. Several times.

"How did you know to expect us here, this particular night?" I asked.

"First, your Lieutenant Plinnit sent some photos up here, asking me to verify it was Darlene Taylor they found dead at your castle."

Leo cut in, "Actually, it's only a tur—"

"Shut up," she said. Then, to me, "He called again, yesterday. He had a number of topics he wanted to discuss. Primarily, he's feeling substantial pressure to find Rosemary Taylor. He told me he's got partial DNA evidence that shows she's still in Chicago, and has been beating up on you, Elstrom. He asked me to keep an eye out for her, if for some reason she came back up this way. I told him I didn't expect she'd ever come back here. He also mentioned that you might be damned-fool enough to pop back up in Hadlow, for reasons comprehensible only to yourself. I laughed at that, saying I believed we'd seen the last of you, as well. That's what I believed, too, until the florist called, not one hour later, to tell me some woman in Chicago had bought expensive flowers for Alta's grave, and that it was a hurry-up order that had to be delivered ASAP. It was then that I began to believe we'd be seeing you after all, and immediately at that."

"No way you would have gone along with a request to open the grave," I said.

"I've never had cause to warrant an exhumation order, nor any reason to approach Darlene about such a thing."

"You never wanted this grave opened anyway, Sheriff."

"That's not entirely true. Ever since I started with the department, I'd see Darlene driving with someone, always in her car, always in the middle of the night. One time or another, everyone in the department has seen him with her, believing he was her special mystery man. Well, after a time, I quit believing that. Thirty, forty years is a long time to be keeping nightly company with a man and not have him be noticed coming or going out at her place, at least once. So I started imagining what else might be going on, for Darlene to be out in her car in the middle of so many nights, and I got to speculating it might be so she could accompany someone who needed to get out, drive around a bit, before going back to hiding during the daytime. That's when I became convinced there was no little fancy man at all, but rather, Alta Taylor, alive and well for all these years."

"Did your grandfather wonder?"

"I think he regarded her death, real or not, as a chance to close the book on an ugly incident."

"An ugly incident caused by his biological daughter."

"That part's only rumor," she said, in an even tone.

"Rumor or not, it was enough to keep you from investigating anything that might reflect poorly on your grandfather."

"Why didn't I stop you two grave raiders after you turned the first shovelful of dirt? That's all I needed for an arrest."

She had a point. She could have stopped us then.

"Because of what didn't come up in my conversation

with Lieutenant Plinnit," she went on. "You didn't mention your suspicions about my grandfather. For that, you were allowed to dig into Alta's grave."

"And because finally, you want to know what's not in this ground?"

"Fair enough," she said. "We haven't been able to find Alta's death certificate. The undertakers that would have done the burial are long out of business, so there's no way to check their records." She pointed to the video camera I'd set on the ground. "However, there will be no video, Mr. Elstrom. Nor is there to ever be any mention of what you've done here. You open the box, everyone gets satisfied it's empty, you close the box and fill the hole. You leave Hadlow, for good."

"Sounds good to me, especially that last part," Leo said, subterraneanly.

"Agreed," I said.

She turned on her bright beam and shined it into in the hole. "I was expecting more of a child's coffin."

"Alta was what, fourteen, when she supposedly died?" I asked.

"Fifteen, but quite small for her age, I've heard. Stunted, actually."

Not so stunted as to not be lethal, I thought, remembering the feral creature who'd taken me down behind the Taylor cottage and again in Sweetie's penthouse.

Ellie Ball told Leo to open the coffin.

The corroded metal box wasn't secured. Leo lifted the lid.

It contained no feed sack, filled with rocks or dirt.

There was a flannel shirt and denim jeans, covering what was left of a corpse, lying facedown.

SIXTY-NINE

WE STARED, STUNNED by a corpse that was not supposed to be there. Leo scrambled out of the hole as if his feet were on fire.

"I want you gone," Ellie Ball said to us.

"I have to know if that's Alta Taylor," I said.

"You will leave. You will never say anything about this, you will never come back, you will never call me."

"I'm going to hang around until your coroner verifies that's Alta."

"You'd rather be arrested for desecrating a grave?"

She whistled with her teeth and lower lip. The people who'd come with her to the cemetery began rustling the leaves behind us. They'd be big men, I imagined, and armed—and loyal enough to do, and say, precisely what she wanted.

"I will call you, Mr. Elstrom," she said.

Leo threw the small tools in the backpack and picked up the shovel and the pick. He'd not made a sound since he opened the casket. He took off toward the gate, shuffling stiff-legged, as if his brain had lost its ability to fully command his feet. I picked up the video camera and hurried after him.

At the truck, he dumped everything into the bed and moved to the passenger's side. His hands were shaking too badly to open the door.

"You all right?" I asked.

He made no sound.

I opened his door, went around, and levered myself carefully in behind the wheel.

"Jeez, Dek, did you see her?" His words came out too high and too fast. "That coffin leaked. Her skin was oatmeal, damp and wet and probably full of bugs. Jeez, Dek, did you see her? I'm never going to sleep again."

He slumped against the door, out cold. He'd had too many hours of driving and too many hours of digging, and too many seconds of looking at a corpse gone to oatmeal in the ground. I drove us the hell out of Hadlow, Minnesota.

Four hours passed. I had no trouble keeping the truck straight on the road, but I couldn't steer my mind in any direction that made sense. I'd come to Minnesota certain that Alta Taylor had done the Chicago killings—right down to eradicating her sister Darlene and George Koros—and the proof of that would be an empty grave. To have found a body made no sense. No matter how I thought, and rethought, the only thing I was sure of was that Ellie Ball was spending the hours since we left racing to dig a new hole for the corpse, and filling the old one, so that no one would ever find out anything again.

She called just after I'd passed Madison, Wisconsin. She didn't say my name, nor did she identify herself. She spoke slowly, and deliberately, and said, "A man. Absolutely, not her." She hung up. It was relief.

Leo woke up an hour later. "I nodded off," he said in a normal voice.

"You nodded off for almost five hours." I rustled the bag I'd brought from Rivertown. "Ho Ho?"

"I need coffee, and something adult to eat."

That, too, was relief. I took the next exit, and we stopped at a McDonald's at a big truck stop. I was no longer concerned about security cameras. Ellie Ball would deny we'd ever come back to Hadlow.

We ate Egg McMuffins quickly and silently, as though afraid to say one word for the flood of them that might release, and took coffee back to the truck.

This time Leo got behind the wheel. Once we'd gotten back on the interstate, he gave me a sly grin. "Who shall we dig up now?" he asked, and I vowed never to underestimate the healing power of McMuffins.

"I heard from Ellie Ball," I said. "It wasn't Alta in that cemetery."

"Who, then?"

"A man. Beyond that, she'll never give anyone the chance to find out more. By now that body has been buried somewhere else, where no one will ever find it."

His fingers tightened on the steering wheel. "What's that mean?"

"Her grandfather knew who was in that box, and who did the killing."

"Who's the oatmeal, and who dunnit, Holmes?"

"Best guess?"

"Fair enough."

"The man in the tin box is Herb Taylor."

"Dead by daughter because immediately following Mr. Taylor's drop from sight, Alta got pulled from school, and was never seen again." He nodded to himself, pleased by his thinking. "It works, circumstantially."

"Maybe not conclusively enough for Ellie Ball," I said. "She hustled us out of there because she wanted to hide the body while it was still dark. She doesn't want a forensic examination."

"She doesn't think Alta was the killer?"

"She's worried it was her grandfather, Sheriff Roy Lishkin," I said.

SEVENTY

A PARADE OF engines woke me just past noon the next day.
I'd slept for only a couple of hours.

I peered out the window. Vans and cars were lining up
to park on both sides of the street. The vans belonged to
television stations; the cars, I supposed, to print reporters.
Benny Fittle was double-parked in the middle of it all. He
was going to work off doughnuts, that day.

I supposed they'd come to hear about my being attacked
in Sweetie's penthouse.

I hurried to get dressed, went downstairs, and made
coffee. It was only after I'd gulped half of my first cup
that someone banged on my door. Banged on my sensi-
bilities, too, as I realized that for all the ruckus outside, no
one else had banged on my door. Nor had anyone called.
The press hadn't come for me. They were gathering for
something else.

I opened the door. Jenny stepped quickly inside. "I've
only got a minute," she said. Her face was flushed beneath
her television makeup.

"What's the rumpus?"

She looked at me, saw I was serious. "You haven't noticed the press outside?"

"They just woke me up."

"You didn't see my report on last night's broadcast, or
see this morning's papers?"

"I was out."

"I broke a corruption story about your city hall last

night. You've got citizens' committees that contain no citizens. They're used as conduits to funnel benefits—hospitalization; life insurance; use of city-owned vehicles; and the biggie, travel expenses abroad, supposedly to study how other cities do things—to the committee members."

"The recipients of this largesse are the lizards?"

"In a nutshell."

"Is that nutshell going to be cracked open more?"

"Eventually, but that's not why I stopped by. Tonight I lead with another exclusive. Plinnit is going to issue warrants for Sweetie Fairbairn. She's being charged with murder, fraud, theft, flight to avoid prosecution, and probably a dozen other things."

"Heavy heat on Plinnit."

"Not just him. The state's attorney and the U.S. attorney are feeling it, too. This case has thick tentacles. Plinnit's got to sling warrants to show activity."

"Heater case, for sure."

"Plinnit might have one with your name on it, as well."

"Might?"

"Does. He's going to arrest you to squeeze you."

"For what?"

"Obstruction, most likely." She looked away, which meant most certainly. Plinnit was keeping her informed.

"Because I wouldn't say it was Sweetie Fairbairn who attacked me in the penthouse?"

She barely nodded.

"He's saying his DNA analysis showed conclusively Sweetie was up there?"

"I heard Plinnit wasn't happy with what he got. I know somebody at Cook County. He heard the DNA showed a mitochondrial relationship—"

"A what?"

"Mitochondrial. Maternal. Like two sisters who have the same mother."

"I've heard of that. Usable in court?"

"Usable for warrants, for now."

I gave her a shrug. It was lying. It was not the time to tell her that Alta Taylor was not in the ground in Hadlow.

She smiled then, a Jennifer Gale television smile, fast and efficient. "I've got to get over to city hall for a one o'clock news conference. My citizens' committee story, remember? News at noon, six, and nine?"

Her high flush had returned. Excitement. Opportunity. I'd seen that kind of flush on Amanda, not that many months before, when she first started imagining doing big things with big donations. Right now, Jennifer Gale had big opportunities.

I opened the door.

"One more thing," she said. "Darlene Taylor was buried yesterday."

I nodded. It was noncommittal.

"I heard you were the only one there, besides the minister, and that you paid for the funeral expenses."

Plinnit must have put a man behind a tree. "I wanted to make sure they didn't drop the coffin."

"Not just the coffin, Dek. You also paid for the cemetery plot, a stone, and that minister. For someone who is broke, all that must have been a reach."

"You're going to use this?"

"Personal interest only."

"Darlene was a victim. Maybe most of all."

She gave that a half-shake of her head, and turned to look out the open door. Newspeople seemed to be everywhere, including several who'd surrounded Benny Fittle.

She stepped outside. "Be careful of Plinnit."

"Personal interest question of my own?" I asked, if only

to delay for a moment more. "Who put Elvis up to that damned-fool salad oil scheme?"

It hadn't been by magic that Jennifer Gale learned of citizens' committees. Elvis was slinking around, offering the Feds something else to make his salad oil problem go away—and he was talking about all of it to Jennifer Gale.

She smiled, shook her head. "Good luck," she said, starting off for city hall.

It sounded like a good-bye.

"Good luck to you, as well," I called back.

As I watched her walk away, I had the thought that I'd like to follow her, at least as far as city hall. The lizards were sure to be frantic, dodging for cover behind whatever spokesman they were about to push out in front of the press. It was something I'd hoped for, since the day I'd moved into the turret.

I'd had enough of public news. I'd had enough of being the news. I went upstairs to my computer, thinking it was better to stay inside, surrounded by thick limestone walls. I pushed my head into the Internet, to find out what I'd missed while I was off invading graves.

Both of Chicago's major newspapers offered recaps of Jennifer's committee corruption story. They'd come late to the story, and details were sketchy. Sketchy or not, I took comfort in the short reports. Broad coverage of corrupt committees, following so closely on the heels of Elvis's oily adventures, offered hope that brighter lights would begin to shine on Rivertown.

Both Web sites also carried updates on the firestorm that followed the news that Sweetie never had any right to give away Silas's millions. So many people were claiming to be blood kin to Silas Fairbairn that law firms throughout the country had begun demanding to see birth certificates, death certificates, and other proof of family lineage before they'd consider taking cases against the recipients of Sweetie's largesse. More than fifty-five lawsuits had been filed in Chicago so far, and many more were expected in the days to come.

After finishing with the major news sites, I moved down to the brackish water of the *Argus-Observer*. Immediately, I wished that I hadn't. They'd run a short piece on Amanda and me, making her out to be a flaky former debutante, working for her father because she could do little else. I was portrayed as an impoverished lunatic, hunkering down in an unheated turret because I couldn't afford to live anyplace else. In my case, I supposed it was accurate.

I called Amanda's office. She was in, and she was furious. "I saw the damned thing. Five sets of lawyers, representing a dozen of Silas Fairbairn's third cousins, are now demanding we escrow Sweetie's gift, claiming she was unduly influenced by you to make the contribution to me. That will shut down everything we planned to do, for years."

"I didn't see this coming." As soon as the words came out, I realized that could have been the mantra for everything I'd encountered with Sweetie Fairbairn: I'd seen nothing coming.

"Maybe you should have," she snapped.

She stopped and took a breath. Then the old Amanda said, "Shall we have that date?"

"You mean at our trattoria?"

"Sure." Hesitancy, though, had come into her voice, a sort of sighing, and I realized that neither of us believed the trattoria would ever be ours again.

Someone interrupted her. She put her hand over the mouthpiece, then came back on to say she had to take a call from yet another reporter.

"Good luck," I said, sounding just like Jennifer Gale.

"Good luck," she said back.

As with Jenny, "good luck" sounded now like "good-bye."

I had no more energy for news. I called Plinnit.

"About those DNA results," I said.

"You've been lying to me, Elstrom. You know where Sweetie Fairbairn is."

"There's an army of reporters outside, waiting for a news conference at Rivertown City Hall. I'm thinking about going over there and telling them about how a police officer might try to deliberately mislead with incomplete DNA. You didn't recover anything from under my fingernails that's conclusive enough to use in court."

"You scratched it off, on that hall carpet."

"That hall carpet," I repeated, but it was for myself. My mind had lurched onto something I'd known before, but was beginning to understand only now.

"What?"

"Back at the Wilbur Wright, you said your officer was cut in the living room, and that's where you recovered the attacker's knife?"

"Yes. What are you thinking, Elstrom?"

"You're sure you recovered the knife in the living room?"

"Right where Sweetie Fairbairn dropped it."

There was nothing more to say. I hung up on him.

Alta hadn't been clawing at the hallway carpet to find a knife. She'd been scratching to find something else she'd dropped. A very frayed old postcard, of a covered bridge with octagonal windows.

Alta had seen a destination in that picture, a place where Sweetie might run.

It took only ten minutes on the Internet to find the bridge. It was in Indiana.

I called Leo. "My credit card's maxed out. Alta Taylor is headed to Indiana to kill Sweetie Fairbairn."

"I have four hundred in my wallet," he said. "Will that be enough?"

I told him I didn't know if there was still time.

SEVENTY-ONE

ACCORDING TO THE INTERNET, Parke County was smack-dab in the middle of the western side of Indiana, and claimed to have more covered bridges than any other county in the state. The bridge with the octagonal windows that spanned Miller's Ravine was built in 1878, and was about smack-dab in the middle of Parke County. It was there, smack-dab in the middle of apparently everything, that I was going to try to find Sweetie Fairbairn.

I took the fast roads, 294 into Indiana, then 65 south, to a maze of country two-laners. My plan was simple. I would work outward from Miller's Ravine in increasing concentric circles, stopping at gas stations and stores and diners, anyplace a newcomer might find work. I was not seeking to ruin any sanctuary she might have found; I would not flash a picture, nor ask if anyone had seen her. I merely wanted to warn her that her sister—sick, runty Alta—was coming for her, dressed as a man or dressed as a woman…and that she liked knives.

It was a fool's plan, statistically destined not to work. It was all I could think to do, at least until Leo's four hundred dollars ran out.

THE BRIDGE HAD been painted since it had been photographed for Sweetie's postcard. No longer a weathered gray, it glistened now, restored to its original red.

I walked through it and back, making echoing footsteps, pausing to admire its odd octagonal windows. It was a fine old bridge, a piece of historic infrastructure protected by people who valued such things.

It must have looked bucolic, maybe even romantic, to a girl or to a young woman on the run from a killing in Minnesota.

I wondered if it had looked the same, years later, to a woman now much older, and running from so much more.

FOR SEVEN DAYS, I worked in circles out from the Miller's Ravine Bridge. The towns were smaller than Hadlow, and had very few stores, but there were intersections to be checked, as well; bumps in the road with a lone gas station or a tiny grocery that might have offered work to a woman.

I worked diligently, and doggedly, sunup to past dark. I slept in the Jeep every other night, ate dry cereal for breakfast, cheese crackers for lunch, and the cheapest diner food I could find for supper—all so most of the money I borrowed from Leo could go for gas.

I worked mindlessly, never letting myself pause to think it was preposterous that Sweetie Fairbairn had run to those smack-dab parts in the first place, that a picture on an old postcard had showed a destination to a woman in trouble.

Never, though, did I let myself allow that my road trip wasn't only about Sweetie Fairbairn, that it also had something to do with getting away from Rivertown and being at the jack—ready for the phone to ring, not knowing who I wanted to hear from most—Amanda or Jennifer Gale. Slipping into such thinking might be to disappear into a dark tunnel indeed, and I wasn't yet ready for that.

I set my phone to go directly to voice mail. Each of the ladies called once, as though in perfect symmetry. Amanda said she was swamped with meetings about the Sweetie Fairbairn fiasco and would probably have to cancel our trattoria date.

Jennifer's message was much more direct: "It was his Ma." She laughed. I laughed as well, at the idea that Elvis Derbil's mother, the mayor's sister, had been the one to suggest he spread his greasy wings and peddle his altered oils beyond Rivertown.

Both Amanda and Jennifer ended their messages by wondering how I was getting on. I did not call either of them back, as I was not at all sure how I was getting on.

Leo called every day, because he knew how I could disappear, chasing impossibilities. His calls I returned because he made me laugh, especially on the evening I decided it was time to head back to Rivertown. I had done what I could with my time and his money, and now I was out of his money.

He sounded unusually chipper. I asked if he'd won a big lottery.

"More fabulous," he said. "Ma's laid up in bed; sciatica."

"That's fabulous?"

"Even Bernard said it was a blessing."

"Bernard, the accountant nephew—?"

"Of Mrs. Roshiska's, who's now in the hospital. Threw her back out."

"From…?"

He laughed a laugh that was almost a shriek, and said he had to go. "I have much to do. I've thrown out the dancing DVDs. Ma's handyman has already taken down the poles and disconnected the special lights. I myself pulled up the gold-flecked floor tiles and down the red velvet drapes. Ma's doctor said to get all the stuff back from storage before Ma gets back on her feet."

"Doctor's orders to stop pole dancing?"

"All praise the doctor."

As with his earlier calls, he hung up without asking if I'd gotten any leads to Sweetie Fairbairn. Nor had he offered to loan me more money to perpetuate my obsession for a second week, or a third. He is my friend.

I had enough money left for one more cheap dinner and two tanks of gasoline. I headed northwest, bound for one last town that evening, and three more the next day on my way back to Rivertown.

Hill's Knob did not look to possess a knob, though where the ground had actually risen might have been obscured by the dense, intertwined weeds that lined both sides of its cracked blacktop main street. No one in the business district was there to mind, since most of the town had burned. Only two buildings remained: an empty old gas station, missing its pumps like Ralph's in Hadlow; and the husk of something that once was a general store, judging by the signs for bait and men's socks that still rested, sun-curled and faded, behind its filthy windows.

The only indication that any commerce was alive anywhere nearby was a billboard for a diner called Blanchie's, five miles farther on. It advertised the best apple pie in four counties. Apple pie would do nicely for dinner, especially since driving five counties away to find better seemed unreasonable.

I drove the required distance, and pulled into the gravel lot in front of a brown-sided, green-roofed building raised up on a cinder-block foundation. The only car in the lot was a twenty-five-year-old station wagon, dotted with at least fifteen years' worth of rust.

It was eight o'clock and there were no customers, just a white-haired grill cook behind a pass-through window, humming along with an easy-listening radio station, and a gray-haired waitress sagging in a pink uniform at the far end of a white Formica counter. She was turned away from me, staring out one of the windows. I supposed that anything of interest was better found by looking out of such a barren place.

Neither of them was a candidate to be the missing Sweetie Fairbairn. That was all right. There would be pie. I sat in a booth by the window.

For several long moments, nothing—absolutely nothing—happened. The grill cook continued to busy himself, mostly invisibly, behind the pass-through. The waitress continued to be absorbed by whatever was outside the far window, though to my eye there was nothing out there but spindly trees, and even those were fading in the tiring sun. Hill's Knob, Indiana, didn't look like anywhere a right-thinking person would run to. People ran from such places, even if the next stop was a place like Hadlow.

Definitely, it was time to go back to Rivertown.

"Best apple pie in four counties?" I called out to the waitress lost in thought, after another few minutes had passed.

"Good enough," she said, without tearing her eyes from the mesmerizing view out the window. Her voice was barely audible, and carried no trace of enthusiasm about the pie.

"I'd like a slice, à la mode, with vanilla."

"Coffee?"

"How much is the pie?"

She mumbled something to the window that I couldn't hear.

"How much?" I asked again.

"Six fifty," she said, a little louder. "With the ice cream."

I would have mumbled, too, if I was looking to get almost nine bucks, with tax and tip, for a piece of pie daubed with ice cream, in the middle of Nowhere, Indiana. Those were Chicago prices, and downtown numbers at that.

"No coffee, thanks," I said.

She continued to sit, staring out the window, as though expecting me to get up and leave, offended by the high prices. Certainly, such exorbitant numbers could explain why the joint was empty. More time passed until finally, when I'd made no sounds to leave, she sighed loudly, got up from her stool, and disappeared through a door into the kitchen.

Another twenty minutes went by, and I'd just begun to wonder if Hill's Knob was so removed that Blanchie had to send someone on a bicycle clear to Terre Haute to get the ice cream when the waitress finally came out of the kitchen and ambled over with a plate. Her face was averted, her eyes behind her red plastic eyeglasses still fixed on the parking lot outside, lit now by one lone dim bulb fixed to the side of the diner. It had gone dark.

She set my pie down, but there was no vanilla ice cream on top, as requested. Instead, there was a chunk of melted yellow cheese.

I thought about reminding her I'd ordered ice cream, but reasoned that might delay my research into the quality of the pie by another fifteen minutes, maybe longer, and by now, I was very hungry.

Besides, the cheese, melted as it was on the pie, did look good.

She walked away.

I picked up my fork, cut the point from the wedge, and brought it to my mouth. It was fine pie, and to my mind, the cheese made it tastier than could any scoop of ice cream.

My tongue puzzled, though, as to the identity of the cheese. It wasn't the usual cheddar or American usually encountered on restaurant apple pie. I lifted off a speck so I could taste only that.

I knew that cheese. The back of my neck tingled. I looked up.

She'd come over with a Thermos pitcher of coffee. She set it down and slid into the booth across from me.

Her forehead was crossed with a dozen deep lines, unhidden now by any cosmetics. Her lips were thin without lipstick, and her breasts were low inside her uniform. If there was a twinkle in her eyes, or a pinch from fear, it was obscured behind those heart-shaped, cartoonish red glasses.

"Around here, folks know to enjoy their apple pie with Velveeta," she said.

SEVENTY-TWO

SHE POURED COFFEE into the two mugs on the table and pushed one closer to me.

I took another bite of the pie. "I'm sure glad I came."

"Will I be glad you came?"

"I can leave, Ms. Fair—"

She stopped me with an abrupt shake of her head, and looked to smile at the white-haired man behind the grill window. He was whistling softly, in tune with Sinatra singing low on the radio, and watching us.

"Gus and I like the name Evie," she said quietly.

"Evie it is," I said. "Forever more."

She took a moment to make up her mind about what was in my eyes, and then asked, "How did you find me?"

Without meaning to, I felt my fingers touch my face. I dropped my hand.

"It took me too long, but I finally remembered a picture postcard of a bridge, on the wall of the only sane room in a very swank penthouse. That postcard disappeared some time after the woman who lived there fled."

"Did remembering that postcard have something to do with the scratches on your face?"

"They're healing just fine."

"I'd written 'Hill's Knob' on the back of that card, so I'd never forget. That man"—she gestured at the grill window—"and his wife had been very kind to me once."

"Alta took that postcard. If you wrote on the back of it, she knows you're here."

The shock I was expecting didn't come. Instead, she looked out at the parking lot, cut from the darkness by only that one dim bulb. Behind us, Sinatra had stopped singing.

"Yes," she said softly, to the glass.

"You're not surprised?"

She turned to me. "You came to warn me?"

"Yes."

Her face relaxed. "She was here."

I waited, saying nothing.

"Two days ago," she said, "she parked right out in front, came inside. It was around closing time, like now. She was dressed in blue jeans, plaid shirt, work boots. I took her for a man, a very short man. I walked up with a menu. She didn't want it. She kept looking at my eyes until finally she just turned and went out the door."

"By then you'd recognized her?"

"Absolutely not. Georgie said she'd died the summer I left. And the years had twisted her face fiercely, Mr. Elstrom. The years, and the anger."

"She just drove away?"

A small noise came from across the diner. Gus had come out from behind the grill window, and had put a hand on the stainless steel coffee machine. He was about sixty, powerfully built, with biceps that hadn't come from turning eggs. I would have bet there was nothing wrong with his ears, either.

His eyes weren't on the coffeemaker. They were on her.

She shook her head at him almost imperceptibly. I had not yet become a threat. He gave her a small shrug and went back behind the grill window.

"She did not leave right away, Mr. Elstrom," she went on. "She stood outside, leaning against her car, an old, beat-up tan thing. After five minutes, I began to wonder if she was sick. Other than Gus, there was no one in the diner, so I walked outside. Whip fast, she was up against me. She had a knife—but first, she had things to say."

Her hands trembled as she refilled our cups from the carafe.

"I was dumbstruck; she wasn't supposed to be alive. I sure never connected her with the TV reports of Darlene being found dead at your home. She started jabbering so fast and choppy I couldn't make out all the words, but there was no mistaking her rage. Or her intent with that knife."

She squeezed both hands around her coffee mug, maybe for the warmth. Two-handed, she brought the cup to her mouth, took a sip, and went on. "Darlene told her I'd gone off to make a fortune, and would come back for them. I might have said that; I would have said anything to get out of Hadlow. Alta said they waited years for me to bring them to a better life. I tried to tell Alta I'd spent most of my years moving from one town to another, waitressing, clerking retail, working always for small wages, barely getting by. She wouldn't hear it. She kept chattering, spit flying out of her mouth, saying over and over it was my fault, them living hellish all those years."

"Then Georgie called them?"

"That rat bastard," she said, looking down at her coffee.

"He was doing well, in your employ."

"Damned right. Several years earlier, he'd seen a picture of me in the *Tribune*. It was right after Silas had died. He came to the penthouse. He said he was down on his luck."

"That was all? He didn't threaten you with blackmail?"

Her eyes got a little wider, but she kept her face under control.

"About what?" she asked, watching my face to see what I knew.

"About anything," I said.

She let it die. "I rented him an office on Wacker Drive,

and gave him a retainer to watch over a few checking accounts. For a long time, it was good enough for him."

"Until suddenly he got greedy?"

"Not so suddenly. I think he'd been waiting since day one for the right opportunity to shake out some big money. He saw his chance with poor Andrew. Georgie came to me, told me he'd discovered Andrew had embezzled a half-million dollars from the Symposium. He said he'd negotiated with Andrew; Andrew would leave, and pay back the money over time. All it took was my blessing. I didn't think to question him, Mr. Elstrom. I was more shocked than anything."

She looked at me with steady eyes. "But then I made things worse."

"By not questioning?"

"By saying something stupid and rash. For some time, I'd been thinking about how burdensome my philanthropic life had become. There were so many requests to investigate, and never being absolutely sure which were worthwhile. I whined at Georgie, saying Andrew was the last straw, that maybe I should give away most of what I had. I could make last, major donations to charities I was already familiar with, and be done with all those hours. At that point, I'd made no final decision, Mr. Elstrom; I was merely feeling sorry for myself, in the wake of what I thought I'd learned about Andrew."

"It sent Koros into action?"

"Like a rocket. He'd already wet his snout with that half million. He wanted more, but he'd have to act quick, before I gave everything away."

"He called Darlene," I said.

"Alta said when he told them I'd hit it rich, it was like I'd cut out their hearts. They didn't need any convincing to come down to Chicago to help. I'd have to pay for those years they lost."

"Alta was telling you all this while she was holding a knife to you?"

"Calm as could be, looking up with her wet eyes and her dead-smelling breath."

I looked at the man looking back at me from the grill window. "Where was Gus?"

"Back in the restaurant, unaware," she said, too quickly.

"He didn't come to the door, wondering why you'd gone outside?" I asked. Gus was too observant, too watchful.

She kept her face calm. "Not a chance," she said.

She took another sip of coffee. Her hands were steady and sure now. "It was a sick idea Georgie had come up with. Apparently, he'd saved a copy of a little novel I wrote in high school, about a clown who died, falling off a roof. I'd given him that copy. It had my handwriting and fingerprints on it, perfect for their needs."

"Sweetie Rose."

She set down her coffee cup slowly. "How could you know that?" she whispered.

"I went to Hadlow."

"Hadlow?" she managed, but we were no longer talking about a high school girl's novel. She was pressing for what I knew of a gas station killing.

"No big deal," I said. "Miss Mason loaned me the mimeographed copy you gave her. It's since been burned."

"Thank you," she said. Then, "Alta had Georgie's copy. It's been destroyed, too."

We were fencing, she and I. I'd been too long going in circles in Chicago and in Indiana; she'd been too long living cautiously, running from Hadlow.

"James Stitts?" I asked.

"I never did see Darlene, but I expect she dyed her hair

to match mine, and Georgie put her in a limousine to be seen hiring Mr. Stitts at his house." She paused, then, "As you reported to me, back in my other life."

"Georgie followed him up on that roof and cut his rope?"

"He was on another roof, taking pictures. They were a little out of focus, but they were meant to leave no doubt who was up on that hardware building."

"A woman who looked just like you, cutting the rope?"

She nodded. "As teenagers, me and Darlene looked like twins. Through a long camera lens, from some distance away, she could pass perfectly for me."

"You saw these pictures?"

For a moment she studied the scratches on my face. Then she said, "Yes. Alta had them in her car, with the negatives, and with that mimeograph of the story I wrote in high school."

"For her to blackmail you."

"For Georgie and Darlene to blackmail me. Darlene told Alta she wanted every nickel I had, but she also wanted me left alive, ruined, so I'd have to live like they did."

"What did Alta want?"

"She wanted me dead. She wanted everybody dead." She shivered. "Alta was the smartest of us all, but my mother used to say Alta was prone to sudden attacks of understandable anger. My father had a sickness in his head. Or an anger. He sexually abused Alta from a very young age, though my mother tried hard to shield Darlene and myself from knowing that."

"And you? Darlene?"

"He never touched us."

"Alta wasn't his child," I said.

"She sure didn't look like Darlene and me. Sheriff Roy would stop by, from time to time, always when my father was somewhere else. I could see Roy's fondness for my mother. I don't know anything more than that."

"Who killed your father?"

"Why do you think he was killed?" she asked slowly.

"He was buried facedown in your town cemetery. He didn't take off."

She leaned across the table. "How can you know that?"

"Traces of your DNA were found on me and a Chicago policeman after we were attacked in your penthouse." Again, without realizing, my fingers had reached up to touch my face. "By then, Darlene was dead. So was Alta, for years, or so everyone believed. That left you as the only person who could have left that DNA. Since I've never seen you as a killer, that DNA meant Alta was still alive. I drove up to Hadlow to take a peek under the ground. A man was in Alta's grave, facedown."

"He was working on a pump. Alta caved in his head with a shovel. We found her standing over him, calm as could be. There was a metal storage box in the barn, meant for long-handled tools. We put him in that, and dragged it to the edge of the woods. Mama and Darlene buried him, while I sat with Alta in the house. She had blood on her, but she didn't seem to mind. Her mind had disengaged from what she'd done. Mama never let her go back to school, for fear of what she might say. She told Darlene and me to say our father had taken off."

"Why put him in the box facedown?"

"We didn't want to see his eyes. Who moved him from our place to the cemetery?"

"For that, we have to talk about the gas station," I said.

She paused, and then nodded.

"Darlene, with Roy Lishkin's unknowing help, moved him," I said. "Your mother's death, and then all of you being seen near that gas station, and then Georgie and you taking off must have set him to wondering. He probably started making unannounced trips to your farm. Darlene must have feared it would only be a matter of time before Alta would let something slip about your father, or the young man at the gas station. So Darlene came up with a way to shut down the gas station investigation, and at the same time, get rid of a potentially risky corpse buried out by the woods. She dug up your father, hosed off the box, told Lishkin that Alta had died and that she was to be buried on the cheap, in that tin box. I doubt Lishkin asked any questions. He must have wanted everything to be over, too. He pulled some strings, and the box was buried quickly, and quietly, at the edge of the cemetery."

"Everybody knows about my father, and Alta, and the gas station, now?"

"Only the current sheriff and a couple of her deputies know who was in that grave. The sheriff won't say anything. Roy Lishkin was her grandfather. She doesn't want anyone pointing fingers at him about your father's death. As far as the gas station, the only ones left who might know anything are Sweetie Fairbairn, who apparently is gone for good, and of course Alta…"

"My father ruined Alta's life, Mr. Elstrom. Her killing him was understandable, in a certain sick way."

"Your mother died just a few months before the gas station."

"Alta didn't kill my mother. She fell, struck her head, just as we told Sheriff Roy." She took a slow sip of coffee. "Will knowing all this really give you peace?"

"Peace is not a reasonable expectancy, but I am more than curious."

"It was one of those spring days that can set the young on fire," she said. "Alta screamed to go along when Georgie came by for Darlene. Darlene didn't see any harm, so long as I came, too, to watch Alta. That was fine with me. There were worse things than riding around in Georgie's convertible."

"The gun?"

"Georgie's dad got death threats from shutting down mills, putting folks out of work. He kept a revolver locked in the glove box. Georgie took it out, waved it around just to show off, and put it right back." Her eyes filled with tears. "He forgot to lock it up. Certainly none of us thought it was loaded."

She took a paper napkin from the chrome dispenser on the table and dabbed at her eyes.

"We stopped at that gas station for Cokes," she said. "Alta was supposed to stay in the car. The rest of us went in. We bought the Cokes, and a Baby Ruth. Alta loved Baby Ruths. We'd just paid, when there was Alta, with that gun. She fired four times. The noise shocked the hell out of her, but she kept pulling the trigger. For the noise, I always thought; she loved the damned noise. At first, we didn't know what she was shooting at; we were looking only at Alta. Then the poor young man made a noise, a horrible, grunting noise. He went down. He was gut shot, bleeding like hell. Georgie was the only one who thought to move. Darlene and me, we were frozen like statues. Georgie grabbed the gun, yelled at us to get in the car. I pushed Alta into the back, damned near sat on her to keep her down, and we flew out of there."

She gave out a small sob.

"Evie?" the man called from the window.

She waved for him to stay away. "I'm fine, Gus. Fine."

"No cops?" I asked.

She pulled out another napkin and rubbed at her eyes. "Darlene said they'd charge her and me and Georgie as accessories to murder. And with our mother so recently dead, they'd start poking around, wondering about our father. They'd find him in the woods, buried like a dog, she said. Georgie got bug-eyed hearing that; he didn't know anything about Alta killing my father. Anyway, Darlene said there'd be more murder charges. Newspaper people would be everywhere. We'd be freaks, dirt-poor sickies from Dirt Bag, Minnesota. We'd be in prison for the rest of our lives. No sir, we didn't call Sheriff Roy."

"You wouldn't have been charged."

"I wasn't taking that risk. I made up my mind right there in that convertible. I was legal, sixteen. If we could get away from that gas station without getting caught, and act normal for a couple of months, I'd be gone at the end of the school year. Besides, no way Georgie wanted to tell, either. It was his dad's gun; his father could be blamed as an accessory, or something."

I touched my side, where I'd been shot. "What happened to the gun?"

"Darlene took it from Georgie. He didn't mind."

"It's gone now, along with the bullets that had been in the crime file all these years. Another loose end Ellie Ball doesn't want lying around."

She looked out the window again, at the darkness. "It was all so self-serving, of course. Georgie and me, leaving, we were looking out for ourselves."

"And Darlene?"

"She was the only one who did the right thing. She stayed in Hadlow, looking out for Alta."

For a minute, neither of us said anything.

"Remember I told you to go to the cops," I said, finally. "That might still be good advice, as opposed to running."

She turned from the window. "We get Channel 8 on cable here. I know what's going on in Chicago. I go back, I'm in court for the rest of my life, trying to explain how

I had nothing to do with killing poor Andrew, Mr. Stitts, Bob Norton, or even Georgie and Darlene. It would take a lifetime to explain all that. Then there's all that money I gave away. Silas had no close relatives; just shirttail people he'd never even met. Court for the rest of my life on that, too. Hadlow? Court there, as well. And me with no money to pay lawyers for any of it. No, I can't go back."

"Especially since the likelihood of Alta ever corroborating your story is…remote?"

Gus had again come out to the counter, and was watching us with unblinking eyes. He looked strong enough to have quickly snapped a knife out of a stunted woman's hand; cunning enough to know back roads that led to empty lands and hidden lakes, places so remote a smart-thinking person could dispose of a body and a car so that they would never be discovered.

"I've already paid plenty, Mr. Elstrom," she said. "I paid with years of being afraid someone would come after me for being an accomplice to the murder of my father or that young man at that gas station. I paid, hiring Georgie Korozakis, knowing he could make up a story about that gas station any damned time he felt like it. I paid, thinking it was poor Andrew Fill who stole my money, then realizing it was my money that got him killed. I paid, knowing Mr. Stitts went off that roof because my sister wanted my money. And I paid, finding Bob Norton lying in my living room, feeling the wet of his life bleed out of him. I paid all that, and it still wasn't enough."

"They never demanded money?"

"I screamed at Alta, knife be damned, 'Why didn't you just ask for the money?' The bitch just rolled her vicious, ugly eyes. 'Georgie wanted you ripened to run.'"

"Ripened to leave it all behind, so he could make it look like you'd taken it all with you."

"I imagine he'd funnied up some documents to let him loot Silas's money with ease."

"Killing you outright was too risky, because that would lead to probate, and Darlene wouldn't get anything if you'd made out a will. You had to be set off running." I nodded in admiration of the plan. "It was an even better scheme than they knew, because you running also took care of the problem of you and Silas not being married. If you were found dead, that would be exposed, and there'd be no money for anyone except his blood kin."

"Too bad they never found that out, the damned greedy fools," she said.

"They threatened to alibi each other for the gas station killing, and say you'd done the shooting?"

"And that I'd killed my father. Plus, they had those pictures that supposedly showed me up on the roof, cutting the rope. Combined with your testimony saying you'd found me covered with Bob Norton's blood, kneeling over his corpse, and Georgie saying I certainly had motive to kill poor Andrew, the case against me would be too damning to survive." She put her head in her hands. "There was nothing I could do but run."

I couldn't help but grin. "Except give away all your money, on your way out the door."

"As I said, I'd been thinking about it anyway. I thought it would stop the killing." She looked at me defiantly, her eyes clear now. "I don't grieve that it led to Alta killing Darlene and Georgie."

"She killed them to get that half million?"

"I don't think Alta found that money, or even cared about it. It wasn't in her car. I'll bet the police will locate it in one of Georgie's accounts. Alta killed Darlene and Georgie to cover her own tracks."

"Like she was going to kill you?"

"No. Killing me was to be revenge, plain and simple. Georgie killed Andrew, but Alta and Darlene, one or the other or both, killed Mr. Stitts and Bob Norton."

She sipped at her coffee, and I finished my pie.

"I don't know what more I can tell you, Mr. Elstrom," she said finally.

"Why not marry Silas Fairbairn?"

Her face brightened at the mention of his name. "He wanted to, brought it up all the time. I kept telling him I didn't want folks to think I was after his money. 'Let them think that, if their nasty minds demand it,' he'd say. I'd say, 'Never mind. We've got each other, as is.'"

"That wasn't your reason, though."

"If it ever got out that I'd been involved in a killing when I was a kid, there would be no end to the scandal. He had me; I had him. It was enough."

A car pulled into the parking lot. An elderly couple came into the diner and took the first booth by the door.

She lowered her voice. "Remember, Mr. Elstrom: Alta came here with a knife."

"There's a policeman in Chicago, named Plinnit," I said. "He's putting warrants out on Sweetie Fairbairn for everything he can think of, right down to assaulting me."

She raised her eyebrows behind the cartoonish red glasses. "Little ol' me?" she asked, forcing a smile.

"The DNA that was found under my fingernails, that partially matches yours? It's enough for some of the warrants. As is a grainy security video from the lobby of the Wilbur Wright, showing you going up to your penthouse, twice, just before I discovered you with Bob Norton's body."

"Twice?" She shook her head. "The first time had to be Darlene."

She watched Gus bring menus to the couple in the

booth. "I helped take care of his wife when she was dying, years ago. He can alibi me for every minute I need, as can his brothers."

"Plinnit can play loose with the facts. For now, he's focused only on your apprehension."

"I know how to travel, Mr. Elstrom."

I started to ease out of the booth.

She put her hand hard on my wrist. "Mr. Elstrom?" she asked.

"This has to be the best place for pie in four counties, exactly as advertised, though I'll never admit to being here to learn that, should anyone ever ask."

We walked together, toward the door.

"No sir," she said, when I stopped at the cash register to peel off some of the last of Leo's money. "In fact..." She went through the swinging door to the back, coming out a couple of minutes later with a box.

"I'm afraid it's all I have to give, now," she said.

I thanked her and took the box out to the Jeep.

For a time I drove, enjoying the steady sound of the engine, and the dark of the night, and the promise that somehow, my life would sort out once I got back to Rivertown.

And, for a time, I enjoyed glancing down at the white box on the seat beside me, savoring the last mystery of Sweetie Fairbairn. Finally, I could stand it no more. I pulled to the side of the deserted country road and opened the box.

Inside, as I'd expected, was an apple pie.

On top, as I'd hoped, were layered several slices of Velveeta.

I laughed with relief, certain that I could not imagine a more righteous resolution to the day.

* * * * *

REQUEST YOUR FREE BOOKS!

2 FREE NOVELS
PLUS 2 FREE GIFTS!

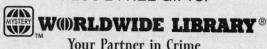

MYSTERY **W⦿RLDWIDE LIBRARY** ®
TM
Your Partner in Crime